The Lion's Cub

Fredrik Bjønnes Lunde

Cover art by Sigrid Aasgaard
Inside illustration by Sindre Opsahl Skaare
Photography by Veronica Høyheim Andresen

www.fredriklunde.no

ISBN: 978-82-999424-0-9

To all of you, whomever you are, wherever you are and whenever you are:
Thank you.

Contents

ACKNOWLEDGMENTS

Writing a book is a journey. For me, I found that I didn't always know where the journey would bring me, even though I knew where it would lead to. I am excited that this is only the beginning of a much longer journey, both for me and those who wish to follow. During the process of making this book I have written, re-written and removed a lot, and a lot of it has taken much longer time than I imagined. Along the way I have had encouragement and aid from a lot of people, and I wish I could thank them all but I've especially been helped by these:

First of all I would like to thank my girlfriend Kristin, for her support through my writing process and for her help in the first editing of this book. I would like to thank my family and friends for always cheering me on in this project, and for understanding that I've had to skip a few plans to make this happen. Arne Kristian Nordhei has been invaluable throughout the entire writing process, being my sparring partner who's given me comments, critique and new ideas. I would like to thank Jacob Telle for the amazing job of editing my work, Sigrid Aasgaard for making an awesome cover and Sindre Opsahl Skaare for other illustrations.

Chapter 1
SURVIVAL

Arkenthan peered through the branches at his latest snare hoping there would be at least a small hare in it. Seeing the trap empty, he felt disappointed and even hungrier. He had been in the forest for two weeks now and still had problems finding good spots to put up his snares. It annoyed him that he still struggled to make his traps work. He went to the trap to see if it was working correctly. He knew that hitting it with a stick would release the thread which would capture the animal. Nothing happened. He set up a new trap and tested it to make sure it worked before leaving for the lake to try to catch some fish. He would need some food soon; his dinner yesterday consisting of about 60 blueberries was upsetting his stomach. The weather was nice though, a warm summer day with barely a cloud in the sky. It made him a bit more cheerful.

Arkenthan had stuck to the lake since the day he found it. He still wouldn't make a definite camp, but until he moved on he told himself "the key to survival is water." It was something his father had told him before the trials. The sun gleamed off the hills on the other side of the lake splitting the light into different colours. The water seemed greener today than it had been before, and Arkenthan wondered why. He didn't have much gear to speak of. He wished he had taken a bit more from home before rushing out the door, but he had been angry and not thinking very clearly. He inspected his fishing rod consisting of a branch, some string and a v-shaped bone for a hook. Digging up the earth near his camp, he found a couple of worms to use as bait before throwing the line into the lake. He removed his boots and put his feet into the water knowing it would probably scare the fish away. It had been such a warm day and the water was well heated, so he just had to do it. *I'll sit like this for about an hour, and then I'll move more towards where the river runs into the lake'* Arkenthan thought. At that moment something pulled at the line very hard, and he was dragged a bit into the water. He quickly got to his feet and started pulling on the line. Standing in the lake and working his way towards land, he struggled to keep his footing. It was a strong fish, telling Arkenthan that he might get a decent meal, which gave him more strength to haul the fish onto land. *I only hope it's not a bonefish'* he thought the very moment the fish jumped out of the water. Pulling hard on the line, the fish landed heavily on land wriggling. Arkenthan was quick to grab a branch to kill the fish. Looking at it, all he could think was that he finally would get a decent meal.

As the fire grew, Arkenthan scoured the forest looking for berries and herbs to spice up his fish. He found a few blueberries and some mushrooms, a few leaves he knew gave good taste, but no roots he knew he could eat. He didn't know much about roots, so the chances of finding any of those were small. On the way back he found a thin bent tree. The tree didn't look damaged, and as he pushed away a tree which had fallen on it, the thin tree quickly flew back up. This gave Arkenthan an idea. He examined the tree, trying to learn what it looked like and started looking for more of the same type. This wasn't a hard task as they seemed to be everywhere. He bent a smaller one easily and as it reached the ground he released it. The tree quickly snapped back up. He smiled thinking *'I guess this is my lucky day.'* He looked around for animal tracks and found what seemed to be a tiny path. Tracks from small game were everywhere on the path. He found the closest tree and set his trap. He cut another tree down with the knife his father had given him when he was twelve summers old. It had been a big ceremony for all the children of his age. Everyone growing to be twelve summers old in the village had to pass the trials set each year. Every year on the day of the sun's turning during the summer, the day the sun was above ground the longest, the elders would throw the trial sticks. These sticks were carved with different symbols. Some were carved with animals, some with plants and some with seasons. All the sticks thrown had its own symbol. "It is the language of the gods," the elders used to say. Reading the sticks took a lifetime of study, and the elders taught one child every five years to become one of the elders. Those children who were chosen would be in apprenticeship all their lives learning to interpret the sticks. To know how to read the sticks the elected child would have to learn about the gods, how they acted and what they stood for. They were the earthbound links between the humans and the gods, and to be elected was one of the greatest honours any family could receive. Each year the elders started the presentation of the results by saying "The gods have this summer decided the trial to be" and every year a different result would appear on the sticks, and the elders would have to know the connections between what the symbols meant and how they landed in combination with others. The year before him had been a cooperation trial where all those who were twelve summers had to hunt down a fjällbear, a bear so big it usually took four warriors to take one down. Less than half the children had returned that year. His trial had been one of survival, where everyone had to live in one type of terrain for one turn of the moon. You could only bring the clothes you normally used, no gear, food or items, so right now Arkenthan felt like he had an advantage. His trial had been five years ago, so he still remembered most of what he had learned in the lone hours in the forest he was assigned to.

He brought the small tree back to camp and started preparing the fish. The herbs and berries he mashed into a paste, and put it inside the fish before wrapping everything in big leaves. He then covered the leaves with mud to prevent them from catching fire. While waiting for the fish to cook, he started carving the tree he brought back into a smooth long stick. At each end of the stick he carved an indent. He made a knot with a loop on a piece of thread and fastened it at each end of the stick which he bent so the thread would be wound tight. He pulled the string and thought *'Wow, I hope it works as well as I am hoping. Cool. I've always wanted a bow. I'll need to find a strong branch tomorrow to make some arrows.'* He was wondering how well the fish had cooked, but decided to let it stay in the fire for a while longer. He went down to the water, took off his clothes and jumped into the lake. The water was getting cold, but still felt very refreshing. He swam a few strokes, then dived down to the bottom of the lake. A muddy ground covered the bottom as far as he could see. When he resurfaced he went back on land and let the sun dry him up while he ate his dinner. The next few days he spent making arrows and practicing his archery skills along with testing out several ways of setting up traps. He kept trying to remember what his father had said the few times they had been in the forest together. How some knots would tighten the rope when pulled, and some would release it.

He started every day by gathering or catching the food he would need. When enough food was gathered he ran along the river or into the forest. He knew that living here in the forest would mean at some point he would have to run from something, and it would probably have to be for a long time. One day, as he was running along the river, he stopped to drink. As he bent down towards the surface he heard a lot of splashing further upriver around a bend behind a hill. The hill made it impossible to see what made the noise. He took a quick sip of the water, snuck into the forest and walked up the hill. As he neared the area where the sound originated from he saw three bears jumping around in the water. *'They look too small to be fjällbears; it's probably a mother teaching her two cubs how to hunt fish. If that is so, I'll not be in any danger so long as I don't startle them,'* he thought as he started making his way down to the river, making sure to make some noise so the bears would know he was coming. He loved taking chances that would normally be very dangerous, it made the blood pump through him and made his head light. When he emerged from the woods he found all three bears looking at him, and he was wondering if it had been a bad idea to go down to the water. They looked more puzzled than angry or hungry, with their heads turned to one side. *'They have probably never seen a human being before'* Arkenthan thought while slowly moving towards a big rock next to the river where he sat down. After a few moments the bears lost interest in him and returned to their fishing. Arkenthan sat in the sun watching how the bears seemed to interact and how the cubs kept trying to copy their mother. He watched as the cubs ran onto the opposite shore and started playing, fighting together while the mother kept a look out for danger. When the sun had travelled a bit across the sky he stood up and slowly made his way back into the forest, again under the observant eyes of the bears. When he was back near the river he started running back to camp. He had spent a long time watching the bears and was not back until late. The last thing he heard before falling asleep was the hoot of an owl.

As the days passed he became gradually more tired of his camp not being of much use other than for catching and cooking food. He had to leave soon, and one day he decided to catch a few fish, gather up his traps and the rest of the gear, then head upriver. "Always stay near water" he told himself. He found a cave which seemed sufficiently big for both him and a fire. He gathered some wood and started a fire by the exit. The moment he put a fish over the fire, rain started to pour down outside the cave. It carried with it a strong scent of every plant and flower outside, and for some reason that made him even hungrier. "Hah. I must have lived too long in the forest if the smell of trees and flowers make me hungry" he told himself. He liked listening to the rain, how the drops sounded like music when they hit different things. He pulled out the rough arrows he'd made and started to smoothen the shafts to make them fly better through the air. He had used some leaves instead of feathers, but these didn't last long, so he reminded himself that he would have to try catching a bird or something else which have feathers. Many things have feathers, he remembered his father telling him. Even some crocodiles have wings. They can't fly, he remembered his father saying, so there was no need to worry too much about an attack from above, but they could leap from hills and glide on the air downwards. The thought scared Arkenthan, imagining something resembling a log with wings floating downwards from a cliff towards him. He sat all day looking out at the rain, occasionally going out to get more wood for the fire. It wasn't until far into the next day that the rain stopped. He left the cave behind and moved further up the river. He soon found an open area close enough to the cave for him to run there in case there was more rain coming.

A few days after getting to the new camp Arkenthan awoke to a loud growl nearby. He slowly sat up looking back and forth. All he could see was complete darkness but he heard loud thuds as something heavy hit the ground. After listening for a while he heard more of the growling and the moving about, and it sounded as if two huge beasts were fighting. Arkenthan pulled a bit back towards the opposite side of where the sounds came from, and hid closer to the trees. He thought *I won't get far in this darkness, I'll have to wait until the sun is up'* and at that moment the ground shook. He sat silently the rest of the night, listening for more sounds, but none came. When the sun arose, Arkenthan felt nervous about the night's events, but he forced himself up and started preparing. Before leaving he collected his traps which contained one hare. He quickly cooked a bit of the hare to get some energy, and then he left. He passed a couple of trees, pushed his way through a bush, and found himself staring straight into the face of a sleeping fjällbear. He felt the blood drain from his face as he remembered all the tales of these bears. This one had a scar across the chin and was missing an ear, but that wasn't the scary part. What scared Arkenthan the most was that the head alone was as wide as he was tall. He slowly backed away into the forest. When he got close to the bush he had come through a few moments ago, a branch snapped under his foot. He froze as he kept an eye out for any sign of the bear waking up. He saw the bear slowly lifting its eyelids and peer around apparently confused and drowsy before the big yellow eye locked on him. *'Shit'* Arkenthan thought, turned and ran. It took a while before he heard the crashing of a huge beast trying to move quickly between tightly packed trees. He heard the bear howl and heard a reply coming from another part of the forest. *There are two of them? Now I'm glad I did all that training. Being able to move quickly between the trees instead of having to break them down or walking around them might give me a chance.'* Arkenthan thought as he kept running through the forest in random directions, trying to shake off the pursuers.

Chapter 2
SHELTER

After a full day of running, Arkenthan had arrived at the foot of a small mountain, and was exhausted. He found a clearing nearby and prepared camp. *'I hope the bears stopped following me'* Arkenthan thought. He knew he wouldn't be able to run for much longer and the bears could tear down trees, so if they were following him nothing he did right now other than resting mattered much. After making camp and starting a fire he looked for places to set his traps, bringing his bow in case he spotted something to hunt. While hunting he kept his attention on the birds around him. Birds, he remembered, had a tendency to help those who knew how to listen to them. They always changed the tempo of their songs when something was around to startle them. So the birds would hopefully warn him if the bears were trying to sneak up on him. He could only find a fox while hunting, but he didn't want to shoot it. Other than that, nothing huntable appeared, and he thought *'Right now I'm glad I took precautions. I hope the hare is still fresh enough.'* While heading back to camp he suddenly heard a low humming. He wondered at this sound and headed towards it. Seeing what it was made his spirit rise – it had been a long time since he had tasted honey. No one in his village wanted to head far into the forest anymore, so they were unable to find any bees' nests. Not after the outbreak of fjällbears in the deeper parts. They always said it was easier to just live off the game they hunted closer to the village than venture further into the forest and risk being taken by one of the bears. What Arkenthan had learned about the bears from the villagers was that they were strong enough to push down a small barn and tended to track their prey for a long time, sometimes up to three days, although Arkenthan thought they might be exaggerating a bit on that point. They tended to say these kinds of things only when they had been drinking moonshine for a while. Why they called it moonshine, he had no idea. At the moment he stood looking at a big bees' nest. The advantage of bees' nests compared to a wasps' nest was that although bees tended to build nests which were harder to approach, the honey would just hang in lumps fully visible. A wasps' nest was enclosed in some thin papyrus-looking thing, and once you tried to poke a hole in it everything inside would attack you. Now a bees' nest would be possible to scavenge from. He decided to come back another time, as he still had some food and bees don't move around too much. When he came back to camp, he put the rabbit on a stick and hung it over the fire to cook. He took a sip from the waterskin and started to pack his gear into the bag in case he had to run again. He wished he had chosen to get some honey, as honey gave you energy very fast, and it lasted for a while. He ate the rabbit and immediately fell asleep.

He bolted upright as the lightning struck, making his heart pound with shock. He had been so tired he hadn't even woken up when the rain started to pour down. Now he would have to find some shelter quickly. He grabbed his gear and ran into the forest towards the mountain. Arkenthan stood looking at the mountain to see if there were any shelves which could bring him some cover. One third of the way up the hill, he spotted an overhanging rock which looked promising. He started climbing, but found that every other step he took made the ground crumble beneath him. After a while he became unsure as to how safe his shelter would be. Spotting some vegetation a bit off to the side he knew the ground would be more stable there rather than going straight up. It would take a bit longer to get there, but the climb would be a lot easier. When he was halfway up the climb to the shelter there were three flashes of light with corresponding crackling sound. The first strike seemed to hit somewhere in the forest below him, the second flashed across the sky and the third struck the top of the mountain so hard it shivered all the way down to where Arkenthan stood. *'It's not safe to be here for long'* he thought. At that moment the top of the mountain broke off and came sliding towards him. Immediately Arkenthan started running back down the mountain. As the rockslide was closing in on him the ground gave way and he fell into a hole which was twice the width of his body, and barely as deep as he was tall. He ducked, and could only think *'If I make it through this without great damage I'll be the luckiest guy alive.'* He was holding his arms around his head to protect it, and as the rockslide started to die out a big rock fell into the hole. If he hadn't protected his head it would probably have killed him. Since he was protecting his head, the rock fell into the hole and hit his arm. It felt as if his arm broke clean off. When the rockslide was over he looked at his arm and noticed it looked alright, but when he touched it the pain shot through his entire body. He thought *'Great, is it broken, or just really badly hurt? Now I have to get out of this hole with only one arm.'* He tried to climb out but the sides of the hole were so slippery and wet that whenever he tried to get a grip he fell back. Sitting inside the hole, Arkenthan hunched up like a ball to try to preserve some heat.

A few hours passed before the rain stopped, but it was still too early for the sun to rise. Arkenthan tested the walls again, but found no point in spending energy on trying to get out when he clearly wasn't going to. He sat down and thought *'Well, at least the bears have lost my scent now, so I doubt I'll see them again,'* then he fell asleep. When he woke up the sun was bright and warm, and he felt his clothes drying with every passing minute. He moved to the side so the sun would hit the wall of the hole in order to dry the soil a bit. He jammed his good hand, fortunately the right one, as he was right-handed, into the wall and dug out small dents to enable himself to climb out. The soil was still too loose to be able to get out, and he had to wait most of the day in order for it to dry enough. When it finally became dry enough his arm made the escape a problematic one. After what seemed like ages he finally managed to get out, and lay on the hill gasping for breath both from exhaustion and from the pain in his arm. When he got up it was late in the evening. He traced his way back to the camp he had made the day before and sat down wondering how he would be able to get a fire going with only one arm. He heard the birds sing their soft soothing songs and lay down on the grass thinking *'What can I do? I'll need some food, but not food I would have to cook.'* He then bolted upright thinking *'The bees' nest! Of course, but without smoke to calm the bees down it will be a pain to get the honey.'* Arkenthan sat wondering what else he could do but found nothing else would really work, so he just had to grab the honey and run. He started looking around for the area of the nest, and eventually found it. Sitting down to evaluate the nest and its surroundings, he knew he had to find the best point of attack. This was so that he could get quickly in and out again. He spent an hour just looking at the nest while the sky became increasingly cloudy. Just as he was about to rush towards the nest, he heard the low rumbling of thunder once more. He remembered having seen, when he was younger, that insects rarely flew around when there was rain. Deciding to wait for a while he hoped that rain would come soon. He didn't have to wait long, and as soon as the rain had built up a bit he slowly made his way towards the nest. Arkenthan looked at the nest for a while taking in how many bees were swarming around it. He noticed how the bees were very active in the dry areas, but how few actually flew into the rain. As he slowly stuck out his knife to cut a piece of the raw honey he felt the bees give him all of their attention. As Arkenthan was looking at one of the bees he felt it staring back at him. For a short time he felt sorry for destroying something they probably had spent a long time making. Arkenthan knew that he had to get some food and this was probably the only way without making his arm worse. He made a quick cut at the top and bottom of the wax comb, grabbed the honey and ran. Thanks to the rain he only got a couple of stings from angry bees. He took the route along his snares on the way back to camp to see if they had caught anything. The last snare he got to had a hare caught in it. The hare was still on the ground and alive, with its leg tied up in the rope. *'With my arm this way it'll be a hard job killing, skinning and cooking it. Maybe my arm will be easier to live with in a few days' time'* he thought, and decided to give the hare some leaves to chew on so it would survive for at least a few days. Back at camp he sat down and smelled the honey. A sweet, rich smell filled his nose, and his mouth watered instantly. The honey tasted slightly different from what he had tasted before. The hunters who had brought honey back to town had purified it and it was only a runny sugary syrup whereas this still had pieces of the hive in it. It was edible, but he had to work his jaw in order to bite through the thick walls of the hive. He saved a lot of the honey for later, as he didn't expect his arm to mend very quickly. From the events of the day, Arkenthan felt exhausted, and fell asleep before the sun had set. The next few days he spent testing how he could do things without his left hand, and he soon developed a way to make fire and set new traps. Trying every now and then to use his arm normally he noticed it started getting better. *'I guess it wasn't broken, but it still hurts to use. I'll just have to train it back to normal'* he thought.

One day, as he was wandering around exploring on the opposite side of the mountain from where his camp was, he found a small cottage which seemed abandoned. He knocked on the door and when there was no reply he wasn't all that surprised. He didn't want to go in though, in case someone only was out for the day or was sleeping. Searching the forest for a clearing closer to the old cottage, he soon found a spot not too far from it. The day grew old as he wandered back to his camp, and it was clear the journey to the new campsite had to wait until the next day. He prepared a big meal so he would have more strength and less to carry the next day. When morning came, Arkenthan awoke feeling excited about the day's tasks. First he would have to take down all his snares. Two of them had caught hares in them, which he killed and brought back to camp. He packed his bag and headed for the clearing while looking out for game trails and signs of predators. For some reason the signs made by predators, broken bones and scratched trees, seemed to decrease the closer he got to the cottage. This made him feel a bit more confident about moving to the new camp. A deer greeted him by standing in the middle of the new campsite. They stood looking at each other for what seemed like a long time. It probably wasn't more than a few seconds before the deer slowly made its way to the edge of the clearing. There it started eating leaves off the trees. As Arkenthan was unable to wield his bow with his arm still hurting, he decided to not start hunting it. Instead he slowly set up camp. When he was finished he looked up and saw that the deer had lain down in the grass and was observing him. It felt a bit awkward, he had never felt an animal observe him before, usually it was the other way around. Feeling slightly uneasy he went to the cottage again to see if anyone was home. There was not a sound from inside when he knocked on the door, and he became more convinced no one was living there anymore. He noticed the garden seemed well tended, but that could be a coincidence. He knew that animals could have eaten it all up. To make sure no one was living there, he wanted to observe the cottage for a few days. When he came back to camp the deer was gone, which pleased him. He couldn't stand thinking he'd have to sleep with a beast watching him.

Three days passed and still there was no sign of anyone else nearby, so Arkenthan tested the door of the cabin and found it to be unlocked. He peered inside and saw a fire-pit in the middle of the room apparently for cooking big game. At the far end of the room he saw a bookcase containing a few books, and several rolls of parchment. To the left was a table and some benches meant for preparing food. The right hand side of the room contained three beds. *'Hmm, it's possible to live here if necessary'* Arkenthan thought. He still didn't want to go inside, but he wasn't that scared of looking around outside. He walked around the house, and saw that it was practically built into the mountain. *'What a strange way to build a house, I wonder how they've managed that'* he thought as he walked around to the other side of the house which held an outhouse. Outside the outhouse there was a well with a lot of water in it, and a bucket on a rope next to it which seemed to be in decent shape. The inside of the outhouse smelled rancid, but several layers of firewood were stacked against the wall. There were some tools there as well, a hammer, a saw, an axe and a few other things he didn't know what was. Arkenthan thought *'If I can live here I'll have what I need for a long time onwards.'* He headed back to camp and made a fire to cook his dinner. As he was about to put a hare over the fire, with his gear spread around the campsite, he heard a low thump. He looked up, alarmed, with his ears on edge. There was another thump, and he heard the bushes shake. A flock of birds flew away close by on the next thump, screaming their alarm. A few moments later the head of a giant wolf forced its way through the bushes. Arkenthan didn't have time to think as he got up and ran. He knew that wolves were fast and hunted whatever prey they could find for weeks, running unceasingly. As he reached the edge of the clearing he heard the wolf growl and leap into the clearing with a crash of broken branches. He kept on running towards the cottage, which now was his only chance of survival. The wolf barked almost like a dog and suddenly the tree behind him exploded into hundreds of splinters. He kept on running thinking *'If it can do that to a tree, what can it do to a thin door or even the walls of the house?'* As Arkenthan crossed the treeline he could feel the wolf's breath on the back of his head, and then, suddenly, it was gone. He kept on running without looking back and crashed head first into the door. He fell backwards, stunned, and as his head hit the ground the world turned and he fell into a daze.

When he woke up the stars were out and he found himself looking at the door to the house. *'Why am I still alive?'* he wondered. Turning around, Arkenthan saw the largest wolf he'd ever seen. He had heard rumours of dire wolves before, but never really credited the size they could supposedly grow to. Now as he stared at the wolf standing on the edge of the woods snarling at him he understood that the stories weren't exaggerated. The wolf seemed afraid to move onto the lawn outside the house, which calmed Arkenthan slightly. He walked back and forth, and a bit closer to the wolf. This showed Arkenthan that he would be safe as long as he stayed on the grass, and out of the wolf's reach. He turned his attention to the door, and was embarrassed to find it opened outwards instead of inwards, which is what he had thought earlier. *'Easy to die out here if you make one small mistake'* Arkenthan thought as he walked inside blushing.

Chapter 3
LEAVING HOME

Arkenthan stood in the cottage waiting for his eyes to adjust to the darkness. He opened the windows to shift the stale air which had accumulated inside the cottage. He got a fire started in the centre of the room and wondered what he should eat. As he went outside to get some water from the well he noticed that the wolf had disappeared. He snuck into the forest and went back to his now old camp hoping the wolf had left in another direction. He found his hare had been chewed on by some animal, but by one that had to be a lot smaller than the dire wolf. Arkenthan collected his gear and went back to the cottage. He put the second hare on the fire and while it was cooking, started cleaning out the dust from the cottage. He found some plates and cutlery in the cupboards and sat down for the first proper dinner in a long time. As the night wore on he kept on cleaning the cottage. When the sun came up from the horizon, he noticed how tired he was and barely managed to reach one of the beds before falling asleep.

When Arkenthan woke up, he couldn't help feeling homesick. The last time he had slept in a bed was the last time he had been at home, and the final day before he had left came back to his memory. He remembered sitting opposite his mother Shaina and his father Iroke, and his mother had told him that "the war against the Kenors is requiring certain people to help in the fight for our country. As you know, our village Dragoria, is known as the black village due to all the blacksmithing being done here. Most accomplished smiths from our village are required to go support the troops with their skills. For this reason, your father has to leave us tonight to go to the war." Arkenthan had wanted to join his father in the war, but he had said "No, you cannot go. I can take you on as an apprentice if you wish to learn the trade, but not in the middle of a war or near a battlefield." "Then I will enrol in the army to fight for our country!" Arkenthan replied, but at this his father had got angry, saying "I won't allow you to go to war, you have to stay at home and take care of your mother, keeping things in order here while I am away." Arkenthan knew this was a lie, as his mother was the one who bought food and prepared it, as well as doing all the cleaning around the house. He kept on arguing for so long his father got annoyed and locked him in his room. While banging on the door, he heard his father tell his mother to keep him locked in the room until the next morning. Arkenthan heard his father yell goodbye to him, but he had been too angry to answer.

The following morning, when his mother had let him out, the first thing he asked her was "Where did they go? What way?" As his mother had refused to tell him, he had gone outside and started looking for tracks of the carriages which would have been heavy with blacksmithing equipment. They were hard to find but eventually, after walking far from the village, he had found softer soil which clearly showed heavy carts having passed quite recently. While running home, Arkenthan tried to figure out what he could say to his mother so she would allow him to go. "Mom, I want to go after dad, to help win the war in every way I can" he tried saying to a tree beside the road. He stood there thinking *'Okay, so this is silly. I'll just have to see how it all works out.'* As he got home, dinner was already on the table. He sat down and ran several conversations through his head, trying to figure out what might work. After a long time, he finally settled on a conversation he liked. It started with him telling his plan to his mother and ended, after several arguments, with his mother agreeing to let him go. Just as he was about to start, his mother said "You're awfully quiet today. Want to share what's on your mind?" At this sudden comment he was so startled, and put off his momentum, that all he managed to say was "Mom, I'm going after dad." When Arkenthan saw his mother's face, he became embarrassed, got up and went to his room. There he started putting some gear he thought would be needed into his bag. After a short while his mother came into the room, already angry, and started to remonstrate with him about his idea. He started arguing back trying to get the upper hand in the discussion, but at the same time continuing to pack his bag. As the evening stretched on, it was clear that his mother wouldn't accept his going, and with this revelation he got so annoyed that he grabbed his bag, ran out of his room and out the door. Outside he could hear his mother both yelling and crying, so he hurried to get away.

He spent the next few days tracking the caravan of blacksmiths from his village. At the beginning of the next week he saw the army. Thousands of people gathered in a huge field with tents and bonfires everywhere. He knew that finding his father in this chaos for now would be impossible. He headed towards the army, and jumped when he heard a voice say "Halt! Who goes there?" Embarrassed that he was so easily scared, he answered "I'm Arkenthan, I've come to volunteer for the army. Where should I go?" "You see the wide spacing between the tents over there?" the guard said. "Go all the way down there to the tent of the captain of the spearmen. Ask him if he needs you" and with that the guard fell silent. Slowly making his way between the tents, Arkenthan closed in on a tent shaped like a spear's head, and he thought *'Well, at least they make it clear where you need to go.'* He stepped up to the entrance and knocked on the sign outside the tent. "Yes?" a voice deeper than he had ever heard before boomed towards him from the inside. He entered the tent and said "I'm Arkenthan and I've come to volunteer for the army." The captain's skin was as dark as his voice, with a bald head and a golden ring in the upper part of his left ear. He had a strange tattoo covering the left half of his face, yellow in colour and resembling a piece of a dream catcher or a spider's web with some additional symbols Arkenthan was unable to identify. He hadn't seen many dark skinned people before. Mostly they were merchants traveling through the village, so he hadn't spoken with many of them. The man stared at him for a while before answering "No." "Why?" Arkenthan heard himself answer, his head dazed by the strong voice of the captain and trying to think of what he should do if he couldn't join the army. "How old are you? Fifteen summers?" the captain asked. "Sixteen sir. Soon to be seventeen." Arkenthan replied, thinking the sir might help him. "And how much combat experience would you say you have?" at this Arkenthan stopped, thinking *The only combat experience I have is with my friends back home, wrestling and making swords and bows out of branches'.* "Not very much, but I've got some experience with traps and general survival skills from the forest I had to live in for one turn of the moon alone for my twelfth summers' trials" he managed to say after a long silence. "Well," the captain replied, "If you had been seventeen with a lot of experience in hunting or fighting I could've taken you. As you have no such experience, you would have to be at least nineteen with only the little experience that you claim to have. So my answer remains, I'm sorry to say, a no. I cannot use you. Come back in a year or two with more experience and we'll see." With this final answer Arkenthan was sent out of the tent without being able to argue any more. *'Come back in a year or two?'* he thought. *'Hmm. More experience. How can I get more experience? At least not from back home, and I can't go home to mom now.'* That had been the day he had decided to live in the forest.

Chapter 4
THIRTEEN TORCHES

Arkenthan jumped down off the bed, eager to start the day in his new house. While he was cleaning during the previous night, he had noticed a hole in the roof which needed mending and a few other things that needed repairs. As he was going to live there now he would have to spend a long time repairing everything and getting the well and the doors to work properly. He chopped down trees to make boards for the roof. When it came to the outhouse, the entire toilet was so rotten that he found it easier to just tear the entire thing down and build a new one.

As the days went by, after he had got the fire going and cooked his dinner, he started reading the books and scrolls lying in the bookcase. Mostly they contained drawings and descriptions of roots and mushrooms and other plants which could be used for various things. It was mostly for food, but some plants were good for making paper or bandages or to be used as ropes. Some again seemed to have a healing purpose. He eagerly read these instructions, how to prepare and use them correctly. Some of the books contained training instructions on how to wield different types of swords both with and without shield, and how to use a bow. He read the scroll about archery so that his hunting might prove easier. He found that after reading the scroll and doing some training he was able to hit what he was hunting much more easily. Only a few days passed before he brought home a big deer. *I'm glad I have the big pit in which to cook game like this, the cottage is clearly made for people hunting their own food'* Arkenthan thought. After bringing the deer home he scavenged the forest bedding for roots, herbs and mushroom to spice up his meal. Thanks to the books and scrolls he could now easily recognize what he could eat and what was poisonous. While eating his dinner that evening, he felt like a king. It was the best meal he'd had for a long time. The meat was soft and easy to chew, and the spices gave it a strong taste without removing the taste of the meat. After he finished eating he went outside to get more water from the well. When he came outside, Arkenthan was startled to see the dire wolf standing on the edge of his garden. The sun was out, so now he could finally see the wolf clearly. It was a huge beast, with a clean pelt which was pure white, unlike most wolves who had grey pelt. The dire wolf had grey pelt on the end of its legs marked off by a brown line. It was a strange sight, yet it was probably the best looking beast he had ever seen. With the sun gleaming off the white pelt, Arkenthan found that he was unable to look away from the wolf. He walked a bit towards it and said "You are quite different from most wolves, aren't you?" The wolf seemed to respond to this, tilting its head to one side as if acknowledging that Arkenthan was there and had its attention. "Greypaws... I guess that's a fitting name for you" Arkenthan said smiling. Before fetching water he went inside and brought a leg of the deer he'd had for dinner outside and threw it to Greypaws. The wolf caught the leg in the air, and settled down to eat it. *I guess the smell attracted him'* he thought as he walked to the well and brought a few buckets of water into the house. Most of the deer remained, and he wrapped it up in some leaves so that it wouldn't become rancid, before storing it for the next day. As he peered outside towards where the wolf had been, he could see it had run off to somewhere else.

The next day Arkenthan figured that if he wanted to join the army he would have to get some sort of training in. Not wanting to only develop raw strength from hauling trees and animals back home, he decided to get some running experience as well. That evening, when he had eaten his leftover dinner, he went to the bookcase to get more hints on archery. When he turned around, he slipped and struck his head against the side of the bookcase. *'Ow, why do I have to hit my head all the time?'* Arkenthan thought as he got up. When he turned around he saw that the entire bookcase had moved slightly to the side, revealing a big crack in the wall. Arkenthan thought *'Great, so after repairing the roof and practically rebuilding the outhouse I now find I have to build a new wall out of rocks?'* Annoyed at the crack in the wall he decided to put repairs off until the next day and started reading more of the books on archery. Taking his bow and arrows he went outside to shoot at a tree. Instructing himself, he spoke out "Okay, so first, stand at a straight angle with the target to your left side. Hold the bow in your left hand and point it straight towards your target. Keep your shoulders low as you pull the string back with your right hand. Aim along the arrow, and release the string." The arrow missed the target by half a metre and flew far into the forest. The next shot he did without the talking, and this time the arrow hit the tree, a bit higher than where he wanted. He practiced until it was too dark to see, and he could feel the new technique helping him to a better control of the bow.

The next morning he sat up in bed and stared angrily at the crack edging out from behind the bookcase. He got up and started the day in the normal manner. He liked keeping his systems going. After breakfasting and making sure he had dinner that day, he took a hike, scouting out areas with a lot of rocks in them so he could prepare for the repairs of the wall. After finding an area containing rocks which looked similar to those in the wall, he spent a few hours bringing different sized stones back to the house. As the day grew older he had managed to gather a big pile of rocks lying in the middle of the garden. He went inside to inspect the entire crack. As he pushed aside the bookcase he could do nothing but stare. *Wow, apparently not just a crack'* he thought *'A big hole leading to a tunnel? Maybe this was a mining cottage of some sort? Hmm.. Looks to be sturdy enough, so it should be safe to enter.'* He fetched a branch to use as a torch and entered the tunnel thinking *'I wonder where it leads.'* He saw torches along the tunnel wall, solid metal torches which couldn't be loosened. He didn't have to go far into the tunnel. After two sharp turns, apparently designed to prevent anyone from seeing far into the tunnel, he entered a room. While lighting the torches around the room it became obvious that this was not a standard mining cave. The walls were polished stone, and at the centre of each wall was a torch shaped like a lion's paw. The room was angular but rounded, and Arkenthan counted thirteen walls making up the shape of the room. Every wall had the same size and look. The only wall not identical to the rest was the entrance one, where the torch was set above the doorway instead of in the middle of the wall. The roof was black with precious stones which, in the light from the torches, resembled stars of different types and colours. The thing that caught Arkenthan's attention was the flat floor with shapes resembling arrows. Around the entire room the arrows pointed towards the centre where a pedestal stood. The base of the pedestal was in the shape of a lion's paw, from which rose spiralling streams, resembling the tendons of a leg, and culminating in a thirteen-sided top, upon which was placed a thick book. The book itself was leather bound with gold inscriptions beneath a lion's head. It was held shut by a gold lock, and the small gold key was stored in a tiny recess in the table, to the side of the book. Arkenthan picked it up and read its title out loud, "The Lion's Cub." He turned the book over and read "The world is being seized by the evil Council. When one of their squads, led by one of the Muriahs, reach the hidden town of Shadowtree, they are forced back by a newly arrived elderly man named Boriam. Jonathan witnesses the fight, and asks Boriam if he can join him when the old man decides to leave town again. The journey leads Jonathan into long unvisited and forgotten lands, through fire and ice and magic, and will forever change who he is, was and ever will be." *'Well, at least I'll have something to do in the evenings now,'* Arkenthan thought as he brought the book with him into the cottage. He put it on the bed before making dinner. *'A couple of rabbits always make a good stew,'* he thought as he dropped pieces of meat into a pot. When the stew began boiling he glanced out the window and saw Greypaws at the edge of the forest. He put his last rabbit on a spit and put it over the fire. He let the stew simmer until the rabbit on the spit was done, and brought a big bowl outside along with the rabbit. "Hey

Greypaws, how are you doing? Here, I cooked a little something for you. I know it isn't much, but that's all I have right now," Arkenthan said as he threw the rabbit to the dire wolf and sat down on a big rock from the pile he had collected. He watched as the wolf smelled the meat sceptically before eating it. After looking at Arkenthan for a while the dire wolf apparently understood that it wasn't going to receive anything else that day, so it turned towards the forest and disappeared. When Arkenthan had finished his dinner he got up and looked at the pile of rocks. *'I'll have to see what I can do about this pile tomorrow,'* he thought as he went inside. He put a few more logs on the fire, sat down on the bed and picked up the book. He looked over the front and back of the book and could now distinguish the old but still strong colour of a clear and deep blue on the leather giving a strong background to the golden writing. The lock opened without a sound, and Arkenthan slowly opened the book and quietly read the first sentence. *'Boriam had been traveling for almost two months before he finally arrived at his destination, the town of Shadowtree.'*

Chapter 5
SHADOWTREE

"Ah, the town of Shadowtree, finally." Boriam said to himself. Now that he could see the town, he realized how it could have such a sombre name. The trees around the entire town were so large that no matter what time of the day, except at noon, it was left in shadow. It was a small town. All he could see were a few farms on the outskirts and the town seemed to consist of only a few buildings. Anywhere else the town would barely qualify to be called a village. *There must be something else going on here as well,'* Boriam thought. *'I wonder why I've ended up here of all places. Doesn't feel like anyone else has been here yet, but that won't last forever. Oh well, I guess I'll just have to see what I can dig up here before going on to the next place.'* He changed his grip on the walking stick, and slowly made his way to town. Upon reaching the town he was wondering how it had managed to stay untouched by bandits. The arrangement of the town was so bad that a band of five bandits could destroy it easily. The only sensible part of it was that they had managed to put the town hall at the end of the main street.

As he entered town he noticed the townspeople staring at him, and some even put their hands on nearby tools or weapons in case of trouble. A grim smile settled on Boriam's face as he thought *'I guess they have had their hardships.'* He saw a man whisper something to a child and then the child ran in between the houses. *'And there the guards are alerted,'* Boriam thought as he turned towards the inn. The inn was a large building compared to the town in general, constructed with beams which appeared charred, but it looked solid enough, and that was all he needed. The inside of the inn was as expected, a dark and smoke-filled room lit up by big wax candles, and a lot of murmuring conversations and laughter. He walked to the counter and signalled the innkeeper. The big man lumbered over "You're a new face here, welcome to Larkin's inn, I'm Larkin, how may I help you?" he said in a tone of voice telling Boriam he was welcome, but would be watched closely. Boriam smiled and said "Thank you, I was hoping to rent a room for a while." The barman stood thinking for a while before saying "Aye, I guess I can manage to get a room for ya. It'll need a bit of cleaning since we don't use it much, it's mostly used for storage now, but there's a bed in there. I have a lot to do here so it won't be ready anytime soon, but if you want to clean it yourself I'll knock a bit off the price for ya." *Hah, I guess visitors died out completely when this town turned into a hidden town,'* Boriam thought as he followed the barman up some stairs. "In here is the cleanest room I've got," the barman said as he pushed open the door. Boriam looked into the room and was met with crates, tables and chairs, and everything was covered in a thick layer of dust and spider webs. At the far end of the mess he could glimpse something which looked like a bed. "Well, I guess I'll just move things around for now so I'll be able to sleep in here, and then finish it up tomorrow," Boriam said. Larkin smiled apparently delighted that he didn't have to clean it up himself. He opened another room and said "You can move things in here if you'd like, and at the end of the hall there's a cupboard with some cleaning stuff."

Later that evening Boriam sat in a corner of the inn lighting a pipe, while listening to the conversations of the townspeople. He kept taking notes in a small book while thinking *There are so many people here, the few houses I saw on the way in can't be holding this many. I guess there are a lot of houses hidden by the trees.'* He looked up and saw that a couple of birds had built a nest upon one of the beams and were fully engaged in the work of feeding their newly born chicks, apparently oblivious to the noise of the inn. A group of men entered the inn, looked around the room and headed towards Boriam. They were ruggedly dressed, except for one man whose clothes expressed a greater importance than the others. "Who are you and why have you come to this town?" the important man said. "I am who I am, neither more nor less than what you see. If you are asking for my name, it's Boriam. As for what I'm doing here, can't an old man do a bit of traveling without being asked a lot of questions about it?" Boriam answered, and with a smile continued "Please, if you wish to talk then sit down. I am eager to learn a bit about your town, it seems like a peaceful place. From your clothes I take it you're the mayor of this town, it would be an honour if you would join me for an ale. My treat, of course." The mayor confirmed his assumption and sat down a bit reluctantly, then said "I am John, I'm sorry for the harsh welcome but you can never be too careful these days. This is a hidden town, well, it used to be at least. We've had a lot of raids in the last few months. I wonder how come so many suddenly know about our fair town? How did you come to know of it?" "Indeed, fair it is," Boriam replied. "From the amount of people here I take it the town stretches further into the forest. It is a fascinating town at that. With your permission I would like to get to know it and its inhabitants. When I was younger I heard legends of the hidden towns, one of which was surrounded by a great forest. I always wanted to know more of the existence of these towns. Now that I am here, I can see why it's so highly spoken of. I learned of its location from someone who has been here many times, but a very long time ago. Other than that I cannot say," Boriam answered. The mayor sat silent thinking for a long time. *'He's probably wondering who I might've heard it from. He'll know in due time, but I can't say anything yet,'* Boriam thought. Their ale arrived, smelling slightly off, but it was welcome nonetheless. After a long journey this was exactly what he needed. The first sip was indeed sour and foul, but he got used to it soon enough. When John finally spoke, he said "From your assumptions I understand that you're a fast thinker and draw quick conclusions. This may be a good thing, or a bad thing. Tell me, where do you stand in regards to the Council?" *'Ah, the Council. I was wondering when he would get to that point, and what a way to ask. I can't tell if they support them or fight them. I'll just have to trust the word of my friend'* Boriam thought before replying with a grin on his face "Well, what can I say. I'm not exactly on friendly terms with the Council, if you know what I mean." Some more thinking was to be done by the mayor, making Boriam slightly uneasy. After a short while a grin and a sparkle appeared in his eyes and Boriam saw the man finally relax a bit. The men accompanying the mayor were sent to other places in the inn, but they made sure to keep an eye on Boriam. Their conversation trailed on to the general state of the world, as John wanted to know the news of what was happening outside. It was long before Boriam was allowed to go to sleep, but he enjoyed the company as it was a long time since he'd had a real conversation with someone.

The next morning Boriam woke up with a sore head. *'Blast the mayor and his excessive drinking,'* he thought. Staggering out of bed, Boriam stretched his limbs, trying to wake himself up. After failing to fully do so a couple of times, resulting in him suddenly waking up in the corner of his room, he finally managed to get downstairs and order some breakfast. For such a secluded town they had a wide variety of food. His breakfast consisted of meat, eggs, bread and fruits. *'I didn't know they could grow fruit in this area,'* Boriam thought as he ate a very tasteful kramsonfruit. It was a fruit which looked like a cactus, but the inside was red and tasted like a blend of kiwi and orange. After breakfast he went out to explore the town.

Boriam sat down in a great circle of trees filled with carts and people, apparently serving as a market. Kids were running around playing and chasing each other. He glanced around to take in the sights and while he was watching, a door suddenly emerged from one of the trees where nothing had been earlier. As soon as a lady had come out of the tree, the door closed and was hidden again. *'I wonder how many of the trees around here work as houses, storages or whatever they are,'* Boriam thought as he looked around the market. He tried to see any signs on the trees as to which were houses and which were not, but ended up getting a headache again and began seeing imaginary signs of houses. As he watched another tree, convinced that he had found an entrance, a door opened at the side of the tree instead of where he had been looking. It all confused Boriam so much that he had to leave the market. He wandered through the woods listening to the birds when suddenly the trees came to an end and a great field lay before him. At the end of the field stood a farm and an elderly couple was busy working the corn and feeding the stocks. Approaching the old couple Boriam said, "Greetings, I am Boriam, I'm new in town, and was planning on staying for a while." "Hallo," They answered apparently unsure of how to greet him. "I was wondering," Boriam said, "if I could work a bit on your farm. It seems you have enough to do here before winter." The old couple stood thinking for a bit, mumbled something to each other before replying "Very well, but we won't pay you much, just so you know it. We don't have much to spare." "But of course, I don't need payment, let me dine with you once in a while, and tell me some old stories of this town of yours and I'll have been paid enough," Boriam said, and to this the old couple agreed.

As the evening went by he cleaned out his room and made it more personal, taking his things out of his backpack. His belongings were a pouch of coins, a few books containing stories of old, and a sword. His shield had been stolen one night when he had been attacked by bandits. He missed it; he didn't really feel like himself without it. '*Uppheim, the thieving capitol of the world, is probably my best chance to get it back,*' Boriam thought. He left his room and strolled towards the market. At this time of the evening all the vending had stopped, and in the clearing were several fires upon which spun roasting boars or goats and other animals as well. There seemed to be an event gathered for the night. "Is there anything special happening tonight, or is this the everyday way of things here?" he asked a nearby man. "Ah, you're the new guy. The town's talking about you. Not often we have visitors here. Well, you're in luck tonight, there's a wedding going to start soon. There're no invitations, so it's open to join whenever you feel like it. The food is a gift from the visitors, along with the pile of things on the far side of the market, but as you're new here I don't know if anything's expected of you. Bringing something will make people more welcoming though, so I would advise it," he said finishing off with a grin. "Thank you, I better go find something then" Boriam said and winked to the man.

As he came back to his room he found that nothing he already had would make a great gift, but chose one of his books to make the gesture. When he returned the wedding ceremony had started, with the bride wearing a leaf green wedding dress, making her look like a sapling. This was common as it marked the beginning of a new life, and the groom would be wearing a brown set of clothes to signify the tree from which the sap grew. These two would be of a higher class in town, as the bride's dress and the suit of the groom was of a very high quality. Boriam looked around the market area, and saw families, couples or friends standing together, but one person stood by himself in the background, watching the process from a distance. He looked young, and should have had many people to be with. Boriam wondered about this and was about to head towards him when the wedding ended and people started moving about, making him lose sight of the boy. People formed a line to congratulate the couple, and after the obligatory people had finished, Boriam felt it was ok for him to line up. He heard the people ahead of him give various blessings and well-wishes, and soon it was his turn. "Congratulations on your marriage, I am Boriam," Boriam said. "I don't have much to offer you, but take this book. It contains a few stories of princes and princesses of an age gone past. It's meant for children, but it's what I've got to give. And for your guests, I offer to tell a story of their choice around the bonfire." The man smiled, looked at the book, and said "We thank you, Boriam, for this gift. This book and a story for the guests is more than we could ever ask from a newcomer. Please, feel welcome at our wedding." At that moment, Boriam's stomach decided to make itself heard, which made the bride laugh and add "And the food is free." Smiling, Boriam turned away from the couple and headed over to the nearest campfire to get some food. He listened to someone telling a story about a rabbit and a bear while he ate his food. As the evening went by he met a lot of people, heard a few stories and discussed a few important topics, as far as important goes when you've had a bit to drink. Before long the sun had set and only the bonfires were left to light up the darkness. As Boriam was about to tell his story he noticed the young man, standing alone again, looking his way. *I wonder what happened here that isolated him so from the others. They seem to tolerate him, but not much more than that,*' Boriam thought as he smiled and nodded to the boy, then got up to tell his story.

Chapter 6
TROLLS

Jonathan watched as the old man looked at him, smiled and gave him a small nod. The old man stood up, and started talking to people, getting them to gather together. Since Jonathan wondered what was happening, he snuck a bit closer and sat down on the ground. He heard the old man say "My good people, newlyweds, boys and girls of all ages, gather together for a story. Can anyone give me a topic to tell a story about?" At this the crowd started shouting words over each other, everything from "A farm" to "Wars" and "Undersea villages". Finally someone, it sounded to Jonathan like a little girl, shouted "Trolls" and the rest of the gathered people agreed that a story about trolls would be fun to hear. As the old man seemed pleased with the topic, he started the story. "As you probably know trolls are made of stone. They keep on growing their entire life, and when they die they are, at least in the north, said to become the rocks and mountains of the world. This happened a very long time ago, as early as the beginning of the world, and even a bit before that. This, my ladies and gentlemen, boys and girls, this is a legend passed down by the trolls themselves, whom I've been fortunate enough to meet. This is a story from the days of old when the grand trolls were wandering among the stars. They were all alike while they were young, but as they grew older, trolls split up into the different clans governed by the six elements. There's fire, water, ice, air, lightning and earth. The looks of the members from each clan were very distinct. When the young trolls came of age, at some hundred years old, their skin would be engulfed in each troll's element. For instance: Those of fire would be covered in flame. Trolls are not born like humans are, there's no mother and father, they are born from the ground they walk on, so until a troll comes of age there's no telling what clan they belong to. Now enough with the background of the story; let's begin. There were two trolls, Stragh'an and Chim'in, who one day happened to crash into each other. These trolls had not yet come of age, and neither could distinguish what clan any of them belonged to. They greeted eachother, and sat talking for five of our normal days. The two trolls grew fond of each other, and when they got home they told their parents about the troll they had met. Now, ladies and gentlemen, I mean parents in the sense that they were the male and female trolls who took care of them during their youth. Their parents did not like this at all, saying that you had to know the clan of the troll before meeting someone you like. The two trolls agreed to never see the other troll again. This promise lasted until the following day when they again accidentally met each other. This time they sat talking for ten days before parting, and they agreed to meet again a few days later. This went on for a long time before their parents found out, at which time they made a tall fence for each of them, far away from the other. The two trolls were devastated, yelling at their parents, while slamming the doors, walls and ground. Not long after they were locked in, the two trolls started showing which clan they belonged to. When they did their parents let them out. The two trolls ran towards each other and met in an open area between the stars, and saw that Stragh'an was from the clan of fire, and Chim'in was turning towards the clan of ice. The two trolls were devastated, as the other now was unreachable. They went each to their own clans, but never forgot the other. Every now and then their paths would cross and each time they remembered the joy they felt in the other. After several years they'd had enough. Chim'in decided she couldn't live without Stragh'an, and ran to him to tell him this. Stragh'an felt the same way, so they embraced each other. As they did so, the ice on Chim'in melted into pools of water. Trolls can't survive without their right element, and so Chim'in died in Stragh'an's arms. The water only put out a bit of Stragh'an's fire, so he survived. When he noticed that she was dead, he screamed at the stars until he lost his voice. As his voice stopped working, he honoured her by wandering around her for the rest of time. After many, many years he noticed that trees and animals had started growing on her body. He felt that the plants and animals were Chim'in's spirit telling him she was still there, even though they could not speak to one another, so he decided to warm them with his heat. As he moved closer and further away from her, he changed her temperature and created seasons for the plants and animals. And that, ladies and gentlemen, is the story of how our world was created."

Jonathan grabbed some food and left for the night. He went to a big tree and climbed it. Sitting in the crown of the tree he thought *I wish I could go to faraway places and see the great races and strange creatures of the world.*' The top of the tree served as his home for the night, and it didn't take long before he fell asleep. The next morning, he woke up to find a squirrel looking at him. "Hello there," Jonathan said, which scared the creature and made it run away. He climbed down and found a drunk man sleeping beside the tree. *It was a late night I see,*' Jonathan thought, smiling to himself. He liked the forest after a big party. All the animals seemed to have been scared further away from the village than normal. A deep silence had settled on the forest, and all he could hear were the birds snacking joyfully on leftover food from the party. He went to the market and found the old man, Boriam, sitting in the centre, apparently asleep. *'Sitting and sleeping? What a strange thing to do,'* Jonathan thought as he passed the old man. He jumped when Boriam suddenly said "Good morning" and managed to say "'Morning. I thought you were asleep." "Apparently, I'm not." Boriam replied "I'm trying to hear all the small sounds around me. It usually helps clear your mind when it's needed." Jonathan grinned and said "Heh, it seems like it's needed after yesterday." He went over to a log and sat down, examining the old man who still seemed to be asleep. "What are you doing here?" He said eventually. "Well, I'm listening," Boriam answered. "No, I mean, what are you doing in Shadowtree?" He said. "Oh, I have done many things in several places. Now, it's your town's turn," Boriam answered, and after a moment said "What's your name?" "Jonathan, and you're Boriam, right?" Jonathan answered. "Ah, a quick one. Not often people catch a name. Well Jonathan, to answer your question more fully, I am looking for something. It can be disguised as pretty much anything. A stone, a plant, a living being or anything else you could imagine. It is something that holds quite a bit of power. Now don't think I just seek power. No, I am here because I am one of not many who could actually find it." At this Jonathan interrupted saying "Even though you seek it because only you can find it, you're still seeking power." Boriam opened his eyes and looked directly at him before saying "Yes, but not for me. It is needed for the imminent fight between the Council and the free world." This brought a silence for a while as Jonathan pieced together what he had heard before saying "You're going to fight the Council? No one has done that for the past twenty years. Are there still rebels around?" "Oh, people might not have officially fought the Council for a while, but there are always people opposing them. But I can't tell you more, I've already said too much," Boriam said before going completely quiet. When Jonathan understood he wouldn't get anything else from Boriam, he got up and left.

Chapter 7
DISTURBING REPORTS

Boriam watched Jonathan go and thought *'I usually don't tell people things like that. I should keep an eye on him.'* He got up and headed towards the town hall. As he pushed open the doors he thought *'I wonder if he's up. He seemed to be in good spirits last night.'* He had barely finished the thought before hearing the sounds of many feet running back and forth inside. He silently walked through the corridor towards what he assumed to be the mayor's office. *'Wow, this place is bigger than it seems from outside,'* He thought as he approached the door to the office. As he reached for the door, it flew open and a maid ran headfirst into him. They landed in a heap, and she sat up saying "Ow, oh, I'm sorry, I'm so sorry. I didn't expect anyone here at this time, after the party yesterday and all. I.. Oh, you're the new guy. I'm Mary, nice to meet you. I liked your story yesterday. Are you here to see the mayor? He's just inside, in his office, I can tell him you're here." Looking down at her lap she noticed that the pile of papers she was carrying had been spread out across the floor. She looked up at Boriam and said "I better clean this up. You go on inside, I bet he won't mind. I hope to hear another story some time." She ended with a smile on her face. *'Wow, she talks a lot, and fast,'* Boriam thought as he got up and said "I should have been more careful of where I was. It was nice to meet you Mary, I'll find the time to tell another story." And with that he entered the mayor's office.

The office was a dark brown colour with thick red curtains over the windows. The walls were covered with bookshelves except for a section which contained small portraits of what appeared to be the late mayors of the town. In the middle of the room stood a big desk upon which lay several layers of documents. "Is everything well?" Boriam asked the mayor. "I am not sure. We've received reports from our scouts that villages near here have been raided lately, by a band of no more than seven people. Would you believe that? Only seven people raiding several villages? These can't be ordinary people." John said before directing his attention to Boriam asking "So what can I help you with today then?" "I was wondering... Do you have any religious sites, places of worshipping the gods you believe in?" Boriam said. This seemed to surprise the mayor, and he sat there blinking his eyes for a few moments before replying "Religious sites? Hmm. Yes, I guess you could call them that. We have some areas which were used frequently before the Council rose to power, but that's about thirty years ago. I can show you if you like, I need some air to clear my head anyways. With the party yesterday and the reports today, it's a miracle my head hasn't blown up yet." The mayor got up and left the office.

Outside he took a deep breath and sighed. "Ah, nothing's like fresh air the day after a big party." He grinned and headed towards a small path at the back of the town hall. The path lead to a small track overgrown with vines, roots and tall grass. "Ugh, there hasn't been anyone here for over ten years I think" the mayor said as he pushed his way through the thicket and up a hill. After a while the path ended at the entrance to a cave and the mayor lit a torch which hung on the wall. As they went deeper inside the cave, Boriam could see a faint light in front of him. Suddenly they entered a majestic room, with benches lined in front of a shrine covered in gold, candlesticks and antlers. "The goat god of the dead?" Boriam said to the mayor. "Aye, I know it's usually believed that this religion is evil, but all there is to it is to live today as it can be. There may be one god, there may be two hundred gods. These are uncertainties. What we know for sure is that death comes to us all, and so we hail it, instead of fearing it. This is not your belief I can see. Do you wish to return to town?" John asked. "No, no. A holy place is a holy place, no matter to which god or belief it is addressed. May I take a look around and make a short prayer?" Boriam asked. The mayor had no objections to this, and he stepped out of the cave while Boriam started looking around inside. He only needed two minutes before realizing 'Okay, so what I seek isn't here.' And with that, he knelt down in front of the altar, and said "Thank you."

When he got back outside the mayor was waiting for him saying "Ready?" When Boriam nodded he started on the way back telling Boriam about the cave. "The cave is a fairly new place of worship, compared to other towns' holy sites. Our town has been, how shall I put it... taking a few breaks from religion, I guess is a decent description of it. There's said to be other caves like this one, but there isn't anyone alive today who knows where they are. There are no records of them to be found anywhere, and believe me, I've been looking." 'Great, and with my luck I'm guessing that what I'm looking for is hidden in one of the other caves. I better ask around a bit and see if anyone knows of any caves at all.'

Arriving back at the town they saw that people had lined up outside the town hall. The mayor sighed and said "I guess it's going to be one of those days" and shot Boriam a tired smile before heading towards the crowd. As the morning went on Boriam found that people were generally too tired from the previous night to manage to think much about caves hidden in the forest. He went to the farm outside town and spent most of the day digging up roots which the old couple called potaters. Boriam found out that they were edible, as lunch seemed to be mashed potaters with some vegetables on the side. The sun warmed him as he worked in the field throughout the day, and when evening fell he was so tired that he went straight to the inn. Sitting in the corner which everyone else seemed afraid of sitting in, he could relax a bit without too many people seeking a conversation. *'I really don't need people to talk to right now,'* Boriam thought as he sipped his beer. His dinner arrived, and consisted of meat, potaters and brown sauce. "Tell me, please, what is in this food?" He asked Larkin. "Aye, the meat is dregnars, potties are plants from underground. The brown sauce... um... Don't ask me about that one. It tastes good, and is supposedly healthy for ya, that's kind of all you really want to know," the barman said, finishing with a nod that silently said "At least it won't kill you." Boriam laughed and said "What is a dregnar?" To which the barman replied "Well, it's a bit hard to explain. I guess it looks like a dragonfly, but has a beak and is able to grip things with its, for lack of a better word, hands. I bet you'll see one soon enough, they return at this time of year." He then lumbered off to serve beer to a group of loud people. The meat was tender with a strong gamey taste. He'd grown used to potaters through his lunch on the farm, and the sauce gave it all a strange softness. He enjoyed the food and was glad everyone kept busy with their own things. As the evening progressed he heard mumbling of the raids which had occurred in the nearby towns, and from all the little pieces of information Boriam could make the assumption that there were two separate parties, one consisting of five people and one of seven. They wanted to make it obvious they were sent by the Council, and they never tried to conceal their arrival near a town. *'Either they are very strong, or very foolish'* Boriam thought. As the conversations began to die out he finished the beer he was holding and went to bed.

The next few days Boriam spent exploring the town and its surroundings as well as helping out on the farm. Hardly anyone in town seemed to even remember there being a cave in which the townspeople used to pray, and even less that there had ever been other caves like it. He spent the evenings telling stories of the past, the time before the Council, or of strange species in faraway places. Usually the youngest people would come to listen, but now and then some of the older generation as well. He would usually see Jonathan, the stranger in his own town, sit amongst the others and dream his way into Boriam's stories. One day, when he had finished his story Jonathan stayed until everyone else had left. "They say other villages have been raided. Young men are being taken from their towns and used in the Council's army," he finally said. Boriam looked at him and sighed "You pick up on more than most people do. That could be dangerous. But I guess there's no use lying to you. Yes, it seems like they have been raided." "Do you think they are going to come here?" Jonathan asked. "Oh, yes. More than likely. Every other town seems to have been raided anyway," Boriam replied, which made Jonathan's face grow stern. "But don't worry, some people say this, and some say that. There's not really anyone who seems to know anything for sure," Boriam said to try and ease Jonathan a bit, but knew it wouldn't help much. *'I can't have them raid this town before I'm finished,'* Boriam thought, then Jonathan said "I don't want to go over to the Council's side. I want to fight them, not help them. I have a feeling that you're just here temporarily. When you leave, can I join you?" This surprised Boriam so much that he couldn't answer anything but "Let me think about it." This seemed to be enough for Jonathan: a grin came over his face, then he turned around and left. *'What am I doing? I can't bring him along, it's too dangerous where I'm going,'* Boriam thought as pictures of the old wars flashed through his mind. *'Oh well, I'll have to give it a day or two before telling him he can't come. I couldn't really say I'd thought about it if I told him now.'* He left the clearing and headed to the inn. *'I mean, it could be nice to have a helper again. Maybe he'll even learn some things. And he seems eager to help the resistance, so in due time maybe he could be useful to have around on our side, not theirs. Bah, why am I thinking this? We'll see what will happen and when,'* Boriam thought at which point he had reached the inn. Inside there was the usual ruckus of rumours whirling about, singing from a table of drunken people, and general joy from having some time off. Boriam sat down at the usual table, and Larkin was quick to bring him a menu. "Tell me, Larkin, where are you from? Your accent is so different from everyone else in town," Boriam asked, and Larkin said "Aye, ye could say that. I come from a small town far to the east. I moved 'ere when the Council just started their conquerin'. I didn't really hold much for their view of things, so I left before they could take over my town. I went in a big circle to the north, and stumbled into this town when I was being chased by wild boars through the forest. Hah! The guards took them down quickly and held a feast since I brought so much food." Boriam saw a joy in the barman he hadn't seen before. "Seems like you were well received in town then," he said with a smile, but Larkin just stood there staring into nothingness. This amused Boriam, and he let the man finish his dream before choosing a dinner and some beer. When he returned with the food Larkin said "I met me wife during that party. Well, didn't meet her as you would say it, I more or less knocked her out when I lifted a barrel of beer and turned around too fast for her to jump away. She was out for a few days, but I brought her the things she needed to get well afterwards, and so I got to know her. She's the one making the food, ya know, she's hardly ever out here, too much to do in the kitchen. Anyways, I've been boring you too long now with my rambling, but thank you for making me remember this. The food's on the house tonight." He turned to leave, but stopped as if remembering something and tilted his head to look at Boriam. "But the drinks you'll have to pay for ya know," he said with a grin, and gave a small laugh as he left the table. The food tasted better than it had done on previous days, and the beer wasn't quite the same rancid goo he'd been drinking earlier. *He must've been really happy to bring out a better keg of beer. Innkeepers tend to reserve their better beer for close friends and relatives only,* Boriam thought as he enjoyed the beer he'd got. He joined a technical conversation about goats for a while, and found he didn't know anything about goats at all. Everything he suggested was met with an initial stare, then a laugh and then a toast to his crazy suggestion. After a while he just shot in crazy ideas out of fun, but the others didn't seem to mind. When the discussion ended, he went back to his table.

After Boriam had been sipping his drink for a while, the mayor entered the inn. He went straight to Boriam's table and sat down saying "Hope you don't mind, I've been so busy with everyone else these last few days, and you are usually pretty quiet." Boriam laughed at this, signalled the barman for a beer and said "Not at all. What's going on?" The mayor just sat there staring at the table. After a while he looked up at Boriam saying "These reports just keep rolling onto my desk. And people are knocking on my door worried about what will happen to their sons or belongings, or for some strange reason goats. People seem very worried about their goats." Boriam laughed at this and said "Just tell people that they are safe for now. They haven't come here yet, and until they do there's no way of knowing what they want." "Yes, but people don't really think about that, as fear seems to run deeper than anything I can say," John said in reply. The noise of the tavern increased through the night, and as the mayor's drinking escalated, Boriam managed to slip away thinking *Oh, no. I won't try to keep up with the mayor this time.*

The next morning Boriam came downstairs to find John at the table in the corner. He thought *Has he been here all night, or has he actually managed to get up this early?* He sat down at the table and said "I'm surprised to see you up and about so early in the morning." The mayor looked at him and said "Well, just because a man seems to be drinking a lot, it doesn't necessarily mean that he is." Boriam smiled and ordered a breakfast. They said nothing as they ate, and just before they had finished eating, a farmer rushed into the tavern and ran to the mayor's seat. He then whispered something into his ears. The mayor signalled his head guard over and said "There's an 02-01, get your men ready." Boriam looked at him and asked "Is something wrong?" and the mayor replied "Well, I guess the time has come. A band of thugs are outside the town demanding to speak with me. Don't tell anyone. The only reason I'm telling you is because you know quite a bit by now. You're of an older generation, so you should rest up here while we take care of this." The mayor left the inn and Boriam thought *Oh well.. I just hope the band isn't any of the Muriahs, the henchmen of the Council. I guess we'll see.*

Chapter 8
THUGS

Jonathan had heard the rustling of the guards' armour, and knew that something was going on. As it was early, not many people were out of bed yet. He made his way to a part of the woods where he could watch the field outside town without being spotted easily. Only two other villagers had heard the stirring of the guards and had decided to check what was going on. He could see two groups of people on the field outside town. One was the mayor and some guards, but the other group he didn't remember having seen before. *'They look mean,'* Jonathan thought as he examined them. He knew other guards were stationed in the trees with bows if it came to that. "What do you want?" he heard the mayor call from the edge of town towards the band of thugs. The one appearing to be their leader, a strong dark-skinned man with orange eyes, answered with a voice which boomed far into the village "We want every young man of this settlement lined up outside the city for a... test. We also want to search the city at our own pace." This intense voice seemed to make the mayor nervous, worrying what they might mean by "test", and he replied "And what if we don't?". The dark-skinned man lifted one arm towards the village and a ball of fire flew from it. Jonathan watched as the fireball flew across the field towards the mayor, dreading what it would do when it struck. The mayor had helped him survive after his parents died five summers ago. Not one of the other villagers would even look at him as his parents hadn't been too popular. He had never managed to find out why. They were outsiders, and that meant a lot here, but that shouldn't make the townspeople hate him. The mayor was the one thing making him feel somewhat welcome in this village, and as he watched the fireball soaring through the sky he noticed he was holding his breath. He breathed again when he saw the fireball strike a tree beside the mayor. *What do they want with us which would make them threaten the entire city to get it?'* Jonathan asked himself. Just as he had asked this question he saw someone wearing a cape green as the woods, and hunched over a cane, walking out of the city towards the band of thugs. He heard the leader saying "Stand aside old man, this has nothing to do with you." At this the

41

old man stopped, lifted his head, removed his hood and said "Thank you". Jonathan was shocked to see Boriam standing there. Jonathan liked the old man. He couldn't say why, but something about the way he acted, the understanding looks he gave every person that talked to him maybe, made Jonathan feel calm. He just stared in disbelief at the way Boriam had walked onto the field between the village and the thugs. Then he heard him say "Thank you. For taking my age into account. Very few have done so in the past few years. But I would advise you, Arnkhand of the Black Raven clan, to turn back from this place. There is nothing for you here, so take your group and move on." The leader of the thugs suddenly looked confused and asked "Who are you, and how do you know my name?" At this Boriam smiled and replied "You don't recognize me? Maybe this will help: I know many things, from far and wide and ancient times. I am who I am, neither more nor less." Arnkhand stood silent apparently thinking for a long time, before saying "You're Boriam?" "I am." Boriam answered. "I heard you joined the Awakened Clan, and I heard all of them were wiped out a long time ago," Arnkhand said excitedly. "The Awakened Clan's members might be dead," Boriam replied, "but the clan itself can never die. It will just be extremely hard to join when, or if, all members are dead." When it was clear that no more of an answer was coming, the leader of the thugs said "I have to make sure that what we're looking for isn't here in this village. Since you are claiming that what I'm supposedly looking for isn't here, I suspect that it actually is. Now stand back and let the young men of this village be brought forth, or I will not hold back against you." The pace of the wind increased slightly, though not enough to be noticed by anyone out on the field, but Jonathan felt it from where he stood. It felt like an omen. A way the world could tell people close by something was about to happen. It made him focus even harder on the field. He saw Boriam smile his kind, calm and steady smile, and then reply "No." At this the villagers started to move about very fast, apparently preparing for an attack. Jonathan didn't exactly hear the word, it was more like a feeling, as if it was his entire body which said no. It made the bones in Jonathan's body shake as it was said, and it was apparent it had the same effect on others around the field. A few moments after the momentous answer from Boriam, three of the thugs raised their hands and each fired their own fireball at him. Jonathan watched the three fireballs soar through the sky towards the old man, and again hoped everything was going to be ok. Boriam looked up at the sky, then smiled. As he looked back down, he bent forward beneath the first fireball putting his cane into the ground with such force that nearby rocks leapt into the air. He made a hand gesture, and the second fireball seemed to be absorbed into is arm. The third fireball took a big turn and started to spin around Boriam, breaking into ever smaller fires. When they were small enough, the wind put them out. The first fireball, having missed Boriam, continued towards the village, but 20 metres away from the edge of town the fireball seemed to hit something invisible. Boriam started to whistle and as he did so, the ground begun to move in patterns towards the thugs. Five metres away from them the ground burst into life with vines jumping into the air whipping around to ensnare the attackers. The vines pulled one man underneath the ground, and locked another man's foot. Three thugs were left, one of them being the leader Arnkhand, who looked at the trapped man in shock. When he saw the man's foot slowly being pulled into the ground he drew a sword and cut the vine before yelling "I will be back with soldiers to finish what I came here for!" At this Boriam replied "Don't bother, by the time you're back I'll have left with what you are looking for. If I haven't, I'll be here to stop you again. Tell your beloved Council there is nothing in this town for you, or for them." Upon hearing these words, Arnkhand screamed with anger.

The mayor treated Boriam to a meal at the town hall, but Boriam felt it was not a show of gratitude; It was as if the mayor wanted more of an explanation from Boriam of what had occurred outside the village. "How did you know who they were and what they were looking for?" the mayor asked. Boriam took a long time before answering "They are looking for the same thing I am..." "Which is?" the mayor interrupted. At this Boriam replied "If you do not interrupt me, I'll tell you everything I know" *'at least everything I am allowed to and want to tell you'* Boriam added in his own mind. "Then begin" the mayor said. "As you know, I am a bit old," Boriam said "I am also a member of the Awakened Clan, the last one of it in fact. It is rumoured that one from our ranks shall be the only one strong enough to take down the Council. Looking at me now, do you believe I am that one?" Boriam raised one eyebrow to indicate that the mayor should respond. "Honestly, I didn't dare hope any of the Awakened Clan was left. And I see what you mean, I did not believe you to be as strong as you showed yourself today." "Alas, I am not as strong as I used to be. I have lost a lot of my strength, and because of that I am unable to do anything about the Council. So in order to do so, I need something. The very same something those thugs were looking for. None of us knows what; it could be a person, or an item, a deity, a symbol, an animal or anything else. All I know is that there is something somewhere in this village, and that the Council is anxious to get it. As for those thugs, they'll probably be back. If I am here, I do not know what will happen. If I am not, you should do what they say because they won't stop until they have searched every stone and root in this village." With this comment the mayor looked worried and said "As you have now stood up to them, won't they be angry at the village for defying them so directly?" "Not if you manage to convince them I acted out of my own self-interest and have nothing to do with this village. If you're lucky they'll mainly focus on a search for me, if you're unlucky they might think you're protecting me and will look everywhere for me at any cost, but that is highly unlikely. Arnkhand is a wise man, even though…" The sentence was interrupted by the door opening. "Ah, Jonathan" the mayor said, "This is Boriam, maybe you've seen him around town?" "Oh, we've met," Jonathan said and continued "I was wondering if I could stay here for the night, there seems to be rain coming." To this question the mayor replied "Honestly I have no idea how you know these things, but you seem to be right most of the time, and of course you can stay here any time you want." Jonathan and the mayor exchanged a few more words while Boriam observed them.

When Jonathan had left the room the mayor returned his attention to Boriam saying "I'm sorry about that, Jonathan has been alone for five winters now, after his parents died when their house burned down. His family wasn't the most popular in town, for reasons I will not go into, but it resulted in no one wanting to take care of him. So I decided to give him some food and shelter whenever he needs it. Other than that I don't know where he stays or what he eats." "He seems like a strong kid. Can you tell me anything else about him?" Boriam asked. "Well, he likes to keep to himself, I don't think there's many people in town who understand him very well, and I don't blame them. That kid seems to know everything that's going on around him. As you heard just now, he said it was going to rain. I don't know how he does it. Everything seems to work out around him though, so I'm not really worried about him." "What did his parents do? Where in town did they live?" He asked the mayor. "They lived in a barn close to the mill by the river. I think they helped out at the farm a little, like you seem to be doing, but other than that, they kept mostly to themselves," he answered. "He's asked to join me when I leave this place," Boriam said which made the mayor raise his eyebrows in wonder and say "Well, that means he trusts you. I've had a feeling he has wanted to leave town for a long time, but he doesn't have anyone to confide in. He has a hard time trusting people, so if he's asked that of you, it means he must trust you," the mayor answered. "My journey will be dangerous and long," Boriam startet to argue but the mayor just raised his hand and said "That won't really matter to him. If he wants to leave, he'll leave. It doesn't matter where to, but I guess he'd rather leave with someone who knows where he's going." Before leaving for his room Boriam said "I think I'll take a look at the place where his parents lived in the morning. When he gets up, tell Jonathan I want to see him at the inn."

The next morning Boriam found Jonathan waiting for him by the table in the corner. As he approached the table Jonathan said "John told me this has become your table." Boriam laughed and signalled Larkin for his usual breakfast. He sat down and brought out his notebook. He drew a flower in it making sure to hide it from Jonathan. Out of the corner of his eyes he saw Jonathan shift on the chair, apparently eager for something. "You're not very patient are you?" Boriam said. "What did you draw in your book?" Jonathan replied. Boriam looked at him and said "How do you know I drew something?" "Well, your pen moved too much back and forth over the paper to be any normal writing. You didn't lift the pen more than a few times even though you crossed much the same area you had already seemingly written something. This means several strokes back and forth on the paper were needed to write what you wrote, or you made a drawing," Jonathan finished and when he saw the stare of Boriam to his reply he looked down and blushed. "Sorry, I tend to say what I'm thinking too fast." "Don't apologize" Boriam said. "You're absolutely right. You seem to be very impatient, and that is not something I need on a journey. What I do need though, is someone who can observe and understand easily. I will give you a task to do for me. Help me find the item I'm looking for, and I'll take you along on my journey. Deal?" To this Jonathan quickly said "Deal, where shall we start looking?" Boriam grinned and said "Not so fast. If we go running around the woods looking everywhere people will get suspicious. And first I will need my breakfast." He finished the sentence as the barman put the food down on his table. Jonathan smiled, leaned back and asked "How did you do that with the fire from those thugs?" Boriam looked at him and said "That with the fire? You should learn to speak in complete sentences. I did many things to the different fires." "Yes, but one ball of fire you seemed to absorb into your arm," Jonathan eagerly replied. "Then that is what I did," Boriam said and, as he didn't continue, Jonathan asked again "Well, how did you do it?" Taking his time, chewing his food, Boriam finally answered "If I explained it, you would try it. If you tried it now, you probably wouldn't be able to do it. And if you'd managed to do it, you'd probably tear this place apart and maybe even pull it into yourself. No matter what had happened it would most likely kill you. It's a fine balance which takes time to master. I can teach you some of the basic things as we travel, but first you must learn something else." "What?" Jonathan quickly blurted out, but Boriam just looked at him, smiling and said "Patience. First there is somewhere I'd like to visit. I heard your parents were killed in a fire a few years ago. My condolences. Could you show me where they lived?" Jonathan was visibly startled by this, looking into the table for a while before saying "I haven't been there myself since it happened. I guess it is time to visit the old place. I would have to go there at least once before I leave town, so why not now? Okay, I'll take you there." Boriam finished his breakfast and they headed out.

Arriving at the scene of the fire made Jonathan have to sit down. A lot of the house had fallen apart. Plants had started growing through the floor, but one wall and some doors were still standing. "This must have been a powerful fire," Boriam commented. Jonathan looked up and said "Yes, I remember we didn't even have time to get out. We were on the first floor, and by the time we noticed the fire, the entire ground floor was burning. My parents barely had time to get me out the window. It was too small for them to get through, but I managed it. As I had to jump down from the first floor I broke my foot in the fall. I had to pull myself away from the fire. As you can see, we're quite far from town, so it took a while before people came here to help. By that time..." Then Jonathan stopped talking, and Boriam understood why. He went inside and looked around. The wall was barely burnt, even though it was standing on the ground floor. He went over to it and examined the wood. Nothing on it suggested it should resist fire any better than the other walls. *Maybe the wind shifted fortuitously?'* Boriam thought as he examined it. He saw, carved in the wood, a symbol resembling a raven's claw holding a ball. Boriam asked Jonathan what the symbol was, and he said "It's a symbol my parents liked, they had it on many things. Why? Have you seen it before?" "Yes, a long time ago," Boriam answered as he walked back outside the ruined building. He looked at the nearby trees, and after a while he found a symbol hidden on the root of a tree. Recognizing it to be the signa of the Council, Boriam said "The fire was probably started by someone standing here. The Council's signa is marked on this root." Jonathan stood thinking before saying "So that means..." Boriam looked at him and said "It means that someone, on the Council's orders, killed your parents."

Chapter 9
STARS IN STONE

Jonathan's head raced so fast it hurt. *'Someone killed my parents? How is that possible? Why would anyone do that?'* He could feel his legs give in, and soon he was sitting on the charred floor of the ruins. Boriam came over and sat down beside him without saying anything. "Do you think someone in town did this?" Jonathan asked. "No, at least not anyone who's still here today. Come on, let's go," Boriam said and got up. Jonathan used the wall for support. As he pushed on the beam to the side of the symbol, it gave way and revealed a small hole. Jonathan stumbled towards the wall as his arm pushed into the hole. Boriam looked at the boy's arm and said "Well, I guess the wall didn't hold up that well against the flames after all," but Jonathan interrupted him saying "Wait, this is some kind of room. There're a few things in here." He pulled out his hand and gave Boriam a ring and a piece of parchment. He put his hand into the hole again and pulled out a strangely shaped knife and a key. A third attempt revealed the room to be emptied. Boriam examined the ring, a golden ring with a dark blue stone with a rune on it. He quickly said "This isn't the item I'm looking for. It's imbued with magic, but I don't think it's harmful to the wearer. I guess it's one of your heirlooms, you should take it." Jonathan took the ring and put it on his finger. A strange tingling went through his body, going from the ring up to his head and out through his feet. "Why did it tingle?" He asked. This seemed to surprise Boriam. He answered "Well, I guess it's possible to teach you something after all. Only some people have a natural gift for magic. Most people can be taught, but few instinctively sense magic. What kind of tingling was it? If it's possible to describe it, of course." Jonathan stood thinking for a few moments before saying "It started in my finger of course, went up my arm and up to my head. After that it went down my entire body and seemed to go out through my feet. It felt a bit like the tingling before a lightning strikes." Boriam laughed. "That's not strange. You see that symbol on the ring?" Jonathan nodded. "That's the rune for lightning. Had it been for fire, the ring would probably have had something to do with flames, and the tingling would make you feel warm. There are

47

many elements in the world, and people have learned to use them in different ways. I can't teach you much right now. As I said earlier, there's something else you must learn first. Now let's see what this is." He finished the sentence by rolling out the piece of parchment. "A map," Boriam said, "Leading to what appears to be a cave. This house is marked here, so it should be easy enough to find." Jonathan looked at the map and burst out "That's not any old cave, it's my cave. My parents took me there all the time when they were alive. I moved there after my leg had healed, I can show you where it is." Jonathan started to head into the forest when Boriam stopped him saying "There's something else written beneath the map. It reads 'In stone is cast the thirteen stars. Let the dagger give light to the stars and the key will fit in the seventh lock." "What does that mean?" Jonathan asked as Boriam lowered the scroll. "We'll just have to see. I am guessing it has something to do with your cave. Please, show me the way," Boriam said. Jonathan nodded, turned around and headed into the forest.

They arrived at the cave when the sun was at its highest. "No wonder not a single person in town knew about this cave. It's well hidden among these trees, and there's no real path leading to it. Shall we go in?" Boriam said to Jonathan who replied "I know, I haven't even been bothered by animals looking for shelter on rainy days." The cave was dark as always, and as Jonathan led the old man into the cave he quickly fished out a flint and lit a candle. Seeing the rest of the candles, Boriam lifted the three middle fingers on his right hand then waved it towards the centre of the room. As soon as his hand stopped, flames ignited each of the candles, lighting the entire room. Jonathan jumped as the candles suddenly started burning, but quickly recovered. He blushed, and to hide it started wandering around the cave. "So what now?" He asked and looked at Boriam. "I guess we will have to look for somewhere the knife fits, or for a way to direct the light using the knife. To be honest I don't know where to start. It might be well hidden, or hidden by being completely visible. I see no light source in here, so I'm guessing we have to use the knife to cut something." They started on separate sides of the room, twisting objects and examining walls, floor and ceiling. After a while, Jonathan brought out a bag of nuts saying "We should probably get some food before continuing. I've picked these over the past few weeks as backup food in case I'm unable to go to town." Boriam brought out some food he had brought on his own and they had a quiet lunch sitting outside the cave thinking what the knife could be used for. "The sun is moving around the back of the cave," Boriam said when they had finished eating. "Which means what?" Jonathan replied. "Which means that there's no way to reflect the light with the dagger. This again means there's something else we'll have to use it for. Let's go inside again and keep looking." Moving back and forth through the room they searched high and low for anything they could use the knife on. As Jonathan passed a candle he had placed on a shelf it flickered. He stopped and watched the flame while it danced back and forth as if standing in a draught. He leaned over and felt the wall behind the candle. "Did you find anything?" Boriam asked from the other side of the cave. "Not really, there seems to be a draught coming from a crack in this wall. I just watched the flame being blown around" Jonathan answered. Boriam came over and looked at the crack, then said "That's probably what we're looking for." As Jonathan just looked at him questioningly, he continued "If you think about it, we're underneath a mountain, and out of this crack there's a breeze. That means the crack has a very short way to the outside, which then could possibly be the way to find the source of light we need. Just try putting the blade into the crack." Jonathan pushed the blade into the crack, and felt it lock into the hole. As nothing else happened he tried twisting the knife. Turning it to one side he heard something snap. Soon after the snap, the cave started shaking and rumbling. Boriam ran outside. When he came back he said "An avalanche. It has taken the top off the mountain." Jonathan looked at the hilt of the dagger in his hand. The blade had clearly broken off during the avalanche. Then he noticed Boriam looking at the ceiling. Looking up, he could count thirteen dots of light glowing in the ceiling. "I guess we gave some light to the thirteen stars," he said as he kept looking up. Boriam looked at Jonathan and said "I think we should blow out the candles." They did so, and as the last candle was put out, thirteen spots of light appeared around the room. Boriam went to the entrance and said "Now this is a game I know. Let me teach you the first thing on this journey. There is a group which is often called the Thirteen. To keep their secrets they usually put up tests or puzzles like the one presented before us. If you look here how the light from one star does not hit where the spot of light is expected to be? That's common in these tests. We'll just have to hope this is one of the original systems. When coming into a room, there are some things to take notice of. If the stars have a specific shape, there is usually some clue to where you should start to decipher the test or code. Or maybe you've found the clue earlier but needed to find the test itself. Here, we have come into a room with a circle. No clue from the stars, but we know to find number seven as it was written on the parchment. Then we follow the wall on the right around the room passing the light from the different stars starting from the entrance and finding the seventh." As he explained, Boriam moved around the room ending up at the spot of light which, when looking into the ray of light, shone from the star numbering seven from the door. They examined the spot and saw a small hole in the wall. "Put the key inside and turn it," Boriam said, and Jonathan did so. The moment he turned the key, a bolt of lightning struck the key and was visibly absorbed into the ring. "Hah, ingenious those parents of yours." Boriam exclaimed as Jonathan stared at the ring in surprise. "How come?" Jonathan asked, and Boriam explained "Well, a common thief would have had a hard time understanding the riddle and tasks, but good ones would. On the other hand most people wouldn't bother putting on the ring, thinking they should sell it at a later point. The only person who would put the ring on, was either someone who knew the trap was there, or someone the ring would hold sentimental value for. Now give the key another turn and we'll see what happens." Jonathan turned the key one more time, and a small door made of stone opened up to reveal a small cupboard. On a shelf were a few items; some rings and another piece of parchment. Boriam read it out "To the finder of this scroll. We are sorry for all the tests, but we had to make sure the finder knew who we were. We are still aspiring, but we are next in line from our respective departments. We have come to fear someone is after us, and if you read this without us being there, it means they have probably succeeded in killing us. If this has come to pass, we hope you have met our son and can grant us one last wish. We want you to bring him to the thirteen to start his apprenticeship. He has been shown things throughout his childhood which will prepare him for the journey he needs to undertake, but only the purest basics. Take the item you seek, and put it to use for good. And finally, Thank you." Boriam put the scroll on the table and looked into the cupboard. The rings, not proving to be what he was looking for, he gave to Jonathan. The only other items in there were two silver cups, which Boriam put in a bag along with the parchment, and a sheathed knife. Pulling the knife out of its sheath showed Boriam a blade which changed colour every few seconds. *This, is what I was looking for,'* Boriam thought, and put it in the bag. "I will need these items, but you keep the rings. I guess we're pretty much done here, we should rest up tomorrow and start the day after. Pack some of the things you want to bring, but not so much that you can't walk for a whole day. I'll head into town and let the mayor know we're leaving. Meet me at the inn the morning after tomorrow, as early as possible. And Jonathan, don't tell anyone that we're leaving, or what we've found here." He left the cave, hearing Jonathan rummaging around for the things he wanted. He smiled and pushed his way through the forest and back to town. On the way he passed the farm where he had been helping out. *I guess I should let them know as well,'* Boriam thought and turned towards the farm. He worked the fields for a while before letting them know he was leaving. As a thank you for helping they prepared a big meal, with fresh corn, potaters, different meats and sauces. It was late before he was able to get back to the inn, so he just went up to his room. The next morning he got up, had breakfast and went outside. The rain was pouring down so heavily he couldn't even see across the road. He knew where he was heading, so the rain didn't prevent him from reaching the town hall. Entering the first room of the town hall, he was greeted by Mary, the talkative woman whom he'd bumped into earlier. She showed him into the mayor's office. After greetings were exchanged, Boriam said "John, I've found what I was looking for. I will be leaving tomorrow morning." John looked at him and said "What about the thugs? They are sure to come back, what shall I tell them?" Boriam looked at the desk for a while before answering "As I said, Arnkhand is a very wise man. If you invite them into town, showing that you won't work against them, he won't let anything unnecessary happen. They will take some of the young men, but they would have done that anyways. He's probably bringing enough men to take me down in case I'm still here. The Council had thought I was dead until now, so I guess their main task will be to find me. Let them know I've left, and they might even forget to take the men from this town. I would say it's a very small chance of that happening though." "Well, if you have to go, I guess this would happen anyways. So what about Jonathan?" The mayor said. Boriam explained that Jonathan would follow him on his journey. "What can I do to help your travels? Where will you go?" John asked but Boriam waved his hand and said "I can't tell you where we'll go. As for the rest, we shouldn't bring anything but what we need. I'm taking what I came here with, and I'm going to get some provisions. I am guessing it will be a long time until either Jonathan or I return here, if ever. So I bid you farewell, and I hope the thugs aren't too harsh with the town." Boriam got up and went to the door as the mayor said his goodbye. Outside, Boriam met Jonathan on the way to see the mayor too. Boriam nodded to him, and set his course for the market.

Having acquired food which would last for a while, Boriam bought a few waterskins and headed to the smithy. He entered the hot room and waited for the smith to finish his work before asking "Do you have a sword?" The smith looked him up and down and said "Aye, I've got one, but I haven't made many swords before, so it's far from as good as it should be. It's the only one I've got, come back in a few months and I'll have made some more to get more experience. I figure more swords will be needed in the future." *Well, a sword is a sword. The kid needs to be able to defend himself,*' Boriam thought, and said "Ok, I'll have to take what you have, but make sure it's well sharpened." Having given the sword a new edge, the smith brought the sword to Boriam's room a bit later in the day. Boriam paid the smith and put the sword in his bag before going to sleep. The next morning Boriam took his bag and his walking stick, and went out of his room. From the top of the stairs he could hear Larkin say "Ho now, haven't you packed a lot! I take it you've decided to leave town? I saw ya wanted to leave a long time ago. I guess this is as good a time as any. Here,

I'll give ya some breakfast as a parting gift."

As Boriam came downstairs, Larkin looked at him and said "Ah. So that's it. You're leaving and taking the kid with ya?" "It was his wish to leave town, how can I deny him that? I figured I might just as well try to help him through to wherever he's headed," Boriam said, and Larkin gave a quick laugh before delightedly saying "Well, I guess I should give you some breakfast as well then." He brought out two plates of food, and joined them while they ate. After breakfast they came outside to the smell of wet plants and fresh mud. They went to the edge of town. Jonathan turned to look back at where he'd grown up. "I'll come back someday. Hope it's still the same as it is now," he said and looked at Boriam. Boriam smiled and said "Who knows what will and will not be? Only time can tell for sure. Come on, let's go." And with that, they turned their backs on Shadowtree and looked at the road ahead of them, winding through the open landscape. Jonathan took a deep breath, and then they started walking.

Chapter 10
EYES IN THE DARK

Arkenthan snapped the book shut and thought *'That was a fitting place to stop.'*
He looked up and said "Oh, wow." As he peered through the window he
could see it was already dark outside. *'I wonder how long I've been reading?'* he
thought as he went outside to get some water from the well. *'It was fun
though, magic, and adventures! I remember my father telling me stories when I was
younger about dragons, magic and princesses needing rescue. Hah, I could hardly wait to
hear more of them. This one seems a bit more advanced than those fairy tales though,'* he
thought as he went inside. He put some logs on the fire and went to sleep.
The next morning he went out to check on his traps and explore a bit more
of the forest. He found a fresh game trail to put his traps by. Not far from
his house he found a small lake with coloured rocks covering the bottom. It
had a green outer ring, and a deep red centre. As it was quite shallow, the
sun was able to warm it up nicely. A few fish with a golden colour swam
around the lake. Arkenthan dived in and relaxed for a while, before lying
down on the grass beside the lake to let the sun dry him off. *'Now this, I
could get used to,'* he thought as he got up from the grass and headed towards
the forest. As he reached the edge of the forest, he heard a crash behind
him. Jumping around he saw a fjällbear come running from the forest and
towards the lake. Arkenthan hid behind a tree as he watched the bear leap
into the lake and splash around in it. It looked so joyful that Arkenthan had
a hard time of it trying not to laugh, but he knew that laughing would only
attract its attention. He didn't feel like becoming dinner today, so after
watching the bear play around in the water for a while he went deeper into
the forest. He was so preoccupied with thoughts of the bear that he almost
walked into a deer. Seeing it just in time, he quickly brought out his bow
and loaded an arrow. The deer turned just as his fingers released the arrow.
Arkenthan watched as the arrow soared past the deer and hit the tree
behind it, alerting the deer to his presence. The deer ran away and
Arkenthan could only go to the tree and pull his arrow out. *'No point in trying
to catch up to it at the moment. I hope the traps have caught something,'* he thought as
he struggled to get the arrow out of the tree. A final pull on the shaft gave a

sharp snap as the tip remained in the tree, but the rest followed Arkenthan crashing to the ground. He looked up at the sky and thought *Thank you, very much. Exactly what I needed.*' Pushing himself off the ground he saw a rabbit hanging in the air above some bushes. Puzzled by this, Arkenthan cautiously crept towards it, to find that the rabbit was suspended from his own trap. Feeling silly and glad nobody was around to see it, he quickly killed the rabbit and took it down. The two other traps he had put up also held a rabbit each. *Wow, a lot of rabbits here. I should learn how to remove their pelts, maybe I can use them for something someday,*' he thought as he headed home.

Arkenthan brought an old barrel from the outhouse into the kitchen and put the rabbits inside. He knew there were mice around, and the more layers he put between them and the meat, the better it was. He went outside and practiced his archery. *Hand to the chin and aim along the arrow,*' he thought as he breathed out slowly. Halfway through the exhalation he held it and let the arrow fly. Two things happened. First a squirrel leapt from the tree he was aiming at towards the neighbouring tree. Secondly his bow snapped sending the arrow far off course. The arrow and the squirrel happened to pass the same position between the two trees at the same time, which sent the squirrel hurtling sideways from its original path with a short surprised squeak. Arkenthan heard the arrow hit a tree further into the forest and ran after it. He found the squirrel hanging dead from the arrow about head high on the tree it had struck. *Hah, maybe that's how I should hunt from now on,*' he thought as he got the arrow and the squirrel down from the tree. Coming back he saw his bow lying in two parts only connected by the string. *Great, not really my day today, is it?*' He scooped up the broken bow, removed the string and went inside. Once inside he threw the leftovers from the bow onto the fire and put the string in the bookcase. He started skinning the rabbits and found that getting a good pelt off them was not as easy as he had thought. He tried two times, both ending up with strings of pelt and a lot of holes. While setting a stew on the fire he went out to cut down another one of the springy trees. This time he had an axe and could choose a thicker tree, both for firewood and to make another bow. He looked through the bookcase to see if there were any scrolls or books which could help him out, but found nothing. He made the new bow a bit thicker than the last one, thinking *This should make it last longer.*' As he went outside to test it, he found it to be a lot stronger than the last one. This allowed his arrows to fly in a straighter line towards his target, increasing the precision. He tired much faster though, and soon had to take a break. He took some of the rabbit pelt he had stripped and made a type of handle for the bow. After eating a warm stew for dinner he fell asleep.

Arkenthan woke up with a jolt, as something slammed into the wall outside his house. It was dark outside and everything seemed quiet. He got up and peered through the window. Not even a breath of wind stirred the leaves on the trees. He used a burning log from the fire as a torch, grabbed his knife and went outside. Once outside, he heard a faint rustling from the trees, and he jumped as an owl hooted. Walking around the house revealed nothing out of the ordinary. There were no marks that he could see on the wall, and he couldn't see anything strange near it. He brought some firewood outside and made a big bonfire. *'Now that I'm already awake, I may just as well experience a bit of the forest when it's dark,'* Arkenthan thought as he was working the flames. After a while the flames had illuminated the entire garden. He put some of the rocks he had found earlier into the flames thinking *'heating these rocks will make the heat last longer than the flames will.'* He went inside and fetched a rabbit. Trying to skin the rabbit made him realize how bad his knife was for doing exactly that, and he started laughing at the shredded pelt he was soon left with. He put the rabbit on a stick and put it over the fire. When the smell of roasted rabbit filled his nose, he made a few cuts in it and seasoned the meat as best he could. His stomach started rumbling, and Arkenthan smiled thinking *'There, there. You'll get some food soon.'* It didn't take long before another rumbling was heard, but Arkenthan didn't feel anything in his stomach this time. He looked up and saw two green eyes in the darkness. "Greypaws, is that you?" Arkenthan said as he stood up. He grabbed the rabbit, cut off a piece for himself, and took a few steps towards the eyes. As his eyes adjusted to the darkness the shape of the wolf's head appeared around the eyes. Arkenthan smiled and said "Don't scare me like that. Here, I'm guessing this is why you came!" He walked as close to the beast as he dared, and tossed the rabbit towards the wolf. Greypaws looked at Arkenthan, then looked at the rabbit and sat down to eat it. As Arkenthan returned to the fire, he saw another pair of eyes on the opposite side of the garden. These eyes had a silvery colour, and the shape seemed to change while he was looking at them. They quickly disappeared into the darkness when they noticed him. *'I wonder what animal that was. I won't go chasing after it now at least,'* he thought as he got back to the fire. Greypaws had finished his food, and had settled down to sleep. Arkenthan watched as the animal's chest rose and sank in a steady rhythm and thought *'I guess this means he trust me. A bit at least.'* The sun had started to rise, and the mountain was filled with red light. As he watched the mountain, he could see a cave which had remained hidden in the normal light of the day. *'Maybe that's the shelter I was trying to reach during the thunder storm'* Arkenthan thought. The light remained a red colour for a while, and as soon as the normal colour appeared, the cave disappeared. *'I have to explore that cave some time, but right now I'm too tired,'* he thought and went to bed.

When he woke up, it was late afternoon. He couldn't see Greypaws anymore, but the grass where he had been sleeping remained flattened, so

Arkenthan suspected he had stayed for a while. *'Maybe this is one of few places where he can feel safe as well?'* Arkenthan thought as he ate his breakfast. Knowing that the darkness would arrive soon he quickly went outside to hunt some more food. It didn't take long before he shot a doe with his new bow, burying his arrow deep into the animal. After putting it into the barrel, he went out again to check his traps. They brought another two rabbits and Arkenthan thought *'I could live off this for a few days. I think I'm going to need a type of storage system. There should be some more barrels in the outhouse. Three days' worth of food should be my goal. I will hunt for what I can, and eat the oldest animals. The doe should last for a few days, even if Greypaws were to drop by.'* When he got home, he brought another barrel into the house to put the rabbits in. He brought a third barrel to keep the pelts he got off the animals in. The doe he found to be easier to skin, but the pelt was still holey and there were stray cuts in it everywhere. As the night quickly arrived he made his dinner and went to bed early.

This night, just as the last one, he was awakened by a loud crash in the wall. He got up and went outside. Again he could see no indication of what had made the sound. He made another fire and sat looking at the stars while he let his mind wander, and then he fell asleep. He was awakened by a searing scream which was so thrilling it made the bones in his body ache. With his heart pounding he sat beside what was left of the fire with all his senses alerted. No more sounds came, but Arkenthan was unable to sleep for the rest of the night. As soon as the sun was up and the cave had disappeared back into the mountain he took his bow and headed for the lake. The water was so cold that he barely managed to dip into it before having to rush out again. It turned his thoughts away from the scream though, so he was pleased. Lying on the grass he let the sun dry him off as he thought about the cave in the mountain *Tomorrow I'll take a hike up to the top of the mountain and look for the cave. Today I should try to get a bit more food stored up, and I'll also have to fill up my stack of wood.'* He got up and went hunting. Catching a raccoon in his snares and killing another rabbit with his bow, he brought the extra food home. He spent the rest of the evening chopping down trees and making firewood from the logs. Having filled the outhouse he brought the rest of the wood into the house. He put the logs in the corner and thought *'There should have been a bin here to fill up with firewood.'* He looked outside and saw it was starting to get dark. After his dinner he read a bit more of the archery scroll, trying to find a few more hints. "Keep your right elbow high as you pull back the string, and keep both shoulders locked in a lowered position," he said to the air as he read the scroll and tried to imagine what it meant. He grabbed his bow and drew the string as if he was going to shoot something. Immediately he noticed his left shoulder started to rise up as he drew the string. He tried again focusing on keeping the shoulder lowered, but it kept rising as he pulled at the string. Annoyed, he went back to the scroll and read "If you are having trouble keeping your shoulders lowered, try lifting the bow and then adjusting the shoulders before drawing the string." He tried this and found that it made it easier to keep the shoulder lowered, even though it rose a little towards the end. The technique also required less energy, letting him aim for a longer time before tiring. He smiled as he set his bow down.

He decided to stay awake for a while that night to see if he could find out what the crashing noise was. For a long time nothing happened. Then, as he was about to fall asleep a piece of the roof fell into the room followed by a rock. Arkenthan sat for a while looking at the rock. *The only thing missing now I guess is pouring rain,*' he thought, but he was lucky enough to evade that. *'So no trip up the mountain tomorrow,*' he thought and went to sleep. The next day he spent pulling trees back to the house so he could fix the roof. Going onto the roof revealed two more rocks, making Arkenthan suspect this was the reason for the crashes the previous nights. He rolled the rocks off the roof and put them in the pile outside the outhouse. He spent the entire day fixing the hole in the roof. By the end of the day he was too tired to even bring the leftover trees out of the house, and he barely finished his dinner before falling asleep. There was no crash of rocks falling on the house this night, but when he woke up, the rain was pouring down outside. He didn't mind the rain though, as his entire body was aching from the workout of the day before. He spent the entire day lying in bed, maintaining the fire and eating. The next day he felt better, but the rain was still pouring down outside, so he spent the day preparing to make a bin to keep firewood in. *I'm glad I stored so much food, having to go hunting in this weather would've been a nightmare,*' he thought as he was piling boards to be used for the bin. He spent the next day finishing the bin as it was still pouring down outside. On the fourth day after he had repaired the roof, the rain stopped. Arkenthan noticed that his food was getting scarce, so he spent the entire day hunting and gathering wood for the bin. That evening he packed his backpack with a knife, some arrows and a flask of water. He also made a lot of extra arrows to keep in the house. *If some arrows get stuck somewhere or I have to run from those I have brought with me, I don't have to spend a long time making new ones. It'll be good to have some spares in case I'm in need of food,*' he thought as he put the arrows on a shelf in the bookcase. He grabbed a rabbit he'd caught and put it on the edge of the garden where Greypaws usually arrived, and then went to bed. The next morning he boiled soup on the meat and bones from a rabbit, and roasted some meat from the doe so he'd have food during the day. After breakfast he brought his bag and bow, and went outside.

Chapter 11
GARANI

Arkenthan saw that the rabbit was still lying on the ground where he'd left it. He sighed, turned round the corner of the house and started climbing the mountain. For a long time he struggled with loose footing before he found a more stable path upwards. By the time he was halfway up the mountain the sun was halfway across the sky. He sat down and looked at the view. The forest reached as far as he could see. There were patches and lines in the forest spread out among the trees. *'Probably lakes and rivers'* Arkenthan thought as he ate lunch. *'I wonder where I started from, where I entered the forest,'* he thought as he looked towards the horizon spreading out before him. He could see the house, and by his calculations he should head a bit more westwards in order to find the cave. He walked west and started climbing again. Every now and then Arkenthan glanced down at the house to calculate where the cave should be. He kept on climbing until he came so high up he should have passed it some time ago. He started going back and forth in a downwards path so that he wouldn't miss it, but again he went too far, and thought he must have passed it. Unsure of what to do next, he went back and forth upwards again, making a wider path. He got closer to the top of the mountain before he sat down to drink some water, eat a bit and think. *'I saw the cave with my own eyes. And even if the cave was just a shadow, there isn't anything capable of casting that type of shadow here.'* He sat thinking for a long time before it started getting chilly. The wind was much stronger here than what he was used to. He got up and stomped about a bit before thinking *'Now that I'm already so high up, I guess I could climb to the top before heading back down.'* He picked up his bag and headed for the top. Arkenthan had to climb the last part of the mountain, and as he got his head over the top he was stunned by the surprising view. In the distance he saw a village at the edge of the forest, and beyond that a small field in front of a big lake. A road leading to the village snaked across the landscape. He climbed all the way up and sat down on the mountain peak. *'Wow, I didn't think I would see the edge of the forest from here. I certainly didn't think a village was so close.'* After some internal debating he decided that the distance from the house to the village would constitute about a day's walk. *If I bring some meat to trade, maybe I can stay there for a night and buy some gear I might need,'* he thought, making himself so eager to get there that he almost fell off the little mountaintop. *'Okay, not safe to jump around up here. I'll have to get back and prepare the journey,'* he thought smiling. He decided that he would need some real meat instead of just rabbits and raccoons, which was all he had for now. He knew that some people would like them, but to get more money from selling meat he would need to at least bring a few legs of deer. When he got back home he inventoried his food and found two rabbits and a raccoon. "Not much here," Arkenthan said to himself as he put the lid back on the barrel. He went out and found another two rabbits in his traps. "I want something other than just rabbits!" he half shouted at the forest. It was getting dark and he didn't really feel like staying out in the woods after the sun was set. As he entered his garden he noticed the rabbit he'd put out had been taken by something, and hoped it was Greypaws. He took the few skins he'd saved up and bound the rabbits together. *'I can eat the raccoon when I get back. This isn't much food, but maybe enough to get me a place to stay overnight,'* he thought as he prepared his bag for travel. He drank a lot of water so that he would wake up early the next day, and went to bed.

Arkenthan woke up before the sun had risen and had to run outside to pee. The sky was starting to brighten as the sun was about to rise. He stood outside looking at the mountain and, as the mountain was bathed in a reddish colour, the cave appeared again. *'That should be exactly where I was yesterday,'* he thought. Seeing the cave now, but not being able to find it the day before annoyed him. He went inside and made a big breakfast. He also roasted some meat he could eat on the way to the village. Having finished eating, Arkenthan grabbed his bow and some extra arrows and went outside. He looked up at the mountain again and couldn't find a single indication as to where the cave was. He sighed and shook his head before starting to climb the mountain. Walking around the slope of the mountain, he could see where he needed to go to reach the village. He looked down the slope towards the dark forest. The thought of walking through it didn't appeal to him, as he knew a bit of what was out there. As he headed away from the mountain the trees grew denser and the treetops closed in on everything, making it so dark that it was hard to see where he was going. He had learned to maintain a direction though, so he knew he was walking the right way. After a while, he heard a thump and a crash a bit to the side of him. Wondering what it was, he snuck closer to the sound and as he put his head around a tree he saw a fjällbear eating a deer it had apparently caught. Arkenthan watched as the bear ate its food. He found it quite fascinating to witness, as the bear ate the entire deer. The bones seemed to crumble to sand in its mouth as it effortlessly bit through the animal. When the bear had finished eating, it went into the woods in the opposite direction of where Arkenthan stood. After imagining what that jaw could do to *his* bones, Arkenthan turned around and silently but quickly walked away from the area. Finding his path again, he kept walking towards the village with his ears pricked up. It didn't take long before he heard rustling noises from the nearby bushes. Putting an arrow to his bow and drawing the string, he crept towards the sound. He could see something brown moving in the bush, and when he was close enough he let the arrow fly. He heard a thud as the arrow struck the animal and as he retrieved it he found a hare stuck to the tip. *'I guess a fresh one will be well received,'* he thought as he put the hare in his bag and kept going. He came to a clearing with a small lake and a river running through it. He tested the temperature and jumped in to freshen up a little. Getting out of the water he didn't wait to dry up, but saw that the sun had already progressed a long way across the sky. He got dressed and walked a bit faster in order to dry off along the way. After another few hours of walking, only stopping to eat, he noticed that it was beginning to grow dark. *'I really wish I could get out of the forest before darkness falls completely,'* he thought. In order to check on his progress Arkenthan climbed a tree. What he found annoyed him. Apparently he'd been close to the edge of the forest, but the swim in the pool had disoriented him. He'd been walking along the edge instead of towards it. *'Wow, I am stupid,'* he thought as he slid back down the tree. Turning in the right direction he spotted a deer grazing a few meters ahead of him. He prepared an arrow and fired it straight through its neck. The deer jumped a bit away from him before falling over. *'Stupid but lucky. I can live with that,'* he thought smiling while he lifted the huge animal onto his back. He could see the fainting light between the trees as the sun was nearing the edge of the horizon. He walked as fast as he could onwards and soon stepped across the line of trees. He found himself a little too far to the west of the village and because of the weight of the animal he had to spend another hour walking in order to reach it.

Arkenthan wandered through the streets of the village, and as he passed them, people would stop what they were doing and stare at him. *'Now I know a bit about how Boriam felt coming to Shadowtree,'* he thought as he saw the the butcher's sign. The butcher was a big man with a thick beard and a strong voice. As Arkenthan stepped inside he said "Ho now, what have we here? Come to drop off some meat lad?" Arkenthan smiled at him and said "I don't have any money, and was hoping you might help me with that?" The butcher laughed and said "I bet you did. Well, that would depend on the meat now, wouldn't it? I see you have a deer there, and they are usually good meat. In addition there's a short supply of game these days as people are afraid to venture into the forest. Say, I haven't seen you before. Just passing through or are you planning to stay here in Garani?"

Arkenthan told the butcher that he lived some way away and had to spend a whole day to get to the village. He said he'd caught the deer in the forest a bit up the road, and would probably be able to get some more another day. This seemed to delight the butcher and he asked Arkenthan if he was returning to the village soon. Arkenthan was about to answer when he thought of a proposal for the butcher. He said "As you know, I don't have any more money than what I can get from the meat which I sell to you. If I were to stay at an inn for a night I'd lose most of that money, if not all of it. I reckon I will bring meat every time I come to the village, sometimes once a week, sometimes rarer. If I knock off the price a bit, would it be possible to borrow a room to stay in while I'm here?" The butcher stood thinking for a long time before gesturing that he should wait in the store. The butcher went into a back room and Arkenthan heard him talking with a woman. When he returned he said "Aye, my wife and I talked it over, and I guess you can borrow the spare room upstairs when you're in town. The meat you bring will attract people to my store, so I don't see any loss in it." Arkenthan thanked the butcher and was guided to the room. It was a small room with only a bed, a chair and a small table. The table stood next to the bed, beside the window. A candle stood on the table which he lit after putting his bag on the chair. Taking the money he had just received, he left his room to explore the village. The sun had gone down, and darkness filled the streets. A lot of people were out wandering between the buildings, and Arkenthan understood that most of the people here sold one thing or another. He spent an hour looking into the buildings to see what was sold before ending up at the blacksmith. It had the same tools his father used in his smithy, but the appearance of the place was completely different from home. It had a grate and an anvil, but that was the only common things. This one had two floors. 'He probably lives upstairs' Arkenthan thought when he saw the stairs. At home, the smithy was a short distance away from the house. This one was messy as well, while his father had to have everything in exactly the right place every time he had finished using it. The place did bring a sense of homesickness though, but he stepped inside without paying it much attention. A wall of heat struck him as he stepped through the door. "Ugh!" he let out before he could stop himself. The smith turned around looking at him. The smith was short with broad shoulders and a surprisingly small head compared to the rest of the man. He had a great black beard and slightly squinting eyes, as if they were too used to look directly at light. "Aye?" The smith said and Arkenthan replied "I'm sorry?" "Well, what can I help you with?" the smith said impatiently. Arkenthan stood a few seconds before realizing what he had come there for. "Do you have a tanning knife? Or some arrowheads?" He asked and the smith looked at the ceiling thinking for a while before saying "I've got a lot of scrap metal I could shape into arrowheads for ya very cheap. A tanning knife though, I have only made two of those before, one for a herdsman who is now long gone, and the other for the crazy old man living deep in the forest." The last statement made Arkenthan pay extra attention. "Crazy old man in the forest?" he asked to which the smith replied "Aye, not crazy as in dangerous, but... Well, he always had a bird on his shoulder, either it was a sparrow or an owl. Hah, once he even had an eagle with him. He stayed for a night each time he came along, and left early the next day. I haven't seen him for several years now, some animal might've got him." "And he lived in the forest? Isn't that dangerous? Maybe he had a house in there somewhere?" Arkenthan asked eagerly and the smith looked at him before saying "Aren't you a curious one? He came out of the forest, and seemed to have no fear of it at all. Beyond that, I don't think anyone would really know where he lived. He did confirm he lived in the forest though, but wouldn't say where." *I might have an idea. But if that's true, then he's not around anymore,'* Arkenthan thought before remembering where he was. "Well, pretend I'm the crazy man and that I've lost the last one. Could you make another? How long will it take for the knife and the arrowheads, and what will the cost be?" he asked the smith who replied "The arrowheads will be very cheap, as I said it will be scrap which I would normally throw away, so a copper piece per arrowhead is enough. The knife will be more expensive though, and I'm thinking between five and ten silver pieces depending on the quality of the handle, edge, protection and so on. The arrowheads will take a few hours to make, but the dagger will take longer." *Five to ten silver pieces. The meat I sold got me three silver pieces, bringing some more meat could get me three silver pieces and fifty copper pieces, but I doubt I'll be able to carry much more than that for a whole day,'* he thought as he pretended to consider the transaction. "How long will it take to make a ten silver piece knife?" he asked and the smith said "A bit more than a week of work. In a hurry?" Arkenthan laughed "No, more like the opposite. I'll be in town maybe once a week, maybe less. Each time I come to town I'll earn two to three silver pieces, which in two more weeks would mean I might have six silver pieces. Would it be possible to have you make a ten silver piece tanning knife, get it when I can pay six, and pay five more as I get the money?" "That would make it eleven silver pieces?" the smith said. Arkenthan nodded and said "And it could be nice to have some better arrowheads later on. Could you see what you could manage for next week? I'll take twenty arrowheads you could make now, and I'll see what you have in a week." The smith agreed to the extra silver piece and told Arkenthan to come back a few hours later.

Arkenthan went into the next shop and saw the entire store filled with wooden sculptures and bows and arrows of different strengths. *'Cool statues.*

Maybe he can teach me how to make a good bow,' he thought before saying "Hello, I'm Arkenthan and I was wondering if I could learn some woodworking from you? I live close to the forest and need to be able to make a bow for hunting and some arrows to go along with it." The woodworker looked him over and said "You seem to have the muscles for it. I won't be able to help you too much, but you can pay attention as I work and after a while you can try making something yourself. If it's usable I can sell it so you don't need to pay for any teaching. If you become good at it I might even pay you a bit. Have you done any crafting at all?" "I've helped my father a bit in his smithy, I'm from the Black Village, so pretty much everyone learns to do it. I haven't done it too much, so I won't say I am any good at it." The artisan laughed and Arkenthan spent the next few hours learning what to look for in trees, what works well for sculptures and what works well for bows and arrows. Eventually he told the artisan he would need some food before it got too late. He explained that he would be in town once in a while, and said he would drop by now and then. He went down the street and found a small tavern where he ate a warm dinner. It reminded him of how much he missed a full meal prepared by someone else. After his dinner he picked up the arrowheads at the smithy and went to the butcher's to sleep.

Chapter 12
ENCOUNTER IN THE FOREST

Waking up the next day he found a bag of dried meat with a note saying
"For the journey home. Thanks again for the delivery." Arkenthan smiled
and went downstairs to say goodbye to the butcher. As he left he travelled
east from the village until he was out of sight, maintaining the illusion that
he was from another town, before looking up at the mountain and heading
south into the forest. The darkness of the forest descended quickly and he
noticed a certain uneasiness come over him which had been absent during
his stay in the village. *'At least it heightens my senses'* he thought as he tried to
find a good reason for having the feeling. An hour had passed when he
happened upon a river. *'Probably the river leading to the lake'* he thought as he
stopped to drink and fill his waterskin. As he looked across the river he saw
a rabbit grazing. He shot it with an arrow, and as the arrow struck, another
rabbit appeared. It jumped towards the shot rabbit, and Arkenthan thought
'I am glad rabbits aren't the brightest of creatures' before shooting that rabbit as
well. He kept on walking, getting ever deeper into the forest.

The day passed with only a few strange sounds and a lot of trees. As
he got close to the mountain, a tree fell in front of him with a loud crash.
Out of the forest came Greypaws. As the wolf noticed him it turned
towards him and started to snarl. *'So the moment I leave the safe area of my house
you'll hunt me again?'* he thought as he looked at the angry beast. Having a
quick internal debate, where he went from being scared to annoyed and
ended up angry, he shouted "NO! I won't let you attack me now! Be quiet
you!" This seemed to confuse Greypaws as he went quiet and sat down
*'Wow, he actually sat down as well as go quiet. I guess he's not used to anyone standing
up to him. Oh, he needs a reward now so he will respond that way at another time as
well,'* he thought. He felt unsure about what was happening, but tried not to
show it. As he put his hand in his bag and got out a rabbit he said in a
calmer voice "Yes, good boy! That's what I want to see. Here, this is for
you." He threw the rabbit to the wolf. It caught the rabbit in the air and laid
down to eat it. While it ate, Arkenthan slowly moved towards the wolf.
When he got close, Greypaws lifted his head and started growling. It wasn't

an angry, threatening growl though, more of a growl telling Arkenthan that if he did something unexpected the wolf was ready to defend itself. Arkenthan decided to move a few steps closer before walking around the wolf in a circle, the entire time with the wolf's eyes on him. When he'd circled the beast he took a few steps backwards away from Greypaws, and then turned around slowly. He quietly started walking away listening intently if there were any sudden movements behind him. Having gone a short distance he stopped and took a deep breath to calm down. When he felt his breathing and heart rate returning to normal, he started smiling. *'That was scary. But now I know he won't kill me if I have something to give him at least,'* Arkenthan thought as he arrived at the lower part of the mountain. Going slightly up the mountainside made the last part of the trip home a lot shorter and soon he was stepping through the door to his, and probably the crazy old man's, house. The house felt darker than when he had left it, as if it had missed him. The walls were very cold and an uneasiness crept over him as he went into the room. Nothing was moved or disturbed in any way, but something troubled him.

He got a fire going in the middle of the room and it didn't take long for the room to heat up. The leftover water he used to wash the pelts he'd stored in the third barrel as they were beginning to smell. After bringing in more water and firewood he went to the bookcase to read more in the book he'd found. Getting close to the bookcase he was unable to spot the book and thought *'Great, so where have I put it, then?'* He pulled everything out of the bookcase in case he'd put something else on top of the book, but was unable to find it. As every book and scroll now lay spread across the floor he decided to make a system for the different shelves. Dividing the top three shelves into fighting, survival and entertainment he separated books and scrolls having to do with archery, sword fighting, spear fighting, herbs, traps, cooking and a lot of other things between the two upper shelves. For entertainment he only found what appeared to be a children's book about a rabbit going to the beach. The fourth, and bottom, shelf remained empty. He looked in the kitchen and under the bed, but couldn't find any sign of the book. *'Where did I put it? Or has someone actually been here and taken it?'* he thought as he sat down on the bed. He went outside to get some fresh air to clear his head, and saw Greypaws sitting at the edge of the garden. "Greypaws, did you eat my book while I was away?" He said jokingly to the wolf. It responded by tilting its head to the side. "Still hungry eh? Ok." He said before he went inside and fetched one of the older rabbits. Coming back outside he said "But this is the last you'll get today." He then threw the rabbit towards the wolf. The throw wasn't hard enough and the rabbit landed a little distance into the garden. Arkenthan watched as Greypaws stretched itself towards the rabbit as far as it could. He couldn't reach it, and Greypaws looked at Arkenthan with a look which said "I'm not doing anything I'm not supposed to" while slowly taking a step into the garden. With the one step, Greypaws snatched the rabbit off the ground and jumped back to the edge of the garden with a crash. Arkenthan started laughing at this and had to sit down on the ground. When he had finished laughing he said "So you will go into the garden if you have to? Maybe you did eat my book." At this Greypaws looked as if he felt guilty about something, and Arkenthan assumed it was because of going into the garden to get the rabbit. Going back inside, he pushed aside the bookcase and lit the torches on the way to the central room. *'Since I don't have the book I might just as well examine this room some more,'* he thought as he entered the room. Looking at the ceiling as he lit the torches he noticed the different torches made the different stars of the ceiling become visible. *Just like the task in the book. Except the stars here don't look like anything Boriam described. Strange that someone would make stars in the ceiling from descriptions in a book,'* Arkenthan thought, looking at the stars. His attention turned to the floor and again he noticed the arrows. All the arrows on the floor looked slightly different from one another, with those proceeding from the same walls having the most in common. Again his eyes followed the pattern the floor made and ended up at the base of the lectern. His gaze continued up the lion's foot which contained incredible details, from the claws to individual hairs in the pelt. His eyes followed the foot onto the plate and stopped at the book which lay there. *'What's that book doing there? I brought the book I found here outside,'* he thought as he walked towards the centre of the room. When he got close enough he read the title out loud "The Lion's Cub". His head started racing with questions ending up with *'So this is the book I was reading, but what is it doing back here?'* He put out the torches and brought the book back out from the cave. He pushed the bookcase in front of the cave and sat down looking at the book. When he opened the book, it even opened to the page he had just finished reading. *'Maybe I've been sleepwalking and put it back?'* Arkenthan thought before putting the book on the bed to make some dinner. He didn't have much left, and decided to stock up a bit the next day. The dinner consisted of rabbit stew seasoned with some herbs he'd found earlier. He didn't know what they were exactly, only that they lent a good taste to the food. After finishing his dinner, Arkenthan threw a few more logs onto the fire and lay down on the bed. He opened the book and started reading *'Jonathan and Boriam walked for half a day before stopping to rest.'*

Chapter 13
THE COUNCIL

They had been walking eastwards, just south of the Rihon mountains. "These mountains are said to be standing at the edge of the world," Boriam told Jonathan. "Hasn't anyone gone to the other side?" Jonathan asked and Boriam replied "You see how tall they are? There aren't many people who would be able to cross such a mountain. And they reach all the way from the western to the eastern coast of the mainland. They even continue a long way into the ocean on either side." They had been traveling through a forest in order to confuse anyone who might be following them. Sitting in an open clearing they rested while eating a bit. "How come you know so much about the world and how things work?" Jonathan asked after a while. "Hah, I've travelled to most parts of the world. I've met people who taught me everything you could ever need to know, and a bit more. Combat specialists, spiritual leaders, kings, trolls and other creatures. And my journey is far from over," Boriam said with a grin. Jonathan sat thinking for some time before asking "Who are the Thirteen my mother and father mentioned in the letter? Do you know of them?" "Yes, I know of them. Most people know of them actually. Not too easy to find though. You will find out who they are later," Boriam answered, and when he saw Jonathan was about to ask again he quickly said "And when you do find out, you will know why I can't say anything about it." With this, Boriam got up and packed his bag. Jonathan did the same, and they headed on. "So where are we going then?" Jonathan asked, and Boriam started laughing. "There are many places we'll need to go. Right now we're heading east. Something was stolen from me, and I have a feeling it's in Uppheim, so we'll have to go there at some point. Other than that, I guess the wind will guide our steps," he replied, which made Jonathan think for a long time. After walking for an hour he said "So we're looking for someone it seems no one knows where are, we're heading east to some town we don't know, and the only sure thing is that we're heading to Uppheim some time during our travels?" Boriam smiled at him and said "We will go where we will go. You have a lot to learn, even before meeting the Thirteen, and I will teach you what I can."

FREDRIK B. LUNDE

The day passed and Boriam told Jonathan of how the plants they passed worked. He described which plants were edible, which were poisonous and which were good for healing wounds. In the evening they stopped beside a small river to camp for the night. Jonathan was shown how to light a fire. He struggled a lot, but eventually got the fire going. "What do you know about fighting? Either unarmed or with weapons?" Boriam asked him. Jonathan looked at him and said "I can't say I've fought much, I hit a guy once with my fist, and I tried archery once, but nothing more than that." Boriam nodded and said "At least you're honest. Any big-city kid would brag about things he didn't know. Now I know where you stand, and I actually believe you. Here, I got this for you," Boriam said and gave Jonathan the extra sword. "We'll practice with sticks until you feel comfortable in a fight. When we're not sparring you'll have to get used to the weight of a sword. Anything can happen at any time, so you'll have to be ready at all times." "We're going to be fighting a lot?" Jonathan asked and Boriam sighed before answering "Yes, I can't see how we can avoid it. You saw the fight which took place outside Shadowtree; those men will be hunting us. In addition to that, the Thirteen are hunted by the Council and anyone who follows them, so finding them will mean drawing the attention of those who hunt them as well." Jonathan looked at Boriam and asked "I've heard of the Council, but I don't know much about what they are or why everyone hates them." "Ah, this is important to know," Boriam said. "Thirty five years ago there were five people, one from each of the great races: humans, trolls, gnomes, the merfolk and the birdmen. There are many more creatures out there with civilizations or small camps, but these five are reckoned to be the five great races. One day, the five people that now call themselves the Council met in a tavern somewhere. There they sat together and started talking about how much they hated the system they were living under. Everyone agreed that something had to be done. They were all masters of the arts of each race, I'll tell you about those some other time. Anyway, these five geared up and started attacking small villages. From each of the villages they took they recruited more men to fight for them, and eventually they could take over larger cities like Uppheim and Tar'miso. They have their main seat in Tar'miso, as it is at the very centre of the world. Everywhere they went, people were robbed of what valuables they owned, and so even though they took control of most of the cities in the world, most people hate what they've done. The systems for living that they've tried to set up haven't worked yet. People are poor and unhealthy in many villages. Since they first started raiding cities, people have gathered in order to fight them. After a few years people started migrating from the cities and gathered in larger numbers. Now there's a great number of people in their army, and when the time comes they will attack the cities of

68

the Council to free the people, and eventually march upon the Council themselves. They just call themselves the Resistance. What I am doing, is wandering the world trying to find things, whether it's weapons, allies or knowledge, which could help in the defeat of the Council." Hearing this Jonathan quickly said "I want to help the Resistance, can we go there?" Boriam laughed and said "We will get there eventually. You still have a lot to learn before you can help them, and besides, didn't you just express a wish to meet the Thirteen?" Jonathan looked at the ground before answering "Yes. I do. But that's mainly because of the letter my parents wrote. If the Thirteen know so much, why don't they help the resistance?" "Oh, but maybe they are. In their own way that is. I guess we'll see when the fighting really starts. For now the Resistance is hiding, so the Thirteen are hiding in their own way," Boriam said. "Now let's see about that sword fighting." He got up and broke off two sticks from a nearby tree. "What would you like to learn? There are three main styles of sword fighting. One where you have a short sword in one hand and a shield in another, one where you have a hand and a half sword, which is a bit harder to handle, but where you can either use one hand if you use a shield or two hands if you don't. There're also great swords, like claymores, which are pretty long and you can't use a shield as you'll need both hands to wield the sword. If you take the point of your arm halfway between your shoulder and your elbow, the distance from there to the ground is the length of a claymore. So you'll have to choose for now what to use, and that'll be what we'll focus on." Boriam finished letting Jonathan ponder on the three types. "I think," Jonathan said "that I'll use the half thing. I know you said it was harder to use, but if it's possible to fight both with and without a shield, I would choose that." Boriam smiled and said "Good reasoning skill at least. I prefer a hand and a half sword as well, so I'll teach you what I know." He threw the stick to Jonathan who caught it mid-air. Boriam showed Jonathan how to hold a sword when fighting without a shield. After going through stances and grips on the stick they prepared for sparring. *I wonder how good he is. He looks old, but he took out those thugs so easily,'* Jonathan thought and saw Boriam moving towards him. The old man swung his stick towards Jonathan's head. He barely managed to block the stroke, but it was so hard that his arm shook from the blow. His hand felt numb and the stick jumped out of his grip and struck him on the head. *'Ouch,'* Jonathan thought as he put his hands to his head. "Pick up your weapon again, and be ready," Boriam said. Jonathan picked up his stick slowly to let the numbness pass a bit from his fingers. He resumed his stance and Boriam attacked again. This time Jonathan managed to parry a few blows before losing the sword. "Move your feet while fighting. As I change my attacks, your stance has to change too. A good fighter can look at his opponent's feet and know where the blow will fall," Boriam said. They kept on sparring until Jonathan was unable to hold the stick any longer. Stars had filled the sky while they were fighting. Jonathans hands felt so warm he had to cool them down in the river. When he returned to the fire, Boriam had put a bag filled with water above the fire and was dropping meat into it. "Won't that start burning?" Jonathan said pointing at the leathery bag. "Well, yes and no. For something to start burning, it needs to reach the right temperature. The water absorbs the heat from the bag as soon as it is received from the fire. If the water were to start boiling, a normal leather bag might catch fire, yes. But this isn't a normal leather bag. This is the stomach of a Golrath, a type of lizard which lives at the edge of volcanoes. They are so resistant to heat that some of them actually live in fire. So this bag won't burn even if I put it in the fire and leave it there," Boriam answered and saw that Jonathan had wrinkled his nose. "So we're going to eat soup from the stomach of a lizard?" He said and Boriam smiled "If that's how you wish to look at it. I've been using this for several years, they are very durable, so everything left by the Golrath is gone a long time ago. Most bags are a type of animal, and it's often the stomach, so you shouldn't be too picky about it. When you get hungry enough you'll eat pretty much anything out of whatever is close at hand. You'll probably see and do that at some point in your life, so why not now?" Jonathan gave up discussing it, and so they ate their food and went to sleep. The trembling of his exhausted hands and the pounding of his heart kept Jonathan awake. He looked up at the stars wondering where they were headed. After a long time, the fire having burned down to glowing embers, Jonathan finally fell asleep.

Chapter 14
TRAINING

Boriam woke Jonathan up by throwing his bag at him. He watched as
Jonathan, confused about the whole situation, slowly turned around and
looked at him asking "What?" Boriam shook his head and said "What if
that bag had been an enemy attacking you?" Jonathan's eyes were red from
the lack of sleep and he was almost falling asleep mumbling "Then I
wouldn't have had a very good time right now, would I?" To this Boriam
answered "No, I guess you wouldn't. Always be prepared to defend
yourself, even if you are asleep." "Okay, I'll have to work on that. The dog
is angry," Jonathan said still mumbling and Boriam looked around before
saying "What dog?" "What?" Jonathan opened his eyes a little and Boriam
said "You said 'The dog is angry.' What dog?" Jonathan looked blankly at
him and groaned while turning around before saying "Never mind, I think I
was sleeping." Boriam laughed and stood up. "Come on you, I see you
haven't slept too well, but we have to get going. I reckon we'll reach
Tresponts by tomorrow if we can maintain the pace we had yesterday."
Jonathan got up slowly, needing several attempts before managing to sit up.
He drank some water from the river and dipped his head in it to wake
himself up a little. His hands were sore and his feet ached, but he didn't
complain about it. They filled their waterskins and hid the residue from the
campfire as well as they could before leaving.

They walked through the forest for most of the day. Jonathan found
the walk boring, as the most exciting thing happening was a squirrel leaping
between two trees. At lunch he sat down heavily with a sigh before a stick
hit his head. "You're dead." Boriam said in a calm voice. "We're sparring
now?" Jonathan asked. "Of course we are," Boriam said. "You have to be
ready for a fight at any moment, even when you're tired. Believe me, you'll
meet with fights when you are a lot more tired than this." He swung the
stick again and Jonathan ducked beneath it pulling out his own weapon.
They sparred for a while, giving Jonathan a few more bruises. He felt like he
started to understand a bit about how to deflect different types of strokes,
but he had a hard time trying to retaliate. *'I'll get you soon,'* he thought angrily

as they sat down to eat. "How long until we get to Tresponts?" Jonathan asked. "We've been walking a bit slower today, but if we keep going we should be there by nightfall tomorrow. Have you ever been anywhere besides Shadowtree?" Boriam asked. "Not really, a few times there have been people coming to town. That's the only time I've seen anyone who hasn't been from Shadowtree," Jonathan answered and Boriam nodded understandingly. "Then you, my friend, have a lot to learn," Boriam said with a smile. After talking a bit about how to behave in other towns, such as what to look out for so you wouldn't get into trouble, they went on. As they went, Jonathan slowly pulled his stick from his bag. Finding a good grip, he swung it at Boriam. He was unable to really say what happened, but he felt the stick being blocked, there was a lot of movement and suddenly he was lying in a nearby bush. "Good attempt, but you made it too obvious. And you should be prepared to defend yourself if your opponent notices your attack," Boriam said and helped him to his feet. Jonathan was still a bit unbalanced, but it soon passed when they started walking again. They turned southwards to reach the end of the forest. As the shadows started to grow longer, they emerged onto a field of bright green grass. "Ah, this will make our trip easier," Boriam said and pushed forward. They walked until the sun set, and then a while longer, before making camp. "You ready to spar a bit?" Boriam asked. Jonathan answered "You're actually asking now?" But Boriam just gave a short smile and nodded. Not wanting to appear weak, Jonathan said "Yes, I'm ready to spar a little" as he got a grip on his stick. "Good, let's eat," Boriam said and started rummaging for food in his bag. It took a while before Jonathan realized what Boriam had actually said, during which time he stared blankly at the older man digging through his bag for food. As the food came out he understood what was happening and said annoyedly "Why did you ask if I was ready to fight when we weren't going to?" "There won't always be a fight, even if you expect one. Anything can happen at any moment in any situation," Boriam answered. "What do you mean by that?" Jonathan asked and Boriam sighed before answering. "You know how a hooded man in a dark alley makes you feel like you'll have to defend yourself, but as you pass him you see he's an old neighbour and the two of you end up having a long conversation? Or how a group can seem to have a good time at a tavern, talking and laughing until one person makes an unfortunate comment and the next day the entire tavern looks like a hurricane has passed through it?" Jonathan nodded a response to both questions. "Well, it's like that. Sometimes you walk through a dark alley and three people might step up in front of you, and you think 'I'm going to die now', and you get ready to defend yourself. When they get close to you, one of them steps up saying 'Here, could you help us out a bit? We're trying to get this cat down from this here tree.' Or some other strange thing you couldn't even begin to imagine they would be saying at that place or situation. That's what I'm trying to tell you: anything can happen in any situation and at any moment." Jonathan laughed trying to imagine how he would feel in the imagined scenario. "I think I see what you mean, but I think it's very unlikely they would be saying that there," he said to which Boriam just smiled and said "unlikely, but possible. Happened to me when I was nothing more than a lad of the same age as you." Jonathan sat down thinking about what he had heard. "Have you ever tried meditating?" Boriam suddenly asked. "No, I don't even know what meditating is. Taste good?" Jonathan replied. Boriam laughed for a long time making Jonathan feel stupid for not knowing. Finally he replied "No, my dear boy, meditation is a way to relax and at the same time sharpen all your senses. It's not easy at first, but the more you try, the better you get at it. It requires patience though, and if you don't have that, meditation will teach it to you. Meditation is something you'll have to learn if I am going to teach you more of what I know. But right now, we'll eat and then sleep. I'll teach you meditating tomorrow when you are a bit less tired and more focused."

The next day came faster than Jonathan wanted it to. He'd finally got some good sleep and didn't want to be awakened when he was. When they had eaten a bit they moved on. "So how do I learn this meditating thing you mentioned yesterday?" Jonathan asked while they walked across the field. "Ah, that. I'll have to teach you that when we're resting. It's a way to relax and preserve energy. There are several stages of it which you'll have to get past before mastering it, but when you do it will help in every situation you're in. The first stage is when you're sitting, on a chair or something else, with your feet steadily placed on the ground and your back straight. You close your eyes and breathe, and while you do so you count every breath you take. If you lose your count, just start over. The amount of breaths taken is not important, but the focus you put on each breath is. This is what you'll be doing tonight after sparring a bit. Each stage will take differing amounts of time before they can be passed, and will be different for each person. We'll just have to see how long you take when you do it," Boriam answered, but then Jonathan interrupted asking "We're sparring tonight as well? But aren't we getting to a town tonight?" To which Boriam just stared blankly towards the horizon apparently thinking about something else before saying "Oh yes, right, I said we'd get to a town tonight, didn't I? Well, we're not going to make that. We haven't walked fast enough each day, but that's ok. We still have food and it gives us more time to teach you what we need to," he said with a smile and continued "But we're probably going to see it a long way off when we make camp tonight, so I can pretty much guarantee that we'll get there tomorrow. If I have calculated the distances correctly, that is." Boriam looked over the fields and towards the forest to the side of them. Then he began telling a few stories. They made Jonathan lose the awareness of how tired he was. He let himself drift into a waking dream, pretending to live out the stories. It took his mind to farms, villages and caves deep in the mountains, and soon the day started growing old again. They stopped to eat a bit, at which time Boriam taught Jonathan how to make knots for different situations, whether he had to tie an animal to a pole or make a trap to catch food. As they started walking again, a wolf came running out of the forest. It stopped a fair distance from the forest and Boriam said "Look at that wolf. Do you think it's old or young?" Jonathan glanced at the wolf and said "I don't know, how could I? Ok, young. Is it important?" "You will see later if it is important or not. For now, what do you think it's feeling?" Boriam asked. Jonathan sighed thinking *How can I possibly have any idea what it's feeling?'* before taking a longer look at the wolf. It ran back and forth turning several times to each side. After a while it noticed the two wanderers and ran back into the forest. "Well, at the end there it seemed scared of us," Jonathan said. Boriam looked at him and said "Yes, at the end, but not really scared. It was just uncomfortable around us when it was all alone." After a few moments of silence, Jonathan asked "So what did it feel then?" It took a few moments before Boriam replied saying "That, I cannot tell you." This annoyed Jonathan and he exclaimed "Because you don't know, or because you don't want to?" But to this Boriam just smiled and started telling another story. Jonathan stayed annoyed for a while, before he started listening to the story, at which point he'd completely lost the meaning of it.

As the darkness closed in around them, they could see a weak light on the horizon. "That, is Tresponts. We'll get there tomorrow. For now we'll spar, then you'll try meditating while I prepare some food." And so they did. Jonathan felt he began to get a bit more control over his sword. He only lost the sword three times, which he felt to be a great improvement. The meditating however, was a completely different story. Boriam said "To meditate, you must first sit in an upright position, with your feet well set on the ground. Then you must focus on your breathing. In order to do that, you should count every breath you take. If you lose your count, just start over." Jonathan found a place to sit, and started counting his breaths *'1.. 2.. 3.. 4.. 5.. Well, this is boring. Wonder why he's so eager for me to do it. Oh, counting, let's see. 8? Ah, crap. I'll start over then. 1.. 2..'* he thought before saying "Are all stages of this meditation as boring as this?" Boriam gave a short laugh and said "Well, it's up to you. Don't focus on how boring it is, but focus on the number of breaths you take. That will help you a lot with that problem." And with that he returned to the cooking and Jonathan kept on meditating. When the food was ready, Jonathan asked "So how long does it generally take to pass each stage of this?" "Some people move onto the next stage after the first day. Some stay on the same stage their entire lives. Often it is so that the stages will be passed more quickly as you reach the higher levels. That's because you then understand more of what it is about, but this is not always the case. For you, it seems you've started to learn, but you've still got a long way to go before passing the first stage. Have patience, and it will work itself out," Boriam answered. Jonathan sighed and ate his food. They didn't stay up very long as they wanted to get to Tresponts as early as possible. The next day greeted them with a clear sky, which brought renewed energy for the last stretch of their walk.

Chapter 15
ARRIVAL IN TRESPONTS

Half the day passed before they reached the gates of Tresponts. "These people like to pretend they're a big city, which is why they have put walls around it and guards at every entrance. If you get into a conversation where, for some reason, you have to mention the size of it, say it's a big city," Boriam said to which Jonathan answered "So they lie to themselves in order to feel important?" Boriam gave a short laugh and said "You're pretty direct in your statements, aren't you?" Jonathan didn't respond to that, but watched as the guards checked the different travellers. "Why do they do that?" He asked and pointed to the guards. "Well, they need to check if someone is bringing something illegal into the city, or if anyone who's wanted tries to get in." Jonathan nodded, and then said "But aren't you wanted by the Council?" To which Boriam said "Yes, but people wanted by the Council are kind of ignored here. The city's under their control, but very few support them, even the guards, so it's likely that they will look the other way as we're entering. But then again, word of me is unlikely to have arrived here already, so it should be easy to get inside the gates." They stepped up to one of the guards who said "Who are you, and why are you here?" Boriam calmly answered "I'm an old man looking for old trinkets. This is my nephew who works as my guard, and in return is learning about the world." The guard examined them both and said "He doesn't look like much of a fighter, and you're an old man, so I guess you won't be much of a danger to the city. You may pass, have a good stay here at Tresponts." Boriam nodded to the guard, and they walked into the city.

From inside the walls, the city looked a lot larger than it had from the outside. Pointing this out, Jonathan was told that wrapping something up in walls or a roof gives that effect. Directly inside the gate was a circular area where the guards were training, along with a board with wanted-posters. They couldn't see any posters of themselves there, and started feeling more relaxed about their journey. "I guess they haven't found out I'm not in Shadowtree anymore," Boriam said. There were two roads leading out of the area. Boriam pointed to them, and said "These two roads each lead to a city gate. There are three gates in the city, and they are connected by these big roads. All the other roads run out from the main ones, and they are connected again by several back alleys. It's a pretty smart system for a small city. The bigger ones wouldn't be able to manage with this kind of system. I guess you'll see when you get to one of the bigger cities. Let's find an inn to stay at." He went down the road with a sign of a bull hanging above it. The other one had a sign of a snake. "The Bull is where most of the butchers' stores and taverns and inns are. The Snake is where the gambling halls, theatres and healers are, and the road connecting the other two gates is the Stag. This is where crafters of different types and official buildings mainly are located. Oh, and the quirky stores. You know the ones where you come inside and see the strangest things, and the air has so many different aromas that your eyes water instantly. They are spread about the city in various back alleys. We have some business with a few of them," Boriam said in a lecturing voice, ending with a grin that made Jonathan shift uneasily. After a while Boriam turned into an alley and said "Ah, the Bull's Horn. This should do well for our stay. Cheap, decent service, not too many fights in a night, might be because of the guards though, and they take payment on arrival, just in case someone has to make a hasty leave of town." "Guards?" Jonathan asked. "Aye, not the city guards no, these here hire trolls to keep order in their inn. Handy creatures, trolls. They can sit staring at nothing for a year with minimal food requirements and still feel amused. When they get paid for a job, they do it so loyally and precisely it feels like you're doing it yourself. So in here, if the owner says someone is making trouble, it doesn't matter if it's one person or twenty, they're going out whether they want to or not," Boriam answered with such enthusiasm it made Jonathan laugh. "You're crazy," He said jokingly and Boriam answered with a smile "Oh yes, but hopefully the good kind of crazy."

Having stepped inside, they heard a tiny voice shout "Boriam! My lord, where have you been?" Turning around, Boriam shouted "Felix! Long time no see! Hey, do you have a room for me and my friend here for a few nights?" Jonathan watched as Felix passed them. From the voice he assumed he was a tiny person, but the only thing Jonathan could think of when he saw the man, was a ball. He seemed to be exactly as wide as he was tall, wearing a leather garment which seemed to be a size too small. Felix had a bald head with big ears and a tiny nose. "Hmm. I believe I could find something for you," the ball said as it wobbled in behind the counter. "Got yourself an accomplice, eh? Is he one of those learner-thingies of yours? You know, student or what you now call it? Never mind, it's none of my business. But you'll have to join me for dinner tonight. The wife'll be happy to see ya." Boriam smiled and said "I am teaching him a bit of what is necessary to know. We'll be delighted to join you for dinner, just leave a note in our room with the time on it. We have some errands to attend to. Do you know if Stephie is still in business?" Felix brought out the key for the room and said "Ah, yes. Stephie's still in business. Not in this city anymore though, but not too far off. She moved to Fisherman's Rest when the Council started going through what the stores were allowed to sell. I guess she would've been in prison by now if she'd stayed here. I haven't spoken to her for a long time though, a year perhaps. Oh my, how the time flies. Anyways, your room is right up there, I'll let you know about dinner in the um.. usual manner." he finished, with a wink to Boriam, and then they were headed to the room. "Usual manner?" Jonathan asked as they came to their room. "Ah, yes. He knows people might be after me at any time, so he hides the note a bit. You'll see later," Boriam answered and Jonathan shot him a suspicious glare before saying "You're pretty often in trouble, aren't you?" As a reply Boriam just smiled and pushed open the door. They put their things down and headed out. Returning to the bar, Jonathan noticed the guard troll standing in the corner. It seemed to be purely made of stone, and its eyes were red flames. "Is that a fire troll?" Jonathan asked Boriam. "What do you mean?" He replied, and Jonathan thought for a moment before saying "In your story back in Shadowtree you said trolls belonged to their own groups, depending on their element. I was just thinking that the troll was a fire troll as its eyes were burning." Boriam looked at the troll and said "Ah, but that was a legend. Yes, trolls have their own elements. The only thing which can kill them, if used as a weapon, is their opposite element, but their elements are not displayed in the same way as in the tale I told. Let's sit down, I have a feeling this will take a while." They went to a table and sat down before Boriam continued. "Every troll's eyes burn. The colour of the flame can change by the mood or will of the troll. Extremely old or talented trolls will have the colour in their eyes shift every few seconds no matter how much attention they are putting into their current task. They must be very tired or wounded before their eyes stop changing. I'm telling you this, because I've only seen two trolls who are able to do this. The first was Krangh'an, the late king of the trolls, the second was Druch'an, who is the troll who is part of the Council. He's not very old, but he is extremely talented at their skill. And no, I don't know his element. You can't know what element a troll is until he gives it away, and this one is very cautious. I'll teach you how to spot a troll's element at a later time." Jonathan looked at Boriam and asked "What did you mean by 'their skill'?" "Oh, mentioned that, did I? Well, you'll learn this anyways. Trolls are elementalists. They can bend the magical elements pretty much however they will. Remember in my tale that I mentioned six elements?" Boriam said. Jonathan nodded and Boriam continued "Well, there are two more. There are no trolls made of these elements, as they are combinations of the

78

others. Before I go on, I must make this clear: the tale was not representing the trolls of today. Trolls far into the past might have displayed their elements on their skin, but these days all trolls look very similar. The two last elements are light and darkness. Fire burns, ice cools. Wind stings, water soothes. Lightning bites, earth shelters. Darkness drains and light heals. That's the eight elements of the world and their opposites. Light is made by combining ice, water and earth, whereas darkness is made by combining fire, air and lightning. For this reason there are no trolls of these two elements." Jonathan sat looking at the table for a while before saying "So for the Council to fall, one would have to kill Druch'an? And the only way of doing that is by having a magician cast the element which is opposite of what he is?" Boriam responded quickly with "Well, that would be the easiest way, yes. The other way to kill a troll is to crush its heart. Each troll has their heart in a different location in their body, so finding it would mean cleaving off bits of hard stone all over its body until the heart was found. So yes, in practicality, the only way of killing a troll is by using magic of the troll's opposite element." "Can I learn magic? Please?" Jonathan said enthusiastically. Boriam smiled at him and said "Studying under the Thirteen involves that, but not from the beginning. Magic is generated from your spirit, and until you have mastered your body, you cannot use your spirit actively. This is one of the reasons I'm teaching you how to fight and to meditate. Fighting strengthens your body, and meditation sharpens your mind." Jonathan seemed to understand as he sat there looking at the table nodding to himself. "Who are the Thirteen?" He said eventually. "That, I will have to tell you at another time, or we'll be sitting here all day. Come on, let's get going. I'll show you around town today so you can find your way around on your own tomorrow while I run some errands."

Chapter 16
DINNER WITH OLD FRIENDS

Stepping outside, they noticed it had started to rain. It wasn't too heavy though, so they pushed on. The city seemed to Jonathan to be mainly white and brown. Brown from tarred logs and white from a type of stone. The stones in the buildings were used to help against fires, Boriam said, as he pointed and talked their entire walk through the triangle of roads. There were smaller roads leading straight out from the main roads, all the way to the city wall. The walls formed as close to a perfect circle as the terrain would allow, so it was easy to find your way around. In the centre of the city stood a castle. Not a grand castle like in the great cities, but a small castle which looked like a miniature version of the bigger ones. Of course, Jonathan had no idea how big other castles were, so to him this one appeared to be huge. It stood on a little hill overlooking the city, and you could see it from almost anywhere in town. There were small shops and places to eat everywhere on the Bull Road. In the middle of the Stag Road there was a beautiful garden with flowers and little fountains and deer wandering around. Jonathan found it very relaxing. Having been used to the forest at home, the city seemed very crowded and noisy. This garden made him feel a bit at home. "I think I'm more comfortable in a forest than in a city," Jonathan said out loud without meaning to, so he jumped when Boriam said "Feel at home here, do you?" Embarrassed he looked down and answered.

After Jonathan had got to know his way around the city, they returned to the inn. Getting to their room Boriam told Jonathan to turn down the main lamps in the room. While Jonathan did so, Boriam went to the lamp standing on a small table on the side of one of the beds and looked inside it. "Nope, not here." He said before turning to the lamp beside the other bed, examining it and saying "Ah, here we go." He turned it on and increased the flame to shine strongly in the now darkened room. Jonathan noticed a lot of dots appearing on the lamp screen, and they cast small shadows all around the room. He saw Boriam turn the lamp screen one quarter turn, then two more, before saying "Well, seems like dinner's in about an hour.

Good timing to get back now then." Jonathan was very confused about this, and asked how he could know that from some dark spots on a lamp screen. Boriam told him to come to the lamp. As he did so, Boriam pointed at the shadows cast on the wall. Several lines of darker spots adorned the wall behind the lampshade. Each of the spots had a small edge pointing to different sides, some spots were filled in and some were circles. "The different spots are the same as letters, as a code. Knowing what the different spots mean will let you know what the code says." Jonathan nodded and asked if he could learn the code. Boriam then started to rummage around in his bag and finally brought out a small book. "Here. I've put down some interpretations of different codes, how to sort and read them. I guess you can have it and can continue filling it in if you see any more codes anywhere." Jonathan took the book and threw himself onto his bed, eagerly starting to read.

An hour later Boriam and Jonathan stood in the main hall of the inn preparing to leave when a tiny person with pointed ears and a pointed nose entered. "What's that?" Jonathan said having never seen anything like it before. "Is he ill?" "Shush! Don't say that, he's a gnome. And they hear extremely well. Every now and then they come out of their caves to sell or buy things. Strong merchants and hagglers, but mainly masters of mechanics and engineering. They invented watches, you know." He finished the sentence by lifting his watch out of his pocket. "The gnomes mainly live in the mountains. They dig deep and wide caves, and some say they were responsible for making the caves the great dragons used to live in." Jonathan looked up at Boriam and said "Great dragons? There're dragons in the world?" "Ah, none of the great dragons are left. They were savage beasts who killed for the joy of killing. Most races hunted them down and eventually killed all of them. They were smart though, and they could communicate with people or trolls or whoever they wished through their thoughts. There are still dragons around, but not the dragons you're thinking of. We're probably passing an area later on in our journey where I know some are living, so I'll try to find one you can take a look at. Gnomes can communicate with and control animals as they wish, but they never misuse them, unlike Chiros. Because they are able to control animals freely, the gnomes were accused of controlling the dragons to kill the other races. We never heard about attacks on gnomes, but personally I believe they lost more people than any other race." Jonathan looked at Boriam and said "Chiros? Who's that?" "He's the gnome member of the Council. He's the one who invented the machines which were used to conquer some of the major cities. He has an army of beasts to protect him at all times." Jonathan sighed and Boriam turned towards him saying "What?" "Well, these Council members seem to be very hard to reach, and even harder to fight.

No wonder no one has managed to kill them yet." Boriam smiled and nodded before saying "Come on, let's get to the dinner. It's just in the house next door, so not much of a hike."

The rain was pouring down outside, and the short trip from the inn to Felix' house left them dripping. Felix laughed as he saw them, saying "Aye, the weather changes quickly in these parts of the world." Jonathan greeted Felix more properly this time, and was introduced to his wife Andrea. As most wives of innkeepers, she was the boss in the kitchen. "You've changed a lot since I was here last," Boriam commented as they entered the living room. "Ah, well, you have to change some things over the course of three years," Felix replied. "My gods, has it been three years? Tell me, what news is there?" Boriam said, and the two of them started a more personal conversation. When their conversation steered towards the old times and how both of Felix' daughters had been married off, Jonathan felt that he would've had to experience their past in order to understand it. Andrea and Jonathan sat talking the way strangers do, where no one really knows what is to be said. She showed him around the house, the study and the library, where Jonathan saw there were many books which were extremely old, and wondered what they were all about. As they returned the two others looked up and wondered when the dinner would be ready. Andrea hurried off and soon returned with a leg of lamb. From the smell of the lamb, Jonathan's mouth watered as they all sat down to eat. "So what are the two of you doing traveling around then?" Felix asked and Boriam said "The parents of Jonathan here left a note to whomever found it, with a request that he joined the Thirteen, so I'm bringing him along looking for them." Felix seemed puzzled at this, saying "Looking for? But.. Aren't.. Oh. Right. I see." He looked around the room and asked "Is there anything I can help you with?" Boriam leaned over the table and in a low voice asked "Can you get a message to Thundir for me?" Felix' eyes widened, but he quickly recovered saying "It won't be easy, but I can try." Boriam nodded and said "Let's do it later." before turning to Andrea and saying "This lamb is delicious, what have you done with it?" And so the talk widened and lasted long through the night, with stories and jokes. Jonathan mainly listened to what the others had to say. He didn't feel he had anything to add to the conversation, except answering direct questions. It was late before they left and as they were preparing to leave, Boriam turned around and said "Tell Thundir the lights are abroad, seeking through darkness as they have before, and sparks are at their tails." Felix' grin disappeared, and a puzzled look crossed his features, before he nodded to Boriam. The old man then said "Oh, and I would like to take a look at a couple of your books tomorrow, if that's all right by you?" This delighted Felix more than having to bring this Thundir a message, and a smile appeared again before they left the house and returned to the inn. Boriam said "Now that you know your way around town, you'll spend most of the day on your own. I'll have to check up on a few things after getting provisions, but I'll meet you back here as soon as darkness begins to fall." And with that they fell asleep.

The next morning Jonathan woke up later than normal. Looking over to Boriam's bed he saw that the old man had left already. Sitting up, he noticed a small stack of coins stood on the bedside table next to a note. It didn't say anything, but was filled with edged lines. Looking at it he suddenly remembered the little book of codes Boriam had given him. He got it out and looked through it. About halfway through the book he found the right symbols. He translated the note to read "Quick thinking. Good! I'm out to get supplies, and then going to Felix' house to look up some information. I have put a stack of money on the table, enough to buy food for the entire day and a bit extra, in case you need it. Have fun today, explore town and learn something new." And with that the note ended. Jonathan looked at the stack of money, put it in his pocket and went to find some breakfast. At the market he bought a roasted newt which he brought to the park they had visited the day before. They both reminded him of home, where the newt was a delicacy he could rarely afford. He sat in the park for a while just listening to the sounds of the animals, the people walking by and the noise of the city itself. After a while he got up and went to the Snake Road. Looking down one of the back alleys he found a very strange store. His nose wrinkled from the smell, but something made him want to enter. Perhaps it was the owl atop its cage, or the old looking bows hanging on the wall. He didn't know why, but something made him go inside. He expected to find a crooked old lady behind a glass ball, but this couldn't have been further from what met him. There was a woman behind the counter, but not an old woman with a wart on her nose, nor a beautiful young woman. This one was as ordinary as you could imagine, and Jonathan thought *Why are you working in a store like this?* He walked around the store looking at medallions and old books when the woman came up to him, staring intently at his eyes. Jonathan felt slightly uncomfortable and said "Hello?" to ease up a little. She made a few hand gestures reminding Jonathan of those Boriam had made outside Shadowtree, and he got worried she was casting some magic on him. After this had gone on for a while he realized she couldn't speak, and was trying to talk to him. Feeling silly at fearing the worst right away, he said "Oh, I'm sorry, I don't understand hand gestures." She gestured for him to follow her to the counter. Passing a stack of swords, shields and diverse armour they got to the counter where she picked up a pencil and wrote "You are on a journey?" Jonathan confirmed her question and she continued "It is important that you complete it. I don't know why it is important, only that it is. Is there anything I can help you with?" *'So that's why you're working in a store like this. You're crazy,'* Jonathan thought, but only said "Ah, thank you, but no thanks. I just found this store interesting, not much I'm looking for" and finished with a "yet." The woman smiled at him, nodded and went into the back room, at which point Jonathan slowly turned around and made for the exit. As he grabbed hold of the doorknob he heard three sharp knocks from the counter. Looking back he saw the woman looking at him. He nodded to her as a "good bye", and she responded by throwing something to him. He saw a small chain soar through the air before he caught it with his left hand and at the same time he seemed to be pushed outside. Not wanting to show anyone what he had been given, he quickly put it into his pocket and headed for the inn. It didn't take long before he got there, and upon entering their room, Jonathan pulled the chain out. On the chain was a small amulet with waves and a rune on it. *'I wonder what this one means?'* Jonathan thought before putting the amulet around his neck. *'Well, that was disappointing,'* Jonathan thought as nothing happened. He had a feeling the amulet was magical, but wouldn't know for sure until Boriam had looked at it. He went downstairs and met Felix at the counter. "Hey, Felix. Is Boriam at your place still?" he said. "Ssh, who knows who could be listening? Aye, he's reading books containing old tales. I think he's looking for something. I mean, he's always looking for something, but now I think it's something more specific," Felix said, and Jonathan nodded before saying "Hey, could I get some dinner in here, or do I have to go out to the market?" Felix smiled and guided Jonathan into the tavern. There he got some meat stuffed between two slices of bread. "Shouldn't there be potaters with this?" Jonathan said, and Felix looked from the plate to the kid a few times before saying "What's 'potaters'?" and Jonathan remembered that the root was unfamiliar even to Boriam, so he assumed they were unfamiliar in the rest of the world. "Potaters are a kind of root I think, you dig it out of the ground, and it's very good to eat. I guess it's not very common outside where I come from," Jonathan said and Felix seemed interested in the root, but was called away before getting to ask any questions about it. Jonathan ate his food and sat thinking for a while, trying to work out what to do next. He paid for his food and went out to the market. At home they usually had some kind of activity at the marketplace in the evenings, but this wasn't the case here. Here, there were still carts and stands selling their goods, so Jonathan bought a small bag of candy. As he went around the cart, he noticed someone he'd seen before. It took a while before Jonathan recognized the dark skin and orange eyes. They belonged to the leader of the group which had attacked Shadowtree. Jonathan saw the dark-skinned man look at him, and he quickly looked away. He crept behind the cart he was standing by as casually as he could, and then started to run.

Chapter 17
TWO MINDS

It didn't take long before he reached Felix' house. He ran inside without knocking, shouting to Andrea and whoever else was in the house that it was him, and ran towards the library. Bursting through the doors to the library he saw Boriam sitting behind the desk looking at an old map. Upon this sudden entry, Boriam looked up, puzzled, and said "Oh my, you look tired. Take a breath and sit down, I'm not completely finished here." Jonathan hurried to the desk only managing to get out "He.. He.. Th.. That.. They.." Boriam looked even more perplexed and quickly said "Calm down, boy. Stand still and take a deep breath." Jonathan straightened himself up, and took two deep breaths before managing to say "He's here. They're here. The men who attacked Shadowtree. I saw them at the market." Boriam's amusement vanished as he stood up. They hurried to the door where Andrea met them saying "Ah, good, I was just thinking of making some food. Will you be staying for that?" Boriam looked at her, and said "I'm afraid we cannot stay. I cannot tell you why, but I would advise you not to tell anyone I've been here." She seemed to be worried by this, but hid it well enough as she nodded and stepped away from the door. They went quickly to their room where they packed their bags with their new provisions and their gear. Shortly afterwards they were explaining to Felix that they had to leave. "So some men attacked the kid's village, you stopped them and now they are after you? You shouldn't have much trouble with some thugs, I believe?" he said to Boriam who shook his head and said "Normally I wouldn't, but one of them was a Muriah, and with the others around it would be tough." Felix then looked at Boriam and said "And I guess the one Muriah was..?" "Aye, Arnkhand." Boriam responded. Felix nodded slowly and said "Oh well, I see how it would be tough for ya then. You should be off now, not let some old innkeeper keep you. Just drop by again at some point, all right?" They agreed to this and left the inn. Taking as many back alleys as they could to evade the main roads they slowly made their way towards the closest gate. This was the south eastern gate, leading onto the open fields. As they neared the gate they saw that a bill had been put up on the wanted-board beside the guards depicting what could resemble Boriam's face. A guard looked from Boriam to the picture a few times before he turned towards the bill and drew a moustache on it. He turned back to Boriam and grinned. Boriam whispered "Thank you" to the guard as they passed him, and he responded with a rumbling cough. Once outside they went as fast as they could to the north-east towards the forest.

They didn't make camp until they were deep into the woods. When they were far enough from town, Boriam felt it was safe to make a fire as long as it was made with dry wood only. Boriam explained to Jonathan that dry wood burned cleaner, so there wouldn't be so much smoke. As they were sitting by the fire, Jonathan asked "What's a Muriah?" Boriam looked at him and said "The Muriahs are the personal lackeys of the Council. They have been trained by the Council themselves to be stronger than most others out there. Henchmen of the Council they are usually called, though they call themselves the Muriahs, which means the Peacemakers in the old language. Sounds nice, but the way they do it is far from it." Jonathan nodded and asked "Do you know this Arnkhand well? Their leader? Felix said he understood it would be difficult for you, so I just assumed you knew him somehow." Boriam nodded and said "Aye, I know him. He's my brother." "What?" Jonathan exclaimed and Boriam laughed. "Indeed, well, more like half-brother. His skin is dark and eyes orange after his father, while I've got light skin and green eyes from mine." "So he's your brother, yet you joined one side and he joined the other?" Jonathan said. "Yes, he was jealous of me for most of his life, for reasons I don't know. So when I joined this side, he wanted to prove that he was stronger, or something, so he joined the other side," Boriam answered to which Jonathan wondered "What did you think of him joining them?" Boriam then told Jonathan about the time he learned that his brother had joined the Council. He was sitting in a temple high up in the Silent mountain meditating when a messenger entered the chamber and told him. "I was more worried about how my parents would take it than how it would affect me. It wasn't until much later, when we had both been through tough training that I met him in battle. We fought more verbally than physically I believe, and we found that one could not kill the other. We parted that day to each our own, knowing that as long as both of us are still alive, this war couldn't resolve itself. Every time we meet we put on a show for everyone around which eventually drives one of us away, based on what we say and do." Boriam sighed and continued "Alas, one of us will have to die by someone else's hand before this war can end." Jonathan felt it was inappropriate to say anything, so he let the old man sit there for a while before asking "But, and don't take this personally, he seems a lot younger than you." "Ah, yes, he is a bit younger. He's 16 years younger than me, and has always looked extremely young. He's based his life with the council around it, so when he called me old man earlier, it was to keep his appearances up," Boriam answered. "Hold on. So you're saying the fight outside Shadowtree was an act?" Jonathan said. Boriam replied by raising his shoulders and say "I did fight them, but not Arnkhand. Fortunately he let me stay until I had finished, but he had to let the Council know I'm still alive. We both know that if he doesn't die, I do and vice versa. Therefore I have to indicate to others where he is, and he does the same about me. That's why I'm now hunted in cities owned by the Council. It's a cruel world, but we've come to accept it." Jonathan was so stunned by what he had heard that he was unable to say anything. "Let's get some rest. We'll have to get as far away as possible tomorrow," Boriam eventually said, and so they did.

They travelled for three days before feeling sure no one was following them. On the third day they made a big fire and sat down tiredly. They sat talking for a while about nothing, and as their conversation slowed, Boriam said "Try meditating again. And don't comment on all other things. Count every breath in and out, and make sure to fill your lungs properly." Jonathan sat meditating for a while and then his mind started to wander again. He noticed this and tried to get back to the counting, but the mind kept running away. He looked up at Boriam and said "Why does my mind keep wandering when I want to focus on my breathing?" Boriam gave a short smile and said "Finally a good question. It's because your mind doesn't receive any attention when you focus on your breathing. It doesn't like that, and so it grabs your attention again by wandering." Jonathan stared into the ground a bit before saying "But how can I need to give attention to my own mind?" "Why indeed?" Boriam replied continuing with "I like to think of it like this: Every person has two minds. The person they are, and with that I mean their soul or existence or their being, and then there's the brain in their heads. They need each other in different ways, where the body needs the brain to survive by processing information which then controls the flow of blood and feelings in the body, the brain needs the body to do the work of actually pumping the blood, moving around and breathing. Everyone is so occupied with the belief that the brain is the only thing they are, that it's become used to having all the attention for itself. When you now start paying attention to your body instead of your mind, it gets annoyed and jealous. That is why it's trying to steal your attention, and it's good at it because you're used to the feeling of your mind having all the control. Now when you meditate and count the breaths and your mind kicks in, focus on what the mind is saying without judging it. When you objectively look at your mind without interfering it, it will eventually be quieter. When it does, you can continue your meditation. By watching what the mind does without objecting, you force it to get used to not receiving attention, and so it will gradually start leaving your head in peace. It will probably only be for a second or two the first few times, but keep doing it, and your head will soon be quiet enough. Now enough questions, get back to meditation." Jonathan went back to meditating and in just a few seconds his mind started wandering. At this point Jonathan thought *'okay, watch the mind,'* at which point he had already forgot what his mind was saying. *'Ugh, I guess I'll have to be quicker at seeing what I'm thinking. Wait isn't this thinking?'* Jonathan thought and again his thoughts disappeared. *'Hmm, strange. Oh, thought!'* He thought, and this went on for a while until Boriam started laughing. Jonathan looked at him questioningly and Boriam said "It's apparent you're thinking about your thoughts, as your face keeps twisting every now and then. Try to imagine that you are outside the brain, which again is rambling on about what it is thinking of. See the brain as a little ball with legs, arms, eyes, nose and a mouth. Watch it as it keeps saying and doing things, and you will soon see that you don't become so affected by it." Jonathan shrugged and went back to the meditation. Immediately his mind started talking again, but this time Jonathan imagined it as a small thing a bit like what Boriam described, but he added a hat and a cane for the fun of it. He saw the mouth of this thing move as the thoughts kept rolling out of it, and the entire thing was so amusing that Jonathan started laughing. He laughed so much that he was unable to sit straight. Lying on the ground when he finally stopped laughing, he opened his eyes and saw Boriam looking at him. He felt his face go red, and he looked down embarrassed. Boriam said "Good, now you know the feeling." Jonathan looked up again and said "What feeling?" "The joy of knowing that you can distance yourself from your mind? Or the feeling of being you instead of your mind?" Boriam said and Jonathan replied "But I was just laughing, because it was funny." Boriam smiled and said "You felt happy." And Jonathan nodded in response. "That's the only feeling the 'true you' can create. All the negative ones, frustration, annoyance and anger is created by your mind so that it can have your attention." Jonathan wondered a bit about this and couldn't really see how that really worked out, but instead of asking more questions he went back to the meditation. As his mind kept getting turned on and off because he switched his focus between his breathing and his brain, he started smiling. Along with the good feeling he felt more relaxed than he usually was, and after a while he could focus on his breathing for longer periods. After a long time he opened his eyes. As he did so, Boriam said "Good, now take up your weapon." He found that the stick they used to fight with had been laid beside him. He quickly grabbed it as Boriam attacked him, and he parried the strike just in time. Getting his balance they fought for a while and Jonathan felt that something was different. It was as if things went slower than they normally did. He could block the strikes more easily, and eventually he even managed to attack once. At this point Boriam jumped a long way backwards and said "Good. Now do you see what meditation can eventually achieve? You've now passed the first stage of meditation, well done. There're twelve to go, but I'll tell you what to do for the next one tomorrow. For now, let's eat and go to sleep, we'll need to go to Fisherman's Rest as soon as possible." Jonathan looked at him and said "How did you manage to jump so far backwards?" "Ah, that would be wind magic. Very handy for moving around quickly," Boriam said. As they sat down around the fire, Jonathan said "You can cast magic? Can you teach me?" Boriam looked at him and said "Yes, I can cast magic of most types. I'm not very good at dark magic, too much pain in that. I don't like dark magic very much. As for you learning it, you will do that eventually. Like I said, it's part of the training the Thirteen pushes you through. About me teaching you, you're not ready yet." "So when will I be ready?" Jonathan asked, but Boriam just shook his head and said "When you don't have to ask that question anymore." As they ate, Jonathan felt annoyed that he couldn't learn magic yet, and was playing out a fantasy in his head of how it would be when he did. In the middle of a heroic jump over a bottomless pit to save someone, Boriam interrupted him by saying "Don't get attached to the desire to learn magic. You would think it's the best thing in the world, but there're limits to it. And if you help one person, everyone else want help too. It will bring a lot of responsibility and a lot of secrecy. Some people will hate you just because you can cast magic, some will try to use you for their own gain. And if you use it to solve all of your own problems, you won't learn anything from it. So you will have to learn how to decide when to use magic and when not to, as well as learn to see how much you have to do in order to succeed at what you're attempting." Jonathan looked at Boriam and said in a mocking tone "How did you know what I was thinking? Can you read my mind or something?" And Boriam responded by giving him a smile. "Wait. You actually can read my mind?" Jonathan asked sceptically. "Ah. Can? Yes. Did? No. People's minds are hard to read. It is possible, but barely so. Much easier to see how they behave to understand what they are thinking." Accusingly Jonathan said "So you can read my mind! How? Can I learn that, then, as I apparently am unable to learn magic?" Boriam laughed and said "I can teach you how to read animals' behaviour, but not how to read their mind. For now, at least." Jonathan argued for a while to make Boriam teach him more things, but most suggestions were brushed aside as either not possible to do, or that he was not ready yet. Annoyed, Jonathan said they should rest, and so they did. The morning didn't do much to improve Jonathan's mood, as the sky had apparently tipped its buckets during the night and rain was pouring down. Even more frustrated,

Jonathan gathered up his things and put them in his bag. The forest couldn't offer them any protection from the weather either, as they had to leave it behind in order to go southwards. They left the safety of the thick forest behind and Jonathan felt his heart beat harder than usual as he now stepped out onto the open fields.

Chapter 18
SWORD AND ARROWS

Arkenthan shut the book and thought *'Wow, glad they got safely out of the city, but I wonder what will happen in Fisherman's Rest?'* He noticed he had been sitting upright on his knees in bed and had been eagerly reading with the book lying across his knees. He got off the bed and his legs were so stiff that he was barely able to walk. He put the book in the bookcase, threw a few more logs on the fire and went to sleep.

Because he had been reading the book so intensely, his dreams were filled with visions of him having to run away from a dark skinned man with orange eyes. He was chased through all sorts of terrain until he finally woke up with a yell and found that he was drenched in sweat. Breathing heavily he got up and sat on the bed for a while before heading outside. The weather was cloudy, but fortunately it wasn't raining. *'I should learn to fight with a sword at some point, but I guess I'll have to do that when I'm in town, as no one ever passes through the forest,'* he thought imagining the tasks he'd be put to in the army. Finding that he'd probably be sent to fight in the archery unit he would not need much sword training, but it would be good to know anyways. He spent the day hunting, bringing home a doe and some smaller game. Having filled his barrels with meat by early evening, he decided he'd need a place to store the meat he wanted to bring to town. He didn't want to keep the meat where he went to the toilet. Using some of the rocks which still lay in a pile at the centre of his garden he made a foundation for a new part of the outhouse. He discovered that he had no idea how to build either a foundation for a house, or a house itself, and decided to get some hints next time he was in Garani. He also decided to make a trip to town the day after the next, after hunting for fresh meat to sell the following day. As the evening grew old and the darkness arrived he was again able to see the cave high up the mountainside. Shaking his head he went inside to make a late dinner and go to sleep.

The night afforded him a quiet sleep, and he woke up refreshed and ready to hunt. As he sat up in bed he looked out the window and saw that it was pouring down outside. He felt his spirit wane as he sat staring out at the weather. Annoyed, he went over to his barrels to check how much extra he had to trade. He would bring a leg from the doe, and at least three of the minor game, two to trade and one in case he met Greypaws again. That left him with most of the doe for the day, but emptied his barrel of minor game. *I can't keep being cooped up indoors every time there's heavy rain outside. I really don't want to go out now, but I'll have to get used to it,'* Arkenthan thought and decided to practice archery in the rain. He would have to be able to shoot in heavy rain at some point, so he took his bow and went outside. It didn't take long for his clothes to get soaked through. Fortunately it was still warm outside, so he didn't become too cold. He shot his first arrow and watched as it hit the ground a couple of meters in front of the target. "Wow!" He exclaimed and thought *'so that's what happens in heavy rain. Well, I'll have to get a lot of practice in then.'* Firing his next arrow, aiming a lot higher, he saw the arrow hit the bottom edge of the target. Frustrated he put another arrow to the bow, aimed at the top of a tree far behind his target, and let the arrow fly. He saw it being whipped around in the air as the wind got hold of it, and then it buried itself in the tree a little above the target. He collected his arrows and started over much closer, building up distance as he got used to shooting in the rain. He eventually managed to hit approximately where he wanted to from most distances. *'Hunting in heavy rain will cover both my sound and my scent, so learning this will help me a lot.'* he thought as he collected his arrows for the hundredth time that day. He was beginning to get cold, so he went inside to warm himself by the fire. As he entered the house he saw that the fire had almost died out. "No! No, no, no, no. Mustn't die, mustn't die," he said as he rushed to the bin and threw a few more logs on the fire. The water from his clothes made a hissing sound as it hit the warm coal, but it didn't put out the fire. Arkenthan watched as the fire grew again, took off his clothes to dry them and started his dinner. He spent the last of his herbs in preparing the doe, and added a few roots for a more substantial dinner. As he stood around the fire cooking he noticed darkness falling outside the windows. After eating he checked his clothes and found them still to be wet. *'Hopefully they'll be dry by tomorrow, and I really hope the rain stops during the night,'* Arkenthan thought as he prepared to go to sleep. Lying in bed he kept thinking of how he would get to town the next morning. If it was raining he would have a lot of trouble getting there, but if it was decent weather he would find it easily again. As he was about to fall asleep he heard something. *'That sounded like something scratching the wall,'* he thought as he forced himself to hear everything around him. No more sounds came. *'Bah, it was probably just a branch blown by the wind,'* he thought as he went back to trying to sleep. His mind kept racing, wondering what the noise could have been, and it took a long time before he was able to sleep.

The following day he awoke feeling surprisingly relaxed. Still lying in bed he looked out the window and saw that the rain had stopped. Excitedly he jumped out of bed and ran to his clothes. They were mostly dry, and the ones that weren't would dry up during the first part of his trek. He prepared some food and water for the journey, and headed out. He quickly went up the mountainside and circled the mountain to get his bearings. Finding his course, he turned down from the mountain and into the forest. The hours passed without him finding any animals to hunt and no surprising events occurred. Eventually he reached the lake he had found the last time he had travelled to town, but this time he didn't stop to take a swim. *'Hah, I am so good at finding my way,'* Arkenthan thought as he passed the lake. He kept heading in the same direction and was soon out of the forest. Looking around he found that he had come out of the forest on the opposite side of town from the last time he had visited, but still far enough away so that no one would see that he came from the forest. He made a mark by the edge so he knew where and in which direction he should enter the forest on the way back.

When he reached town he headed straight to the butcher to sell his meat. "Well, well, look what we have here," the butcher said as Arkenthan stepped through the door. He helped Arkenthan unload his bag of meat, and counted up the price for it. As he didn't bring as much as last time, he only got two silver pieces. Before he went up to his room Arkenthan turned to the butcher and said "Hey, what's your name? I don't think I got it last time I was here." The butcher turned towards him with a hand stretched out and said "Name's Jonas. And yours is?" Arkenthan shook his hand and gave the butcher his name before heading to the room he was borrowing. Throwing his things onto the bed he left the store as soon as he was able to. First he wanted to drop by the smithy, and as he entered the blacksmith with the giant beard smiled and welcomed him back. "I haven't quite finished the knife fer ya, but I've got some better arrowheads, as you requested. These'll be easier to fit onto the shafts, and they are a bit sharper. For thirty arrowheads though I'll have to take one silver piece." Arkenthan nodded and paid the smith before asking "I wish to join the army when I'm able to. Before joining I think I should practice some fighting. I already know how to hunt with a bow and arrow, but I was wondering if there was anyone in town who could teach me to fight with a sword?" The blacksmith stared vacantly into the ceiling and said "Hmm. No, I don't know of anyone who's an official teacher of sword fighting. Oh, wait, I think the man living across the street used to fight in a war some time ago. He's taught a few of the city guards I believe. Come, I'll introduce ya to him." And with that the smith walked across the street and knocked on a door. Arkenthan followed close behind, and was met by a tall man with one eye. The missing eye trailed a deep cut down his chin. The man was slightly red as if he had been interrupted while working out. He was introduced to Arkenthan as Johannes. "So what do you want boy?" Johannes said. *'That's a rude way to say it,'* Arkenthan thought before saying "I heard you might have fought in a war before?" "Yes, that's how I got this." And with that he pointed to the scar along his chin before asking "What of it?" Arkenthan was stunned for a moment by the harshness of his speech, and had to force himself to keep talking. "I am planning to join the army when I'm able to, but first I would like to know how to handle a sword. Therefore I'm wondering if you could teach me how to use a sword?" Johannes looked at Arkenthan and said "No." Before slamming the door shut. Arkenthan looked at the smith with a questioning look, making the smith shrug and say "Aye, he's a bit grumpy these days. I have no idea why. Well, he's the only one I know of who could teach you, but it's not like I know many people here that well. Ask around, maybe you will find someone, or you could join the city guard. There you'll get some training." Arkenthan thanked the smith and turned towards the woodworker's shop. Spending a few hours there he was able to make a few decent arrows with the new heads. "Not bad those," the woodworker said. "Strong shaft and sharp edge. You're often out hunting? I hear the forest is dangerous these days, giant beasts roam ever closer to the edge of the forest. At least, that's what they say." Arkenthan nodded and said "Yes, I met a huge dire wolf in there just last week. I got away though, evidently." He finished with a grin and continued "How much are these materials I've used now? I'd like to pay for them so I can take the arrows with me." The woodworker named his price and Arkenthan paid for them. As the darkness fell, Arkenthan started to get hungry. Heading towards the tavern he had used last time, he passed the smithy. As he passed, the smith shouted at him and told him to come closer. He went inside and the smith headed to a big barrel in the corner saying "I remembered this after you left earlier. As you want to help our country in the war you can have it for free," and he pulled out a sword. Arkenthan stood looking at it while the smith brought it over. It was probably the worst sword he had ever seen. It was poorly made, unbalanced and chips had broken off the edge around the entire sword. Seeing the boy's stare, the smith said "Aye, it's in bad shape. It's one of the first swords I ever made, and I haven't had the heart to throw it away. It won't survive a war for long, but it's possible to use for training, whether you find a teacher or have to teach yourself. Of course, I could make a better one, but that would cost you more than you can afford. For now at least." Taking the sword, Arkenthan thanked the smith and swung the sword a few times before leaving the smithy.

The next day Arkenthan woke up as early as ever. Heading downstairs he met the butcher before leaving for home. "Off again, then? I hope you'll be back soon, my customers got crazy last week when we had some nicer meat in stock. I expect they will be the same now. I don't think anyone suspects it's you who bring the supplies, but I don't know how long that will last. If they had suspected though, I guess they would be lining up outside already." "Well, as I said, I'll probably be able to visit once a week. I'll try to bring some more meat, but I don't know how much I can carry. I'm off now, I'll see you next time," Arkenthan answered and left the store. He left town the same way he had arrived. While leaving, he saw a man staring at him. He wasn't an old man, but he wasn't very young either. Something about him made guessing his age a hard task. Arkenthan wondered why the man stared so intently at him. Before he could ask, the old or young man turned and left. Puzzled by this, Arkenthan kept heading towards where he should enter the forest. After an hour of searching he finally found the mark he had made, and headed in between the trees. As he got deeper into the forest and the darkness closed in on him again, he felt nervous and stupid for feeling that. *'Come on Arkenthan, you've been living here for a long time now, just entering the woods shouldn't make you nervous,'* he thought, but couldn't help feeling nervous about the forest when he knew exactly what creatures lived there. He arrived at the lake, and again he just kept on going. The sun had climbed high in the sky before he stopped for lunch. He didn't stop long, and was soon on his way towards his house again. An hour after he had stopped for lunch he could see the mountain between the treetops. Finally thinking *'I'm home soon'* Arkenthan heard a loud growl to his right. Quickly turning his head he saw a fjällbear staring at him between the trees. As the bear started to sprint towards him, Arkenthan ran as fast as he could towards the mountain hoping the trees would shield him enough for him to get home. He also hoped that the bear would feel the same way that Greypaws did. Hearing the bear crashing through the trees reaching ever closer, Arkenthan reached the mountain and ran upwards. He heard a sharp yelp from behind and the crashing of the bear stopped. After running a while without any noises behind him, Arkenthan stopped and looked backwards. *'I wonder what happened to it? I'm not complaining, I don't really want to get eaten, but I wonder what stopped it in case it could stop me too. Bah, no use thinking about it, maybe it just hit a tree which was too strong or something,'* Arkenthan thought as he turned towards the house and kept on running. It didn't take long for him to reach the house. As he entered the garden he gave a sigh of relief. Once there, he felt completely safe from everything. *'Yes, there are a lot of dangerous creatures in here, but I must say the forest is a very relaxing place to live,'* Arkenthan thought as he walked to the door and entered the house. He spent the rest of that day filling the woodbin and carrying water from the well. As the night fell, Arkenthan went to the bookcase to find *The Lion's Cub*. Again he was unable to find it, even though he searched through all the shelves. *'I wonder...'* Arkenthan thought as he pulled the bookcase aside, fetched a torch and entered the tunnel and then the central chamber again. Not bothering to light the torches around the room, he went straight to the pedestal. Atop the pedestal, with the key beside it, lay the book. Arkenthan shook his head and thought *'So the book got back here again. Have I brought it back, or did it somehow travel back here by itself when I went to town?'* Arkenthan found the event extremely puzzling, and brought the book back out from the cave. When he came into the house again, Arkenthan's stomach made its hunger heard. Due to all that had happened since he got back, he had forgotten to make any food. Heading to the barrel he found that there was not much food left. *'It'll have to be enough for today, and I'll hunt tomorrow,'* Arkenthan thought as he put a spit with a small piece of meat above the fire. Standing by the window he watched as the darkness grew. He saw the big pile of rocks in the middle of the garden and felt annoyed. *'Okay, I'll have to do something about that pile soon,'* Arkenthan thought. The moment he finished the thought, the two silvery eyes he had seen earlier appeared at the edge of the garden. He went outside to get a better look at what animal they belonged to. As he came out, he saw the eyes rush up to the treetops. *'Is it just a bird?'* Arkenthan thought, but noticed that the tree was bent. As his eyes got used to the darkness he saw a giant shadow hanging onto the tree, and he thought *'Wow. That is a big and strange creature.'*

Chapter 19
BEESTINGS

Arkenthan slowly stepped backwards into the house and closed the door. Sitting down on the bed he thought *'I wonder why I haven't seen that before, or even heard of something like it?'* He sat there for a while before his stomach twisted with hunger, and he remembered his small meal. When he had gone to bed he was unable to sleep as every time he closed his eyes he saw the shape of the creature. The long body, the big pointed head, the claws on its feet, the protruding eyes and the long tail. He had only seen the contours of it, and Arkenthan assumed that was worse than seeing the real creature. Only having seen a darkened version made his head come up with ever more terrifying suggestions as to what the creature might be every time he came close to falling asleep. The hours passed as Arkenthan lay tossing and turning in bed.

The next morning Arkenthan woke up late in the day, without even remembering having fallen asleep. He didn't feel very well, but forced himself out of bed to go hunting. In his traps he found dead animals which had been eaten by something, so he relocated them in case the predators would return to the same traps. The day didn't continue well either. He stumbled as he finally saw a deer, making a noise so that it ran away. The rest of the day passed quickly without any sights of animals besides songbirds. *'I have to find some food soon,'* Arkenthan thought as he entered a clearing. *'Wait. I've been here before. This is where I stayed before living in the house,'* Arkenthan thought, and started visualizing the forest as he turned around. *'That means the river is a day's march in that direction, the house is in that direction, the pool of water is in that direction. Oh, the beehive! It's got honey, and it is in that direction!'* Arkenthan excitedly thought as he started running towards it. When he neared the hive, his head kept racing for a solution to how he would get a hold of some honey. The sun was out, so he wouldn't receive cover from any rain this time. He bent down a small distance away from the hive to get an idea of how it was built. It was a lot easier to see what it looked like with the sun above him, and he soon located the spot where he had last broken into the hive. The bees had been busy it seemed, as the area was almost filled in again. He saw that the hive had a large section which hung without protection of any kind. *'Okay, my only choice is to grab that part, cut it loose quickly and run for the lake. I wish I had the sword here,'* Arkenthan thought as he prepared to run. As he was about to attack the hive, he noticed a big bush with thick leaves standing not far away. Thinking the leaves could give him some protection from the beestings he wrapped some leaves around his arms, legs and stomach. He would have to keep his hands free in order to grab the hive. He looked over his bee armour and then looked at the hive. *'Okay Arkenthan. Time to move,'* he thought and started to run. He quickly arrived at the hive and made a cut around the protruding piece of the hive. As he grabbed it, his fingers sunk deep into the hive and he felt several bees sting his fingertips. He screamed, pulled the piece from the hive and started running towards the lake. While running he saw several bees sting his arms and legs, but luckily the leaves protected them. *'Oh, dear gods, don't let there be a bear by the lake,'* Arkenthan thought as he ran through the forest. A short while, and many beestings later, he broke through the edge of the clearing leading up to the lake. Arkenthan ran towards the lake and saw three scared deer jump into the forest on the other side. *'Ugh, typical bad luck,'* he thought as he threw the piece of honey onto the ground and jumped into the lake. He dived in as deeply as he managed, and only got up for a short time to get some air and listen for the buzzing of the bees. After diving beneath the surface ten times he was no longer able to hear the bees hum. Slowly swimming towards the edge of the water he saw only a few bees swarm around the honey. Unwrapping one of the leaves on his arm he used it as a tray to carry water. He threw the water on the leftover bees to reach the piece of the hive. He wrapped the hive in a few leaves and noticed his hands, fingers and neck starting to throb in pain from all the stings. He jumped into the water and felt it cool his pain immediately. While pulling himself onto land one of the remaining leaves he had wrapped around himself got scratched, and a red misty liquid started to trickle from it. Arkenthan found this very strange and used one of his fingers to smell the liquid. It felt cool to the touch, and as his hands, neck and other parts that were stung started to burn again, his finger didn't. He quickly covered both his hands in the sticky goo, and felt the pain recede. Arkenthan was so pleased with this discovery that he forgot about the honey until he was about to leave for home. A sting on his leg reminded him of the reason for his past pain, and he hurried to get the piece of honeycomb. While walking back home he applied more of the sap from the leaves as the stings began to hurt again. *'I wonder what plant this is?'* Arkenthan thought. When he got home he grabbed the scrolls depicting different plants and their healing properties, but none of them displayed the leaves he had in front of him. He thought *'I guess I'll have to ask someone in town next week, I should save a few leaves for then.'* He put the leaves on the bottom shelf of the bookcase. They were so long that they took all the space on the shelf, and even though he only had two of them, the others having fallen off during his sprint through the forest, he estimated that the shelf would only have room for about eight or nine on top of each other. He pulled out the piece of honey and put it on the bench. Taking a knife he cut strips off it, eating some and putting some in a bowl for storing. He glanced out the window and dropped his knife. Outside he saw a deer passing the garden, heading into the forest. He quickly grabbed his bow and went outside, making sure he didn't slam the door. Sneaking into the forest where the deer had gone he soon caught up with it. A stag with gigantic horns stood proudly between the trees some distance in front of Arkenthan. He loaded an arrow and aimed at the animal. He let go of the arrow and watched as it soared high up between the branches. *'Darn it Arkenthan!'* he thought *'it's not raining now. The old way of aiming...'* From the sound of his bow and the arrow hitting the branches overhead, the stag was alerted and was now looking towards where Arkenthan stood. He was covered by a tree, and it didn't seem like the stag noticed him. He quickly put another arrow on the string, aimed and let it fly. With quick reflexes the stag bent low as it turned away from the sound of his bow. Arkenthan watched as if everything was moving slowly while the arrow flew just above the back of the stag. He felt annoyed that he had misused the first arrow the moment the stag made the first leap in the opposite direction. Arkenthan watched as the stag's leap put its head directly in the path of the flying arrow, and he heard the arrow hit the stag's head. The animal dropped to the ground instantly. It took a while before the realization sunk into Arkenthan's mind as it raced to comprehend what had happened. Then he laughed. His eyes watered and his stomach started to hurt while he staggered towards the animal. Sighing as his laughter subsided, Arkenthan marvelled at the arrow. *'I am glad I'm close to home, this is a big animal,'* Arkenthan thought as he finally started to calm down. Lifting the hind legs of the animal he wondered if he would be able to even shift it the short distance home. As he pulled with all his strength the animal slowly moved towards the house *'Ugh. Come on! It's just like pulling one of the bigger trees you've brought home. Except they weren't limp,'* he thought to motivate himself. After what felt like a year, Arkenthan finally pulled the animal into the garden. He got the animal further into the garden just in time to be out of range from Greypaws' claws. Arkenthan turned as he heard the growling, and when he saw who it was he said "You have a knack for knowing when I have food, don't you? No, don't growl! Stay there and you'll get a piece." He headed towards the house and thought *'This will make for a bloody kitchen. That's why I need the extra part of the outhouse.'* He looked at the outhouse and thought *'crap,*

I forgot to ask how to build the addition to the outhouse,' he turned towards Greypaws, pointed at the ground where he stood and said "Okay, stay!" before he turned towards the house and brought the stag inside. Making sure the fire was burning brightly he started to cut the stag. He cut a big piece off the leg, weighed it in his hand and went outside. Looking towards where Greypaws had been standing he saw that the wolf had left. Feeling slightly disappointed Arkenthan turned towards the door, and out of the corner of his eye he could see something white. To the side of the garden, almost by the slope of the mountain sat Greypaws looking at him. Pointing at the wolf Arkenthan said "When I tell you to wait somewhere, you wait there." Greypaws bowed its head, and Arkenthan thought *'hah, as if he'd understood me. Okay, here goes.'* He headed towards the wolf with the meat stretched out in one hand. As he got close to the beast, Greypaws lashed at him with a paw. Jumping backwards out of its way, Arkenthan put up the other hand with a finger stretched out saying sharply "No! Bad wolf!" As Greypaws put down its paws again Arkenthan moved towards him once more. Again the wolf lashed at him, and again he jumped out of the way. After three more attempts, Greypaws let Arkenthan come closer. Aware of the beast's every move and preparing to jump in different directions, Arkenthan kept moving towards the wolf. When he was close enough, making sure to hold the meat as if he was presenting it, Arkenthan watched as Greypaws bent down towards the ground, stretched its head towards the meat and snatched it out of his hands. Arkenthan smiled and said "Good boy! Was that so hard?" He saw Greypaws keep an eye on him, and he didn't want to get attacked by the wolf, so Arkenthan slowly took a few steps backwards before turning towards the house and walking as normally as he could through the door.

After closing the door he had to hold onto it to support his shaking legs as he took a few deep breaths. His hands were shaking so badly he barely managed to use them for support, and his head felt as if someone had bashed it with a club. He staggered over to the bed and lay down thinking it had been one of the scariest and yet most extraordinary experiences he'd ever had. After a long while he sat up in bed and felt his entire body still shaking. Trying to calm down Arkenthan sat in bed taking several deep breaths thinking *'Deep breath in, deep breath out. Hey, this is almost like the meditating Boriam was teaching Jonathan. Oh, and this is the mind I guess. Okay, all attention on the thoughts while it's talking.'* He failed to focus on either the breathing or the thoughts which appeared, but as he sat there breathing in and out he felt the muscles in his body relax and his head start to feel more normal. Standing upright on steady feet again Arkenthan thought *'Well, I'm not shaking anymore. Might be because of the amount of time I was sitting there, or maybe it was the meditating. I think I'll try it again some other day, but right now I'm hungry!'* He cut a big piece of meat off the deer and hung it over the fire. Remembering the honeycomb he went to the bench and finished cutting it. *'I wonder how this will taste?'* Arkenthan asked himself as he brought the bowl of honey to the meat and smeared it on the top. After waiting for the honey to get stickier so it wouldn't fall off, Arkenthan turned the spit to put honey on the other side of the meat. He did this a few times before letting it all finish cooking. Making a small cut in the meat he checked that it was done. He took his first bite, and it made Arkenthan forget where he was. The strong taste of the meat combined with the sweet taste of the honey made his mouth water even though he was already eating.

That night, Arkenthan had another dream. He saw three shadows standing on a hill, and as his viewpoint moved to above the shadows he saw a huge army beneath the hill rushing towards them. His viewpoint turned around and Arkenthan saw another army coming up towards the shadows from the opposite side. When the two armies crashed into each other, Arkenthan woke up with a jolt. He looked around the house a few seconds before realizing where he was. Outside the sun had come out, but the windows were wet, so he assumed it had been raining during the night. He went outside to get some water, and as he came out the grass seemed dry. This puzzled Arkenthan so much that he walked around the garden a bit. What he found were some spots where the grass was dry and some spots which were wet. Confused, Arkenthan looked up and saw Greypaws lying by the edge of the garden where he had been fed the night before. "Good morning. Had a good sleep?" Arkenthan said to the wolf. Greypaws stretched his limbs, looked at Arkenthan and went into the forest. Arkenthan stood looking to where Greypaws had entered the forest and thought *'Not even a "thank you."'* He grinned at himself and said "Arkenthan, it seems you've been too long in the forest." Then he carried some water inside.

Chapter 20
A DIFFERENT VIEW

Arkenthan spent the entire day hunting. Every once in a while he saw something white between the trees and wondered if Greypaws was watching him as he hunted. *If he meant to attack me, he probably would've done that already,'* Arkenthan thought as he crept through a set of bushes following a game trail. The day had gone well so far, and he'd already dropped off handfuls of smaller game at the house twice, and one deer. The animal he was now following seemed heavy though, and Arkenthan assumed it would be a young deer. As he peered around a big tree he saw that this wasn't the small deer he expected. What he was looking at was a huge pig with giant tusks from both its upper and lower jaw, long hair falling from its spine and a tail like a cow's. *Whoa, a Great Boar. I've only heard of those in tales. I'll have to be careful with this one,'* Arkenthan thought as he looked the boar over. He found that even though it was huge compared to a pig, he would probably be able to bring it home. He put an arrow to the bow, aimed and fired. He watched as the arrow soared through the sky, hit and barely manage to penetrate the skin of the beast. *'Crap'* Arkenthan thought as the pig jumped, turned and charged straight at him. As the boar ran at such a high speed and weighed a lot, it had no way of stopping or turning quickly when Arkenthan jumped behind the tree. After a long slide, the boar stopped, turned towards Arkenthan again and attacked once more. While the boar had been trying to stop, Arkenthan had managed to put another arrow to the string, and as the boar started running he fired it. The arrow hit the boar in its right shoulder but the beast didn't seem to notice. Watching as the boar kept coming towards him, Arkenthan had nothing to hide behind. Instinct was the one thing which made him jump aside just before the boar hit him. Once again the boar had too high a speed to be able to stop, and as Arkenthan drew another arrow he watched as the boar ran head first into the big tree. The tree fell, and the boar rolled onwards a bit and then lay still. Arkenthan quickly pulled his knife, ran up to the beast and cut its throat. As he did so, the boar quickly jolted awake, stood up and ran a short distance before falling again. Arkenthan stepped shakily towards the animal and when he reached it, he made another cut. This one didn't provoke any reaction from the beast, and putting his hand in front of the nose he could not feel any breathing. *Phew, finally dead,'* Arkenthan thought as he pulled the arrows out with trembling hands. He had to sit down for a while before his body stopped shaking, and as it did, he got up, grabbed the boar's legs and pulled. Nothing happened. He put his entire weight against it and it was slowly dragged across the ground. *No. No, no. Did I miscalculate the weight this much? How?'* Arkenthan thought as he realized how heavy the boar had been. He wouldn't leave all of the boar behind though, and he cut off a large piece of meat and cut its legs off. They proved heavy enough for him and he got tired walking back to the house. Dropping the meat off he ate a bit of food he had prepared earlier in the day, and took a bite of honey. He got some renewed energy from the honey and headed out to the remains of the giant animal again. As he arrived at the fallen tree he followed the tracks of where the boar had ran, and looked at the mark where it had fallen. Where it no longer was lying. Arkenthan saw no marks from the boar being dragged along the ground. *Must have been picked up by a fjällbear or some other big animal. Or Greypaws. Of course, it must've been him. If he's been following me all day he would've seen that I left it behind, and grabbed the opportunity,'* Arkenthan thought and shook his head smiling. *'Oh well, I've got too much food today anyways. Maybe I should sell one of the legs in town, but then I'd have to take a trip tomorrow.'* He went back to his house, turning the question of whether he wanted to take a trip into town the following day over in his mind. When he was half way through the garden he caught something out of the corner of his eye. Turning, he saw Greypaws standing above the boar. As he watched the wolf, he had a feeling the animal was smiling at him. *'Come to gloat, or to help?'* Arkenthan thought as he turned towards Greypaws. Stepping towards the wolf he said "Are you helping me? Good boy." When he got closer to the boar Greypaws stepped backwards allowing Arkenthan to take the pig. "Thank you. Stay there," Arkenthan eagerly said and carried the rest of the boar inside. Grabbing two hares he went outside and stepped towards the wolf. As he came close, Greypaws gave a low growl telling Arkenthan that he was feeling unsure of the situation. With that Arkenthan stopped, put down the hares and stepped back. Greypaws sniffed the hares before pulling them closer and settling down to eat them. Arkenthan built a fire outside and put up a spit with a piece of the boar on it. He watched Greypaws eat while his food was cooking. He saw how the jaws of the beast easily chewed through the muscles and bones of the hares and imagined what those jaws could've done to him. The thought gave him goose bumps, so he tried thinking of something else. Looking at the tree he used as an archery target he thought *'Why only archery?'* Then he went inside to get the sword he'd received in town and the first scroll on how to fight with a sword. He practiced the first three steps for a while, twice managing to scratch his own legs with the sword. After training he poured a bucket of water over his head, sat down by the fire and ate his dinner. Greypaws had long since finished his food and was diverting himself by gnawing on a small tree. Arkenthan found this amusing and he thought *'Just like a dog.'* He finished his dinner after Greypaws had disappeared into the forest, so he let the fire die out before heading inside. He put the sword in the corner beside the beds and looked at his barrels of food. *'I won't be able to eat all of this before it gets old. I'll have to take a trip to town again. Okay, I'll go tomorrow to get it done,'* Arkenthan thought. He cut the nicer parts from the body of the pig, the ribs and shank, and put them in his bag. He put in a leg from the boar and a leg from the stag he shot earlier in the day as well, and added a hare in case he met Greypaws. He didn't think the wolf would attack him anymore, as he had feared the first time they met, but it would be good to have Greypaws associate Arkenthan with free food. He went to bed early to get a good start the following day and was about to fall asleep when he remembered the leaves. He jumped out of bed and hurried to the bookcase where the leaves lay, rolled one of them up, and put it carefully in the bag.

Arkenthan had got a very early start this time, and he took a short trip up the mountainside before starting his journey to eat breakfast while the sun came up over the horizon. The entire forest was filled with a red light making it look like several torches were placed among the trees. He sat looking at the forest for the half hour this light lasted. *'It can be very scary here sometimes, but this beats living in a city packed with people and buildings,'* he thought before heading out. As he walked to the city he began to recognize some of the areas he was walking through. The thought of being able to recognize where he was, anywhere in the forest, made Arkenthan smile. *'I'll have to do some more exploring,'* he thought as he pretended he had tricked some enemies into the forest and was sneaking around to scare them. It took a while before he realized that he was actually sneaking around, and that he moved a lot slower while doing so. Feeling silly he increased his pace and let his mind wander. As the day went by he kept on going, but started to take slight turns out from the path and then back again. He did this to try to familiarize himself a bit with the surroundings, but he often found he felt lost and had to walk back slowly in order to find his original path. He didn't get to the lake until late afternoon, at which point he stopped to rest his feet. After eating a bit he relaxed and tried to meditate. He started counting his breaths, in and out, and again he found his mind wandering. *'What was it Boriam had said? Your mind is trying to get your attention? See the speech as a small thing talking,'* he thought as he tried to remember what the book had said. Soon he started picturing everything as a ball with a small face and a big mouth. The ball also had legs, and it kept running around a room shouting for his attention. Arkenthan laughed to himself as he sat there by the water. After he finished laughing, he went back to meditating, and started to imagine it was the ball which was talking and not himself. It took a long time before he managed to coordinate the thoughts to the speech of the ball, but when he did manage it, he thought *Well, at least I've tried it. I'll have to continue some other time though, it's starting to get late.'* He hurried on, through the rest of the forest, and soon came out onto the open road. He marked his entrance point, turned left and headed into town. As he entered town an old man with a long grey beard and grey hair pointing out in every direction looked at him and said "Oh! It's you! I.. Oh.." He then looked quickly back and forth before running down an alley. *'Quick for his age'* Arkenthan thought *'What was that about?'* Arkenthan kept puzzling over this until he reached the butcher. He waited outside for several customers to exit before going inside saying "Hello Jonas." Jonas looked up at him questioningly. "Yes, I'm back early. Made a good catch yesterday which wouldn't keep until next week," Arkenthan said, and Jonas nodded to him. Arkenthan put his bag on the table and let the butcher take out the meat. "My, the leg of a deer, a hare, a piece of meat and leg from what? It looks like a pig, but it's big." Arkenthan looked over and said "Ah, yes. It's a boar. Big tusks on it, forgot to bring those. Anyways, I couldn't bring the entire thing as it weighed more than me." The butcher stared at Arkenthan for a while before saying "Boars are hard to find these days, only live deep into the forest. Are you saying it's safe to go into the forest?" As Arkenthan didn't really want many people poaching in the forest he quickly said "Oh, safe? No. Not safe, but I have my ways in there and they usually get me out safely." Jonas nodded suspiciously and pulled out the wrapped leaf. Looking at it, the butcher asked "Is this a spice or something?" Arkenthan hurried over to the butcher and took the leaf out of his hands carefully. "No, no, this is just a leaf I found which helped my beestings. I'm glad you reminded me of that one, do you know if there is anyone meddling in medicines in town?" He asked and the butcher quickly replied "Aye, there's one. Helena is her name. Calls herself an apothecary, whatever that might mean. You know the street behind the store here? If you follow that all the way you will see a store with a sign, showing a very strange cup with some flames underneath. That's where she'll be at. Here, I think this should pay you more than you deserve for this meat, but boar's meat is something I've been missing for years, and I know I will earn my money back. Now head out to Helena's, but be aware, she can be a bit eccentric." Arkenthan looked at the pile of coins he'd gotten from the butcher and thought *'Wow, I'll have to hunt boar more often. This is five silver pieces and twenty copper pieces.'* Dazed by the amount of money he'd got, he went out quietly. As he came out of the store he thought *'What does eccentric mean? If he warned me about it, then it could be dangerous. Still, he had more of a joyful look on his face. Bah, I guess I'll see when I get there.'*

As he wandered down the street he got a different view of how most people in town actually lived. He had thought most people in town were wealthy people who could eat what they wanted whenever they wanted it. Looking along this street however, at the houses falling apart and people hunched over small fires, made Arkenthan reconsider his view of the town. After a long walk down the street he got to a store with big windows and a sign which could resemble the one Jonas described for him. As he looked through the windows, Arkenthan could see shelves of ointments, potions and herbs. A lot of the jars were empty. Suddenly a young woman came running out from the back room, grabbed a few bottles, turned around and disappeared back into the back room again. Wondering what she was doing, Arkenthan went inside. The air was filled with every scent Arkenthan could imagine. Most of them were rancid and made him cough, but some were sweet as honey. Arkenthan stood looking around the room at the bottles thinking *'I should have one of those for my honey.'* Then the young woman appeared again, mumbling something for herself, and passed Arkenthan without noticing him. She picked up another bottle and hurried to the back room. Arkenthan snuck up to the back door, opened it, and was immediately frozen by what he saw.

Chapter 21
DRAGON'S BLOOD

In front of him Arkenthan saw a man covered by red blisters and sores lying on a table, apparently in pain. The young girl and an older woman was running around him, seemingly to help. They talked so softly and quickly that Arkenthan was unable to understand them. "Excuse me? Is there anything I could do to help?" he said. Both of the women looked up at him and said "No. Go out to the front room, and one of us will be there soon." Arkenthan backed out of the room and sat atop the counter. After a while the younger girl came out from the back saying "I'm sorry about that, it's just a bit stressful." Arkenthan nodded and said "What's wrong with him?" The girl sat down sighing and said "He got an infection in his foot. Now it's spread to his entire body. It'd be difficult to handle at the best of times, but these days it's hard to come by supplies. Oh, I'm sorry, I'm just rambling on and on. Hi, I'm Johanna, what can I help you with?" Arkenthan gave Johanna his name and said "Johanna, I found this plant while hunting in the forest. It helped lessen my pain when I was stung by a nest of bees, and I was wondering what it was, and if it could possibly be sold here?" He brought out the rolled leaf and unrolled it. Johanna looked at him saying "You were hunting in the forest? Isn't that dangerous?" Arkenthan raised his shoulders and indicated she should look at the leaf. She picked up the leaf carefully and directed her attention to it. Within a few seconds she said "Wha.. Could this be?" She grabbed a pin and made a hole in the leaf. Soon an orange-red liquid spilled forth from the hole. She took a drop of it on a stick and put it into a flame which went blue. She gasped, cut off half the leaf and ran into the other room. *'It was that good?'* Arkenthan thought as he watched the girl disappear. She soon came back out, grabbed an empty bottle, a mortar and a few other instruments. A long time passed, before the young girl returned from the back room smiling. "Thank you. Thank you, thank you," she said. Indicating what was left of the leaf she continued "That leaf, comes from the bush called Dragon's Blood. It is very rare, and the leaves are very sought after by people like us. They are very good for removing pain, healing wounds and curing poisons. It can be used for most problems and sicknesses, and for that reason people have picked everything they could find. You must have gone very far into the forest in order to find this." Arkenthan saw an accusing look on the woman's face and said "I guess I got lucky with this one. I shall see what I'm able to get for you, but if it's that rare I can't bring much of it." Johanna nodded and said "A half leaf goes a long way, so I'll make you a deal. If you bring one whole leaf, I'll take half for the store, and I'll make a potion out of the other half which you can have. I'll even teach you how to do it, but it takes quite a while to make, so maybe next time. That is, if you're able to get more. My mother, Helena, is right now preparing the other half for the man you saw. He will need all of it to get well, so if we could have a small piece of this part as well we could have some in stock for the next person who needs it." Arkenthan looked towards the other room and said "Take the entire leaf. This one's free." And he winked at Johanna. "I'll try to get some more, but I'm not that often in town. How long do they last before you can't use them anymore?" Johanna eagerly thanked Arkenthan and said "Oh, you can pick them and bring them at a later time, they don't dry out like other plants, so even after several turns of the moon they are still almost perfect. Of course, the fresher they are, the better." "Okay, I have one more leaf at home, but I believe I won't be back until next week. I'll try to stay for two days so I can spend one day learning how to make this potion." Arkenthan said and started for the door when he remembered "Actually, do you have any spare jars? I have some honey at home and need something to keep it in." Johanna smiled and said "Now you have honey as well? Why, you must have gone really deep into the forest." Giving a small laugh she continued "So you want a jar. Hold on, I'll see what I've got." Johanna disappeared behind the counter and Arkenthan could hear the rustling of drawers and ceramics. Eventually Johanna appeared again holding a small ceramic jar painted in many colours. "Here," she said smiling "You can have this one. It's not much, but it's the only one we've got. Consider it as a payment for the leaf." Arkenthan thanked Johanna for the jar and left the store.

Outside the store, Arkenthan was met by a contrasting wall of fresh air. He had become used to the stale air inside the store and was now surprised by the fresh air outside. He headed back to the butcher's store where a queue had formed. *Is that because of the meat I brought, or is this the time people go to the stores in this town?'* Arkenthan thought as he decided not to push his way past the crowd and instead head towards the smithy. He felt at home there, and maybe the knife was finished. As he walked down the street he saw the old man again. "Hey!" Arkenthan shouted, and as the old man saw him, he whistled a tune and turned into another back alley. Arkenthan ran to the alley and saw four doors before a brick wall. Knocking on all of them produced no results, and he soon gave up trying to reach the old man. He went back out onto the street and continued his stroll towards the smithy.

When he arrived, Arkenthan saw that a big note had been hammered into the door saying "Back in five" and Arkenthan wondered where he had gone off to. After a few minutes the blacksmith returned beaming with two handfuls of meat. *'It would seem word spreads fast in this town,'* Arkenthan thought as he greeted the smith. "The butcher sent me a pigeon saying he'd got some great meat in stock, and boy has he. You should run and get some while you can," he said, to which Arkenthan just smiled. "I heard he did. What meat did you get?" Arkenthan asked. "Oh, he had the finest deer leg I've seen in a long time. I had to get some of it. But he also had some wild boar in, which I hear is excellent, so maybe I'll have to go back soon to get some of that," the smith said and continued "But here's me rambling on about my business, what can I help you with lad?" Arkenthan shook his head and said "No, no. I don't mind. I was just popping by to see how everything is going. Hey, what's your name? I don't think I caught it the previous times I've been here." "Aye, name's Horace, pleased to meet ya. You're wondering about the knife, aren't you? I'm almost done with it, if I push on into the night I'll have it done by tomorrow morning. Do you have the money we agreed on?" Arkenthan nodded and held out eight silver pieces. "I got a bit more this time, so I can pay a bit more than we agreed on for the first payment." Horace nodded and took the money. When Arkenthan turned to leave the smith said "Hey, you've spent some time in a smithy before, haven't you? Maybe you could help me with a little something. Need someone else to hold it steady while I hammer it into shape." Since Arkenthan had nothing else to do, he decided to help the smith.

He learned a bit about working with metal and soon understood how much work every little job was. After two hours, Arkenthan was unable to hold his arms up, so Horace said "It's a good workout for your body. You might normally manage to hold these up for much longer, but with the continuous hammering your muscles are beaten into place. You managed to work longer than I expected though. A lot longer than anyone who has helped me before. Feel free to help out again, if you want to." He ended his sentence with a rolling laugh and Arkenthan staggered tiredly out into the street. *'I hope the queue outside the butcher's store is gone,'* Arkenthan thought as he made his way to the store. When he arrived there was one person left inside, so Arkenthan stood waiting outside for him to leave before entering. "Ho now, did you meet Helena?" Jonas said, and Arkenthan told the butcher of how there was a sick man there and that he'd only met Johanna. He explained to the butcher that the leaf he had brought apparently was exactly what the man needed to survive. He left out that it could be used for pretty much anything, and that it was extremely rare. "Well, I've been helping the smith with an iron fence for the past two hours, so I'm dead tired. Do you sell snack pieces of roasted meat here?" Jonas understood that he was tired, and said "I'm sorry to say that we don't have any roasted meat here, but I'll tell you what. If you buy a small piece of meat, I'll chop it into even smaller pieces and have my wife roast them for you. Arkenthan thanked the butcher for this offer and bought some meat worth the extra twenty copper pieces he was carrying. After a short while Arkenthan brought a bag of roasted meat up to his room and lay down on the bed relaxing his arms. *I wish I had the book now. Next time I come here I'll bring it with me,*' he thought as he ate some roasted meat and stared at the ceiling. Drifting into sleep without knowing it, Arkenthan woke up the next morning with the bag of meat still beside him, his arms sore and the sun blinding his eyes. Sitting up in bed he looked at the bag of meat and thought *I guess I have lunch.*'

He went downstairs and was met by Jonas and a few customers. "Oh, hello. Who are you then?" an older lady said to him but before Arkenthan managed to say anything Jonas said "Um, he's um. My sister's hm. Son. Yes, my nephew." Arkenthan looked between the old lady and the butcher then nodded to the lady. "Aye, he's in town once in a while, so I've let him use the spare room upstairs while he's here." The old lady looked him over and seemed to accept the explanation as she turned towards the counter and looked at some meat Jonas had laid out for her. Feeling he had to say something, Arkenthan moved towards the door while saying "Well uncle, I'll be off now, see you next time I'm in town." Jonas gave Arkenthan a wave goodbye and then he was off. Hurrying to the smithy he quickly received the knife and ran to the other end of town. Not wanting to get tired too early he slowed down to a normal walking speed as he left. There were a few heads which turned, but not many paid him much more than a glance. As he left town he looked up at the sky and thought *It's going to be dark by the time I get home. Oh well. Dark old forest, here I come.*' He didn't walk long before reaching his entrance mark, and he soon found himself at the pool of water. He kept his bow ready in case something happened, but otherwise he just focused on walking onwards. A few times some animal jumped out a little ahead of him, but he never had sufficient time to prepare an arrow and fire it. As the sun set Arkenthan had the mountain well in his sights and saw it being bathed in a blue light. *Wow, that's beautiful,*' Arkenthan thought. When he got up the slope of the mountain he stopped and gazed upon the stars for a while as he snacked on the few pieces of roasted meat left in his bag. It was a quiet night and he slowly made his way towards his house. For some reason the forest didn't seem as scary as it used to. *I guess I'm starting to get used to it,*' Arkenthan thought and smiled. As he came inside, he spent a long time lighting the fire, and then went to the bookcase. Realizing the book was gone again he smiled and nodded to himself knowing exactly where it was. He didn't bother to get it yet, but went to sleep instead.

Arkenthan woke up late in the day feeling refreshed. Looking outside he saw the blue sky had disappeared behind a layer of clouds, and thought *'Maybe it'll rain tonight?'* He peeked into his barrels of food and found that he wouldn't need any new supplies for several days. He put a hare and a piece of meat from the boar aside in case Greypaws decided to drop by, and went outside to stock up on water. *'If it starts to rain, it's good to be prepared'* Arkenthan thought as he pulled the bucket out of the well. He spent the day chopping trees and cleaning his house. He wanted the trees for the planned addition to the outhouse along with a little firewood. He lined the planks he got out of the trees along the wall inside the outhouse and thought *'There, if it starts to rain they'll be dry.'* He knew he wouldn't be able to build the entire addition that day, and the skies had turned darker while he was working. Looking up at the clouds Arkenthan thought *'I'm glad I took my time today for this. If it rains tomorrow I can read the book knowing I've prepared myself for after the rain.'*

As the darkness fell, Arkenthan put a stew over the fire and took out the knife he'd got from the smith. It was smaller than he had thought it would be; the handle was of a normal size, but the blade was much shorter. The blade was also very curved and Arkenthan wondered why as he kept looking at it. It was thicker than he had imagined but assumed that was for durability. He fetched a rabbit and felt the knife easily cut through the skin. Twisting the knife sideways he followed the pelt of the rabbit and soon understood why the knife was so curved. The long strokes the blade allowed him to make gave the pelt an even cut which made it much easier to cut a whole piece out of it. He still struggled to get a good pelt from the rabbit, but he found it was easier to get larger pieces from it. He knew that as soon as he had amassed a bit of experience using it, he would be able to skin pretty much anything quickly. *'Skinning animals won't just give me good pelts which could be useful, but it leaves more of the meat behind, bringing in more food,'* Arkenthan thought as he tested how close to the skin of the pelt he could cut without ruining it. He knew how much meat was lost using his normal knife, and he could see there were a lot more saved with the knife he held. Feeling tired, Arkenthan put the knife down on the bookcase and smiled at the leaf lying at the bottom while shaking his head. As he lay down to sleep, his stomach reminded Arkenthan that he'd forgot to eat his dinner. Annoyed at this, he quickly ate the stew and threw himself onto the bed. His stomach didn't seem to like the sudden rush and he soon had to run outside. As he opened the front door he was hit by a strong wind, whipping rain in his face and he thought *'Great, that's just… Great…'* By the time he got back into the house, he was soaking wet. Before he could go to bed he had to hang his clothes to dry and get warm. The next morning Arkenthan got up and looked out of the window. It was still raining outside, so Arkenthan nodded, smiled and went to the bookcase. Having pulled it aside he got a torch and went inside. After a short while he returned with the book, pushed the bookcase back in place, and sat down on the bed. It rained for two days, during which time Arkenthan read the book only interrupted by his meals. Arkenthan silently read *'Boriam and Jonathan spent the next few days walking through open fields, which were only interrupted by small farms now and then'.*

Chapter 22
DARÚN RIVER

In the evenings, Boriam instructed Jonathan in the next level of the meditation. "You've now understood how to focus on your breathing as you meditate. Going forward you will have to look even deeper within yourself, by feeling your own heartbeats. This requires an even greater silence in your head. The heartbeats are very hard to control, while the breathing is something you can do manually. Listening to your heart pushes away your mind even more than listening to your breathing, but thus the more your mind will try to fight back." Jonathan nodded while Boriam spoke. Boriam watched as Jonathan meditated and after a while said "If you can't listen to your heart for long, change your focus to your breathing. As soon as you lose focus on one, try the other. Only when you're able to feel your heart continuously during meditation are you finished with this level." Jonathan nodded, but Boriam felt he hadn't quite understood it. *'Oh well, learning by doing I guess,'* Boriam thought as Jonathan went back to meditating. It was apparent that Jonathan had to keep switching his focus between the two levels as he alternated between having a normal breathing rhythm and taking deep breaths. After a while Boriam instructed Jonathan to only do the breathing meditation. *'Making him get used to having more focus will let him find the way more easily through the levels of meditation,'* Boriam thought as he prepared the practice sticks. After a while Boriam saw Jonathan's shoulders lower themselves, and knew he was deep into the meditation. "Good, know that feeling, and get ready to use the focus for the upcoming fight. Catch," Boriam said as he threw the stick towards Jonathan. Not having enough time to react, Jonathan only managed to open his eyes and begin lifting his arms before the stick hit him in the head. He quickly recovered after falling over, preparing for a fight knowing that Boriam could attack at any time. And so he did. This process repeated itself every night while they walked across the open fields. As they now had so much more space to fight, they could move about more freely, and Boriam could teach Jonathan more easily how to stand and move. When Jonathan had become better at fighting, Boriam showed him some flourishes. "A flourish, is a set of

113

movements combined into one action," Boriam explained as he showed a combination of swinging and stabbing the sword towards a pretended enemy. After Boriam had taught him the flourish, Jonathan practiced that for some time while pretending to fight an enemy. At the beginning of this training, Jonathan used the stick to practice, but he soon tried using the sword he'd been given. "Using the sword will help you get used to it and get to know how it behaves when you swing it. Soon we'll spar using real, but dulled, swords. We'll buy some training swords in Fisherman's Rest, but we won't get there for a few days, maybe a week." Jonathan nodded and kept practicing. After a while he said "It's very different to fight with a sword. It's so much heavier than the stick." Boriam nodded and said "That's why we'll have to train using swords. The longer we're walking around, the greater the chance of someone recognizing us, and with that attack us. So you'll have to learn, if not how to single-handedly defeat an attacker, then at least how to stall an enemy from hitting you until someone comes to your aid. And you won't be able to even do that, unless you get to know your sword."

They usually spent the night in the open air, but one night they neared a farm, so they decided to try their luck. Having knocked at the door they heard a lot of noise from inside before a man opened. "Whaddaya want?" The man, to Jonathan's amusement, managed to mumble and scream at the same time. Boriam thought 'Great, a drinker. Have to be careful now.' He said "Hello sir, we're wandering across these plains and was wondering if we could stay in your barn this night?" The man looked at Boriam apparently proud and yelled "That's right! I'm the sir around here! Why should I let you? Are you sent by the Council or sumth'n?" Boriam saw Jonathan almost start to laugh and quickly said "We do not follow the Council. It's rather the opposite, I'm afraid. If we can stay in your barn, we won't need a campfire to heat ourselves." The man suspiciously examined Boriam and said "So not from th' Council?" to which Boriam shook his head in reply. "Good!" the man said as he straightened himself up, his voice completely changed. "I find it much easier to deal with the Council's men when they think I'm dead drunk," he said grinning. Boriam laughed and politely asked again if they could borrow the barn. "Ah, yes, yes. Stay as long as you like, as long as you don't cause any trouble." They thanked the man and went into the barn where they quickly went to sleep.

Boriam was woken by the man knocking hard on the barn door. "Yes?" Boriam answered him, and the man said "There are torches in the field, heading this way." Boriam thought for a while about what this could mean, and had a suspicion. "Is that good or bad? Well, as you wake us up in the middle of the night I assume it's bad, but how bad is it?" Boriam asked. The man entered the barn and spoke in a lowered voice "Let's put it this way. There are many people wandering around at night, and that's ok. But there're very few who wish to announce their arrival by carrying torches. That's only for the soldiers of the Council. So I'm wondering now, how interested are the Council in getting a hold of you guys? Don't they care about you, or are you the reason they are here?" Boriam nodded and asked "How many torches is there?" The man looked at the ceiling of the barn and answered "There are several along the horizon, but they're grouped in twos. I'm assuming two of them are going to come here." Boriam sighed and said "Jonathan, wake up." As Jonathan jolted awake, he pulled his sword and said "Sparring now?" Boriam laughed and said "In a way we might be, yes. Thugs of the Council are closing in." "At this time of night? In how long will they be here?" Jonathan said and the man said, looking between his two visitors "You're that wanted by the Council? The moment you see soldiers you anticipate fighting?" Both Jonathan and Boriam looked at the man questioningly. The man sighed and said "I'll try to get them moving on, but they might pop in here to check. You should probably dig a bit into the hay and hope they don't torch the place." The man left the barn and went inside the house. Boriam started digging and Jonathan asked "We're actually going to dig down in the hay?" Boriam looked up at him and answered "Absolutely. The best way of getting someone off your tracks is to let them pass by you quietly. If you have a choice between fighting and any other way of getting out of a situation, choose the other way. And remember this, there's always another way than fighting, you just might not have the time to find it." He then kept on digging, and soon Jonathan found his own spot to dig. A few minutes later they were covered in hay, and Boriam had managed to make a small hole to look through.

A long time passed before he saw two torches walk past the barn. The hay covered the sounds, so Boriam was unable to hear what they were talking about. He could, however, hear that the man in the house was dead drunk and thought *'Wow, that's good acting.'* After a bit of arguing where the drunken mumbling of the man had grown louder, Boriam saw the two torches walking away from the house along the barn. Nearing the door of the barn one of the men said loudly "'Oy, Strum, the drunken one said he hadn't seen anyone, but what if they just snuck in here? I say we check it out quickly and be on our way." The torches turned to the door and it opened. Two young men in armour entered the barn and looked back and forth. The men were so noisy that Boriam didn't think they would hear anything even if they stood still. When the men began to move into the barn he felt a bit less secure. He saw the two men head towards the haystack, pull their swords and stab at the hay in various places. *'I hope Jonathan sees this. If they move too close to him he'll need to defend himself,'* Boriam thought as one of the men walked towards where he assumed Jonathan was hiding. Having paid attention to the man heading in Jonathan's direction, Boriam hadn't noticed the man heading towards himself. Noticing the man just as he stabbed, he was unable to do anything besides focus on not flinching. The sword barely passed between his legs, making a small cut in his right thigh. Boriam heard the other man say "Come on, let's get out of here, I don't think anyone's here." He saw the man above him, apparently oblivious to the fact that he'd hit someone, look up, nod and follow the other man towards the door. Before heading out the man who had scratched Boriam's leg stopped and looked around again. The other man had reached the door and shouted "Frank, let's go!" Frank turned towards him and answered "Aye, be right there, have to take a piss. The old drunkard won't notice." Strum laughed and said "Okay, I'll head back into formation." He left and Boriam saw that he was heading away from the barn. Frank stuck his sword into the ground and peed on the wall of the barn. When he finished, he yanked the sword out of the ground and started wiping the dirt off. "Ey Strum! There's blood on my sword!" Frank shouted, at which point Boriam quietly crawled out of the hay, took aim at the man and threw his sword. The man mumbled "Where could this blood come from? Unless..." He turned and managed to see Boriam standing in the hay, and assume a surprised look on his face, before the sword hit him blade first in the chest. Boriam heard a cough before the man fell on his back. He saw Jonathan emerge from the hay before saying "Wow, that was awesome!" Turning towards the boy, Boriam said sharply "There is nothing awesome in killing!" Then in a slightly more normal tone said "I said it before, try to avoid it if you can. Right now I couldn't, but I could do so even when he stabbed my leg. That's the emotional control you'll need to learn, that even when someone strike you, it might not mean that you need to strike back. Now let's get out of here in case the other one comes back." They snuck out of the barn and were surprised to find the man from the house standing outside. "I saw two of them go inside, but only one coming back out. I began to wonder what was happening, but I have a decent guess as to what happened. Leaving me to clean it up, are you?" he said accusingly. Boriam and Jonathan looked at each other before Boriam turned towards the man saying "Please?" The man started laughing and sighed before saying "Aye, you two bugger off, I'll deal with it. His buddy went straight south, so I'd advise you to head slightly east before turning that way. Didn't see any torches eastwards, but that doesn't mean there weren't guards around." Boriam nodded and said "There's always a chance there are people looking for us, we'll just have to follow what seems to be the safest path." The man looked at him and said "You're what they would call wise, aren't you?" Boriam gave a short laugh as Jonathan and he turned eastwards. He looked at the man and said "I wouldn't say wise.

Understanding I might be, but wise? No." He grinned and started walking. After a long time Boriam stopped and said "Let's camp here to be rested for the day tomorrow. We'll be easier to spot in daylight, so we should be well rested for what may come. And don't light a fire. It will just attract attention." Jonathan didn't argue and quickly threw his bag on the ground to use as a pillow. Boriam soon did the same.

The following morning Boriam woke up to the sound of running water. Sitting up and looking around he noticed they had been camping beside a small river. *Was I so tired yesterday I didn't even hear the river?'* he thought as he examined the landscape. "Wake up, Jonathan! We have to move!" He shouted at the still sleeping boy. Jonathan jumped awake saying "What, who, where? Are we under attack?" Boriam looked at him and said "No, we're not. Not directly anyways. There're two things. One: I just wanted to check your reaction. Two: This is the Darún river." Jonathan put his hand on his head and said "Ugh, you woke me up for a river?" "Yes. This isn't just any river," Boriam answered. This comment seemed to wake Jonathan up a bit more, although he tried to hide it. "And what's so special about this river then?" Jonathan said sarcastically. Boriam looked towards the river and said "Well, it's dried out." Jonathan turned towards the visibly flowing river and said "I think you and I have a very different view on what 'dried out' means." Boriam grinned and said "You see the steep rise in the field to our south, going across the entire horizon?" Jonathan nodded. "You're pretty lucky to be here now. You see, every fifteen years for one single night the Darún river begins to run. It will keep on building up during the following day. By the time darkness falls on the following night, this entire field will be a lake all the way down to that rise you see." Jonathan looked thoughtful for a while before saying "So what you're saying is that by the end of today this entire area will be under water?" "That is exactly what I'm saying," Boriam confirmed and Jonathan continued "And unless we want to be under water by that time we'll have to get to the horizon and up a steep hill?" Boriam nodded his response. "Great, same old thing then. Something is chasing us and we have to hurry to get away from it," Jonathan said which brought a short laugh from Boriam. "The good thing though," Boriam said "is that Fisherman's Rest is only about half a day's walk south of the hill you see. But yeah, to reach the bank before sunset we'll have to hurry." They hadn't unpacked anything and were soon ready to start walking again.

Chapter 23
ESSENCE OF MAGIC

Having spent half the day walking, Jonathan turned around and saw that the edge of the river had been following them. He estimated they had got about half the way to the banks to the south. "We've spent half the day getting half the distance. If we keep this up we should be ok," he said. Boriam turned his head towards Jonathan and said "Yes, and no. We should be by the banks by the end of the day. However, you have to remember that we'll be more tired towards the end." Jonathan sighed, and Boriam said "But I guess the worst part is that it is said that this entire area will be flooded by nightfall. So by then we will be tired and have to swim or wade while carrying all our things." Jonathan looked up and said "It is said? You haven't seen this before?" Boriam shook his head and said "This is an event which happens for one week in the middle of summer every fifteen years. Very few are able to experience it, and fewer are able to remember exactly how long ago the last flooding happened. Fifteen years is a long time to remember a single event like this. You'll understand as you get a bit older." "I hate that sentence. Adults or older people use it all the time, and especially when they're unable to explain something. It's as if they're saying 'you're too stupid now, but maybe you'll be smart enough later.'" Jonathan kept feeling irritated by this for a while until Boriam said "Shush, did you hear that?" Jonathan's thoughts stopped as he strained to hear, and he soon heard a strange sound. The sound started with a splash and went over to a small pop. They turned around but couldn't see anything except the plants standing above the water. They kept on going for a while until they heard the sound again. Turning around they still couldn't see anything. *What can it be?'* Jonathan thought as he looked across the water, and then it happened again. The splash sent a big area of water shooting skywards, and in the now waterless area the pop made a plant appear. It happened so fast Jonathan barely registered what really happened, except for the falling water. Where there had been just water before, there now stood a plant, fully sized with big leaves standing out. "Wow. Can I call that awesome?" Jonathan said to Boriam who nodded and said "That even I will describe as awesome. Wait, is that…?" Boriam then looked like he was deep in thought until Jonathan asked "Is that what?" "Huh? Oh, nothing, nothing. We should keep going." Boriam said and turned. Jonathan sighed and followed him. As the day went by, Jonathan noticed the pace of the water increasing behind them.

They were getting close to the banks now, but the water had caught up with them. It was ankle deep, and made their walking a lot harder and slower. As the evening wore on Jonathan could feel the water crawling up his leg. When the water was waist high and he was tiring quickly, he hit a rise in the ground. Having been looking into the water for steady ground he now looked up at the banks. "Finally!" He said but Boriam said "The more water there is, the more slippery the hill will be. In order to get up now, we'll have to run to quickly get to the dry areas." Jonathan's spirit waned and he considered just waiting for the water to rise all the way before climbing out, but when Boriam started to run, so did he. They made a lot of noise as water flew everywhere, and the ground gave way beneath their feet. Struggling for some time as they ran up the hill, Jonathan finally found dry ground which sped him upwards. At the top he laid down on the ground. Boriam came up the hill smiling and as he reached the top said "Good job. You've managed to utilize the extra energy you have for this final sprint." Jonathan needed some time thinking this over before saying "Wait a minute. You stopped running half way up the hill!" Boriam nodded and said "Yes, you didn't need to run the entire hill." "Wha..? But you said we had to run to get up!" Jonathan said annoyed. Boriam laughed and said "I didn't say you had to run up the hill, I only said you had to run to get to the dry part." Jonathan stared blankly thinking back at what Boriam had said, without finding any way to argue with his statement. "The way you said it suggested I had to run the entire thing!" Jonathan shouted. Boriam put his hand up to silence him and said "Always listen to what people are actually saying. People might say one thing and mean something else. Some people say exactly what they mean in a way that others will understand wrongly or differently. Understanding what people mean is the key to survival in this world." What Boriam said made Jonathan feel that it was true. He didn't understand what he thought was true about it, he just knew that it was, as if a part of him shouted the same thing silently in his entire body. The experience surprised Jonathan so much that he just stood there blankly staring across the water. A splash and a pop from the water, throwing a lot of water into the air right in front of him jolted him out of his dreamlike state as he jumped from the shock and fell flat on his back. Boriam laughed and helped him up before saying "Come on, let's make a fire to dry us a little." "But won't that alert the guards that we're here?" Jonathan said. "Yes, but either they are far away in the middle of the water somewhere, or they have made it to the bank as well. If they have made it to the bank, they will probably patrol it. Patrolling it will bring them here, so the more prepared we are, the better. All we can do now to prepare are the three gets." "The three gets?" Jonathan asked. "Aye, get dry, get warm and get food."

As the darkness filled the sky and the stars emerged, the plants on the water kept making the splash and pop sound. Jonathan couldn't sleep, and after a while the sounds made Jonathan laugh. For each time the sounds came he laughed even more. "What's so funny?" Boriam said in a strict voice. "I don't know!" Jonathan said gasping for air. "It just makes me laugh, and the more times I hear the sound, the more I laugh." This went on for a while before he finally managed to stop laughing. The laughing had made him more tired, and he soon fell asleep. His dreams were filled with strange things that Jonathan didn't remember in the morning, but he did remember that each time a new thing had appeared it had made a splash and a pop sound. Waking up he felt as tired as he had the night before, but was surprised that he had been allowed to sleep in. Looking towards what was left of the fire, he saw Boriam staring across the water. He turned towards the water and froze. Spread across the water were hundreds of giant flowers in all the colours of the rainbow. "What has happened?" Jonathan asked. "Oh, good morning," Boriam said excitedly. "These are the Tendúril flowers. They are thought to be extinct! The seeds live and grow for many years underneath the ground, and as soon as there is enough water above ground, they shoot into the air. First they become the stems we saw yesterday, and then during the night they grow into the flowers you see before you. Would you mind staying here for today?" He asked and Jonathan thought *If something makes him this excited, it's probably good to have seen it. I'll probably have to dig a lot to find out why though.* He then said "It would be nice with a quiet day, and Fisherman's Rest won't go anywhere, but why do you want to stay until tomorrow?" Boriam looked at him and said "Even though we stay here, it won't necessarily be a quiet day." And Jonathan thought *'Of course not,'* before Boriam continued "But that being said, I believe you would want to be here tomorrow. Today the flowers start preparing their seeds. Tomorrow, well, you'll see tomorrow."

Jonathan rebuilt the fire and started to prepare some food. Grabbing a piece of meat he noticed that the bag was almost empty. "Hey, we're nearly out of food!" He said but Boriam replied "Yes, I expected as much. Don't worry about it. We'll have enough for today, and we'll get to Fisherman's Rest tomorrow evening. We'll only starve for half a day, which pretty much everyone does once a week these days." Jonathan nodded and asked "Is it far to Fisherman's Rest?" Boriam turned towards the fire and pointed southwards. "Do you see the tiny black spot by the lake at the edge of the horizon?" Boriam asked. Straining to see where Boriam was pointing, Jonathan finally saw it and nodded. "That's Fisherman's Rest. It will take us a little less than a day to walk there, even on empty stomachs." Jonathan blinked twice before lying down on the ground, waiting for the sparring stick to arrive. He was prepared when Boriam threw it at him and he caught it in the air, jumped to his feet and rushed at the old man. Boriam seemed surprised at this and barely blocked Jonathan's strike. "Always be prepared for anything, old man," Jonathan said mockingly, but in a few more strikes it was clear that Boriam had the upper hand. Jonathan focused on blocking Boriam's strikes, but eventually he lost his sword. "Don't put too much effort into just stopping your opponent's blows, or you'll end up losing your sword. Look for gaps in your opponent's attacks and strike there." They sparred for a long time, and Jonathan got the upper hand a few times. As soon as Boriam noticed this though, the old man took it back. "You put too much effort into thinking about who is in charge of the fight, and not about what you are doing in the fight," Boriam said which made Jonathan think even more about it for a while. After some time it felt like he stopped thinking at all, and his focus changed to every strike he did. It felt like he was back to meditating, his head swimming in a haze and everything seeming to slow down. He saw more easily how Boriam was striking him and he soon managed to hit the old man's stomach. At this point his head returned to normal. "Good strike there," Boriam said, and Jonathan answered "Thank you. I don't know how I did it, but it felt like my head was somewhere else. Everything moved slowly and I just knew where to swing the sword, or stick that is." "Hmm," Boriam said before attacking again. This time a few strikes were exchanged before Jonathan's stick flew out of his hands. "Let me guess. That feeling you had is gone?" Boriam asked which Jonathan confirmed. Boriam taught Jonathan more about movement and flourishes during a fight. They didn't stop until it was dark around them, and seeing what the other was doing had become difficult. "We'll practice how to fight in the dark later, when you have learned more about your own strength," Boriam said, at which point they stopped fighting and settled down to eat and sleep.

Jonathan jolted awake as something gave off a loud bang. Startled, he looked around for the cause of it. He turned towards Boriam and said "What wa.." Another bang interrupted him and he looked towards the water. *What in the name of the gods is happening?'* Jonathan thought, but soon found the answer. One of the flowers' petals curled up and created something which looked like a cocoon. The plant stayed this way for a long time before the cocoon suddenly exploded, sending a tiny ball of something flying through the air. The ball landed in the water a slight bit away from the flower and quickly sank to the bottom. "Is that..?" Jonathan said and pointed towards where the ball had flown. "The seed? Yes. Marvellous, isn't it?" Boriam answered. Jonathan could do nothing but stare at the lake as another plant started to curl up. When this plant exploded the seed was sent in their direction, landing with a loud thumping sound and boring into the ground. Jonathan picked it up and turned it over a few times. A crack had appeared in it, and as he showed it to Boriam the old man said "You should open it. I remember having heard there's something special about these seeds, but I can't remember what it is." *'Let's hope it's edible, because we need some food soon,'* Jonathan thought as he took his sword and started to peel the seed. Testing the pieces he broke off there didn't seem to be anything they could eat. As he kept peeling another seed landed hard on the ground beside his left foot. Looking at how hard the seed struck the ground, he imagined what it would do if it had actually hit him. What he didn't notice was the glowing green gem he was unwrapping from the seed. Boriam, however, did. "Wow, so that's where they come from! Hah! I knew there was something about these seeds," he exclaimed eagerly. Jonathan looked puzzled at Boriam before looking into his own hands. He picked up the gem and held it towards the sky. He could see through it, but it was as if something swirled around inside the gem. "What is it?" Jonathan asked. "It's a seed apparently, but it is also something you'll need later on. Here, look," Boriam answered and pulled out a necklace with seven of the same type of gem, all in different colours. "Of course it's a seed, and ok I'll need it later, but what is it?" Jonathan pushed on. Boriam seemed reluctant to answer, but said "It is, hmm, an essence." Jonathan kept pushing with "An essence of what?" Looking for a way to circumvent the question, Boriam finally sighed and said "An essence of magic. Raw and pure magic. Very rare." Jonathan looked at the gem and thought *'An essence of magic? What does that do?'* He picked up the seed which nearly struck his foot and started unwrapping it as he said "Tell me about these seeds or essences or what they really are. Why will I need them later on?" Again Boriam sighed and began speaking. "An essence of magic is something solid which is made of pure magic. Sometimes it will be a mess of magical elements combined in the item which will give it a tainted colour and make it very unstable. Then there's the other side, where the item is made from a single magical element and has a very pure glowing colour. The one you found is green, and is made from wind magic. Touching an item of pure magic gets you directly in touch with that element. It enhances your ability to use that type of magic, but it only applies to the first elemental item you touch. Applying several items of the same element does nothing for you." Jonathan finished unwrapping the seed and held up a purple gem. "What element is this one then?" he asked, and Boriam said "That's based on lightning magic. You're off to a good start, but we should hope that some more land ashore."

"Why? Can't we just wade out to where the seeds land in the water?" Jonathan asked, but Boriam shook his head and said "No, as soon as the seeds hit the water, they become hard as steel. You won't be able to break it open. And we can't leave and come back later, because the seed itself eats the magical core. It stays alive for about an hour after hitting the ground in the hope of rolling into the water. After that hour is up, the magical essence is gone." Jonathan nodded and said "So we should walk up and down the edge of the water here in the hope that we find a stranded seed?" Boriam nodded and told Jonathan to go one way before turning the other way himself.

Chapter 24
BLACK AND WHITE FLOWERS

'How lucky can this kid be?' Boriam thought as he walked along the water's edge. He listened for the explosions of the flowers and whenever he heard one nearby he looked up to see where the seed was heading. *I stayed in training for 20 years before even seeing one of these. Bah, no use fussing about it. Oh, there's one,'* Boriam thought and picked up the seed. He quickly peeled the shell and found a deep blue gem. *'Water,'* he thought as he put the small stone in his pocket and kept on walking. He looked at the closest flower and saw it starting to curl up. He felt for the direction of the wind and put his hand in front of his face with one finger stretched out. He then pointed it towards the ground, before making a circular motion with it. He watched as the still curling flower was pushed around and ended up pointing straight at him. Boriam smiled, and the flower exploded. He picked up the seed and took off his necklace before putting his thumb to his forehead. Focussing his mind on the seed he cycled through the different energies of the various elements, looking for the one which corresponded to the seed. *'Another water,'* Boriam thought and threw the seed into the lake. For a while he continued this procedure, pushing the flowers and looking for the seed's element. He ended up finding one fire and one ice before heading back.

As he was nearing their campsite he looked towards the water and saw that a flower was about to explode. Not managing to push the flower in time, he instead focussed on the seed. When the flower exploded, Boriam saw the seed fly along the edge of the water. He quickly forced the air to blow the seed towards the shore. Noticing that the seed would still probably hit the water, he put his thumb to his chest and felt the earth magic fill him up. Pointing towards the ground, Boriam released the magic and stretched the bank out where the seed was landing. As he pulled the ground back with the seed on it, he noticed that this seed was different from the others. All the others were a dark brown, but this one had a bright golden colour. *'Could it be?'* Boriam thought and looked towards the camp. He saw Jonathan sitting by the fire with four brown seeds. *'Might just as well,'* he thought, picked up the golden seed and went to the campsite. Nearing the fire, Boriam said "Here, this should get your attention." He then threw the golden seed to Jonathan. The boy caught it in the air and looked at it for a long time. "Looks quite different from the others," he said eventually, and Boriam nodded saying "Yes, I think it is one of the rare ones. Open it." Jonathan did so, and soon revealed a transparent, glowing white stone. Jonathan looked at it for a long time before saying "Let me guess, light?" Boriam confirmed this and said "It is very rare because it requires the combination of the correct three elements in identical amounts. Equally rare is the black one. I have all the elements except the black one in my necklace." Boriam sighed and continued "Let's hope we find two. Here, I'll boost our chances a bit." He saw that there was a group of flowers close to each other which was about to explode, so Boriam spent a lot of his strength in turning the flowers towards them. He got them into position just in time for the explosions, and soon Boriam and Jonathan had to run from a volley of heavy seeds which were hard as stones. Returning to their camp, Jonathan picked one up and was about to start peeling it when Boriam said "Okay, hold on. What elements do we have now?" They both laid out the stones they had, and Boriam found that they had two red, three deep blue, two light blue, one white, one green and one purple. Boriam nodded and said "Red is fire, deep blue is water, light blue is ice, white is light, green is air and purple is lightning. So we need orange, which is earth, and two of the rare black one which is dark. I can sense what colour the stone inside is, so I'll check the seeds to see if they are the ones we need. If they aren't, we should throw them into the water so they can become flowers." Boriam did this, and found one orange, but all the others were thrown into the water. "You should go try to hunt something we can eat, this will probably take some time," Boriam said to Jonathan who questioningly said "Hunt? With what? A sword isn't exactly easy to hunt with." Boriam went over to his bag and thought *I should have something here. Maybe this? No that won't work. Oh, I have those.*' He pulled two strings out of the bag, separated them and gave them to Jonathan. "This one you can use to set up a trap," he said as he pointed at one of the strings and continued "Now this one, is a fishing line. The best you'll ever find. You cast it into the water and it curls into a hook. When the fish bites it, the hook bites the fish back, and it's strong enough for most types of fish." Jonathan looked at Boriam and said "What do you mean it bites the fish?" Boriam smiled and said "With a normal hook, when the fish get stuck it start to thrash around in the water to shake itself off. Often it manage to break free or break the line. Here, when the fish gets stuck to the hook, the hook digs into the fish. As the fish wriggles to get loose, the hook wriggles also, and digs deeper into the fish." Jonathan looked surprized, but he didn't bother to ask any more questions before he turned around and went to the edge of the water.

Lowering the end of the line into the water made it curl just like Boriam said it would. He looked up at Boriam before swinging the line back and throwing it into the water. He tied the end of it to a root which was sticking out of the ground, and took the other cord with him to hunt for food.

Boriam kept his focus on the flowers to see if any were ready to explode. He didn't find any close together, so he focused on single flowers instead. After an hour he'd gathered and checked over 30 seeds without luck. He noticed something moving in the corner of his eye, and looked to the side. For a short while nothing happened, but then the rope started jerking back and forth. He quickly went to the line and pulled at it. It was a big fish, and Boriam struggled to get it ashore. When he finally managed to get it out of the water, he sat down taking deep breaths of air as the fish wriggled around. Then the head of the fish exploded. Boriam blinked several times trying to find a logical explanation for the exploding head. After a while he gave up, got up and went over to the fish. When he got there he saw that the head hadn't really exploded. It had only looked like it exploded, as it had been squeezed flat very suddenly. Boriam found the reason for the sudden squeezing of the head embedded in the ground. It was a seed which was now coloured red in some areas by the fish blood. Boriam saw the colour spread from the blood into the leaves giving them a slightly purple colour. *'No. Is it really?'* Boriam thought and looked up at the sky. The sun was bright and not a cloud was to be seen anywhere. *'Hmm,'* he thought and focused on the seed again. After letting the blood spread the purple colour all the way around the seed, he started peeling it. As he got through the layers he found that the purple colour had spread to the entire seed. The centre stone was now completely black, slightly transparent and glowing in a way which nauseated Boriam. *'I didn't know black could glow, but that's the only way I can describe this,'* Boriam thought as he put the seed with the others. Looking at the water he soon located another flower which was about to explode. Concentrating all his focus on the seed he started using the wind to turn it around. Boriam managed just in time to see a slight golden colour on the seed before it hit the water. Boriam smiled, and took out his sword. A big explosion came from the water where the seed had landed, and soon a white flower which was bigger than all the others appeared. *'Wow. I've never seen anything like that before. I wonder what seed that will give,'* Boriam thought as he stared at the flower. *'It will be some time until that one explodes though, but when it does, we shouldn't be too close,'* he thought as he looked for more flowers about to explode.

"Help!" Boriam heard Jonathan yell. The boy came running towards camp with a wolf chasing him. Boriam whistled a tune and vines shot out of the soil before slamming into the ground in front of the wolf. The wolf stopped, wondering what was happening, before seeing Boriam. Seeming to understand that it would have trouble dealing with two people, the wolf turned and ran back the way it came. "Thank you," Jonathan said gasping for air. "How did you manage to get that after you?" Boriam asked, to which Jonathan replied "What do you mean?" Boriam looked around before saying "Wolves live in forests. I can't see any forest nearby. So where did you find it?" Jonathan nodded, finally getting his breath back, and said "Yes, well, there's a cliff over there. It leads to a forest. I'm just glad the rest of them didn't follow me. I, oh.. Wow.." Jonathan stood staring at the big white flower. He pointed at it and said "What? Who? How?" He looked at Boriam who started laughing at his confusion. "That, is a flower, Jonathan," Boriam said before continuing "It is the flower of a light element. I've figured out how to get light and dark centres. Light is produced when magic works on the seed while it is flying through the air. It might have something to do with the combination of magic and clear sunlight, but who knows? Anyways, to produce a dark seed I think there has to be blood on the seed. It might have to be that it hits blood as it lands. See that fish over there?" Boriam said and pointed at the fish. Jonathan nodded and Boriam said "A seed hit its head as I pulled it on land. It turned purple as I was watching, and when it was completely purple I opened it to find this." He took out the black seed and let Jonathan examine it. It seemed to have the same effect on Jonathan as it did on Boriam, as the boy turned away from it after a short while. "That was nauseating. Is all dark element things like this?" Jonathan asked. Boriam answered "I've only seen this one, so I don't know. The others look like they are supposed to, so I am guessing this is correct." Boriam sat down and got the fire going again. As he prepared the fish he said "Now we only need one more dark one, and I would like to throw a dark seed into the water, just to see what the flower would look like." Jonathan nodded and said "I wonder what seed these flowers will shoot out. But the flower is big, won't the explosion be powerful?" Boriam agreed to this, but said the flower had only just appeared, so it probably wouldn't explode for some time.

They ate the fish with the explosions of the flowers in the background. As they were finishing their dinner a seed landed beside them. Boriam quickly drew his sword and made a cut in his arm. Jonathan watched in surprize as Boriam let the blood drip onto the seed. After a few moments, Boriam blew on the wound and first the blood stopped flowing, then it began to close. They kept their eyes on the seed to see if it worked, and it did. Soon, a purple colour started spreading across the seed. When it was completely covered in a dark purple colour they peeled the seed to find a black stone within. They both smiled and without saying anything they both started walking along the shore, waiting for another seed to drop. It didn't

127

take long before one arrived, at which point Boriam again cut his arm and let blood drip onto the seed. Having healed his wound, Boriam picked up the seed, brought it back to the camp and threw it into the water a little to the side of the white flower. A few moments later a huge explosion happened underwater, throwing a big halo of water into the air. With a loud and deep pop the black flower appeared. "If the pop was that loud, how will the explosion be?" Jonathan said. Boriam nodded and said "My thoughts exactly. We should move camp a bit further away, just to be sure we stay safe." Jonathan agreed, and soon they had moved a bit down the shore. *'Let's see how prepared he is. This is an obvious time I could attack, and if he isn't prepared now, he won't be prepared when it isn't so obvious,'* Boriam thought. He quietly pulled his stick from his bag and swung it at Jonathan. Jonathan pulled his sword, cut the stick in half, span around and swung the sword at Boriam's stomach. Boriam quickly pulled his sword and parried the blow.

Chapter 25
THE LION'S CLAWS

Standing with their swords locked, Boriam said "Ho now, good strike. Ready to fight with a sword I see. Okay then." He attacked again. Jonathan jumped backwards thinking *'I don't really feel ready, I just couldn't find my stick.'* Parrying several of Boriam's strikes, Jonathan started feeling more confident about handling a sword. A long time passed before he dropped it. Lifting the sword off the ground he noticed that the edges were jagged. "Hey, why is my sword this jagged? It's as if tiny pieces have been broken off from it." Boriam came over and looked at it before saying "That is the reason for the need to sharpen your sword all the time. Most swords chip a little, but good swords primarily become blunt. Not much you can do about that. A good sword will grow dull with use, but let you sharpen it over and over without wearing it down too much. A bad sword will suffer marks to the blade, and eventually break." Jonathan looked at Boriam and said, slightly disappointedly "So this is a bad sword then? I guess yours just goes blunt." At that moment there was a loud bang which made them both jump. They turned and saw something fly through the air and land with a heavy crash on land. They looked at each other, then ran to where it had landed. Jonathan was quicker than Boriam and reached the hole in the ground first. "Can you see it?" Boriam said as he approached the hole. "No," Jonathan said "there's nothing in here. Just dirt and rocks." He stepped back letting Boriam see. "Nothing? This isn't nothing." Boriam said and lifted a medium sized rock out of the ground. "This, is an extremely rare material. Combined with the material I'm guessing will come out of the black flower, this becomes a metal which is very light and extremely durable. My sword is made of this material, so to answer your previous question, yes it would have been dulled had it been made with a normal metal. As it is not, my sword won't dull." Jonathan looked at the piece of rock in Boriam's hand then said "So if we get the piece from the black flower we can make a sword like yours for me?" Boriam thought for a moment before saying "Yes, and no. You see, these flowers have supposedly been extinct for hundreds of years. Many of the races of the world grow very old, but I do not know of anyone living today who would have the ability to blend these two materials. It would have to be someone able to control magic freely at the same time as he or she is able to forge perfectly a blade. It will have to be made in a fire so hot no ordinary human would be able to stay close to it. In addition to this, the one doing it will have to sharpen the sword while forging it, as sharpening it after it cools off will be impossible. So now you see that yes, it is possible, but no, I have no idea who or what would possibly be able to do it." Jonathan looked at the rock disappointedly before saying "Then how was your sword made? It's stayed sharp for a hundred years?" Boriam sighed and said "This is only a tale, but it's the only information passed down to me. Once, there was a troll named Starr'an. He was of the fire element, and the two hundred years he had lived he had focused on making the best weapons in the world. One day, he found these materials and felt that one was infused with light magic, and the other with dark magic. As they were physical materials and not raw magic he thought it might be possible to combine the light and the dark. Everyone who heard his idea laughed at him. He soon shut himself into a cave deep inside a volcano. As his element was fire he naturally had a high tolerance to heat, but the lava was too hot even for him. While digging out the caves it is said that he met a great dragon. Having told it his story and what he wanted, the dragon understood what Starr'an was thinking. With his flames the dragon managed to get the materials to such a temperature that even the elements of light and dark would blend. After many failed attempts, the troll succeeded in making a sword. Perfecting his ability he had soon made a few weapons, but his materials had run out. He did not know where he could find more of the materials, so he was unable to make any more. Emerging from the cave he gave the weapons to the members of the Clan of Lions, because they had sworn to protect the world from what might come. Here the swords have been passed down through the centuries. Over the years the members of The Clan of Lions named the weapons The Claws of the Lion. As every creature, plant and thing in the world is unique, so are also the weapons of the Lions. By looking at its shape and make, one would know which member owned a specific weapon. And to answer your earlier question, yes, it's stayed sharp for about seven hundred years." Jonathan noticed his mouth was open, and quickly closed it. *'Seven hundred years and still sharp?'* Jonathan thought and said "Who are The Clan of Lions? Are you a member?" Boriam looked at Jonathan and said "Yes, I'm a member. But don't tell anyone about it. No one knows about the Lions anymore, except the Lions themselves. The only reason I'm telling you, is because the other Lions have been hunted down and killed by The Council, and I guess you are the closest one to becoming a member. As for who they are, now that's a story for another time." Jonathan sighed and said "Everything you say has to be continued at another time, why? We have time now while we wait for the other piece, don't we? And don't say I'm not ready yet!" Boriam stared across the water for a long time until Jonathan said "Well?" Boriam looked at him and asked "Well what?" "Well, what's your answer? Why can't I hear about everything now?" Jonathan said impatiently. Boriam looked confused and said "But you told me not to say it." Jonathan blinked a few times before saying "I told you to give me an answer which was not 'you're not ready yet'." Boriam nodded and said "Then I cannot give you an answer yet. Don't worry, it will come, but not for some time. Go and try to meditate for a bit, you need it." Jonathan had grown angry now and stomped towards the new camp where he sat down heavily. *Why does he need to keep things hidden from me all the time? I can understand that I can't say anything to anyone, but why can't he then say anything to me?* Jonathan thought and punched the ground. *'Ow.. Rocks...'* he thought as he looked at his hand. Taking a few breaths he managed to calm himself enough down to start meditating. As he was still upset, he first focused on his breathing. After what felt like ages he was able to focus on his heartbeats.

Finally sitting calmly hearing his heart beat, he felt a slight breeze which pulled him into a dreamlike state. When he felt the rate of his heartbeats slow down, a massive explosion pulled him abruptly out of his calm state. His heart started beating so strongly that he grabbed his chest to calm down. Looking around he saw Boriam run down the hill and plunging into the water. After wading a bit out from shore he bent down and picked up what looked like a rock. Jonathan found this very amusing, and nodded before shouting "The second piece?" Boriam looked at him and raised his thumb before returning to camp. When he arrived, he put the two pieces in his backpack and said "Let's bring them with us, in case we think of something. You ready to leave?" Jonathan nodded and packed his bag. Half an hour later they were on their way to Fisherman's Rest. On the way Jonathan admired the sword hanging from Boriam's belt, and thought *His sword looks ordinary enough. He said every sword looked different, but I wonder how different?* He looked up at Boriam and said "You said the Lions have been killed? If no one knew of them, how could they have been hunted down?" Boriam got a wondering look on his face and said "People knew of them, but they are known to most as The Enlightened Clan, or by some other name. It has many members, but the leaders are promoted to Lions, and at that point get to know of the Lions' system. The other members are under continuous tutoring by the Lions, and along the stages of teaching they follow what the Lions call the Lion's Path. They start off as each Lion's cubs and grow within the clan, or family if you want to call it that. As you are now being tutored by me, you are in our system called my cub."

Jonathan thought about this for a long time before saying "You have many members? Yet everyone's been killed? Every single one?" Boriam shook his head and said "No, when the leaders were killed, the other members abandoned the clan. Only those who had got far in the teachings stayed and fought, but they were killed as well. I believe many wish to return, but feel unable to do anything and thus stay in hiding or abandon the teachings completely." Jonathan nodded and said "Every Lion had their own weapon? What happened to them? Are they hidden somewhere?" Boriam shook his head again and said "Every Lion had their own weapon, and some of them had their own shield. I had a shield as well. It was stolen one night, but I'm determined to get it back. As for the weapons, the ones who killed them took them, and are probably using them for their own evil acts." Boriam got a sad mine on his face, and Jonathan thought it best to not rip up old pain. "I'm going to hunt them all down and take back the swords," Jonathan said to himself. Boriam smiled and said "Do not seek pain, or that is exactly what you will find." Jonathan stared blankly into the air unable to reply to this comment. They walked in silence for a long time before Boriam again started telling one of his stories. Darkness fell and the stars lit the sky. Boriam pointed out the great constellations and said he'd tell Jonathan about their significance later, as they were now entering Fisherman's Rest.

Chapter 26
THE VILLAGE ATOP THE WATER

Jonathan stood looking over a small village. It lay on top of the water, each house built on wooden poles driven into the bottom of the lake. Boards were placed between the houses as a road above the water. Boats of different types were tied to the road between the houses. "What kind of boat is that?" Jonathan asked and Boriam replied "Those boats are canoes, two men use oars to push the boat through the water. That one there is called a sailboat, they use the wind to move forwards, so people on board don't use so much energy getting around. Come, it's late. We're staying in here, and you can explore tomorrow." Jonathan looked over the building they had arrived at, and read the sign. "Fisherman's Inn" he read and thought *'Of course it's called that.'* He shook his head and entered.

The following morning they had a quick breakfast at the inn before heading out. "We need to find out where Stephie has set up shop. Knowing her aversion to people, I have a feeling we should look for the most hidden and secluded building in the entire village," Boriam said. Jonathan looked around and said "This Stephie is a shop owner, but doesn't like people? Something's wrong with that picture." Boriam laughed and said "Yes, I know what you mean, but that's how it is. She has supported the Lions with information for as long as I can remember." "So she's pretty old then?" Jonathan said to which Boriam replied "You'll see. Don't call her that, though. You'll make her angry." Jonathan understood this and started looking around. While he stood looking towards one of the piers, a man stepped out of the water. His skin was green and blue, and Jonathan noticed it was covered in what looked like small stones. His eyes were angled and slim with a green colour. Jonathan had a hard time figuring out whether the eyelids went up and down or sideways, as they seemed to do both. On his elbows the man had tiny wings, and his feet were wide and flat. A folded piece of cloth was fastened to one of his legs from a belt at his waist down to his foot. Jonathan pulled on Boriam's arm, and when he got the old man's attention he asked "Is that a merfolk?" Boriam looked up and said "Very good, that's exactly what it is. A merman to be precise.

133

Fascinating creatures, the merfolk. Do you see the eyes? They have two sets of eyelids, one going sideways and one going up and down." At this point Jonathan interrupted with "I was wondering about that, why do they have that?" Boriam nodded and said "The sideways layer is possible to see through. They don't have eyes which water themselves. When they are on land they have the inner eyelids closed, blocking out some of the light and keeping their eyes moistened. When they get into the water, both the eyelids stay open, allowing the merfolk to see far in the poor light underwater. The cuts in the neck are called gills, and just like fish they use those to breathe under water. In contrast to fish though, the merfolk are able to breathe on land as well. You see how he wobbles when he's walking? They are not very quick on land, but in the sea they move effortlessly through the water. Thanks to the flat and wide feet and the fin they make from the cloth attached to their left leg they are extremely quick. Steering is hard with just arms, so in order to manoeuvre they have the wings on their elbows and a fin along their entire spine." Jonathan noticed he was staring as the merman walked past them, but was unable to take his eyes away. The merman noticed this and blinked to Jonathan and gave him a grin displaying several sets of jagged teeth. This scared Jonathan and he quickly looked away. He heard a bubbling rolling sound behind him and when he looked back he saw the merman was doing something which reminded Jonathan of laughing. "Did he just laugh at me?" Jonathan asked Boriam who replied "Yes. Yes, he did."

They kept going along the wooden road until they passed a store. They bought something to snack on as they slowly made their way through the village. Eventually, Boriam stopped and glanced between two houses and said "Hah, typical Stephie. Come on!" He then started to climb along a wooden platform between the two buildings. Jonathan looked at the old man climbing between the houses and thought to himself *You may be old, but you take the least logical routes for an old man.'* After observing Boriam some more, Jonathan followed, a bit more easily, between the houses. He soon found himself in a wooded clearing behind several houses. A big pile of stones shaping a cave created an entrance into one of the houses. Embedded in the stones above the entrance was a wooden board with symbols he'd never seen before. "What does that mean?" Jonathan asked and pointed to the sign. Boriam looked at it and said "Oh, that. Just a joke really. It's in a way saying that you've actually used your eyes since you found this place, or that you're very stupid for wandering behind all the houses." Jonathan didn't understand the joke, but nodded to keep going. Boriam stepped up to the cave and looked inside. "She's out it seems. Come on, let's wait inside," he said and bent down to get into the cave. *'So we're choosing to wait inside a small cave when we could stand out here in fresh air and have room to move around? Okay then,'* Jonathan thought before going into the cave. After squeezing through a tight tunnel Jonathan emerged in a big room with a desk and several bookshelves containing strange things. Jonathan picked up something looking like a tiny claw and asked "What's this?" Boriam came over to where he stood and said "That looks like a bat's foot. Stephie creates festivities' items like fireworks, but in secret she meddles with potions and poisons. Bat's feet are used in many potions." Jonathan looked at the tiny foot and said "I've never seen a bat before." "No?" Boriam asked surprized. "It's like a.. Hmm.. A mouse.. Yes, a black mouse without a tail, and it has leathery wings." Jonathan had a hard time imagining what it looked like, and while he stood staring at the tiny foot a gnome came walking through the cave. Jonathan saw it was a female gnome, with three golden rings in one of her nostrils, long golden hair set in a ponytail and clothes which reminded him of old stories about pirates. The gnome jumped when it saw them and said "Oh, sorry, I didn't expect anyone being here. Well, congratulations on finding this place, I'm Stemophiniadorona. Welcome to my Stephie-store, the store with Steph and stuff." Boriam smiled and said "Still not tired of the old phrase?" Stephie looked at him and asked "Are you one of my regulars or something?" Boriam sighed and said "Stephie. Has it been so long you don't even recognize me?" Stephie looked at Boriam for a while before saying "Boriam!" And running over to give him a hug. "They said you guys were dead, what's going on?" Boriam sat down beside the gnome and said "Yes, everyone else is, as far as I know at least. I pretended to die, and was lucky enough to have them believe me without thorough testing. It was thanks to your potion that I didn't die from the poison in my soup, you know. Of course, I knew it was poisoned, but I figured that if they thought I was dead it would be easier for me to get around unnoticed." Stephie nodded and said "What poison was it?" Boriam smiled and said "It was your famous gut blower." The gnome looked shocked at this and exclaimed "But the antidote to that was just experimental! You still took the poison?" Boriam sighed and said "I'd just heard of several friends' deaths and was far into the darkness when I thought 'The worst that would happen is I die an extremely painful death, possibly I'll survive and the Council will leave me alone.' So I poured the antidote into my cup of water, drank it and sat reading for a while before eating my soup." Stephie made big eyes and said "So what happened when you had eaten it?" Boriam thought for a while before saying "Well, my stomach nearly exploded. It made a loud bang and a shockwave went through my body. Then I passed out and woke up in a gravedigger's workshop." The gnome laughed a light thrilling laugh which made Jonathan smile even though he found the story shocking. Stephie went to the desk and seemingly for the first time noticed Jonathan because

135

she said "Who're you then? Can't say I remember you from the early days." Jonathan gave her his name and Boriam said "His parents' last wish was for him to follow the Thirteen's teachings. Therefore I've decided to guide him along until we find them." The gnome stood thinking for a while looking Jonatan up and down before saying "Yes. I see. Well, what can I help you guys with then?" Boriam put out his hands and said "We need some information. News of the world, where to go for our next search. You know what I mean, the usual." The gnome lady nodded and thought for a while before saying "Okay, I get you. I'll have to sum things up first, and check on my sources, so come back in a few days and I'll have something for you." They thanked her and left the store. Outside Boriam sighed and said "She always asks for a few days to sum things up. I have no idea what she sums up, and from where, but the results are always helpful. Come on, let's see what this village has to offer." They climbed back out between the buildings and Jonathan was soon staring across the lake. Boriam explained that it wasn't always this calm, but since there was no wind today there were no noticeable waves. Boriam explained a bit more about how the sun and the wind worked together on the world, but Jonathan didn't understand this. He kept wondering how the sun could make the wind when he had learned as a kid that the gods made the wind. Because of these contradictions he soon forgot what Boriam was saying. "Hey, how are these buildings able to stand on the water? Won't the logs rot when they stay in the water for long?" Jonathan asked eventually. "That is true, they will rot if they are put into the water. But the normal logs aren't in the water. There are trees growing from the bottom, which stand just above the surface. The logs holding this entire village up are resting on these trees. If you put your head over the edge over there, you can see the logs resting on the trees," Boriam said and pointed towards the edge of the road. Jonathan lay down on his stomach and peered beneath the village. "Wow," he uttered as he could see beneath the entire village in any direction. He saw thick roots sticking out of the water everywhere, and on top of them lay logs and tree trunks carrying the entire city. From the underside of the village, Jonathan could see where the roads and houses curved. He could also see bigger or smaller logs holding the different sized houses and roads up above the water. Boriam led Jonathan around the city and showed him how the boats worked. Jonathan had never been on a boat before, and by the looks of them he was quite sure that he'd hate it. He liked having solid ground underneath his feet, and the boats on the water didn't seem anything like solid ground. He shrugged and Boriam said "We'll probably take a ship out of here, so get used to the idea of boating." Throughout the day Jonathan saw many things he had never seen before, like a bird without feathers. "It's a bird which flies under water," Boriam said when he'd asked about it. *This is a strange place. A village on top of the water and birds flying in the water? Everything's turned upside down,'* Jonathan thought as he was starting to get a headache. Another curiosity was the food. He'd never tasted this thing called squid before, which Boriam of course recommended. He couldn't say he enjoyed it much, first spending ages cutting the pieces, and then the same amount of time trying to chew it before having to flush the pieces into his stomach with water.

As the darkness fell the stars began to shine, and the moon threw stripes of light across the water. Near the shore, small glowing insects began to fly around. Jonathan was unable to stop staring at them, and as he walked onwards while looking at them, he walked off the edge of the road. He gasped for air as he struggled to get his head above water. No one had been around to teach him how to swim, so he had no idea how to stay afloat in deep water. His foot struck something in the water, and he soon understood it was one of the roots. Balancing on the root he managed to get his head above water and cough up a lot of it. After calming down a bit and getting more control over his balance, he soon heard Boriam shout for him. "Hey! I'm down here!" Jonathan yelled back, a slight panic in his voice. Boriam peered over the edge of the road and said "What in the gods' names are you doing down there? Come on, there's some stairs if you swim along the road here for a bit." Jonathan looked up at Boriam and said "I've never learned to swim." Boriam didn't hear what he said and replied "Sorry now, what was that you said there?" Embarrassed Jonathan said a little louder "I never learned to swim!" Boriam looked at him and said "But how are you staying afloat then?" Jonathan lifted one arm and said "I'm standing on one of the roots in the water! Will you help me up or not?" Boriam laughed and said "Alright, sure. Hold on, I'll get a rope." *'Hurry... I can't say I like this,'* Jonathan thought. After what, to Jonathan, seemed like hours, Boriam returned with a rope. As Jonathan finally climbed back onto the road, Boriam asked "How did you manage to fall off the road? Weren't you walking just behind me?" Jonathan looked at the shore where the glowing bugs were, and said "I was looking at the bugs there. Then I didn't see the turn in the road and walked off it." Boriam laughed again and said "Well, pay attention in the future. So you've never learned to swim?" Jonathan confirmed this and Boriam continued saying "Well that's something you'll *have* to learn." Jonathan nodded and asked "I want to learn it, but why do I have to? I mean... You said it in a way which made it seem like swimming was very important to learn." Boriam nodded and said "You want to eventually learn magic. In order to learn the different elements, you'll have to know how they feel on your body. You know how it feels when it's searing hot or biting cold? If not we'll have to make you feel that as well. Anyways, when you learn to move while your body is covered in any element, and your meditation has reached a certain level, you will be able to feel how the elements affect your body. As you understand this, you will learn to feel how the different elements behave and with that you'll eventually learn to control them." Jonathan interrupted Boriam and said "It seems extremely hard to learn magic, yet there are so many magicians in the world. Have everyone really been through this type of training?" Boriam shook his head and said "No. Magic is actually easy enough to learn, anyone can do it." Again Jonathan interrupted with "Anyone can do it? Then why can't I learn something now? From what you're saying I don't have to 'be ready' in order to learn it." Boriam put up his hand and said "Let's go somewhere we can't be overheard." He then stood up and walked down the road.

Chapter 27
A MESSAGE IN STONES

Jonathan followed Boriam back to Stephie's store, and as they arrived at the small gap between the houses, Boriam said "She's closed the store." and pointed to a pile of stones. "Oh well, it's safe enough to talk here, I guess. We can't go to the inn, as there're always people listening there." Seeing Jonathan's face Boriam quickly said "There're always people listening in inns. That's why people go there. To speak a lot of nonsense, and hear a lot of secret or personal information." Jonathan nodded and said "So tell me what you were about to say." Boriam sighed and started talking. "Magic is very easy to learn for most people. You seem to have an almost unnatural knack for sensing it, so you would probably have an even easier time learning it than most people. The problem with learning it in the way everyone else does, is that you can only do a little bit with it. Those who specialize in fire magic are able to control up to ten fireballs at a time, and that is pretty impressive. The Lions have created a new way of learning magic, which is passed down in the chain of Lions. It is much harder to learn magic this way, and the student will have to learn a lot of other abilities and tune his or her body to be able to use magic in this way. On the other hand, this way of doing magic lets the user have almost complete control of it, only limited by their energy level, physical strength and imagination." Jonathan blinked a few times and said "What do you mean by free control of magic?" Boriam pointed towards a building and a bolt of lightning shot from his fingertip towards the wall. Before reaching the wall, the lightning gathered into a ball. Droplets of water started appearing in the air surrounding the lightning, and after a few seconds the droplets connected together. Soon the lightning bolt was enclosed inside a ball of water. Jonathan could see the light from the lightning inside the ball as the surface of the water turned to ice. The ball of ice then grew a bird's head and wings, before exploding into flames. The flickering of the lightning through water and ice inside the bird gave the flames a strange hue which amazed Jonathan. The burning bird flapped its wings a few times then everything disappeared. As Jonathan looked at Boriam, he noticed the old man was breathing heavily. "Are you all right?" Jonathan asked to which Boriam replied "Yes, but controlling four individual elements at the same time is extremely hard. That's the most I am able to do though." Boriam sat down to rest and Jonathan said "What else should I know?" Boriam looked at him and said "Tell me, do you remember how it felt when your house back in Shadowtree was burning?" Jonathan looked at Boriam and said "I somewhat remember. I remember the burnt smell and some of the heat, but it was a long time ago. Why?" Boriam nodded and said "The two ways you can learn to know fire, is either by going as close as possible to a volcano, or be inside a burning building. Which you have." Jonathan interrupted Boriam at this point saying "So what you're saying, is that I can learn fire magic? Now?" Boriam seemed annoyed about the interruption, but didn't make much of it, as he said "Well, that would depend on whether you are able to remember the feeling of how the heat hit you and behaved." Jonathan thought for a while and said "I don't know, maybe. Is there any way I can remember it better?" Boriam nodded and said "If you meditate." Jonathan stared blankly ahead, and said "How can I remember how something that happened in the past felt like when I have to focus on my heartbeats or my breathing?" Boriam grinned and said "That's what the other levels are for."

Back at the inn they grabbed a bite to eat before Jonathan sat in their room meditating for the rest of the night. He felt a slight progress after a while where he started to feel his heartbeats calm down. "Why does my heart calm down when I manage to meditate on it for a long time? I mean, it's natural that it starts to calm down when I'm just sitting here. When I'm thinking about things and I get back to the meditation, I notice that my heart's been racing a bit. As I start to focus on the heartbeats again the heart starts to slow down. Why is that?" Boriam had been sitting looking at his sword and now looked up at the sky, apparently thinking. After a short while he said "You're getting close to ending this level, but you haven't mastered it just yet. The heart behaves much like your mind. It wants your attention. When you look at your mind, it goes quiet. When you look at your heart, it slows down. It's as if the heart is trying to get your attention, but is unable to grab it in the way your mind does. For that reason it beats faster. When you manage to put enough focus on the heart, it calms down, feels that you're giving it the attention it needs. And with that, the calm sets in. Keep meditating now. Tomorrow I'll put you through a test to see how far you've come." 'A test? He can actually test if I've managed to meditate? What kind of test is that?' Jonathan's head raced with questions which made meditation very hard. As his head started to quiet down he heard a low rumbling sound. As he looked up he saw Boriam lying on his bed snoring louder with every breath. A few times it got so loud Jonathan almost started

140

laughing. On the floor beside the bed lay the old man's sword. Sneaking over to it, Jonathan grabbed the handle and lifted. It didn't move. He put all his strength into lifting the sword and yet he barely managed to lift the handle off the ground before his fingers gave in. The sword slammed back onto the floor with a loud noise. Jonathan jumped as Boriam said "Don't do that." Jonathan looked from the sword to the old man and then back at the sword before saying "How can you wield the sword so easily? It's so heavy I can't even lift it off the ground." Boriam opened his eyes, looked at the sword and said "It's not that it's heavy. It just doesn't want to be lifted off the ground right now." Jonathan didn't understand this comment and said "What do you mean 'it doesn't want to be lifted off the ground'? If I attacked you now, you wouldn't be able to use your sword?" Boriam put up a finger as to make a point and said "Ah, let me rephrase that then. It doesn't want to be lifted off the ground by you." Again Jonathan looked between Boriam and the sword and thought *You really are crazy aren't you?* He then said "So how can I use the sword if I have to? If we're attacked and I only have your sword at hand, what would happen?" Boriam thought about this for a while before saying "A very good question. I would say you would be in a lot of trouble, really. The sword chooses the one it will follow. As long as that person is alive, the sword will only wish to be wielded by him or her." Looking at the sword, Jonathan said "But you said the swords were passed down in the line of Lions. If the sword chooses its owner, there must be a way to influence the choice." Boriam grunted and said "You're too quick for your own good, you know. Yes, I guess you're right. The sword won't choose any owner until the person who is to be its owner makes the right sacrifice. Well, sacrifice might be wrong. Offering, perhaps. Anyway, in order to make one of these weapons yours, you first have to make sure it doesn't have a living owner. When it doesn't, the sword will let you transport it as you wish, but it will never be used in a fight. As you probably understand, this is a good test. If you can't lift it, the owner is still alive somewhere. I know what you're about to ask next, but that will take a long time to explain, and it's better to teach you that directly." Jonathan got puzzled by this and asked "What was I going to ask?" Boriam gave a short laugh and said "You were going to ask what kind of offering and how to do it, and that takes too long to explain now. For now we should rest, it seems we have a lot to do tomorrow." And with that he went back to sleep. Jonathan lay awake in his bed for a long time thinking about what he had learned. As he was unable to sleep, he tried meditating while lying down. As he felt his heart rate slow down he saw different coloured spots behind his eyelids and thought *is that because my heart is slow, or is it just something my mind creates?* He tried focusing on it, and as he kept looking at it, he felt like he was pulled into the colour. After a while a green colour appeared in front of his eyes. The new colour expanded and he saw a pink colour appear in the same spot where the green colour had appeared. These two colours kept appearing and expanding for a while until Jonathan started making out shapes. Suddenly he saw tall mountains stretching as far as the eyes could see. Green grass and trees beneath the mountain and a clear blue sky. As he kept watching, a big and black cloud came over the mountain.

Jonathan woke up early the next day with no recollection of ever falling asleep. Boriam was sitting in a chair staring out the window. "You look concerned," Jonathan said. Boriam raised his shoulders and said "Just have a bad feeling." Jonathan let the old man stare out of the window for a while before suggesting they go get some food. The thought of food seemed to cheer the old man up a little, as he eagerly left the room. In the dining room Boriam told Jonathan that he had heard several men with armour wandering outside the inn during the night. Having finished their meal, Boriam led Jonathan out of town to a field nearby. "We should get some practice done today before getting the supplies we'll need for the road ahead. Later on tonight we'll go to Stephie's store to hear what she's got for us." Jonathan nodded and said "Didn't Stephie say she needed a few days? It's only been one day now, so isn't going there tonight a bit early?" Boriam agreed, but explained that as armoured people were arriving in town it would be best to leave as quickly as possible. As Jonathan could understand this well enough, he didn't argue any further. They sparred for a while before Jonathan was told to meditate. "This is so you will get a bit more energy, use all of your senses and be more focused," Boriam explained, and let him do the meditation. After a while Jonathan felt his breathing and his heart slow down. When he felt his heartbeats were slow and strong he opened his eyes, looked at Boriam and nodded. The old man seemed pleased with this gesture as he got off the ground and pulled his sword. Soon they were fighting more vigorously than Jonathan could remember them having done before, and he was beginning to wonder if the old man was actually trying to hurt him. For some reason Jonathan didn't feel scared by this thought, but managed to keep the fight going. He got a few cuts on his arms and legs which weren't deep, but they seemed to tire him quicker than he thought they would. After a long time Boriam jumped away from the fight to show that the fight was over. He sheathed his sword and went over to Jonathan saying "Good! A strong focus and better technique than usual. You're getting better." Jonathan smiled tiredly as Boriam healed the wounds they'd received during the fight. Having finished healing the wounds, Boriam said "Now you'll have to run around this field for a while." Jonathan looked at the old man wondering if he was joking, but seeing nothing of a grin in his eyes he started a light run in a big circle around the field. Finishing one lap he passed Boriam who said "The slower you run, the longer you'll have to be running." Increasing his speed Jonathan thought *'He's going to tire me out completely? He's probably going to say we will have to spar again when I'm dead tired.'* Letting his mind race on, quarrelling about what tortures Boriam was going to put him through, he soon started breathing heavily. After a few more laps, getting very tired and dripping with sweat, Boriam told him to run back to where he was standing. Having a hard time standing straight Jonathan took deep breaths of air. Boriam grabbed his arm and soon said "Good. Now, feel your heart and calm it." Jonathan looked in disbelief at Boriam before sitting down trying to meditate. He felt his heart beat quickly and heavily as his mind argued about how wrong this all was. Focusing on his mind he quickly quietened it, which let him focus more on his heart. Soon he felt a sharp and strong beat of his heart which forced a sound like "Ugh," to escape from his mouth. The entire feeling made the muscles in his back tighten, which again forced his upper body to straighten for half a second. He opened his eyes, breathed heavily and suddenly felt his heart beating calmly and evenly. He looked at Boriam questioningly. Boriam grinned and said "You've now passed level two of the meditation. What you just experienced was a forced reset of your heart. It's where your heart compresses three beats into one, then skips the next two beats. This forces all of your muscles to jump, before relaxing again. The exercise puts a great toll on your heart, so I wouldn't recommend doing it very often. Actually, you should do it as little as possible. Doing it often will break your heart down and kill you, so it should only be used for emergencies." Seeing Jonathan's face at this comment he quickly said "Oh, but don't worry. Doing it once now won't hurt you. It lets you know how it feels, so you can do it more easily later. Now come on, you should clean up a bit before we go to Stephie's shop."

When Jonathan was ready they headed to Stephie's store. With his muscles aching, Jonathan found it hard to climb the gap between the houses. He almost fell into the water below, but they soon stood in front of the store. At least, what had been the store earlier. Now it was just a scattering of rocks, seemingly laid carefully around the area. Jonathan saw Boriam walk very carefully between the rocks, looking back and forth. "What is it?" Jonathan asked which seemed to pull Boriam out of some sort of trance. Boriam said "Oh, this? Well, it doesn't look like much, but it's actually a very rare code. Stephie is a master of codes, and she invented several of those in the little book I gave you. Give me a few minutes to translate this one." Jonathan nodded and sat down with his back to one of the houses where he fell asleep. Jolting awake as Boriam started speaking he felt like he had slept for several hours. "Say that one more time. How long was I sleeping?" Boriam looked at him and asked "Were you sleeping?"

Jonathan looked back and forth before saying "No?" Boriam laughed before saying "Okay, I've just been rambling on about this code, but it's not very important. I've decoded it now though, care to hear what it says?" Jonathan nodded and stood up. Boriam pointed towards the rocks spiralling inwards as he said "I had to leave, but the three hold the information, one shall tell and one shall listen, so the two will see the right path."

Chapter 28
THREE WAY CROSSING

Boriam watched as Jonathan stared blankly into the air for a while before saying "Okay, that didn't tell me much. I'm guessing Stephie knows you can understand it?" Boriam nodded and said "I don't understand all of it, but some of it I can decipher. The three are often said about three rocks standing at the crossing of three small roads. I'm guessing there is something to be found near those rocks." Jonathan sighed and said "So more traveling then? How long will it take us to get there? A week? Two? Are we leaving now?" Boriam raised his hand to quieten the boy, saying "It won't be that long. Tonight we'll get the provisions we'll need for going onwards, and tomorrow morning we'll take a ferry upstream. From the ferry we will have to walk for about an hour before getting to the rocks. So it's not very far. After we get to the rocks I do not know how far or how long we'll have to walk, so we'll have to be ready for anything." Jonathan nodded and Boriam thought *'If you want to be on this journey, you'll have to accept that we're going to do exactly that.'* They climbed out from between the houses, with Jonathan seeming to miss his steps every now and then. Boriam thought this was a lack of balance, and made a mental note to teach the boy some things to improve it. Once they were back on the main road again, Boriam led the way towards the market area. They bought a hooded cloak for Jonathan, and Boriam explained that a hood was a very quick way to hide one's face from prying eyes. Turning a corner as they headed towards the ferry, they were passed by two guards in armour carrying the emblem of the Council. Fortunately the guards didn't seem to be looking for anyone in particular, and let the two pass without a second glance. Carefully making their way onwards they slowly approached the ferryman. He nodded at them and said "I'm not leaving until tomorrow I'm afraid, be here early, seems like it'll be crowded." Boriam nodded and in a low voice asked "What's with the armours? Hear anything from them?" The ferryman leaned in and replied in an equally low voice "Haven't heard much, but there seems to be a lot of them gathering somewhere. Worried about'em are ya?" Boriam lifted one eyebrow and tilted his head slightly, which gave a deep laugh from the ferryman before he continued "I don't think they'll bother ye much, most of'em seem pretty green at what they're doing, although some of'em act like a hotshot for having the shiny armour. You know how young lads are when seemingly given some responsibility." Boriam nodded and gave the ferryman a coin as appreciation. They quietly made their way back to the inn before saying anything.

As they entered their room, Jonathan asked "Are we going to take the ferry with a lot of the Council's men? Is that really smart?" Boriam stood thinking for a while before saying "I think it is, yes. We'll have to buy a bottle of rum to pass around, and they'll be the best friends we could have on this journey." Seeing that Jonathan was about to argue, Boriam continued "Look, you heard the ferryman. They're greenhorns, new to the army, so they don't know who they should look out for. We'll take the ferry for two stops upriver, and then get off. Maybe they're going that way, and maybe not. They won't think much of us getting off there anyways." Jonathan sighed apparently against the notion of traveling with those who were hunting them, but seemed to accept it. Boriam went to the door and said "I'll get the rum, you should meditate." Before he got to opening the door, Jonathan said "On what?" Boriam blinked a few times before saying "What?" Jonathan coughed and said "On what? You said I finished the second stage, so what's the third?" Boriam turned towards the boy and said "Ah, right. Just keep doing the second one. I don't have time to teach you the third right now. You can never finish any stage of meditation, only get ready for the next, so you can perfectly well do it more." Then he left the room. *'So impatient. Can be a good thing, but it usually isn't. I guess I'll have to see how he turns out when he learns a bit more,'* Boriam thought as he headed outside. He passed a few more guards and overheard the words "...excited to go, but a bit scary." Boriam smiled for himself thinking *'Indeed not much experience. A good thing.'* He went to a store and bought a decently sized bottle of rum. *'Poor quality of course, they won't know the difference,'* Boriam thought laughing silently.

Getting back to the room he saw Jonathan sitting on the bed meditating. He pulled out a glass from his backpack and poured some rum into it. He felt the liquid burn his throat as he emptied the glass. He missed the feeling, but the quality of the drink annoyed him. He coughed once with the dryness in his mouth. "What is that stinging smell?" Jonathan suddenly said. "It's the rum for the soldiers. Never tasted it?" Boriam answered, and Jonathan said he'd never drunk anything alcoholic before. "Right, you're having a sip then. You should at least have tried it before we give it to the soldiers tomorrow," Boriam said and poured some for the boy. Boriam watched as Jonathan took a small sip of the drink. The boy's mouth wrinkled up and his body shook from the taste. Boriam laughed and said

"Ghastly, yes? Always is, the first time you taste something strong. Even beer which is not so strong will taste horrible. But with time, and with an acquired taste, you'll learn to like it." Jonathan looked at Boriam and said "I don't know if I want to acquire this taste. The soldiers actually like this?" Boriam shook his head and said "Probably not. But they are greenhorns, which means they'll do anything to seem tough in front of their comrades." Jonathan shook his head and said "Idiots." Before he could say anything else, Boriam said "Idiots they might be, but if a person is not tough in the army, he will quickly be put where he doesn't want to be, which is directly in front of the enemy's spears. Acting tough is a means of getting yourself higher in the hierarchy of the group, in this case the army." Jonathan sat thinking for a while before asking "What's a hierarchy?" Boriam remembered he was talking to a young man who'd lived most of his life without anyone to teach him anything. He explained to the boy that a hierarchy is the order of command, but that it could be either official order like in the army, or social order where one in the group assumes the position of leader, and others fill other social jobs within that group. When he had finished talking it was dark outside, and Jonathan had got a few more drinks on the argument that he should at least get to know the taste before the next day. "What if the soldiers hand you the bottle during the trip? You'll have to drink to blend in, and it's not too charming if you make that face every time you drink it." Jonathan had somewhat understood the reasoning, but didn't like the pressure he was being put under to drink. He agreed to have a few more sips to get a bit more used to the taste.

Morning brought a beaming sun and no wind. *'Will be a slow trip without a wind, but at least the sea will be calm,'* Boriam thought as they headed to the ferry. As they arrived they saw the boat was starting to fill up, so they hurried the last stretch of the road. Right after they had got on board, with a few more groups of men in armour still on the way, the captain left the mooring and steered the ship out of the docks. As Boriam predicted, getting the ship out of the docks took a long time. Boriam went up the ladder to the captain and asked "How long do you think it will take us up to the Three Way Docks?" The captain nodded and said "About three hours." Boriam looked at the captain and said "But that's what it would normally take us. How do you intend to make that happen?" At that moment they cleared the entrance to the docks, and Boriam felt a slight pull on the boat. The captain smiled and said "Well, with the soldiers needing transport the Council has been generous with the payments. So I hired a bit of help from our underwater friends. They'll pull this boat upstream without any trouble." Boriam thought for a while before nodding and headed back to Jonathan. When he arrived Jonathan expressed the same concerns about time that Boriam had, so Boriam explained to him what was going on. The boy nodded as he quickly understood how the merfolk helped. It did help a little in explaining it all, when the boat went sideways before straightening up the correct way.

Boriam and Jonathan were sitting in a corner of the deck, avoiding the guards' attention. It worked for a while until a guard came walking over asking who they were. "Oh, just an old man and his nephew," Boriam said to the guard. The guard nodded and said "I thought so. But then again, that's what most people say when I ask them, or a version of it anyways, so who are you really?" Boriam sighed and said "Most people might say that, but some people actually mean it." The guard looked at Boriam and said "Well, I don't believe you." Boriam sighed and said "Whether you believe me is your choice. So what now?" The guard nodded, apparently pleased with the position he'd got Boriam in, and said "Well, if I don't believe you, my buddies and I," the guard gestured towards the rest of the boat before continuing, "will have to take action. Maybe even arrest you for falsely identifying yourselves. Unless you can persuade us otherwise, of course." The guard ended his speech with a slow laugh. Boriam coughed silently. "Well, how about this then? We don't really have any use for it, so it would be nice if someone could take the dead weight off our hands," he said as he opened his bag and pulled out the bottle of rum. The guard grinned at Boriam and said "Ah, I guess we could help you out with that little problem." He lifted the bottle out of Boriam's hand and said "Have a nice trip with your *nephew*." Boriam heard the extra pressure on the word nephew, and got a feeling the guard didn't trust him very much. *'As long as he doesn't make any trouble for us it doesn't matter,'* he thought as he watched the guard lumber towards his comrades. He looked at Jonathan who nodded and went to the port side of the boat, looking out across the water. Boriam sat for a while looking at the people taking the boat. There was an elderly couple who managed to stay out of the guards' attention. A group of younger men was soon their centre of attention. At first the men seemed to be picked at, but after a while they were invited by the guards to join them. *'Pretty good at recruiting, those guards. Maybe that's why they travel?'* Boriam thought as he got off the deck and joined Jonathan. As he approached, Jonathan said "Do these things always make you feel sick?" Boriam looked out across a silent sea and thought *'You get seasick from this? You should try when there are actual waves.'* He said diplomatically "People can tend to get seasick, some easier than others. It all depends on how tall the waves are." Jonathan stood looking at the water for a bit before saying "There are no waves." Boriam nodded and replied "I know." "Oh," Jonathan said as he realised he must be very easily seasick. Boriam slapped his back and said "Don't worry, you've never been on a boat before. You'll get used to it after a while." Jonathan breathed heavily and said "I think I'll have to lie down for a bit." He then went back to where they were sitting and lay down on the deck of the ship. Boriam stood looking at the landscape passing by, reminiscing of old times when things were easier. When all he really had to do was travel between towns to give aid in planting crops, help in courts and gather information. He sighed and sat down at a table nearby. He heard metal striking metal and he quickly stood up and turned around to see what was happening. He soon sat down again, watching as the guards tried teaching the newest addition to the group how to handle a sword. *Because they have been accepted into the army they think they know everything about sword fighting?'* Boriam thought laughing to himself as he watched the one guard after another show off some impressive looking, but very simple and basic, movements. Boriam watched as the group started sparring, and saw the different guards stumble around as if on one leg as they swung the swords they had been given. *'I'll give them that: it does seem like they have some basic skill with the sword, but they have no idea about movement in a fight,'* Boriam thought as one guard tripped over his own boot. He smiled as the guard struggled to get back on his feet. The red face of the guard turned around quickly and must have noticed Boriam smiling because he stomped over to the table yelling "What are you laughing at old man? Want me to cut your tongue out?" *'Ah, the youth and their need to seem strong after failing at something,'* Boriam thought as he put his hands up and said "You haven't been too long in the military, have you?" The guard looked taken aback as he shifted his stance before saying "How do you know that?" Boriam nodded at the guards' feet and in a low tone said "You should turn by putting the opposing foot behind the other in a circular motion. And you should start a sidestep by putting the foot closest to where you want to go further out before following with the other. This way you won't have one foot crashing into the other, which again will prevent you from falling. Other than that, you should practice your balance." The guard scrambled for words before saying "How dare you tell me what to do and what not to do? I tell you what to do!" Boriam coughed once and again said in a low tone "That's why I talked so low. So the others wouldn't hear the hints I gave you. If you follow them you should turn out better than any of the others I see here. Now pretend you're pleased with my humility and stride back to the others." The guard didn't know what to do, so he ended up doing exactly what Boriam had said.

The next hour passed with the guards training a bit but otherwise nothing exciting happened. Jonathan slept for most of the trip, only awakened by the thump created when the boat hit the landing at their first stop. The older couple left the boat, but all the guards remained. *'It wouldn't be surprising if they are getting off where we're getting off. Still, there are a few more stops after ours. If they're getting off at the next stop though, we'll have to let them walk on before we go,'* Boriam thought as he looked at the impatient group of guards trying to make the time pass.

Jonathan woke up just before they arrived, claiming to feel a little better. "Can't you just remove the sickness with magic or something?" Jonathan said but Boriam quickly said "Ssh, don't say that so loudly. There is a law passed down by the Council stating that anyone who are able to perform magic, and isn't helping them, is an enemy of the Council. So if anyone finds out I can use magic, they have to attack me. I would probably not have too much trouble with these guys, but it would be nice if we could avoid a fight." At that moment the boat hit the landing and Jonathan read a sign and said "The sign says 'Three Way Docks', why is it called that?" As they stepped ashore followed by all the guards Boriam said "That's because of the roads crossing up ahead. It's pretty famous actually. Now hold on, we'll let these guys go ahead first." They walked to the side of the road letting the guards pass. As they did so, the guard who'd taken the rum grinned at them before turning away. Jonathan and Boriam slowly walked down the road after the guards, letting them gain a bit of distance. The guards arrived at the crossing and took one of the roads.

Boriam and Jonathan arrived at the crossing a little after the guards had left. Looking at the three stones Boriam pointed to each and said "Do you see the carving in the stones?" Jonathan nodded and said "They look a bit like faces." Boriam looked at Jonathan and said "What makes you think that?" Jonathan stepped into the centre of the crossing and looked at the three stones for a while before saying "They look only slightly like faces. That one there," Jonathan pointed to one of the stones and continued "Looks like a head covering its ears while staring ahead. And that one over there seems to cover its eyes while shouting something. The last one looks like it's covering its mouth and nose." Boriam went to Jonathan's side and looked at the three stones. "You know, you are absolutely right. They do look like that. I've heard people mention these look like people, but I was never able to see it. Until you pointed them out now." Jonathan smiled and said "What was it Stephie wrote again?" Boriam sighed and pulled out his notebook before saying "You really should get yourself one of these." Finding the right page he read the text he'd written down. They stood thinking for a while before Jonathan said "It said that one shall tell and one shall listen. Do you think she literally means that this statue here, which is shouting, and this one here which is silent has some kind of information about them?" Boriam nodded and said "Good thinking, let's find out." He then went over to the listening statue and walked around it a few times before saying "I can't really see any marks on them which could indicate a code, so there must be something hidden around here which holds the information." Jonathan joined him and after a long time he said "These

150

statues are very thoroughly done." Boriam looked at him and asked what he meant. "Well," Jonathan said "look at where the ears are. There's a small hole exactly where it's supposed to be. They must have been looking more like people a long time ago, but the weather probably wore them down." Boriam nodded and stared at the holes Jonathan pointed out. Going over to them he tried putting his finger inside, but they were too big. Jonathan asked what he was doing, and Boriam replied "I was just thinking something might have been hidden inside these holes, but I can't get my finger inside. You try it." So Jonathan tried, but his fingers were too thick as well. Looking around they soon found a small stick. The left ear revealed nothing, and they didn't hold high hopes while trying the right ear. Pulling the stick out a small corner of a sheet of paper peeped out of the hole. Trying a few more times they eventually got the piece of paper all the way out. "Good, then I guess there is something else about the screaming statue as well." Boriam looked at him and nodded his agreement. It didn't take long for them to find the hole in the throat of the statue, and pull the sheet of paper out. They folded the two pieces of paper out and put them next to each other where they were torn apart.

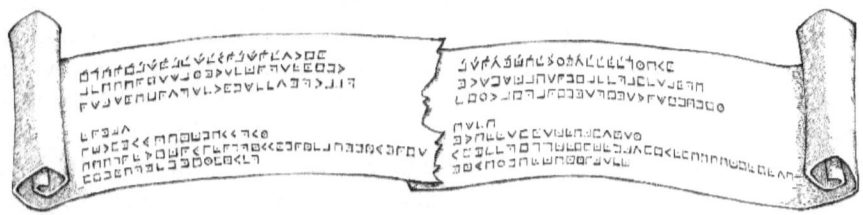

"What does that mean?" Jonathan asked but Boriam shook his head and said "I have no idea. It looks like a simple replacement code, but I've never seen it before." Jonathan nodded and said "What was the last part Stephie wrote, maybe it can help us?" Boriam brought out his book again and read "So the two will see the right path." Jonathan looked at the third statue and said "I'm assuming it has something to do with this one. As it's staring down that path there, could it be simply saying we're to take that path? But why should she have to tell us where to go in the other code when she probably could've written it on these notes?" Boriam nodded and said "That's some good thinking Jonathan, I would say you were right about having to go down this path. As for the other question, I have no idea why. Maybe she knew I wouldn't know this code? We'll have to work on it as we move, seeing as she left so quickly maybe she's trying to tell us that we will have to hurry to wherever we'll have to go." Jonathan agreed, but pointed out "We shouldn't walk too fast though, that's the way the guards went." Looking around a few times Boriam said "You do notice things very easily, don't you?"

Chapter 29
THE WOUNDED BEAST

Arkenthan shut the book and thought *'I've never seen a code before. I wonder how they will solve it? Oh well, I'll have to look at it later. Right now I have to stretch my legs.'* Arkenthan rose from the bed to find his knees had fallen asleep from sitting wrongly in bed reading. His supply barrels were starting to empty and the little food he had left was tasting off. *'That can't be healthy,'* he thought and decided to get rid of the lot. He went outside and was met with a fresh and humid air which awakened his senses. The sun stood in the middle of the sky behind a thin layer of clouds. He took an hour to walk around the forest, registering how the rain had given a freshness to everything. He stopped by his traps and found a few smaller game, which he brought back to the house. *'I guess it's about time for breakfast,'* Arkenthan thought smiling at his own joke. When he got home he quickly prepared some food and got ready to start hunting. Just outside he was met by a bark, which Arkenthan quickly identified as belonging to Greypaws. The wolf was sitting at the side of the garden looking at Arkenthan. "Hey, Greypaws. Sorry I haven't been around for a few days. What have you been up to?" Arkenthan said and Greypaws tilted its head to the side with one ear upwards and another down. This made Arkenthan laugh and he said "I'm going hunting, are you going to follow me as you normally seem to be doing?" He slowly made his way to the edge of the forest, prepared an arrow and left the safety of the garden.

Having walked around the forest for a few hours, with nothing in his traps and nothing to hunt, he decided to start exploring a bit. He went west from his house into the dense forest. Passing small trickling rivers and ponds he came to a hill. In the middle of the slope was a clearing with a single tree. The tree had been cut down, but Arkenthan estimated the tree stump to be as wide as the house he was living in. As the height of the stump was lower than the nearby trees, Arkenthan wondered if this was the reason he didn't notice it from the mountaintop. He saw that the roots of the tree lifted the entire trunk off the ground. Roots had been intertwined to create a wall around the entire space under the tree, but between some of

152

the roots there seemed to be a small passage leading underneath it. Peering inside from a safe distance, Arkenthan found it to be too dark to see anything, and thought *'I wonder how many things live under there?'* He was curious to see what it was like underneath such a huge tree, but he decided to stay out of it. He turned away from the tree and saw Greypaws standing at the edge of the clearing. Arkenthan looked around and thought *'I wonder why he is afraid to enter these open places?'* Examining the area didn't tell Arkenthan anything and he soon decided to leave.

The sun was about to set as Arkenthan entered his garden. He hoped he had enough to eat that evening as he hadn't managed to hunt anything that day. Making a stew he made sure to add more water than usual so he would have some for the next morning as well. He went outside while the food was boiling and noticed it had gone dark very quickly, and that it felt colder than usual. *'Is that because of the rain from the past few days, or is winter starting to get closer?'* Arkenthan thought. *'If it is, I better get some warmer clothes.'* He looked at the short pants and the torn sleeves on his arms and sighed. Turning around he was once again able to see the cave up in the mountain, and he saw a big creature moving outside it. Arkenthan found it too dark to truly see what it was, but something told him that it was the strange creature which had climbed up the tree. He reminded himself that he had to look at the tree, in case it had made any marks on it. He shook his head and went inside.

The next morning Arkenthan found it warmer outside. After reheating the stew from last night and eating it, he took his bow and went outside. Feeling slightly disappointed that Greypaws wasn't there to meet him, he quickly turned and chose a new route. He soon found himself in the clearing where Greypaws had first hunted him and chased him to the old house. *'Hmm, I wonder if the bees have managed to rebuild their nest?'* Arkenthan thought and headed in their direction. Crouching down a few steps away from the nest he saw there was still a big piece missing, but the work to repair it had already been going on for a while. Arkenthan nodded thinking he should let them fill it up before attempting to take anything again. He turned away from the hive and saw the Dragon's Blood plant. *'I wonder if they would be easy to plant somewhere else?'* he thought, *'It would be good to have it in my garden. I should ask in town the next time I'm there.'* Looking up he saw something move in the bushes close-by. He snuck closer and saw a small creature looking like a beaver stirring on the ground, looking for roots or similar food. It hadn't noticed him yet, so Arkenthan readied an arrow and shot the creature. *'I wonder how this one tastes,'* Arkenthan thought as he retrieved the animal. He thought the creature might last two days, but no more, so he put it in his bag and went on. Taking a trip past his traps he found a few more hares which he soon brought home. He went to the small lake not far from his house and swam for a while. The sun had warmed the water nicely, and Arkenthan let himself forget the time as he lay in the grass beside the lake. When he had dried up, he went to the edge of the clearing and found a long stick. Taking a thread he always carried in his bag, he made a fishing pole. He didn't really think the pole with the rough string and a hook from a branch would catch anything, but he wasn't in need of food for the day and sat by the bank relaxing. He heard the bushes behind him rattle and something made a sound like "Eep" before it was gone. Arkenthan had never heard a sound like that before, and wondered what kind of animal could have made it. He sat wondering about the noise for a while until something pulled on the fishing cord. It wasn't a strong pull, and Arkenthan assumed it was a small fish. *'It's actually good that it's only a small fish, I don't think my fishing rod would survive a big one,'* Arkenthan thought and laughed at the fact that his fishing gear had actually caught something. Getting the fish on land he thought *'This might be a good starter for my dinner. Just to make it a bit fancier.'* He remembered where a few herbs were located, and after picking these, Arkenthan brought the fish home along with his fishing rod. He looked forward to the dinner he was going to have while he gutted the fish outside the house. The smell of the fish made him think *'I wish I had done this while I was near the lake.'* What he pulled out of the fish he stored in a bowl which he later carried a bit into the forest to get rid of. On the way back to his house he saw a small creature sitting on the path. Annoyed that he had forgotten to bring his bow Arkenthan picked up a stone and threw it towards the animal. The stone bounced off the ground a bit to the side of the path. The small animal got scared from the sound of the stone and quickly went in the opposite direction. Arkenthan sighed and went on. As he passed the area which the creature had run towards Arkenthan heard a strange sound, then a thin screech from something. Wondering what the sounds were he entered the forest. Pushing his way through the bushes he soon saw the animal, which he now noticed was a badger, hanging from one of his traps. *'I guess that's another way of hunting small game,'* Arkenthan thought as he killed the animal and brought it home. Having several smaller animals ready he figured he should take one more day of hunting before making a trip to the city.

Having spent a full day hunting and not managing to find anything other than small game, Arkenthan stood in his garden thinking *'I wonder where all the bigger animals has gone?'* He counted seven smaller game in total, and figured it would have to be enough. He liked staying in the forest, but he had some things he needed to find out.

The next day Arkenthan found himself overlooking the forest from the mountain when a flock of birds suddenly rose to the side of him, and he heard something heavy running towards him. *'Oh, no. What now?'* Arkenthan thought as he prepared to rush back to his house. A few seconds later a white blur passed the tree line a little ahead of him and he half shouted "Greypaws?" The running animal went quiet. Looking quickly around him, still ready to run home, he listened for any sounds of the beast. Soon, the white head of the wolf emerged from the trees and Arkenthan felt easier. Watching as Greypaws stood at the edge of the forest Arkenthan saw that his front leg was bleeding. "Have you been fighting something?" From where he stood he couldn't see if it was a bite mark or something else. When Greypaws lay down trying to lick the wound without success, Arkenthan stepped towards the wolf. As he came close, Greypaws started growling telling Arkenthan he was uncomfortable with the situation. Arkenthan stopped and sat down in front of Greypaws, looking at the wound. After a while the wolf lowered its head as it calmed down, and again Arkenthan took the chance to step closer to the wounded leg. When he got close enough to touch the leg, Greypaws lifted his head ready to strike if it had to. Arkenthan raised one hand towards the nose of the wolf and let Greypaws smell it. He had heard dogs had to identify the person which is petting it before allowing them close, so Arkenthan hoped this was the rule for wolves as well. Greypaws sniffed the hand and made a biting motion towards it, and as a response Arkenthan said "No! No biting." Lowering its head, it seemed like Greypaws understood the command given to it, so Arkenthan nodded and petted the wolf on its head. A low growl came from Greypaws, but nothing more happened. With his heart pounding so hard he couldn't even hear the growl, and white spots started dancing in front of his eyes, Arkenthan couldn't believe he had actually petted Greypaws on the head. Finally regaining his senses Arkenthan slowly put one hand into his bag, under the watchful eyes of the wolf, and pulled out the leaf of the Dragon's Blood plant. Greypaws sniffed the plant apparently wondering what this was, and pulled his head back when Arkenthan brought out a knife. Using slow movements so he wouldn't scare the animal, Arkenthan proceeded to cut the leaf in two and peal one side of it. Using a bit of string Arkenthan attached the leaf with the sticky side towards the wound. This seemed to relax Greypaws a little, as he smelled the leaf on the wound before laying his head on his other paw. Arkenthan nodded and scratched the wolf behind the ear before standing up. Raising his head Greypaws looked at Arkenthan. "You stay here and get well," Arkenthan said before turning away and heading towards town. As the day went by Arkenthan got a feeling Greypaws was following him. Every now and then he heard something heavy set its foot on something. *'He's usually much more quiet though, maybe the wound makes him more noisy?'* Arkenthan thought still walking onwards. When he reached the lake he took a quick bath before moving on. Soon he had reached the edge of the forest.

He turned towards town and walked straight into Jonas. "Ow, I didn't see you there, what are you doing all the way out here?" Jonas looked at him for a while before saying "You just came out of the forest. What were you doing in there?" Arkenthan looked back and forth a few times before saying "Hunting?" Jonas coughed signalling he didn't believe that. Arkenthan nodded and said "It's the shortest way from home." "And where exactly is home?" Jonas pressed on. "Why so inquisitive suddenly?" Arkenthan asked slightly annoyed. Jonas pointed at the forest and said "Because something is going on in there these days. The scouts have spotted huge animals getting closer to the city. Some hunters have come back missing an arm or a leg, and some haven't returned at all. The few who have returned say something must have stirred the animals to come this close." Arkenthan sighed and said "I guess I can tell you but you cannot, under any circumstance, tell anyone else. And we have to go somewhere no one can hear us." Jonas looked at Arkenthan sceptically before saying "Okay, I won't tell anyone, but I can't guarantee people won't hear us if we go somewhere in town. People patrol the border of the forest now, that's why I'm here now, so someone might meet us here as well." Arkenthan nodded and thought *Where to go when people can hear us everywhere?'* His mind drifted to the lake not far into the forest and said "I know of a place, but it's inside the forest. It's not far, but it's probably going to get dark by the time we get back here." This seemed to scare Jonas a little and he started walking back and forth apparently thinking. Arkenthan watched as the big butcher kept walking in a circle waving his arms as if discussing something with himself. He had almost started laughing at the sight when the butcher turned towards him, sighed and said "Okay, I'll follow you. Lead the way." Arkenthan coughed once when he heard this response. He hadn't thought the butcher would actually follow him into the forest. He didn't reveal this thought though, but nodded before heading into the forest. *'I guess it's good that someone in town knows what's going on. Maybe he can tell me if he hears anything I should know,'* Arkenthan thought as he pushed his way through the forest. The butcher seemed scared of the forest, as he was making so much noise that any animal would hear them a long way off. "Have you ever been into the forest?" Arkenthan asked to try to calm the butcher down a little. Jonas made a strange sound and whispered "No, I've lived here all my life, but the forest has never been safe to enter." Arkenthan smiled and said "Well isn't this exciting then?" Jonas shook his head and whispered "No, well yes, but having lived my entire life knowing I should never enter here makes everything more scary than exciting." Arkenthan stopped in front of a bush and the butcher did so as well. "Well," Arkenthan said and continued "then it's time for you to see what it's all about." He then pushed the butcher in front of him into the clearing with the small river running into the pond.

Chapter 30
STATE OF THE WORLD

Jonas looked around him and said "Wow, it's beautiful." He turned to look at Arkenthan as he said "Are there more places like this in the forest?" Arkenthan smiled and said "Yes, but those I've found are far away from here." Jonas nodded and looked back across the pond directly at a great white wolf which was snarling at him. Arkenthan saw the butcher's face become white, and he followed Jonas' gaze towards the wolf. "Ah, forgot about that one," Arkenthan said to which Jonas turned towards him and said "You know of.. um.. that?" Arkenthan laughed and said "Well, yes. And that, is a he. I've named him Greypaws. See the paws?" Jonas nodded as Arkenthan passed him, stepping towards the wolf. "Don't make any sudden movements, he's not completely tame yet, so I can't guarantee what he will or won't do. As long as you're calm I think I'll be able to handle him though," Arkenthan said as he got close to the wolf, at which point the butcher interrupted him saying "Oh by the gods, that wolf is the same height as you, how can that be?" Arkenthan reached out his hand to Greypaws for him to smell and said quietly "You stay here. This is a friend of mine, so it would be nice if you didn't eat him." He then turned towards the butcher and said "I am guessing it's a dire wolf. I had only heard of them before this one tried to eat me. We've got to know each other quite a bit since then." Arkenthan pulled a rabbit out of his bag and gave it to Greypaws before going back to the butcher. They sat down on a log on the ground and Arkenthan asked "So what do you want to know?" Jonas sat staring at the lake, the grass in the clearing and at the giant wolf which was watching them. "Where do you really live?" Jonas asked and Arkenthan nodded and started looking around. Pointing at a giant and sturdy tree he asked "Are you able to climb that?" The butcher raised his shoulders saying "I guess I could try, but I can't promise anything." Arkenthan nodded and watched as the butcher went to the tree and started climbing. When he had gotten a bit up the trunk of the tree the butcher asked "How far will I have to go?" Arkenthan looked at him and asked "Can you see anything above the trees?" To which the butcher said "Almost." "Well, then you're almost there," Arkenthan said and waited until Jonas said he could see above the other trees. Pointing in the direction he imagined the mountain to be he said "Do you see the mountain in that direction?" The butcher confirmed this and Arkenthan said "At the other side of that mountain, at the foot of the mountain itself is a small house. That is where I live." Jonas returned from the tree and said "The forest stops at the mountain?" Arkenthan made a grunting laugh and replied "No. This way was the shortest route to the edge of the forest, and it takes over half a day to walk." Sitting down on the log Jonas asked "Why do you live out here? Do your parents live here as well, or just you?" Arkenthan sighed and started telling the story about how his father had been called to war and how Arkenthan had followed trying to join. "The war is nasty business. Every now and then a few soldiers come through town, and they say each side gains a bit and loses a bit every now and then, so they barely move at all. Some of them are going to the war, and some are returning from it. Most of those returning are missing an arm or a leg," Jonas said before asking "Why didn't you go back to your mother? I am sure she misses you." Arkenthan looked at the ground and said "My mother is always opposed to what I wish to do. And when I never get to do anything I get annoyed, while she gets angry. This lasts for a while until one of us leaves the room in anger. I'm sure she is better off with me being here." Jonas shook his head saying "A mother is never better off with their son away somewhere she doesn't know. Even if all she does is argue with him. She only does that because she cares about you and wants to keep you safe, you know." Still looking at the ground Arkenthan said "She probably thinks I'm with my father now, helping in the military." Jonas coughed and said "She's probably heard from your father and understood that you're not there. She might think you've become lost, eaten by animals or robbed by bandits." Arkenthan sighed and said "So what should I do then? Believe it or not, I actually like living here. I've learned more in the last months than I've done in several years at home." Jonas stood up and said "Well, when we get back to town I'll get you some ink and some paper. Then you'll write to your mother and say that you are okay, and living in a small house while getting ready to join the army. You don't need to say exactly where that house is. I'll give you the address of my store so she can send an answer to you." Arkenthan blinked a few times before saying "Okay. I can do that. As long as she won't arrive demanding that I come home. I hope you won't tell anyone where I live?" Jonas nodded and said "Aye, I've already promised you that." They stayed talking for a while before heading back. As Arkenthan had predicted it got dark while they were in the forest, and Jonas was even more anxious while they walked back to the road.

Back in town the two of them were met by a group of guards who stopped them asking "Jonas, where were you? You didn't return when you should, and you weren't near your patrol route. Everyone was worried something bad had happened." Jonas lifted one hand and said "I'm sorry if I got everyone worried, but I met my nephew here and we sat talking for a while and I guess I lost track of time." The group of people kept asking why they hadn't just stayed near the route, which would be logical, and Arkenthan couldn't really argue with this. Jonas seemed to be prepared for this though, and managed to evade all of the more penetrating questions. After a while they were allowed to go on, and they were soon entering the butcher's store where a slim woman of the same age as Jonas greeted them by yelling at the butcher. Jonas tried to calm the woman down. He called her Marie, and Arkenthan assumed it was his wife whom he'd never met before. When she eventually directed her attention to Arkenthan wondering who he was, he talked as politely as he could while explaining that he was the one who'd been borrowing the room upstairs. After being cross-examined by the woman for a while, Arkenthan was given some ink and some paper and Jonas told him to go to the room and write a letter while the butcher started working on the game he'd brought. Going up the stairs Arkenthan assumed they were starting to argue again, but imagined it wouldn't be as fierce as when they had entered the store. He just hoped the butcher wouldn't say too much, it seemed like people weren't very welcoming to the idea of anyone going into the forest, much less living in it.

Sitting down by the table in the room he started writing a letter to his mother. It started out saying he was fine and that she shouldn't be worried, but he soon tore the letter up and started again. He started the letter with where he had left the house. He wrote how he'd been annoyed that he had left home so angry, and what he had thought about saying in order to join the army. He wrote how the army had rejected him, but that he had chosen to get more experience by living in the forest. That he'd met Greypaws, a wolf which he was now becoming good friends with, and that the wolf had helped him hunt to survive. He wrote that the house in the forest was so peaceful that he really felt at home there. Watching the letter become a pile of sheets telling about everything which had happened, he was wondering what she would think of it. Without mentioning anything about the cave in the mountain or the book he'd found, he finished the letter remembering to ask how she was doing, and asked how his father had been getting on in the war. Finally he slowly made his way downstairs and found that the fight was over. Jonas looked up from his work and smiled at him. Seeing the pile of sheets in Arkenthan's hands the butcher asked "Did you write a letter or a book?" Arkenthan looked questioningly at Jonas who laughed and said "You've been at it for almost three hours." Looking at the watch hanging on the wall he noticed it was very late, and that he was very hungry. The butcher's wife entered the store and smiled at him. "I hear you're my 'nephew' now. Now I haven't heard anything about who you are, but if Jonas think it's best to keep it hidden, I have a feeling I don't want to know. As long as it's not illegal, of course. If it is, you're out of here." She ended on an angry tone, but she quickly recovered her equilibrium and expressed that she didn't mean to be crass. Arkenthan nodded at her and asked Jonas what the address was to the store so he could add it to the letter. "Have you eaten yet?" Marie said. "No ma'am," Arkenthan replied, still being as polite as possible. "Well, then you'll have to come have some food. I can't let my nephew starve, can I?" Marie said as she pushed him out of the store and into their house.

Arkenthan was shoved into a chair by the table and watched as Marie hurried back and forth setting out plates as well as making food in the kitchen. "I heard you're supplying us with meat? How do you get it?" Arkenthan thought for a while eventually saying "I hunt it." She stopped and looked at him saying "Not in this forest do you? It's become so dangerous!" Arkenthan nodded and said "Where I go it's not that dangerous. Danger is near of course, but I think I would feel safer there than closer to here. Especially from what I heard from Jonas." Marie nodded and kept on with the preparations saying "So where are you from?" Arkenthan had to think for a long time trying to hide where he was living now. He eventually said "I'm from Dragoria, The Black Village. My father was a smith there." Marie looked at him and said "Was a smith?" Remembering how he'd said it he quickly said "Oh, sorry, he still is a blacksmith. However, right now he's been called out to fight in the war. Or make weapons for the army or something." Marie nodded and said "The war against Xi'n Tze?" Arkenthan looked up and said "No, against the Kenors. Are we fighting the Xi'n Tze as well?" Marie lifted her shoulders and said "It is quite a long time since I heard about the war against Xi'n Tze. How well do you know the geography of the world?" Arkenthan had to admit that he hadn't paid much attention to geography in school, so Marie explained "Our world, Alonia, consist of seven countries. Six of the countries surround a seventh, which is our country Orugonas. All seven countries want power in the world, and so they always wage wars against their neighbours. All of the countries have only three neighbours they have to defend themselves against, except for our country which has to defend itself against all the others. For this reason our country has always focused on getting a strong military as well as diplomatic standing in the world." Here Arkenthan interrupted asking "What do you mean by diplomatic standing?" Marie nodded and said "I mean that we're very good at discussing our way to peace instead of fighting. Sometimes the countries we've come to peaceful terms with ask us to help them solve problems with their neighbours as well. But if the negotiations don't go anywhere, the country we're talking to often attacks us. For that reason we have to have a strong military as well. I understand that's where you're headed?" Arkenthan confirmed this and sat thinking for a while before Marie said "Here, eat up. Then you should rest for tonight." Arkenthan looked at the food she had given him and felt his mouth watering while his stomach started growling. Marie laughed a low but thrilling laugh and sat down by the table. While Arkenthan ate, he asked if she would have a problem with him staying for a few days. "A few days? Hmm. I guess you can do that. You seem like a good guy, but why? Have a lot of errands to do?" Arkenthan nodded and said "I found some herbs in the forest when I was hunting and Johanna, Helena the apothecary's daughter, said it was good for cleaning wounds and curing illness. She offered to teach me how to prepare it, but it would take a full day to do. Traveling home will take me half a day, so I would like to not have to walk there during the night." Marie smiled and said "Johanna is a nice girl. Okay, if she said she will need you for a day then I guess you should have a place to sleep as well. I'll go tell Jonas." Arkenthan thanked her and finished eating his dinner. He took several scoops from the kettle and figured he should try to make something like this back home. When he finished his meal, he carried the plate back to the kitchen before heading for bed.

Chapter 31
TWO SMALL BOTTLES

The next morning Arkenthan headed early to the apothecary's house. *'I hope she has time to show me how to prepare the leaf,'* Arkenthan thought as he walked quickly through the back streets of Garani. Soon he could smell the strong scent of the store and he began reconsidering spending the entire day there. *'I guess I'll get used to the smell soon enough,'* he thought as he opened the door. Johanna was lying with her head on the counter fiddling with something. "Hello?" Arkenthan said when he'd entered the store. Johanna looked up, beaming, saying "Oh, hello, sorry about that. I didn't hear anyone come in." Arkenthan smiled at her and said "Maybe you could hang a bell on the door. That way you will hear when someone enters." Johanna went blank for a few seconds apparently imagining how that would work. Returning to the real world she said "That could work, good idea. So what can I help you with?" Arkenthan approached the counter and put the leaf on the table saying "Well, there's this." Johanna looked at the rolled up leaf. Opening the leaf and looking at it she said "Oh, it's you. I am sorry for not recognizing you, it was really hectic here the day you came by. Have you cut this?" Arkenthan looked at the leaf and remembered using some of it to put on Greypaws' leg. "Ah, that. Yes, a friend of mine had a bad cut on the leg, so I took a chance, peeled the leaf on one side and tied the juicy side onto the wound." Johanna smiled at him saying "I guess you have an easy time learning things. That's exactly what I would have done if I hadn't had an ointment of this." Arkenthan smiled proudly towards the sky, which made Johanna laugh. She went to the back room and brought out several instruments for making potions, most of which Arkenthan had never seen or heard of. Pointing at the different things she named them and got Arkenthan to repeat the names back to her so he would learn them. "It is a good thing you've come here today, not much has happened the last few days and I was really bored. So thank you," Johanna said with a smile. She then spent half the day telling Arkenthan how to refine the leaf into an ointment using the different instruments. Having finished the explanation she got her mother to bring them some lunch.

Having almost finished their lunch, the door opened and a man stepped through it. Johanna jumped out of the chair and said "Johannes! Welcome, are you well yet?" *Johannes? Where have I heard that before?'* Arkenthan thought as the man answered her question. "Come," Johanna said and guided the man over to Arkenthan saying "This is the one who brought in the medicine you needed." Arkenthan turned towards the man and said "Oh, it's you." Johanna looked at Arkenthan and said "You two know each other? And you don't need to be so sullen." Johannes laughed and said "No, no Johanna. It's all right, I was even more rude to him, if I recall correctly. You're the sword kid right?" He directed the question to Arkenthan who nodded. "Ah," Johannes said "well, at the time I was weak and thought I might die. I didn't have much time to be polite to random people. I'll tell you what, I'll teach you how to fight with a sword. I'll even make it free of charge seeing as you saved my life. I've run a fencing school before so I usually take payment for it." Arkenthan looked from Johanna to Johannes a few times before a smile spread across his mouth. He thanked the man for the offer and told him about how often he would be in town. Johannes scratched his short beard and said "Usually you'll have to practice every day, so I guess I'll have to find something for you to do while you're at your own place. Wherever that is." Johannes looked at Arkenthan and nodded before turning to Johanna saying "I'm in a bit of a hurry, so I'll have to go now. Thank you again for saving my life." As he turned, Johanna held out a potion and said "Drink this tonight before going to bed, and tomorrow when you wake up. It tastes bad, but it should remove the rest of the illness." Johannes nodded to the girl and left the store. Johanna looked at Arkenthan and said "Learning to fight with a sword?" For some reason Arkenthan started feeling guilty about this, but said "Yes, I'm hoping to help the military, so I figure I should learn how to fight with a sword. I'm good with a bow, but what if I don't have a bow at hand? I'll have to be able to defend myself." Johanna nodded seeming a bit sad before saying "You don't have to fight to help the military, you know." This comment set Arkenthan back a little as he stuttered to respond saying "Y.. I.. Yes. I know. My father is a smith there, but I don't know a profession like that, so joining in the fighting was all I could think of." Johanna nodded and said "They need people tending the wounded as well." Arkenthan thought for a while before agreeing, and Johanna said "Come on, let's teach you how to make this ointment." Arkenthan followed her back to the counter where the leaf and all the instruments were placed. With Johanna's help explaining and guiding, Arkenthan worked his way through the process of refining the necessary parts of the leaf. After several hours of work Arkenthan dripped the first drops of a clear red liquid into a small round bottle. "Good, this is very good. Only a few drops will fall into the bottle every now and then, that's why this step takes so long. The entire distilling should fill this bottle, so keep at it," Johanna said. Arkenthan kept moving the bottle, with what was left of the leaf in it around above the flames to even the heat out. On top of this bottle was a glass tube which went upwards before turning downwards. The apparatus puzzled Arkenthan, and he asked about what it was. Johanna said "This is a small distillery. You boil the liquid to either remove something you don't want in there, or to extract exactly what you want. The liquid boils out of this bottle, and soon what we want runs down this tube and into this next bottle." Johanna pointed to the different parts as she spoke but Arkenthan felt like there were a lot more to it than what she was telling him.

He watched as at first the drips were slow, with minutes between each drop, but after some time the drips were much more frequent. Towards the end of the process the drips became slower again. As it slowed down, Johanna removed the potion and said "We don't want the last drops. When this," she held up the bottle and said "is finished coming out of the tube, something else starts to come out of it. We only want this part, so the rest we can throw away." She brought the bottle containing the rest of the leaf outside and emptied its contents. Coming back into the store she looked at the potion they had made and smiled saying "We actually got quite a lot out of that leaf. Look at this potion. It's very sticky, and so from this bottle there will only come a few drops out at a time. That's very handy for this potion. Since we now have extracted the healing substance from the sap, it is so much stronger than using just the sap of the leaf itself. In a small amount of lotion, I would put two drops of this. For a bee sting I would smear one drop over a large area around the sting, and for a small wound like a cut in the finger I would put either three drops in a lotion or one drop straight onto the wound. It will hurt, but it will help. Since I've helped you with this I will take half of this bottle here. And I'll give you a basic lotion which you can use to mix this into." She poured half the potion into another bottle which she handed to Arkenthan. He looked at the bottle and said "A basic wound will need only one drop?" Johanna nodded and said "You expect to get injured a lot?" Arkenthan laughed and said "Who knows? No, I was just beginning to understand how ill Johannes was when I brought the other leaf." Johanna nodded and looked at the floor. Looking outside, Arkenthan noticed it had become dark. He looked at the bottle he'd got and sighed before turning to Johanna saying "I should go, it's dark outside so I should get to bed. Have to leave early tomorrow." Johanna smiled and nodded before giving him a hug. Baffled by this, Arkenthan went to the door and opened it before remembering what he was going to ask. "Do you know if this Dragon's Blood plant is easy to grow? Is it possible to move it, for instance from the forest to the garden?" Johanna thought for a while, staring into the air, before saying "I think you can cultivate it in the garden. Hold on, I'll ask my mom, she knows this better than me." She disappeared and remained in the back room for a while. When she returned she said "Yes, the plant has long roots, and as long as you get all of them it should be all right to move it. But it doesn't like much sunlight, so plant it somewhere shady, and not too close to other plants." Arkenthan thanked her for the advice and said good bye again. As he stepped outside his senses seemed to wake up, letting the fresher air fill his body with a tingling sensation. The first breath of air he took made him cough, so he took a few breaths before heading back to the butcher's store.

Arkenthan was woken up by a sharp knock on the door and Jonas saying "Hey, forest boy, wake up! A scout's been injured by something in the forest. I think you should check it out." Arkenthan looked at the ceiling unable to remember where he was at first. He thought *Someone's been injured in the forest? And I should look at it? Is he afraid Greypaws hurt someone?'* Getting out of bed he hurried outside to meet the butcher. A crowd was outside the store arguing over what to do. Arkenthan stepped outside and saw a man apparently bitten by something huge lying in the streets. He heard the argument between the guards on where to take him. Arkenthan sighed and said "Pick him up and follow me." A guard turned to him and stared angrily at him before saying "And why should we follow you then?" Arkenthan headed towards the alley towards Helena's store and said "I probably know more about the creatures in the forest than you do, and I also know of someone who treats people for a living. So follow me. Now!" He ended in an angry tone before turning away. The guards were so surprised by this that they stood staring blankly into space for a few seconds before picking the man up and following Arkenthan. Soon they were outside Helena's and Johanna's store, knocking hard on the door to wake them up. After some time Helena put her head out the window on the second floor and shouted "What?" Arkenthan stepped backwards and said "There's someone here who needs your help." She looked at him and said "Arkenthan? Okay, if you think it's important then we're coming down." She looked further up the road and saw the injured man being carried by four guards. Her mouth made an o shape and she quickly turned, shouting "Johanna! Things will get busy!" She then shut the window. A few minutes later the door opened and the guards carrying the wounded man were guided into the back room. *Please don't let it be Greypaws. Please don't let it be Greypaws'* Arkenthan thought as he watched the ladies cleaning the wounds. It seemed like the man had received a scratch across his back, and something had bitten across his stomach. The guards argued about what could have done this, and they started naming different animals living in there. "The size of the bite and claws are huge, so it has to be a big animal. Maybe it's a fjällbear?" One of them said. Another joined in saying "It could be, but there have been tales of a huge white wolf wandering the woods. It's said he's the only one of his kind in this forest, and that this has made him secluded and angry." Arkenthan interrupted the man at this point saying "If a wolf has done this, the bite will be pointy. A bear would have a much more stubby mouth, leaving a more rounded mark on him. We'll have to see when they get him cleaned up a little." Hearing this the second man said "But this wolf is nothing like a normal wolf. How would we know what kind of bite he has? Maybe he can change shape? A demon wolf!" Arkenthan thought *How can someone jump to that conclusion out of nothing?* He said "If it had been a demon wolf, wouldn't it have attacked the city a long time ago?" Another man stepped into the room and said "Aye, I heard Phil met the white wolf one time, and the wolf just looked at him before going its own way. If it had been evil I don't think Phil would've been around today." Arkenthan smiled thanking the gods that someone was keeping calm. The second man started arguing again but the third man said "Martie, you're starting to panic. Step outside and relax a little. Clear your thoughts before coming back." Martie looked at the third man and said "Yes, colonel. Right away." He then left the room. Arkenthan looked at the colonel and said "Colonel of the guard?" The man nodded and said "Locke. You're the one responsible for getting Bull here?" Arkenthan nodded. The colonel looked at the wounded man and said "Thank you. We haven't had a dedicated doctor in this city since the last war broke out. I didn't know of this place." Arkenthan looked up as Johanna shouted for him to get the bottle. *The bottle?* Arkenthan thought before remembering the bottle of Dragon's Blood. He quickly left the room, got the small round bottle and brought it back to the two women. He sat down on a bench next to the colonel who said "You don't seem very afraid of the forest." Without thinking, Arkenthan answered "I'm not. People should be, though." Locke looked at him and asked "And why is that?" Arkenthan looked at the wounded man and said "People don't walk in it with proper respect for it. It makes them sloppy, and gets them hurt." The colonel smiled and said "You're right. So how would you like to join the city guard as a scout in and around the forest?"

Chapter 32
GREYPAWS ENTERS GARANI

Arkenthan sat looking straight ahead of him thinking *'I can't join the guards here, I'm hardly around.'* To the colonel he said "Ah, no. I'm not from around here." Locke nodded and asked "So where are you from?" Struggling to find something to say, Arkenthan eventually said "I'm from the Black Village." The colonel coughed before saying "Then you're a very long way from home, which means you probably stay somewhere nearby, so why not join us then?" Looking uncertainly around Arkenthan thought *'Crap. How am I going to get out of this one? I could tell him I live in another town? No, he'll just ask which one and I have no idea what towns are nearby.'* The silence lasted a long time making Arkenthan feel slightly awkward. He ended his inner debate on the sentence *'I'm going to have to tell him, aren't I? How many people am I going to tell on this trip?'* He then sighed and said "Let's go somewhere no one can hear us." The colonel looked at him, nodded and guided him out of the store. He went down the street before opening a door. Inside sat three men of the guard preparing for their shift. "Get out," the colonel said and, with a quick scramble, the three men were out the door. Locke sat down at a table and gestured to one of the chairs. Arkenthan nervously sat down and began telling his story. After finishing his tale, the colonel sat with his mouth open before saying "So you actually live in the forest?" Arkenthan confirmed this and the colonel said "Have you noticed anything strange in there lately? Something which can explain why all the beasts have come here?" Arkenthan shook his head saying "No, I haven't." Thinking for a while before continuing, Arkenthan said "There is one thing though. The larger game seems to have disappeared from deeper inside the forest. Maybe they've fled to the outskirts?" The colonel nodded and said "That could explain why these beasts have come here. Well, thank you for your help. Is there any way I can contact you? I might need some information at some point." Arkenthan told Locke where he was staying which made the colonel laugh before saying "So you're the one supplying the butcher with all the good food. I guess you're more important to this town than I assumed."

After asking a few more questions, the colonel led Arkenthan back to the store. On the way back the colonel sighed and said "I just wish people wouldn't listen to tales like the one circling about the great white wolf." Arkenthan smiled and said "That one actually exist." The colonel stopped and slowly turned towards Arkenthan before saying "It's real?" Nodding, Arkenthan said "He's not mean though. As long as you aren't mean to him, he won't be mean to you." Staring at Arkenthan, Locke said "How do you know it's a he?" Arkenthan looked at the colonel and said "He's sort of my pet." The colonel burst out laughing and eventually managed to say "He's 'sort of' your pet?" Arkenthan heard the extra pressure on the words and said "Yeah, well, I haven't tamed him completely yet. He lets me pet him once in a while though, so I'm making progress." Shaking his head, Locke mumbled "You're crazy," before opening the door to the store. Inside was the scared man, who looked up at them. The colonel looked at Arkenthan and said to the man "I guess you were right, the wolf does exist. But it's not a mean beast, so as long as you don't scare it you won't be eaten." The man's face grew a little paler and he stuttered "H-h-how d-do you know t-t-that?" Locke pointed at Arkenthan saying "Seems like this guy meets him pretty often." Arkenthan looked at the now shaking man and nodded before saying "I've actually named him Greypaws." The man whispered the name "Greypaws." Which seemed to calm him down a little. Whispering the name a few times, he soon turned towards them and said "What if Greypaws attacked Bull?" Arkenthan sighed saying "I really hope not, I kinda like that wolf. We'll take a look at the wounds and let you know." The colonel led the way into the back room of the store where the two women had bandaged the wounded man. The guard standing by the door saluted the colonel who asked if everything was well. The guard looked at Arkenthan before asking his colonel "Shall we take this somewhere else?" Locke looked at Arkenthan before shaking his head saying "Naw, he can know." The guard nodded and said "They say the bleeding was bad, but the medicine this guy brought would save him. While they bandaged him, Bull woke up and said two words. 'Huge' and 'bear'. Before passing out again." Arkenthan felt himself exhaling heavily and his heart settled slightly. The colonel nodded at Arkenthan and he understood that it was a notice to tell the guard outside. He stepped out and said "It was a bear. Bull woke up and told the guard in there before passing out again. He's going to make it though, just give him a few days." The guard sitting on the floor smiled and looked at his hands where he'd been picking his nails. Arkenthan stepped into the back room and said "His brother?" The colonel nodded, turning to Arkenthan and asked "What do you know of these huge bears? When he says huge, what does he mean by that?" Arkenthan thought for a while before saying "The wolf everyone seem to have mentioned, is about the same height as me, which is pretty big. The bears are fjällbears, and they are probably as wide as I am tall, so they truly are huge. They will run for a long time when they first start hunting someone or something. If you want to survive, you'll have to run into dense forest, which will slow them down a bit, and run as fast as you can towards somewhere you know is safe, or at least hope is safe. This man here is extremely lucky to be alive." The guard looked at Arkenthan in awe saying "How do you know all this?" Arkenthan looked at the wounded man before saying "Because I've been hunted by them a few times now, and I'm still alive. The wolf saved me a couple of times I suspect, but some of the times I've barely gotten away." The colonel laughed and said "And you still do what you do." The guard looked between the two of them looking very confused. The colonel turned to Arkenthan and said "If you come across any of my men in there, can you observe how they act in there? If they act wrongly tell them how to do it, will you?" Arkenthan blinked a few times before asking "Why would they care to listen to me? I'm nobody to them, and they are a group of guards." Locke sighed and nodded, apparently understanding what Arkenthan meant. Arkenthan on the other hand thought *I have a feeling it's as it was described in the book. If a nobody walks up to a group of people who feel like somebody, they won't listen to the person.*' Colonel Locke said "Go back to the butcher's store and tell them I've told you to stay in town for another day. Tomorrow I'll have figured something out." Arkenthan nodded to the colonel and the guard before saying goodbye to Helena and Johanna. He then went back to the butcher's store.

Arkenthan lay in bed thinking, wondering how long he was going to have to stay in town for. He missed the forest, the quietness, the smell of it and how he could do exactly what he wanted to do. Here he had to follow the rules and regulations of the city. Jonas knocked on the door and entered saying "How'd it go? Colonel Locke seemed pleased that you took charge of the situation." Arkenthan looked at the butcher and asked "He's been here now?" Jonas nodded saying "He dropped by explaining that you had to stay for another day, and told me to say thank you for all you did for Bull." Arkenthan nodded and lay down in bed. As Jonas was about to leave, Arkenthan asked "Did you send the card yet?" Jonas grinned at him and said "The book you mean?" Arkenthan jokingly looked at the floor before nodding. The butcher laughed and said "Naw, the postal services open tomorrow, so I'll have to take it then." He then left the room to let Arkenthan go to sleep for a few hours.

When he woke up, Arkenthan tiredly went downstairs to the store. Jonas was serving some customers and asked Arkenthan to help wrap the meat in paper. Having done so, Arkenthan watched how Jonas stripped the meat from the animals. "Want to learn how to do this correctly?" Jonas asked, and Arkenthan nodded eagerly. As Jonas was about to start the demonstration, colonel Locke burst through the door. It took him few seconds to locate Arkenthan. "Come, quickly!" he said *'Why does everyone have to drag me somewhere quickly?'* Arkenthan thought as he followed the colonel. Asking what was the problem, Locke said "There're a lot of scared people in the market." Arkenthan wondered what that had to do with him, and the colonel seemed to understand his wonder because he said "It would seem your pet has wandered into the village. I got my men to keep the townspeople away, but there's only so much they can do. I'll have to contact you later, but right now I think you should take him far away from here." Arkenthan stopped and said "I don't have my things, they're still at the butcher's." The colonel explained that he would get someone to fetch them for him. At that moment Arkenthan heard the screams of fear and anger, and he began to dread what was happening there. They passed the woodworking store, and Arkenthan dropped in to fetch a long wooden pole. The woodworker had called the pole a bamboo, which Arkenthan didn't know what was, but he understood it was strong. The woodworker was out, so Arkenthan told the colonel to explain some of what had happened to him when he got back. Locke asked how he could know so much about a foreign village. Before Arkenthan was able to answer they turned the corner and were met by a big crowd shouting towards the centre of the market square. Arkenthan saw that the square was near the forest, and figured that if he was able to calm the beast he would only have a short trip to make before they were safely away.

The colonel made a path between the masses, helped by his guards, bringing Arkenthan to the front of the crowd. Seeing the great wolf, Arkenthan noticed that it was very scared, and trying to get out of the ring of spectators. If he didn't do anything quickly, Greypaws would attack someone and the guards would shoot him. Trying to shout at the crowd to be quiet, he quickly noticed that no one noticed a young man shouting at the crowd instead of the wolf. This annoyed Arkenthan so much that he felt the anger rise to his head. He leapt into the ring with the pole above his head, and with all his strength, he slammed the pole flat on the ground. The sound was so loud it made his ears ring, and as the sound resonated off the walls of the nearby houses Arkenthan could hear people go quiet. Standing up he noticed every person looking at him in awe and fear. He pointed the pole at the crowd and said aloud "Be quiet you idiots. If you make noise, it will get scared. If it is afraid it might attack. Just stay back!" He then turned towards Greypaws and slowly walked towards him. The wolf snarled at him, and he firmly said "No! No snarling!". When he got close to the beast, Greypaws snapped his head towards Arkenthan trying to bite him. Arkenthan had foreseen this however, and quickly turned the pole to hold

Greypaws back. Holding on to the middle of the pole, Arkenthan steered one end of the pole in front of the wolf's nose, and the other end on its jaw. The pole bent as the wolf tried to reach Arkenthan unsuccessfully. Pushing against the pole, Arkenthan got a springing effect like that from his traps, pushing the wolf further back than he meant to. Getting more time to act, Arkenthan twisted the stick to point towards Greypaws. Getting the wolf's attention again, Arkenthan shouted angrily "No! Stay there, and be quiet you! No attacking!" Greypaws bent low as if to attack again, but all he did was snarl at Arkenthan. Again Arkenthan shouted at the wolf. This went on for a long time, with Greypaws lunging for the boy several times. Each time the wolf attacked, Arkenthan managed to get the pole in the way. Some of the times he only managed to block the attack just in time. For every time the attack stopped, Arkenthan moved a little closer to the wolf, and he felt the tension of the crowd watching them. After several attacks the wolf seemed a lot calmer, seeming to feel more safe and understanding that Arkenthan didn't want to hurt him. Still not sure what Greypaws would do, Arkenthan was careful about approaching the beast. As he slowly got closer to Greypaws, Arkenthan could feel the eyes of the people around them, but he didn't look away from the wolf. Holding one hand out as he pulled the pole to the side, Greypaws started snarling at him. When this happened, Arkenthan stopped and said "Greypaws, no! No snarling, and no attacking!" Upon hearing what Arkenthan usually called him, Greypaws seemed to wonder what was happening, and let Arkenthan come closer. Holding his hand out, Arkenthan let Greypaws smell his hand and as he did, the wolf put its head closer to the ground showing that Arkenthan could approach. Finally getting to pet the wolf, Arkenthan began feeling he was a bit more in control of the situation. Breathing out heavily, he felt his muscles relax and he said to the wolf "Come on, let's get you out of here." He then pushed on the wolf's head to signal it should turn around. After some persuasion Greypaws seemed to understand what the boy wanted and he turned to the part of the market edging towards the forest. Leading the way, Arkenthan walked in front of the wolf. The crowd parted immediately as they approached, and as they did so, Arkenthan saw his bag on the ground in front of them. He picked up his bag as they passed it, and soon the two of them were into the forest again.

Chapter 33
STINGING MUSHROOMS

'I need to take a break from town,' Arkenthan thought as he walked beside Greypaws. "Let's give them some time to calm down. You can't enter town like that, you know. At least not until they get to know you," Arkenthan said, and Greypaws seemed to understand because it made a small whimper. Arkenthan looked up at the sky and thought *'At least it's still early morning, we should get home long before it gets dark.'* He put a hand on Greypaws' side, which seemed to surprise him because the wolf jumped slightly sideways, tripping over his own feet and rolling into the bushes. Arkenthan laughed. He laughed so much he fell and was unable to get back up. His eyes watered over and he had to rub them several times before being able to see. Getting his vision back, Arkenthan saw Greypaws sitting in front of him with his head turned to one side. *'I guess I really can feel safe around you now. If you didn't attack me now, you never will,'* Arkenthan thought as he scrambled to his feet. He talked to Greypaws about nothing the entire trip home, wondering what the townspeople would be thinking about him.

He'd brought all the food from the house when he left for town. Running outside he shouted "Come on, Greypaws, we'll need some food!" Greypaws seemed to agree on this as he barked and crashed after Arkenthan into the forest. The traps yielded three small game, which Arkenthan figured would be enough for that day. He could take one for himself and let Greypaws have the other two. Back home Arkenthan made a big fire in the garden before entering the house to clean the food. Having done so, he returned outside and hung it above the flames to cook. While waiting, Arkenthan attempted what the book had been describing as meditation. Remembering what to look for, he noticed how his mind kept racing ahead of itself, and he also noticed how, as he focussed on it, the mind went quiet. He started hearing things much better, and soon he started feeling how his heart beat. As his mind started racing about, he struggled to keep his focus. He opened his eyes and took a deep breath. Arkenthan felt as if it was the first breath of air he had taken in a long time, and he looked around as if in a haze. He was much more focused though, and he looked at the pile of rocks still lying on the grass. Looking at Greypaws he thought *'Hmm. Why not?'* He started arranging the rocks in a big circle, walking around a confused Greypaws to measure. He soon had a big circle with a smaller circle attached to it. The ring was big enough for Greypaws to lie comfortably inside. When the game finished cooking, Arkenthan put two of the animals in the smaller ring. This seemed to confuse Greypaws, as he put his head to the side. Arkenthan pointed at the meat while looking at the wolf and said "Here, boy. Here's your food." Greypaws went along the forest to the edge of the big circle, which he sniffed sceptically. He walked back and forth for a while, looking between the ring of stones and Arkenthan who started to laugh. "Okay, I'll do this for you," he said and stepped over to the point where the forest was closest to the ring. Removing a few of the stones, Arkenthan made an entrance for Greypaws. The wolf sniffed the entrance to the ring of stones, and decided to take a chance and step into the ring. He looked at Arkenthan, who smiled. Greypaws bent down and smelled the food before picking it up and walking out of the ring again. Arkenthan sighed and turned to his own food. Remembering the honey he'd got a long time ago, he went inside and brought the bottle he'd received from Johanna. He spread the honey on the meat before it was finished cooking, so that it had a glazed layer.

Arkenthan finished his dinner with a sigh. He lay down in the grass and thought *'It's good to be back in the forest.'* He looked to the side and saw Greypaws lying by the edge of the forest squinting at the sun. Greypaws looked at Arkenthan as he jumped up and shouted "Come on, you!" He then ran into the forest. It didn't take long before he heard the crashes of the wolf behind him. Arkenthan ran as fast as he could towards the lake and as he came out of the forest he jumped as high as he could, landing in the water. He rose to the surface just in time to see Greypaws suddenly noticing the lake. Arkenthan watched as the wolf dug a long trench of dirt leading up to the lake trying to stop. Greypaws' speed had been too high however, and as Arkenthan thought he was about to stop, the wolf tipped forwards and into the lake. Arkenthan watched as the great wolf scrambled for a while to get out of the water. "I thought wolves liked the water," Arkenthan said to Greypaws who answered by shaking the water out of his pelt. Arkenthan climbed out of the water and sat down next to Greypaws who was now lying on the grass resting. He tried meditating again, and felt he got more of a hang on it, even though his mind kept interrupting.

The two of them got home as it turned dark and Arkenthan noticed how he didn't even think about the dangers of the forest at night. He looked at Greypaws who lay by the edge of the forest. Sighing, Arkenthan shook his head before going inside. Bringing a few of the pelts he'd stored outside, he spread them out inside the ring of stones, which made Greypaws very curious. The wolf came over and smelled the ring of stones as Arkenthan was working. Greypaws kept stepping into the ring getting in the way of Arkenthan's work. After struggling to put them all down, wrestling the big wolf, Arkenthan watched as Greypaws finally settled down inside the ring. Having said good night, Arkenthan went inside and remembered he hadn't been home for a few days. The fire at the centre of the room had burned out, and he had to spend an hour in the dark trying to start it again. He spent most of his strength on the task, so when he finally got a big fire going he sat down on the bed and fell asleep.

The next morning arrived too soon for Arkenthan. Extremely tired, he stepped outside and saw that Greypaws was gone. This made Arkenthan feel a bit lonely, so he sat down by what was left of the fire, and fell asleep again. His stomach woke him up several hours later, when the sun was in the middle of the sky. *'I don't feel like hunting today,'* Arkenthan thought and decided to look for roots, berries and herbs. He brought his bag in order to put his pickings somewhere, and headed into the forest. A long time passed before he found anything, but eventually he found an area with different kinds of berries. At the edge of this area Arkenthan found some fallen trees with mushrooms underneath. *'I wonder if they are edible?'* Arkenthan wondered as he examined them. Something his mother had told him a long time ago sprung to mind. It was "Whenever a mushroom is poisonous, if you cut the stem and put the cut edge on your tongue, it will sting." Arkenthan shrugged and thought *'Why not?'* He then cut a mushroom and put it on his tongue. The effect was immediate. It felt like someone put a sword through his tongue, and he quickly removed the mushroom while spitting at the ground. *'Wow, it's that strong?'* Arkenthan thought as he found a new type of mushroom and cut it. Putting it to his tongue gave a slightly weaker effect, but it still stung him. Rummaging around looking for more mushrooms he eventually found one which didn't sting. *'Or have I grown too used to it?'* he thought sceptically. He decided to cook the mushrooms for a long time, in case that helped.

He spent the day digging up roots, finding mushrooms and picking berries. His traps only had one small rabbit in them, but he figured the roots, berries and mushrooms would fill up his stomach sufficiently. Back home he grabbed a few of the sword fighting scrolls and went outside. He found his stance and swung the sword in an arc pretending to strike and parry with an enemy. He tried to end each attack in a correct stance, which at first led to him tripping over his own feet. After an hour of training he managed to hold a stance through several attacks and blocks. He finished his session battling one of the trees at the edge of his garden. The tree fell, marking the end of the session, at which point it was starting to get dark.

'No use wasting it,' Arkenthan thought looking at the tree before getting an axe to chop it into firewood. Having brought the logs into the house Arkenthan went into the cave and retrieved the book. He lay down in bed and started reading *'Boriam and Jonathan kept following the group of guards.'*

Chapter 34
A CODE UNRAVELLED

Every now and then they could see the guards, at which point they would slow down to let them get a slight lead. "Can't we just pass them?" Jonathan asked and Boriam thought *'Yes, we could but...'* Out loud he said "I have a feeling we want to follow them." Jonathan sighed and said "Another bad feeling?" Boriam grinned and said "Well, as the bad feeling began with all the guards in Fisherman's Rest, I would say it's still the same bad feeling." Jonathan laughed and said "All right, then. Still the bad feeling. Which way are we heading anyways?" Boriam shrugged and said "There are several villages and cities this way, so it could be any one of them. Who knows what will be the task to do there. We really have to figure out what this code is telling us." *'Let's hope we haven't gone too far by the time we figure it out,'* Boriam thought as they kept walking. He pulled out the pieces of paper and looked at them. Turning them upside down he didn't really see much difference, so he said "I assume these figures are letters of the alphabet. Do you know which letter is the most used one?" Jonathan shook his head and guessed "A vowel?" Boriam nodded and said "Good, there are few vowels and every word needs one, so yes. The vowel 'E' is the most used letter of the alphabet. If we count all the letters, you could assume the letter E is the most common symbol. Of course we can't be completely sure, but it is a good assumption, and therefore a good start." Jonathan started counting the symbols and Boriam noted down what he said in his notebook. When the symbols were counted, there didn't seem to be any specific symbol which was used more than the rest. Boriam sighed and said "I guess the code is a bit more complicated than that." As darkness fell around them they could see the guards stopping to make camp. They sat down and lit a fire to cook food on. As the stars began to appear, Jonathan and Boriam both sat pondering what the code could be. Finally Boriam said "Bah, I need sleep. We'll keep working on it tomorrow." Jonathan agreed and prepared to go to sleep.

The next morning Jonathan gasped as he woke up. Boriam asked "You're all right?" to which Jonathan replied "I know it." Boriam lifted one eyebrow and said "That was a question, not a statement." Jonathan looked at him and said "What? Oh, no. I understand the code! It's the very first alphabet my parents taught me. It was so long ago, I had forgotten all about it." Boriam blinked a few times before saying "So what you're saying is that you know the code that Stephie wrote to us? Then she probably wrote it in that code for that exact reason." Jonathan thought about this for a while before saying "But how could she know what I've been taught when I was a child?" Boriam shrugged and said "I don't know how she knows most of the things she does, but she still does. She keeps saying 'The spirits guide us' though, so who knows, maybe they do tell her something? Now. How do you read this code?" Jonathan nodded and started to draw as he said "You know the game three-in-a-row?" Boriam did not, so Jonathan continued "I think in some areas they call it 'Tic-Tac-Toe' or something. Anyways, you make two parallel lines like this, and then you cross them with two more lines. In the game you put circles or crosses in the squares. With this code, without any outer edge, you fill in two letters in each square. So the symbol with a line downwards and a lower line pointing to the left, is an A. If you have a mark in the middle of the symbol, it means B. Then you fill out the code as you go on. I don't know what the line on top of the first letters is though." Boriam nodded and drew the system in his notebook before saying "What about these V shaped ones or the circular ones then?" Jonathan looked at where he was pointing and said "Ah, draw a big X. Continue filling in the alphabet at the top, then left, then right and then at the bottom. The circles I have no idea what means." Boriam marvelled at the simplicity of the code and how the entire alphabet could fit in the squares. "So the dotted symbols are the second letter of each square?" Boriam asked and Jonathan nodded eagerly. Standing up, Boriam said "Here, take this pencil. We'll solve the notes while we go. From the setup of the lines I think this is the first note. You can have this one, as you were the one to come up with the code." This made Jonathan smile and he accepted both the pencil and the note.

Having started walking they quickly arrived at what had been the guards' camp. After looking around for a while, Boriam said "The fire's gone cold. They must've left very early, probably while it was still dark." Jonathan nodded and suggested they keep moving. "Do we have to hurry in order to catch up to them, or can we just walk normally and see if we catch up to them?" Jonathan said, and Boriam answered "No, I don't think we need to hurry to catch up to them. Maybe they even have scouts behind them. If they do, then it will be suspicious if we run after them, or sneak around too much. Right now we should just assume they've gone too far ahead, and if we happen to meet them it will at least seem like a coincidence." Jonathan understood what he meant and started working on the coded note. After a while Jonathan said "This note is just a lot of letters. I can't make much sense of it. I assume the spacing between the words has been removed, but this still don't make any sense." Boriam, who was working on his own note, nodded his agreement, and said "Maybe it's spelled backwards, or every other letter or something?" Jonathan looked at him and said "Every other letter? How can that be logical?" Boriam shrugged and said "I don't know for sure, but maybe it's one letter from each note after the other? Read the first letter on your note." This was an I, and Boriam continued with A, and Jonathan said M. Boriam read "iam? Or maybe 'I am'? This could seem right. Wow, this must be important. Stephie always puts another layer of code in if it is important." Jonathan smiled and said "We should translate all the symbols now, and then solve it when we stop tonight." Boriam laughed and said "You'll manage to wait that long? It's still early, you know." Jonathan shrugged and said "I guess I'll have to. It will be hard, but then it'll be something to look forward to." They walked on for a while translating the letters. When he finished his note, Boriam started telling another story. After a while, as Boriam was about to finish his story, they arrived at a fork in the road. "Which way now?" Jonathan asked and Boriam thought *'Indeed, which way. The ground looks more stomped over here, so maybe the guards went that way?'* He pointed at the path turning to the right, and said "It looks like a lot of people have passed this way recently. I suggest we head down the same road, and if we find out we should go back, then that's what we'll do." Jonathan looked from one road to the next and said "I have no idea where we're even heading, so I'll just follow you. How do you know a lot of people had passed here?" Boriam pointed at the road and said "People usually don't see the small hints around them. You see how the sand of the road has been whirled up and deposited towards the side of the road? You can't see that on the other road over there. That's one of the clues. I'll teach you more later on. Come on, let's head off."

They went on and having followed the road up a small hill, they could see two guards on the road ahead of them. "Are they waiting for us?" Jonathan asked quietly, but Boriam answered "Just stay calm, maybe they're waiting for another group of soldiers." Boriam could see the group of guards walking further along the road and didn't believe his own suggestion. As they approached, one of the guards said "What are you doing here? Have you been following us?" They drew their swords and pointed them at the travellers. Boriam put his hands up and said "We haven't been following anyone! We're here merely by coincidence." One of the guards said "Where are you headed and what is your business there?" *'Well, aren't you nosy,'* Boriam thought as his mind raced to find a good answer. Giving up on finding one, he sighed and said "You know what, we haven't really decided yet. We're just two travellers, one old and one young. That's really all we are." The guards looked sceptically at Boriam and said "You'll have to buy food. How do you get the money for that?" Boriam shook his head and said "As I said, I'm old. I haven't always been a traveller. I used to buy and sell things, and now that I've got a bit to spend I'm doing some traveling. This is my nephew, and he's working as my guard. In exchange, I'm paying for his traveling as well." The guard looked at the two of them and said "There's something familiar about you, but I can't figure out what." *Oh no, let's hope it isn't from one of the posters,* Boriam thought and cheerfully said "If you've been to Uppheim, maybe you've been to my store? It's just to the east of the lesser market." The guard looked thoughtful but seemed to accept the suggestion. He said "Very well, we're moving a squad a bit ahead of you, so you'll have to slow down to fall some distance behind us. When we make camp later on, you'll make camp. And we will be keeping an eye on you." Boriam blinked a few times wondering what was going on, but he didn't want to ask, so he nodded and gave his assent to the guard. As the guards made their way after the rest of the group, Jonathan and Boriam stayed where they were. After a while, Boriam quietly asked "Did you hear what he said?" Jonathan looked at Boriam and said "That we had to slow down?" Boriam shook his head and said "He said they were moving a squad." Looking up at the guards, Jonathan said "What's the problem? Isn't that the same as a group?" Boriam nodded and said "Yes. A group in the military." Jonathan looked back at Boriam and said "Military?" Boriam sat down and thought *The military usually only move squads when they are gathering an army. If they're gathering squads, it means some city will be under siege soon. We'll have to find out where they're going.* He looked up at Jonathan and said "They are probably going to attack a city very soon." The boy looked at the sky and sighed, saying "Which city do you think it will be?" Boriam shrugged and explained that a bit further onwards was an area directly in the middle of eight cities, and that only three of them were under the control of the Council. "It could really be any one of them, although a couple of the cities are unlikely as they are pretty huge." Jonathan nodded and said "So you're suggesting we try to find out which city is going to be attacked, and then try to warn them?" Boriam smiled and said "I wish it were as easy as that. I would like to, but I don't know how we'll manage to find the camp, get in, find the information and get out again unnoticed. It would be a nightmare." He sighed and suggested they started walking slowly. "No use waiting too long when you can just walk slower than them," he said, and so they did.

Evening came and as they made camp, they saw the light from the guards' camp further along the road. Jonathan asked if they should light a fire, and Boriam said "They already know we're here, so there's no need to hide. We should make a small fire to cook our food at least, and to get enough light to solve this message." Jonathan made the fire while Boriam prepared the food. Because they had been walking more slowly than anticipated, Boriam said their food supply would run very low by the time they were near any of the towns. "You assumed we'd spend just the minimum number of days to get somewhere? Isn't that badly planned?" Jonathan asked to which Boriam answered "It might be, but no matter which way we would've gone it would have been about the same amount of days before reaching a town. Now come on, let's translate this code." They sat down and Jonathan read out every other letter from each note as Boriam wrote them down in his book. When he had finished reading, Jonathan sat waiting as Boriam started to fill in the spaces between the words. Eventually he looked up and said "Okay, the text reads 'I am sorry I had to leave, they were after me. You will have to go to Draios Strag. I have seen darkness falling over it, and a Lion carrying the sun lights everything up again. For the boy' and then there's just random letters afterwards. I guess the next part is only for you, so she's put another layer of code on this part. You should keep the notes for yourself, and try to solve the bottom text as we go." Jonathan looked at the notes and mumbled to himself "Another layer? How important is it that Boriam shouldn't even see it?" To Boriam he said "What's Draios Strag?" Boriam looked at the boy and said "Draios Strag is the capitol of the human race. It was a gift from the gnomes. In their language, Draio is the word for city, and Strag means mountain. Draios Strag would translate to City of the Mountain." Jonathan sounded disappointed as he said "We'll have to go all the way up into the mountains to get there?" Boriam laughed and said "No, no. It's not a city in the mountains. It's a city made of a mountain." Seeing Jonathan's expression, he said "The gnomes spent over a decade carving the inside and the outside of a small mountain into a huge city. The walls of the city and the buildings are not placed on the ground as in a normal city, but they are carved out of the very ground on which they are standing." Boriam looked at what seemed to be a confused boy as Jonathan said "So what you're saying is that there was a mountain that the gnomes shaped into a whole city?" Boriam nodded and said "It'll be easier to understand when you see it." Jonathan nodded slowly, seeming to think about this before asking which way the city was. Boriam sighed and said "The quickest way would have been to turn left at the split we met earlier. Right now I think it's quicker to walk for half a day to the great crossroads ahead, and turn there. It's not too much of a problem that we didn't turn at the last split in the road." They sat discussing what the message from Stephie could mean while their food cooked. As they ate Jonathan asked "You said the Council must be gathering the military to attack a city. And Stephie wrote that a darkness was falling on Draios Strag. Do you think the Council is planning to attack Draios Strag?" Boriam shook his head in response, and said "As the city was made out of a mountain by the gnomes, the city is nearly as strong as a mountain. Until now the Council has only been attacking minor cities, towns and villages, as far as I know at least. If they were to attack the city, they would need a huge army." The boy nodded and said "What if the Council has such an army?" Boriam looked at the sky and said "An army that size is unheard of. Even when the great wars raged and the humans and the merfolk had formed an alliance, their army wouldn't have been big enough to attack Draios Strag. What I mean is: of course anything is possible, but based on earlier actions from the Council, it is very unlikely that they have such an army." Jonathan smiled and said "Good! I know we'll have to fight the Council eventually, but I honestly don't think I'm ready yet." Boriam looked at Jonathan and said "Then we should practice, no?" Jonathan grabbed the hilt of his sword in case Boriam attacked. Boriam laughed and said "No, no. With the Council's guards probably watching us, practicing fighting will only get us in trouble." Relaxing, Jonathan said "So what should I do to practice?" Boriam sighed and said "You know what to do to practice. You have to meditate."

Chapter 35
THE GREAT CROSSROADS

Jonathan looked at the old man and thought *'Meditate? That's practicing? Maybe I'm learning something important through the meditation now?'* To Boriam he said "Am I learning the next part of meditation now?" Boriam nodded and said "You won't only learn what is required for the next step, the next step will only take today to finish." Jonathan blinked a few times and asked "It's that easy to do? Why don't people do this more often then?" Boriam smiled and said "It really is very easy, but you must be able to do the other two stages before getting the desired effect out of it." Jonathan nodded and asked what to do. Boriam grinned and said "I will have to explain every single step to you. This is more of a procedure than a meditation. Once I've explained every single step to you, I'm not allowed to say anything until you've completed the procedure." Jonathan asked sceptically "What does the procedure do to me?" Still smiling, Boriam said "It unlocks your soul." Jonathan's mind raced *'Unlock my soul? Isn't the soul only a part of who we are? Isn't it just there? Is it locked up somewhere inside me?'* Boriam laughed and said "I know what you're thinking. I had the same questions when I went through it. Yes, right now the soul is a part of you. But you will see what I mean afterwards, don't think about what I said now." Then Boriam began explaining. "For this part, you will have to lie down on your back, without having your feet or arms touching either each other or your body. Don't force it out from your body, but keep them comfortably relaxed beside you. Keep your eyes closed through the entire procedure. Start the meditation by listening to your breath. When you know you have done this for long enough, listen to your heartbeats. Keep your mind quiet through the entire procedure. When you are finished with the second part where you listen to your heartbeats, the third part starts. In this part, you will have to inhale through your nose for seven seconds. Then you hold your breath for three seconds, before exhaling through the mouth for seven seconds. At the seventh second of exhaling, start the procedure again. After a while you will feel dizzy and your head will start to feel foggy. Don't be alarmed by this, but keep doing the procedure. After a while, a tingling will move from your head and down towards your chest. Observe this tingling and will it to move to different places of your body. Start with making the tingling go down your left arm. Following this, you must move the tingling into all of your fingers, and let it fill the entire arm. Expand the feeling to your left leg and toes, before continuing to your right foot and toes, and on to the right arm. When all of your limbs are filled with a tingling feeling, fill your chest and stomach. Keep doing the procedure while all of your body is filled with this feeling. Let the tingling get more and more intense, as if you're refilling your body with liquid. When you feel that the body is completely full, start shrinking the tingling feeling. Compress it to a dense lump of the feeling. Compress it as much as you can until there is a very tiny ball of it inside you. Keep the procedure going, and fill up the compressed ball until it doesn't change anymore. After this, open your eyes and start breathing normally. Then I will explain what this small ball inside you is." Jonathan nodded and lay down. Just before he started the meditation, Boriam said "Feel your body become heavy. As if it's pushing you onto the ground." Again Jonathan nodded and then closed his eyes. Starting with the breathing, he quickly felt himself relax, but he couldn't feel that he was being pushed into the ground. When the first step was finished, he switched over to listening to his heartbeats. The moment he did so, it felt as if his entire body fell asleep, becoming very heavy. He smiled quickly to himself, which broke the concentration and he didn't feel as heavy anymore. Spending some more time he soon got the feeling back, and this time he kept listening to his heartbeats. When he noticed that he had a steady rhythm to the beats, he started the breathing exercise. At first it was hard managing to spend seven seconds breathing in and out, and at first he forgot to hold his breath for three seconds. When he got the hang of it, he started feeling strange. Only four breaths into the method his head was dazed, and he felt like shaking it to wake up. Soon, just as Boriam had explained, a tingling started in his head. At first he didn't manage to shift it around inside him, but after what felt like ages the tingling spread from his head and down to his chest. At this point he was able to will it around as he wished. It was a strange feeling, and he almost started laughing, but something prevented him from doing so. He assumed it was the foggy head which made him unable to do anything except look at the moving tingling. He did as Boriam had explained and eventually managed to fill his entire body with this feeling. When he had done so, the feeling felt weak, as if it was stretched out. With every breath, however, he felt something being added to it. Soon, he could feel the tingling in every muscle in his arms and legs, and the feeling increased ever more. After what seemed like hours he was unable to feel any difference and he wondered if this was the limit. He mentally nodded to himself, which was a new experience to him, and started forcing the tingling inwards. Pushing and pushing, he felt the feeling increase in his chest as the feeling was compressed into a tight ball the size of a pea. When he had compressed as much of it as he could, he felt like the ball was a bit lower than his heart, at the centre of his chest. Continuing the exercise it felt like the ball got heavier. After a while, Jonathan noticed the ball seemed to change colour. The mass he felt inside him swirled between red, blue, green and pink, before ending up as a sort of golden colour. At this point a jolt shot through him and he took a deep breath from the shock. He opened his eyes, which had watered during the exercise. He lay quietly staring at the sky. It looked so much more blue than he could remember. He felt the earth move underneath him, and he heard birds sing even though there were no trees around him. *'Okay, the procedure makes you go crazy?'* he thought. Lifting his arms was a chore, and he felt he had to use all of his strength to do it. As he lifted the arm, he could feel every muscle in it working. He slowly sat up and looked around as the world was swirling before his eyes. When he breathed, it felt like he'd never breathed before in his life. He had forgotten that Boriam was there, but even though the old man started talking he didn't jump. The voice was just there. Boriam said "Focus on your hands, fingers, legs and toes." Jonathan did so, and the moment he mentally looked at his limbs he could feel that they were alive. He felt how his muscles worked as he closed his hands or lifted his legs. He looked at them in wonder, and Boriam said "I see you really have completed the third step. Congratulations." Jonathan looked back at the old man and said quietly "So what about this lump in my chest?" Boriam nodded and said "That is the point where the true you is. Your soul, your being. Whenever you have to make a choice about something, don't feel what your mind is saying, listen to what that point says. The ball itself is an energy deposit. Having completed step three, the energy in that spot should last for up to seven years. That is, if you don't use it of course. Did you notice a colour to it?" Jonathan nodded and said it was golden. Boriam smiled and said "Not many reach the golden one, they often stop at green or purple. I guess you reached the golden one because your parents taught you something when you were very young. This colour represent your magical finesse. Your ability to sense the energies in and around you. Now that you've completed this stage, I am willing to teach you a bit of magic. You won't learn much for now, but you were in a fire when you were small, so I'll teach you how to make fire." At this, Jonathan eagerly leaned forward to hear what the old man was saying. Boriam said "Imagine the fire you were in when you were younger. Use what you have learned now to force your muscles and nerves to remember the heat from that fire. To help you, you can hold your hand over the fire here." Jonathan did this, and at first he could only imagine the fire. He put his hand over the flames and searched for how the fire felt to his hand. When it was stinging a little he started to move the feeling up his arm, to his back and across the rest of his body. Boriam said "When you have a good feeling for how the flames live, grab a stick and point it at something." Jonathan found a stick and pointed it at a nearby rock. Boriam said "Good. Now feel the living fire inside you being forced into your hand, and as the pressure there increases, shoot it out through the stick." Jonathan imagined he gathered together all of the fire inside him and pushed it into his hand. It felt like his hand was going to explode. He pointed the stick at the stone, and forced the fire with one blast of energy out through the stick. The tip of the stick said 'poof' and a small stream of smoke came out of it. Then Jonathan fell asleep.

The next morning Jonathan woke up with his head and his hand hurting. His head was foggy as he stood up grunting and Boriam said "Good morning. Had a nice sleep? How are you feeling?" Jonathan sighed and said "In pain." Boriam laughed. Standing up, Jonathan asked "Was the little poof all I did? It felt like my hand was going to explode." Boriam nodded and said "You did it correctly, but you only focused on pushing it out to the tip of the stick, not to maintain it after you had pushed it out from the stick. It will take time before you manage this, but you should practice every day." Jonathan asked why he had fallen asleep, and Boriam explained that as he spent a lot of his energy on building and casting the fire, his body received a shock from the loss of energy. This shock resulted in his body reacting by suddenly falling asleep. Jonathan didn't really understand what he meant by this, but asked "Will I fall asleep every time I use magic?" Boriam smiled and said "At first, yes, probably. Until you master your focus, you will lose a lot of your energy. As we walk you should try to reach the ball of energy you created inside you yesterday. Notice how it feels and how it reacts to you. When you find out how, you will be able to use the energy stored there to do magic, lift heavier things than you normally could or refresh your senses and muscles." This Jonathan understood and as they packed up and left their camp he probed Boriam for more answers. For once he felt that the old man was willing to actually tell him something useful. They passed the camp where the guards again seemed to have left early in the night. After a while Jonathan asked "Why did I use a stick when I did magic? It seemed like a wand the old tales of magicians talk about." Boriam answered "At first it is very hard to make the magic go where you want. You need something to direct your focus in the right way. That's where the wand, as you mentioned, comes in. Then you can point at what to affect, and be able to do that. The thing you point with doesn't have to be a stick. A normal thing to use is your sword. It's ready when you fight, and it's something you are used to wielding. It's already a part of you, or at least supposed to feel like it." Jonathan eagerly asked "So

185

anything can work as a wand? My sword, a battle staff, even a whole tree if I am able to lift it?" Boriam laughed and said "Yes, even a whole tree. But I would think you would expend your focus on actually lifting the tree rather than pointing it at something specific. After training for a while, you will be able to create magic without using anything to gather your focus. But this will be a long time still." Jonathan sighed and said "Nothing you teach me is easy, is it?" Boriam didn't respond to this, so Jonathan wandered along thinking about how he had felt when he had tried to do magic. After some time, Boriam said "When you walk now, feel how your legs, back and arms work together. See them as individual parts belonging to the whole you." Jonathan blinked a few times and thought *So I shall see inside me how the muscles work?* He did this, and found that for every step he took, several muscles he didn't even know were there worked together to move him forwards. After some time Boriam laughed and said "Good, but you don't have to walk so fast." Jonathan looked around and saw Boriam a space behind him. "I didn't even notice I was walking quicker," Jonathan said as Boriam caught up to him. The old man smiled and said "That's one of the advantages of focussing on the muscles you use. They are able to move quicker than they normally could, without using more energy." Jonathan looked at Boriam and said "Without using more energy? How is that possible?" The old man laughed and said "Okay, it uses more energy, but the energy is taken from the storage inside you. Normally your muscles have an energy storage of their own, so when the energy is taken from somewhere else, you won't feel tired even though you move faster or longer." Jonathan stood thinking for a while about this as they walked on. After a while he asked "How long until we get to the crossing?" Boriam sighed and said "Once we're on top of that hill there, we should see it." Jonathan nodded and looked forward to being able to see their goal. He felt like it would aid his motivation to get there.

Jonathan noticed that he was quickly climbing the hill. His feet were tired, and he was getting sick of always having to get somewhere in a hurry. He looked forward to seeing the crossing where they were supposed to turn. Reaching the top of the hill he stopped and stared onwards across the field. "Oh, gods!" Boriam said as he got to Jonathan's side. They couldn't see the crossing. They couldn't see much of the field beneath the hill either. They could see a road which should lead out of the crossing, so nothing was actually wrong with the field below them. That is unless you counted a greater amount of people than Jonathan could ever have imagined as something wrong. Jonathan didn't even bother trying to count the tents. The mass of people stretched from about an hour's walk from the hill and all the way to the horizon. "How's that for an army?" Jonathan said and turned to Boriam.

Chapter 36
THE GRAND ARMY

Boriam's head hurt as he thought *'I really don't want to go to war now, I've done that enough in my life. Why does it keep happening?'* He sighed and said "Yes, that is a big army. I don't know if it is big enough to take Draios Strag though. It could damage the outskirts severely, but they shouldn't be able to take the city itself." Jonathan asked "What if they have people inside the city, who prevents it from finding out the attack is coming?" Boriam nodded and thought *'If a war is coming and they don't know about it, it is possible the city could fall. It is very unlikely, but they should get as many allies as possible to help.'* To Jonathan he suggested crossing the field to the next road leading out of the crossroads instead of going through the camp where someone would probably recognize him. "We'll have to get to Draios Strag as soon as possible. We'll have to walk both day and night, only taking small breaks." Jonathan nodded and found a path leading northwards down the hill from the road. The path led onto a marshland with puddles of water everywhere. Every now and then a frog would appear, croak and disappear again. They didn't talk as they went, in case the army had scouts hidden somewhere. Boriam assumed the army already knew they were there, but for now they let them wander the marsh as they pleased. Several hours later, with dripping shoes, they arrived at the next road leading out of the army's camp. Boriam sighed and said "Let's hope we can remain on the road until we get there." Jonathan agreed to this as they set their backs to the camp and headed down the road. It didn't take long before two guards on horseback caught up with them and asked why they had gone through the marsh instead of through the camp, so Boriam said "We saw the camp and felt like we would be unwelcome there. We didn't want to cause any inconvenience, so we went around instead." The bigger of the horsemen scowled at Boriam and said "And where are you going?" *'Crap. What other cities lie this way? Durums... No. Gren.. No,'* Boriam thought as his mind raced to the few maps he'd seen and said "We're going to Ilsberg, and after that onwards to Cornuris." The guards looked at each other as if having a mental conversation before the bigger horseman again spoke "You're just going from place to place? For what reason?" Boriam put his hands out and said "I've been around quite a bit in my day, and I've always told my nephew here about the places I've been. He wanted to see them for himself, so I'm taking him there." The guard looked sceptically around the immediate area and asked "Just the two of you? You're not afraid of bandits?" Boriam laughed and said "At my age there's no use being afraid of everything. As far as bandits go, I believe they are further south, closer to Uppheim." The guard nodded and said "That might be true, but there're always some around. If I were to attack you, you wouldn't have any way of stopping me?" *'A subtle, yet direct, way of asking if we would be a threat?'* Boriam thought as he sized the guard up. He said "My nephew is starting to learn how to use a sword, and I already know how. If you alone attacked us, we'd probably manage to fend you off. If you brought your army over there, we'd have some problems." He ended the sentence in a mocking tone and the guard gave a quick laugh before finally saying "Your nephew should join us in the military then, if he wants to learn how to fight." There was an underlying tone to the statement which Boriam didn't like, so he replied "Ah, yes, he is thinking about it. But not right now. It looks like you're getting ready for a battle, and he doesn't want to be thrown into it as quickly as that." Boriam stood patiently looking at the guard as he did some thinking. *'A military person who is actually taking his time to think. A rare one,'* Boriam thought just before the guard found out he couldn't manage to find any more questions. Reluctantly the guard let them pass and be on their way. The two guards turned their horses towards camp and left.

When the guards were out of hearing range, Jonathan said "I didn't think the guards would let us go." Boriam looked back towards the camp and said "They didn't really." Jonathan also turned and saw the small group of soldiers exiting the camp from the side entrance. He looked at Boriam and said "Those guys? But they're not following us." Boriam nodded and said "To trick us into thinking they will leave us alone. Did you see the dog?" Jonathan hadn't, so Boriam continued saying "It's a dog bred to track people. They set off in a different direction so we wouldn't be suspicious, and then from a slight distance they will follow us and see if we go where we said we would." Jonathan sighed and said "It's getting dangerous, isn't it?" Boriam nodded and they went on in silence.

A long time passed, and the sun was about to set when they reached a river. *'Hmm. We should rest now and get ready for a long walk tomorrow. If I'm correct, they won't attack us until we pass the crossing between Ilsberg and Draios Strag,'* Boriam thought and suggested to Jonathan that they should set up camp. When Jonathan asked about why they weren't going to walk all night, Boriam explained his assumptions. After some discussing and a lot of thinking, Jonathan agreed to set up camp. Boriam cooked a small dinner as

Jonathan tried to focus his energy. He picked up a stick and pointed it at the ground a little distance away from him. Once more the tip of the stick said 'poof' and he felt extremely tired. Not having instantly fallen asleep, Jonathan put it down as progress. They sat around the campfire discussing how Jonathan could manage to cast some real magic. Jonathan didn't understand too much of what Boriam was saying, but he understood that as soon as he was able to do it with one element, doing something with the others would be easier.

As Boriam had assumed, they were allowed to sleep through the entire night without being bothered by the soldiers. When they had packed up their camp and was starting to walk, Boriam said "At normal speed, we'll be at the crossing between Ilsberg and Draios Strag just before nightfall. We should make a camp a little before then, and eat the rest of our food." Jonathan looked questioningly at Boriam and said "Eat the rest of the food? Why?" Boriam nodded and said "We'll leave enough food for breakfast, but we won't be able to eat again until we get to Draios Strag. I assume the soldiers are still following us, or maybe they are already at the crossing waiting for us. The moment we turn to Draios Strag instead of Ilsberg, I believe they will attack us. More food in our bodies, means more energy to run, and less weight to carry." Jonathan understood what he meant, and didn't ask any more questions. Boriam started another story, about a little troll wandering out into the world. "How do you know so many stories?" Jonathan asked as the story finished. Boriam shrugged and said "I've been around, and these stories are the stories traditionally told in the training regime of our order. There is always some information in them, both hidden as well as directly, which you will have need of in the future. At first, my stories won't be that important to listen to, but it's smart to do so. Eventually I will be talking about more important things, and you will have to listen to every part of them. Maybe even listen to them several times." Jonathan nodded and said "So right now I don't have to worry about really listening to the stories. Good, I can worry about the great army following behind us." Boriam laughed and said "Worrying has never helped anyone. Makes your mind think about all the possibilities where one could fail. In the end you'll realize that nothing you plan for will actually happen, and only the moment will be what is important. Get used to this way of thinking and you'll be free from a lot of problems." "You can't just get used to not worrying until you do something," Jonathan said mockingly, but Boriam only asked "Why not?" Jonathan started arguing that you couldn't just stay calm when you knew something bad was about to happen. Boriam nodded and said "Worrying is a feeling. Feelings are imaginative things created by your mind, and the feelings your mind creates are always negative. When something sad happens you cry, but if you cry for something which has already happened, it's because the mind is reminding you of what has happened a long time ago. You already know that the mind can be stilled. If you do this at the times these feelings come, you will notice the moment you are in, and see that nothing is really wrong right now. At that moment your feelings will die and your emotions will take over." Jonathan interrupted, saying "Aren't my feelings and emotions pretty much the same?" Boriam shook his head and said "I think of them as different. The feelings are the things your mind is telling you to feel about, usually, something which has already happened. The emotions are usually what your body is telling you to feel about the moment you are experiencing. The past can be ignored when your mind is quiet. The moment will always be noticed when you learn to quieten your mind." Jonathan blinked a few times and asked "There are feelings that you can categorize under emotions too. From what you're saying, I mean." Boriam looked at the sky trying to figure out how to explain it differently. Eventually he said "Well, feelings are something you feel. While emotions are something you are. I usually don't compare it to emotion, but I figured it was easier for you to understand it. You feel sad, you are happy. You feel annoyed, you are at peace." Jonathan went quiet and didn't say anything for a long time. Boriam figured he'd understood a bit of it, and was still trying to figure it out completely. After a while, Jonathan said "People are sad some times as well." Boriam sighed and said "Yes, I guess you could say that, but that can only be truly used for someone who's sad about something happening right now." Jonathan lifted an eyebrow and asked "Right now?" Boriam shrugged quickly and said "Well, yes. Whenever the now is at the time of the sad occurrence." Boriam didn't think the boy truly understood what he meant about it, but Jonathan kept quiet after this.

After a long time, Jonathan said "It looked like something moved in the forest over there." Boriam looked up and saw the small forest they were approaching. He said "Good, you're starting to pay attention to your surroundings. The movement might be the guards following us, or maybe it's just an animal of some sort. Let's hope it's the latter, I don't think we'll get all the way to Draios Strag unharmed if we're attacked as soon as we approach the forest." Jonathan looked towards the forest again and asked "You can't do something about them?" Boriam sighed and said "Oh, I think I will have to do something, at some point. But I'm hoping not to have the need for it too much before getting to Draios Strag." Jonathan didn't argue with this, and watched as the sun crept closer to the ground. "Are we at the crossing soon?" Jonathan asked and pointed out that the sun was about to go down in the horizon. Boriam agreed and said that the crossing should be around the edge of the forest. He led Jonathan onto the field a bit away from the forest saying "We should make camp and eat the rest of our food. We'll probably have to run tomorrow, and the less we have to carry, the faster we can run." Getting a feeling they were being watched, they decided to take turns sleeping. "It won't be too good for the sprint tomorrow, but it will be better in case bandits actually are around these parts. They won't be as willing to attack us if they see that someone is paying attention."

Chapter 37
THE LINIMA

Nothing happened that night, but Boriam still felt keeping a guard was a smart thing to do. They packed up their camp, ate the rest of their food and started walking. As they walked along the forest Boriam could hear birds chirping, and thought *'Those aren't normal birds for this area. Still, it's very well done.'* He whispered this to Jonathan so the boy could start learning a bit about areas of the world. They turned the corner Boriam had mentioned, and could see the path turning a little away from the forest before the crossing. Boriam breathed a sigh of relief knowing that, even though arrows would reach, it would be harder to get struck by them. "Are you ready?" Boriam said to Jonathan as they neared the crossing. The boy nodded and Boriam could see him bracing himself while he asked "Will it be a long run?" Boriam replied "Yes, an hour and a half at least. You will be tired, but try to save as much of your energy as possible. Spend some of the reserves you stored in order to go further." Jonathan nodded understanding what Boriam meant. *'I really hope he'll manage to run for that long,'* Boriam thought as they stopped at the crossing. Still nothing had happened and they looked around as if wondering where to go. They still couldn't see anyone by the forest. Having got a short rest, they started the next part of the trip. They had only taken a few steps before an arrow struck the ground in front of them. *'Ah, and so it begins,'* Boriam thought as he turned around telling Jonathan to run. He saw several arrows in the air heading their way. He pointed at the ground and felt the magic well up in him. As the arrows got close, Boriam lifted his arms and clapped his hands together. This released the gust of wind he had built up, which blew the arrows back towards the forest. Then he turned and ran.

He could see that Jonathan was out of reach of the arrows by now, and again he pointed to the ground, letting the wind magic fill up inside him. He jumped, and the magic rocketed him forwards to where Jonathan was running. Landing heavily he forced his legs to move him forwards. Running besides Jonathan, he heard the boy breathe heavily and started wondering if he would manage the long run. He heard a dog barking behind them, and he put his thumb to his chest before, in mid-run, he put his fist to the ground. The earth magic connected him to the ground and he felt how the dog was running towards them. Or, as it seemed to Boriam, the dog was trying to run towards them, but was held back by something, or someone. *They probably haven't had time to take it off the leash. At least that's a relief,*' Boriam thought as he ran to keep up with Jonathan.

Half an hour passed and Jonathan was starting to slow down a little. Boriam spoke some encouraging words to the boy as he tried to get his speed up. Some of the things he said were just reminders of what might happen if they stopped, so he didn't really feel like they were encouraging, but they made Jonathan increase his speed slightly. Boriam felt his chest ache as his breath started to get heavy, and he thought *'Aging and having to run for one's life isn't such a good combination.'* He took big gulps of air as he forced his body onwards, every now and then sensing the ground to find out how far behind the pursuers were. They seemed to maintain the same pace as them, which puzzled Boriam. He knew that they should be able to gain on the two of them, or at least their dog should be able to take them down if it was released. *'Maybe I scared them with the magic I used to repel the arrows?'* Boriam asked himself.

They ran up a hill, and as they came to the top, they could see Draios Strag. Jonathan slowed down for a quick stop, gaping at the city as if being put in a trance. Boriam reminded him what was following them, which seemed to pull Jonathan to his senses. They knew they still had a long way to go, so they kept on running. Another half hour passed, and Boriam noticed the pursuers were starting to gain on them. He assumed they would be caught up with about half way to the city, so he wondered what they should do. After some grumbling Boriam said, breathing heavily "We'll run as far as we can. They will catch up with us, but I'm not sure where. We'll have to fight when they do." Jonathan barely managed to talk while he ran, and managed to gasp out "Okay." Boriam was annoyed that they were this close to the city, yet wouldn't manage to get there in time for safety. For some reason their pursuers had managed to increase their speed even more, and were starting to close in on them.

Eventually Boriam sighed and said "Okay, just stop. We'll need to have some breath left for when the fight comes. Get ready though, so quickly meditate to get your breath back." Jonathan fell and grunted as he hit the ground. Boriam pulled his sword and prepared himself as the boy started to rise from the ground. Boriam watched as Jonathan shakingly pulled his sword and got ready. Thinking this would be a tough fight, Boriam put three fingers in the air to prepare some fire magic. As he suspected, the enemy stopped, drew arrows and fired. Boriam looked at the seven arrows flying through the air. Feeling how the arrows were disturbing the air, he knew exactly where they were when he released the magic. Seven small explosions happened in the air simultaneously, blowing up all the arrows. The explosion didn't seem to affect the attackers as they quickly gained ground on them. As the first pursuer reached them and prepared to strike, Boriam raised his sword to block the blow. The clash of the swords made a loud noise, and Boriam looked sternly at the man while pushing backwards. Suddenly the man was struck by an arrow. As the man fell, Boriam blinked a few times wondering what had happened. He saw two more of their attackers fall with arrows in them, and wondered where they were coming from. Their pursuers seemed to have received good training, as they didn't mind much about their comrades dying in front of them, and were soon upon the two travellers once more. Boriam noticed Jonathan managing to fend off two of the attackers, and he focused on the two attacking himself. Having got rid of a few attackers already, Boriam managed to take down the two he was fighting. He saw an arrow hit one of the men attacking Jonathan. With only one attacker left, Boriam raised his hand to signal the archers, wherever they might be, to stop shooting. *This is Jonathan's fight,'* Boriam thought as he watched the boy fending off the attacker again and again. Boriam stood ready to attack in case Jonathan started having trouble, but he found the boy was doing fine considering it was his first real fight. The archers seemed to have understood the signal Boriam made, as he now could see two of them slowly standing up from the tall grass and walking towards them. As Jonathan's fight dragged out, Boriam thought *'He would not have survived this long in a war.'* He greeted two men carrying bows who wondered what was going on with Jonathan's fight. The two fighters seemed to be equally matched with every attack and parry, and Boriam found it amusing to watch. He told the archers "The boy is named Jonathan. He hasn't been using a sword for very long, but I think he's doing really well. I'll probably have to jump in soon though, so I'll have to pay attention. Don't want anything to happen at this point." The archers nodded and stood looking at the two fighters. Suddenly an arrow pierced the enemy's leg, and he fell to the ground. Jonathan was so focused on the fight he didn't seem to understand what happened, but as the man fell, he thrust his sword into the enemy's chest. As the man fell away lifeless, Jonathan turned a pale colour and stepped backwards dropping his sword. Boriam nodded and left the boy to himself as he turned to the archers. A third man was lumbering across the field towards them. "It was lucky you were here, we wouldn't have managed very well without your help, thank you." One of the archers looked at Boriam for some time before saying "You seemed to do pretty decently for an old chap." *'Old chap? What..'* Boriam thought and remembered where he'd heard that kind of speech before. "You're the Linima?" Boriam said and again received a searching stare before the archers nodded. "Our people were hunted by the Council. Some of us joined them, but most of us resisted. A lot of us died for that. The few who are left came here to be safe." Boriam nodded and said "But you're not very safe anymore, are you?" The man seeming to be their leader said "We seem to have a lot more bandits than usual these days, like the ones who attacked you." *Bandits. So they don't know,* ' Boriam thought as he looked between the three archers. The third archer was a woman with soft blonde hair with curls at the tips tied behind her neck. Boriam said "These weren't bandits. I need to see the king in Draios Strag urgently." The archers looked at one another and said "Many have said they needed to see the king. Some of them were bad, and almost made it to him. Why should we let you into the Great Mountain?" Boriam sighed and said "These people, although they might be dressed as bandits, were not so. Their clothing must be intended to trick you into believing they are. In fact, these men have followed us since we circumvented an army at the great crossing which is two days' walk to the south. From the size of the army, we wondered if Draios Strag knew about this. As it doesn't seem like it, there must be someone inside the city who prevents this information from reaching the king. This leads us to believe the army is set to attack Draios Strag." The archers looked at Boriam sceptically and said "Why should we believe you? There have been no signs of war here, and there has been no word about anything like this inside the city." Boriam reached into his shirt, pulled out a necklace and said "I am Boriam. You know what this necklace means. I know that it could've been taken from my dead body and used by the enemy, but that's all I've got to prove anything. Either you trust us, get us to the king and survive, or you don't trust us, kill us and die in the attack happening later." A frantic speech in a foreign language occurred between the three archers until their leader said "Okay. Lia will get you to the king. She knows the shortcuts you'll need inside the city to get there quickly. She'll tell the king that Miron here has headed to the place you claim to have seen this army. He is quick, and can run for days, so we should be able to verify the information soon enough if it's true." *The stealth and speed of the Linima are legendary. If any of it is true, we might actually have the information by tomorrow,* ' Boriam nodded and said "Thank you, make sure to stay safe, we need the information as soon as possible." Miron nodded, turned and ran. He went quicker than anyone Boriam had ever seen, and he found himself staring at the man speeding across the ground in front of him. Lia tapped his shoulder and gestured for Boriam and Jonathan to follow her. Boriam bowed to the leader, who headed back into the tall grass beside the road. Hurrying across the ground towards the city, Lia told them "The city has been wondering where all the traveling merchants and the usual crowd have got to, so it is a bit on edge. Many of the stores are awaiting deliveries from elsewhere, so their owners are a bit grumpy. The information the two of you have for the king would explain what is happening."

They approached the city, and Jonathan said he understood why it would be hard for anyone to attack the city. The gates were so big two trolls could walk comfortably beside each other at their full height, and the door for the gate itself was a meter thick slab of rock which was lifted from the ground. Boriam pointed at it and said "If anyone attacks, the guards above can cut a single rope, and the stone will come crashing down, held in place by the grooves at the side of the door." Jonathan looked wherever Boriam pointed and explained, and the similarity between Jonathan's face and the face of a child going into a caramel store sprung to Boriam's mind. He smiled, and kept pointing out details about the city, how some of the houses looked like mountains in their own right, and how every single house flowed organically into the ground. "Why is everything here white?" Jonathan asked, and when Boriam gave him a puzzled look, the boy explained "All the mountains I've seen have been grey in colour. If this city is carved out of a mountain, why is everything white?" Boriam laughed and asked "Have you ever heard of marble?" Jonathan had not, so Boriam said "It is a very strong type of rock, which is completely white. Only a few pieces of grey are in it. Once you polish it, you will get a very smooth and clean surface, as you see over there." He pointed at the wall of a building which was gleaming in the sunlight. Jonathan nodded, apparently understanding what Boriam had said. The archer asked "Is it long since you've been here?" Boriam nodded and said "Oh, it must be ten years or so since I was here last." Lia nodded and said "Then you're in for some changes. The king died a few years back, so his son took over the throne. He's made some mistakes, but not too grave ones, and he has learned from them. I think he can become a good king." *'Can become?'* Boriam thought as he started to become sceptical to how much the new king would listen to him. *'Oh well, come what may...'* he thought as they entered a tunnel he couldn't remember having seen before. Lia must have seen Boriam looking at the cave, and said "The king, in his early days, was attempted assassinated. So to make things a little more difficult for his enemies, he asked the gnomes to make these tunnels. There are several spread across the inner walls of the city, each leading into a sealed part of the castle. The king will have access to all the parts, but will only stay one day in each place. The other rooms the tunnels go to have guards in them, who will kill or capture anyone who enters." Boriam felt impressed by this, but hoped they took the right tunnel. He would have to ask how they knew which to choose later on. Lia pushed open a door to a great room with guards lined behind the entrance and along the walls of the room. Lia was approached by one of the guards, and she quickly whispered something to the man. The guard looked up at the two travellers and quickly entered through a huge doorway. They waited less than a minute before the guard opened the great doors and said "The king will receive you now."

Chapter 38
A SHRILL SCREAM ON THE MOUNTAIN

Arkenthan jumped out of bed and ran outside. The book had been so exciting that he hadn't noticed how much he needed to go to the toilet. As he crashed through the door he noticed Greypaws jumping upright in his pen, preparing to run after Arkenthan into the woods. As Arkenthan returned from the outhouse, Greypaws looked like he was wondering what was happening. Glancing upwards Arkenthan noticed it had grown dark, and went back inside to sleep. The next morning Arkenthan got up and felt drained of energy. After debating with himself for a while, he noticed his bag was still full of roots, mushrooms and berries. *'Did I forget to eat dinner yesterday?'* Arkenthan thought as his stomach screamed. He clenched his stomach with his hand, and carried the bag to the kitchen. Having looked over the scrolls of mushrooms, he found that only one of the ones he'd picked were poisonous. *'Glad I didn't eat that, then,'* he thought as he prepared the food. Boiling everything together, mashing some of the roots, he got a thick soup which was rich in flavour. He missed the taste of meat though, and decided to get some hunting done that day. When his breakfast was finished, his stomach seemed satisfied, even though it did feel a bit angry. Stepping outside he noticed Greypaws had gone. *'Probably out hunting?'* Arkenthan wondered and put his bow across his back. He stepped into the forest and immediately saw a deer. *'Well that's lucky,'* Arkenthan thought and quickly but silently got his bow out. The arrow hit the deer, but not exactly where Arkenthan had hoped, so the deer jumped frantically into the forest. He could hear the crashes as the deer fled inwards, and he cursed under his breath before running after the animal. He had hit the deer well enough, so the blood made for an easy trail to follow. As the sounds of the animal quietened, he slowed down and snuck onwards along the path the deer had taken. It didn't take long for him to see the deer lying on the ground apparently too weak to move any more. He didn't want the deer to suffer, so he put another arrow in it where he knew the animal would die right away. Arkenthan sighed and stepped over to the dead animal. The first arrow had been broken during the flight, but the tip could be reused and the second arrow was whole. He looked around and wondered where he was. At the same time another deer wandered close by, but with the newly shot animal in front of him Arkenthan didn't see the point in hunting another one. He didn't plan on heading back to the city for a while, so he didn't need that great of a storage. This deer would feed him for about a week. Grabbing the feet of the animal Arkenthan noticed it was way too heavy for him to carry. *'I wish Greypaws were here, maybe he'd carry it for me,'* Arkenthan thought and reminded himself that he would probably have to teach the wolf to carry some things. Imagining how he would have felt himself, Arkenthan imagined the wolf would be opposed to being suddenly loaded with things like a mule. He started chopping off the legs of the deer and tied them together using a string. Hanging the four legs over his neck he got up and started running back to his house. He didn't know where he had been, but the trail was still fresh, and the path was easy to see. As he loaded the legs into one of his barrels, he found a longer piece of rope and entered the forest again. Getting back to where he had shot the deer he was surprized to find that the deer hadn't been taken by anything. He tried lifting what was left of the deer and found it to be a decent weight now that the legs were gone. Even though it was easier to carry, Arkenthan spent a long time bringing the deer back to his house. Entering the garden, he was met by Greypaws who watched as Arkenthan cleaned out the deer and carried the leftovers into the forest. As he put the remains down, Arkenthan saw Greypaws step up to them and sniff the pieces. Using his paws, the wolf dug out a few of the parts that Arkenthan had thrown away, and ate them. *'I might not need to throw those kinds of things away when he's around,'* Arkenthan thought as Greypaws happily lumbered behind him.

When Arkenthan got back to his house, he roasted one of the deer legs, packed his bag with the food and some firewood, and went outside. He turned to the slope which led up the mountain and called for Greypaws to follow. He climbed upwards for a few hours before sitting down looking across the forest. Now that he knew where it was, he noticed the giant tree on the hill some way away, but wasn't surprised he'd missed it the last time he was up there. Walking a bit further upwards and around the mountain he had a view of the edge of the forest and of Garani village. If he strained his eyes he thought he could see movement, but he assumed this was his imagination. Back on the opposite side of the mountain he lit a fire. *'I don't really need the people from Garani to see where I live,'* Arkenthan thought as he tended the flames. Having got a good heat on the fire, he put the leg on a stick over the flames. While waiting for the leg to reheat, he walked a short circuit around the mountain and looked at Garani. The sun was so low now that the mountain cast a long pointy shadow. Right at the tip of the shadow lay the village. "Wow. That is awesome," Arkenthan said and thought *'I wonder if anyone in the village knows that? There should be a way to capture moments like this, so you could show them to other people.'* He sighed and watched as the shadow passed the village before returning to his meal. Greypaws lay quietly on the ground, apparently enjoying the sun as it rolled across the sky. Arkenthan took the leg off the fire, and cut a big piece from it. He was unsure if he would manage to eat all of it. Grabbing the rest of the leg, he stepped over to Greypaws and put the leg in front of him. Greypaws looked at Arkenthan as he went back to his piece of meat. The wolf seemed sceptical to the meat since it had been heated, and tested it a few times. Soon enough he sunk his teeth into it. Arkenthan grinned before grabbing his own piece of meat and doing the same. He marvelled at how long it had been since he'd been that messy with a meal. He felt like a wolf having felled a target after days of running. Eating the meat quickly and eagerly, it didn't take long for his hands to be full of grease from the meat. He finished his meal with a sigh and suddenly noticed how full he was. He sighed once more, and lay down to rest his stomach. A loud crack made him bolt upright. Another crack soon followed, and Arkenthan noticed that Greypaws was chewing the remains of the leg. He lay down and gave another sigh as his heartbeats and breathing returned to normal. His stomach ached, and he tried to relax while he watched the sun roll onwards towards the horizon.

Arkenthan was jolted awake without knowing he'd fallen asleep. He cursed as he noticed it had grown dark while he was asleep. Greypaws was still resting besides the embers of the fire, and Arkenthan had a feeling the wolf had been on guard while he slept. Greypaws stretched his legs when Arkenthan got up. "Come on, let's get back home. I don't want to be here too long in the dark," Arkenthan said. Greypaws tilted his head looking towards Arkenthan. He got the feeling the wolf wasn't actually looking at him, but somewhere behind him. Turning slowly around, Arkenthan stood face to face with the strange creature with the silver eyes. It had scales along all that Arkenthan could see of its body. Huge claws protruded from its paws and it had an ancient air which struck Arkenthan. The tip of the creature's face, where there were two great holes for the nostrils, blew a stream of air into Arkenthan's face. He screamed. So did the creature. A shrill and loud scream which carried across the forest. The creature then hurried up the mountain and disappeared into what Arkenthan assumed was a cave. He didn't think much of this though, as he turned and ran in the opposite direction down the mountain. Greypaws came crashing down the slope behind Arkenthan. He ran for half an hour, almost jumping his way down the mountainside, before getting to his garden. Arkenthan ran inside and jumped into bed. He stayed there until the shaking stopped. Then he lay there until his limbs were under his command again. After this, he slowly went outside again to see Greypaws sitting at the edge of the garden. "Don't grin like that. Why didn't you try to scare it away?" Arkenthan said half annoyed and half jokingly to Greypaws. The wolf tilted his head and Arkenthan said "Is it behind me again?" He then quickly looked behind him, but was met with the expected emptiness. *Why didn't you try to scare it away?'* The question remained in Arkenthan's head, and his mind searched for what the reason could be. It drifted to the scrolls in the bookcase, and he quickly went inside to look at them. There were several scrolls picturing different animals. Looking through them, he finally found something that looked like the animal. He read out "Unable to produce its own heat, the lizard spend most of the day in the sun. Most types of lizard are carnivorous, mostly feeding off insects or small rodents like mice. Some types of lizard feed off plants instead of meat. The average lizard is about 30 centimetres long, but they can become up to one meter." Arkenthan looked at the ceiling and thought *Well, this one was definitely more than that. Maybe Greypaws knew it only ate plants, and therefore didn't see it as a threat? It did run away when I started screaming, instead of attacking me.'* He pondered for a while before starting to feel tired.

The next morning Arkenthan went back up the mountain, finding the campfire from the night before. He looked upwards trying to find the cave the lizard had run into. Trying to remember what had happened the night before, he looked at an area he assumed would be the right one. *The huge creature must have a pretty big cave to hide in. It shouldn't be much of a problem to spot it when I'm nearby,'* Arkenthan thought and started walking. The cave couldn't be far up, as the creature had disappeared quickly when he had screamed. Remembering what direction the creature had run off to, Arkenthan kept walking. It wasn't until he had almost reached the top of the mountain that he felt that something was wrong. He turned around and thought *There's my camp far below, this is the direction the creature ran. So where did it run off to?'* He felt annoyed that he had missed the cave, and headed back down, circling back and forth. When he reached the campfire again he sighed. His head was aching with confusion, so he sat down to rest and ponder. It didn't help that his mind kept going in what he felt was the wrong direction. He started meditating, thinking it would help. He soon quieted his mind and went over to focusing on his heartbeats. He recognized the feeling described in the book, and soon felt completely at peace. After sitting like this for a while he could start hearing the wind and the nearest rivers, and he started wondering if the resetting of his tiredness described in the book could actually be done. *I'll have to test it,'* Arkenthan thought, jumped up and started running down the mountain like the night before. Reaching the bottom of the mountain, entering his garden, Arkenthan felt tired. He didn't think he was quite tired enough, and continued running in a large circle around his garden. After a while he reached a point where his legs didn't want to carry him anymore. Before his body collapsed, Arkenthan stopped and gasped for air, making the spots disappear from his vision. He sat down and started focusing on his heartbeats. At first his mind complained, but he soon quietened it. Then a shock went through his entire body. It felt like something kicked him hard in the chest, and he struggled to breathe. Clutching his chest he felt like it lasted for several minutes, even though he knew it only lasted for a few seconds. When the shock passed, he felt that his heart had a steady rhythm, and his breath was easy. He stood up and noticed his limbs felt fine, as if he'd just rested. He felt extremely hungry though, and thought *'I guess everything didn't reset itself.'* He went inside and drank a mug of water, and put a leg of the deer on the spit over the fire. He assumed Greypaws would be outside when it had finished cooking. He grabbed his bow and sword, and stepped outside. After shooting several arrows at a target, he unsheathed the sword and adopted a stance. He fought an invisible foe for a long time, until his stomach twisted so hard he fell over. Having forgotten about the food he went inside to a smoke-filled room with a charred leg above the fire. Arkenthan lifted the leg down, and tested the meat with his knife. Luckily, the meat was only burned on the outside, and the rest was good enough. He cut the outer layer off the leg, where the charred meat was. What was left of the leg was just enough for Arkenthan who thought *'Wow, I don't think I've ever eaten this much. That must be the downside to what I did earlier.'* He cleaned the rest of the leg, and brought the bone outside to Greypaws. The wolf eagerly started chewing the bone, and it didn't take long for it to start cracking under the strong jaws of the beast. Arkenthan smiled and lay down in the grass beside the wolf. *'I'll have to go to town soon,'* Arkenthan thought, reminding himself that he had to start learning how to fight with a sword.

Chapter 39
FENCING LESSONS

A few days passed, as Arkenthan gathered wood and hunted for food to trade in town. When he felt that he had enough food, he put a large amount of it in bags across Greypaws' back, and led the wolf towards town. At first the great beast resisted the bags, jumping around to throw them off, but eventually he accepted the weight and followed Arkenthan. *'Let's just hope he will follow me all the way to town,'* Arkenthan thought and put a hand to Greypaws' side. Hours passed as they walked through the forest without anything special happening. As they entered the area where the lake was, Arkenthan stopped. *'That was a strange sound, wasn't it?'* he thought and looked around him. Again he heard the sound, and this time he thought it was someone laughing. It came from upriver, so he slowly made his way in that direction. As he turned a bend in the river, he saw someone at the edge of the river. The creature, which Arkenthan thought resembled a tiny human, looked up and quickly disappeared into the forest. Arkenthan blinked a few times and tried to recollect what he'd seen. It looked like a little girl, with a big head full of curly hair. The hair had branches and moss in it, and he had a feeling the girl's nose wasn't quite the way he expected. He couldn't remember exactly why though, as the rest of the memory disappeared from the short encounter. *'Who was that?'* Arkenthan thought as he turned back to where Greypaws stood waiting. The wolf tilted his head as Arkenthan approached. "I don't know Greypaws, something strange is going on in this forest," Arkenthan said and started to take the bags off Greypaws' back. He pulled out a piece of meat and gave it to the wolf as a reward for carrying everything all the way. He grabbed the heavy bags and felt glad he didn't bring it all alone. The weight even threatened to drag him to the ground in the short distance to town. He put another piece of meat down in the clearing and told Greypaws to stay there. *'Let's hope he actually does it this time,'* Arkenthan thought as he slowly walked through the remainder of the forest.

When he stepped out of the forest, a cart came rolling up the road. "Ho, now. Heavy bags ye got there. Need a ride?" the driver said and

Arkenthan thought *Well, why not?'* He nodded to the driver and lifted one bag at a time onto the cart. Sitting down beside the driver his mind returned to the little girl in the forest. It wasn't until they got to the edge of town that the driver said "Quiet guy, you." Arkenthan looked at the man questioningly, and the man said laughing "You haven't even said where you're heading." Arkenthan looked at the approaching village, and said "Just in there. To the butcher's." The driver nodded and left Arkenthan to his own thoughts until he stopped outside the butcher's door. Arkenthan thanked the driver and unloaded his bags. Jonas came outside and saw Arkenthan with the overloaded bags. "How did you manage to get those all the way here?" Jonas asked and not wanting to alarm the driver of the cart, Arkenthan said "Oh, you know. A friend helped me most of the way." Jonas nodded and said "And this friend of yours didn't want to join you here?" Arkenthan grinned and said "He's had a bad experience with this village. I don't think he'd want to enter here for a while." The butcher laughed and lifted one of the bags inside the store. Arkenthan thanked the driver again who nodded and drove on. After carrying the last bag inside, Arkenthan helped the butcher sort out the meat. "Nice catch this, I just hope I'll manage to get it all sold before it goes bad." Arkenthan looked at the sorted meat and said "Well, it seemed like it all went quickly last time I was here, so why not now?" The butcher grunted and rummaged around in his till. Soon he returned with a small stack of money. Arkenthan counted eighteen silver pieces and looked at the butcher. "For getting all this here, you deserve that," Jonas said and started loading the meat into his storage before looking up saying "Oh, colonel Locke has been asking for you. You should head over to their tower and ask for him." Arkenthan nodded and went up to the room with his things.

Arkenthan was already running down the street when he thought *Where is this tower anyways?'* He stopped and looked around wondering where he was. A man passed him, so he asked "Excuse me, I am heading to the guards' tower, but I don't really know where it is. Could you help me?" The man looked at Arkenthan and said "Ah, the forest boy! Oh, uhm.. The tower is down this street and to the left. Near a small plaza." Arkenthan blinked a few times and said "What do you mean by 'forest boy'?" The man lifted a finger and said "No, no. Can't talk now, busy busy." He then ran off down another street. When the man had disappeared, Arkenthan remembered it was the same man whom he'd chased into a blind alley where the man had disappeared. "Strange," Arkenthan muttered to himself and turned back down the street. Not long after, he was knocking on the door to the tower. It wasn't a big tower, as Arkenthan had imagined, but more of a rounded house with a pointy roof. It looked like a tower though, and Arkenthan imagined it as a big tower which had sunk into the ground leaving only a height of two floors sticking out. He laughed at himself just as a guard looked through the peephole. The guard looked at Arkenthan and the boy stared straight back at the guard. "You're the guy with the beast," the guard eventually said. Arkenthan continued to stare at the guard who said "What is your business here?" Arkenthan explained that the colonel had been asking for him, and that he was to seek him out at the tower. The guard opened the door and said "I'm afraid the colonel just went on patrol along the forest edge. He's probably at the outskirts of the city by now. I'll tell him you dropped by." Arkenthan nodded and said "Thank you. I'll probably be leaving again tomorrow though, so he'll have to find me before then." The guard nodded and closed the door. Arkenthan turned away from the tower, and made his way to the smithy to say hi to Horace. He seemed to have grown an even bigger beard since Arkenthan saw him last, but he didn't comment this. Eventually he turned across the street and knocked on Johannes' door. The man took a long time before opening his door, but Arkenthan forced himself to smile when he eventually did. "It's you," Johannes said and Arkenthan got the feeling he wasn't very welcome. "You said you would teach me sword fighting?" Arkenthan said as he put out his hand. The man nodded without taking it and stepped aside, letting Arkenthan enter.

The entrance had several swords hanging on the wall. To each side of the hallway were rooms where Arkenthan assumed Johannes was living. The man led Arkenthan through the hallway and out a back door to a great empty square. Surrounded by buildings, Arkenthan understood why he hadn't seen this place before. Johannes grabbed two wooden swords and stepped into the centre of the plaza before turning towards Arkenthan. "I do not claim to be the best swordsman in the world. I am far from it, but I am one of the best in this village. First, I will test your skills. This will tell me why you wish to learn sword fighting. I will not train those who wants to fight in order to fight, but I will train those who will fight for the fight." Johannes said and Arkenthan blinked a few times unable to understand what the man meant. Gesturing Arkenthan towards a spot, Johannes threw one of the wooden swords to Arkenthan. As he did so, Arkenthan had a flash of something he'd envisioned while reading the book in his house. It was of the sparring Boriam and Jonathan had done, and that Boriam always attacked without Jonathan being prepared. As the sword flew through the air, Arkenthan turned to grab the sword and was immediately ready for an attack. It happened exactly as Arkenthan had assumed, but it didn't happen with the force he had anticipated. That is, it happened a lot more forcefully than he had imagined. Arkenthan missed the parry, and received the sword of Johannes straight in his stomach. He gasped for air as the sword struck, and he rolled away to recover. Having barely got his breath back and risen to his feet, the next attack came. It was exactly the same attack, so this time Arkenthan managed to parry it the way he'd taught himself from the scrolls. Johannes seemed surprized by this, and when he attacked again, Arkenthan had taken the time to find his stance. He managed to parry a few more attacks before the sword was thrown out of Arkenthan's hands. "Good!" Johannes said. "I can teach you some things. Who taught you to use a sword? Your grandfather?" Arkenthan shook his head and said "I've never really fought with a sword before, only mock fights with an invisible foe. Why?" Johannes put a hand to his chin and looked at Arkenthan. "Go back to your stance again," he said and Arkenthan did so. Johannes walked around Arkenthan poking and prodding him, but didn't say anything. Eventually Arkenthan said "Finding anything interesting?" Johannes grinned and said "I've seen your stance before. Only the very old sword masters use it. It's so old that very few people know about it. The technique itself is very efficient, but it is so hard to master that people don't bother learning it. The fact that you have this stance naturally tells me you're keen to learn swordsmanship, not just learn how to fight." Arkenthan looked at his stance for a while before looking back at Johannes asking "You can teach me how to use this stance effectively?" Johannes sighed and said "Alas, I can not. I know a bit, which will help you understand it better, but I only saw this as a child. I can't teach you many useful things for this technique. I don't think there are many people left in this world who could do that really." *'Only the scrolls in my house then?'* Arkenthan thought. "So what can you teach me in order to learn more?" Johannes attacked. Arkenthan was not ready, and received a hard smack to the back of his head. "I can teach you to be ready, and to get used to your sword." Johannes said. *'Ow. Is this generally how to learn sword fighting or something? It seems every teacher just suddenly attacks the student,'* Arkenthan thought and got ready. When the next attack came, he was expecting it. He tried to remember what the scroll had said about parrying and attacking, but as Johannes attacked, it all disappeared. "When I know how to do something, for instance how to block your attack, why do I forget what to do the moment you actually do attack?" Arkenthan asked and Johannes smiled before saying "I have a feeling you know more about fighting than you think. But what you're saying is common. In the heat of battle, all your senses turn to what is happening where you are. Your mind is too slow to react during a fight. This is why you have to teach your muscles how to fight, not just your brain. When your muscles know this, you are able to fight effectively and precisely." Arkenthan nodded, and Johannes attacked again.

By the end of their session, Arkenthan felt bruised and battered. Reaching the bed above the butcher's store he fell asleep even before he had lain down. The next morning his muscles were sore, and he felt weak as he stepped down the stairs. He helped Jonas out in the store for a while before finding that it was time to go home. By then he had warmed up his muscles a little and figured he should get moving before they stiffened, or he'd never get back. Before leaving town, he went to the guards' tower again and asked for the colonel once more. Again Arkenthan got the message that the colonel was out on patrol. Arkenthan sighed and left the village. With the bags empty, it was a lot easier to walk back to where he'd left Greypaws the night before. As he entered the clearing he saw that Greypaws had left. "Not really surprizing," Arkenthan mumbled to himself and thought *'I really hope there're no bears or anything around. I don't think I can run for very long today.'* He sighed and started walking. An hour into the forest he heard something running next to the path. He couldn't see anything, but was sure something was there. *'It's not heavy enough to be a bear, or even any big game. It must be smaller, but not a rabbit or a badger,'* Arkenthan thought as he tried to analyse the sounds coming from beside him. As he walked on, the sound of running feet followed him. "Hello?" Arkenthan said in a low tone. No answer came, not that he'd expected one. He heard some bushes rustle further along the path. Looking ahead he could see something running across the path, but he was unable to say what it was. Feeling like something was watching him, he slowly made his way onward. Suddenly an "Eep!" and a crash was heard, and Greypaws stepped onto the path. Looking at the beast, Arkenthan could see no signs of alertness or danger. *'If he's calm, I guess I should be too,'* Arkenthan thought and greeted the wolf. He still had the feeling someone or something was watching him, but he felt safer now that Greypaws was with him. His muscles were starting to get very sore and very stiff now, and Arkenthan spent a lot longer than usual getting home. Once in a while he thought he heard the crash of something big beside the path, but nothing tried to prevent him from getting home.

Chapter 40
CHALLENGING A FJÄLLBEAR

That night Arkenthan dreamt of his mother. She was looking out the window of their house, holding a pile of paper in her hands. He saw her get more paper and start writing something. Soon, a bird knocked on the window, and his mother gave it the paper with writing on it. The bird then flew away. The dream followed the bird soaring high above the ground, across fields and forests. It passed a great field where two armies stood on either side. As his view closed in on the two armies the sky turned dark and heavy. The dark sky sank lower and lower until it engulfed the two armies, at which point Arkenthan woke up with a jolt.

Upon waking up, Arkenthan quickly sat up in bed. As his muscles were still sore, they made him lie down again to relax. The dream made him miss both his mother and his home town. *I wonder how she is? Maybe the pile of paper she held symbolized the letter I sent her?*' he thought and started to hope his mother would reply to him. After a while he slid out of bed and stood wobbling on the floor. *I don't think I'll get much done today,*' Arkenthan thought as he barely managed to move the kettle from the kitchen bench to the fire. He massaged his arm as he waited for the water to boil. He noticed the sky outside was a pale colour, and mist lay over the ground. "Creepy... I like it," Arkenthan mumbled to himself. He opened the door and smelled the cool air outside. '*Oh, no. Winter must be getting close,*' Arkenthan thought and went back inside. He went to the bookcase and found a blank piece of parchment. Using coal from the fireplace he noted down that he had to fill his stock of wood, and get herbs and roots before winter truly arrived. He hung the piece of paper on the wall by forcing a knife into one of the cracks. *I'll add to it as I go along,*' he thought as he went to his barrels. He still had a lot of meat, so he picked up a whole leg of the deer he had shot some days earlier and went outside. "Greypaws!" he shouted trying to get the wolf to come. He had to call a few times, but after a while a white furry head poked out of the forest. Arkenthan smiled and said "Here, you've probably already eaten, but if you want it you can have it." He then went to the wolf's pen and put the meat beside it. It didn't take long for the leg to be picked up by the wolf, and Arkenthan could soon hear the sound of bones crushing. "I really am glad you don't try to hunt me anymore," he said airily to the wolf. Turning one eye the wolf kept a watch over Arkenthan as it ate. He sighed and went inside to prepare his food. He threw several pieces of meat and herbs into the now boiling pot of water before laying down in bed. He immediately fell asleep again.

This time he dreamt about six crows. Each crow was, as crows are, black, but instead of the white or grey line they each had their own coloured line. They were picking on a giant walnut, poking holes in different parts of it. He didn't feel they were picking on it to get to the food though. When a crow had finally managed to make a hole in the shell, it jumped to a new spot and began anew. Arkenthan suddenly felt scared as the crows kept tearing down the shell, and he ran towards them scaring the crows away. The crows attacked him, and in response he pulled a sword which was hanging by his side. The fight was a long one, but eventually he raised an arm and one of the crows burst into flame. At this, the rest of the crows fled. Arkenthan sighed and went to look at the nut. He picked it up, and from inside the shell he saw a small man climbing out to greet him and thank him. As he saw the man, Arkenthan woke up from his dream. He blinked a few times looking at the ceiling. He wondered where he was before remembering that he had fallen asleep while waiting for his food. "My food!" Arkenthan half said to himself as he sat up in bed. His muscles were still sore, but not as much as earlier. He flexed his fingers and looked at the kettle. It was overflowing, spilling a lot of water and stew onto the flames beneath. All the water threatened to put the fire out. "Aaaah!" Arkenthan yelled as he ran to the fire pit to save both his food and his fire.

The sun had come out, warming the world and scaring the mist away. *'I guess this is one of the last days I can, without freezing, swim in the lakes. I'll have to go there when it gets a little hotter,'* Arkenthan thought, sitting on the roof of his house, savouring the sun. A small stone bounced off the roof and landed beside him. Arkenthan looked carelessly at it and saw similar stones spread across the roof. He got up and started picking them up. Having gathered all the stones on the roof, Arkenthan started throwing them towards the well. He gave himself one point for each stone which fell into the well. After half the stones were thrown, he hit one into the bucket. *'That's got to be worth three points at least,'* he thought, amusing himself. In twenty stones he got nine points, and figured he would have to get better than that. Lying down on the roof of his house, he felt the sun warm his sore muscles.

After lying there for a while, he got down, grabbed his bow and sword and entered the forest. With Greypaws following him, Arkenthan noticed how peaceful the forest made him feel. A bird sang to his left, and was answered by another bird to his right. He sighed, and turned towards the little lake with the coloured rocks. As he reached the edge of the forest, Arkenthan noticed that he wasn't the only one planning to go for a swim that day. Several different animals were grazing by the water's edge, and some were jumping into the lake. He saw the water splash into the air as some of the animals jumped in. There were several hares in the grass, a few deer with cubs, two strange looking big birds which Arkenthan had never seen before, and a few other types of game. Greypaws came up to him and Arkenthan could see the wolf preparing to attack. "Greypaws, no," Arkenthan said in a calm tone. "Today we're just here to relax. If you want to hunt, do it somewhere else." He put his hand up in front of the wolf and it seemed like Greypaws understood him, as he stood up and stopped the low growl he had started. Arkenthan stepped calmly into the clearing, and as Greypaws followed, every animal seemed to notice that they were there. Arkenthan stopped and made Greypaws stop as well. *'I don't want to scare them away from the area for when I have to hunt them,'* he thought, and sat down. The sun was shining where he sat, and he sighed contently marvelling at the playing animals. Greypaws laid down beside him, and some of the animals seemed to relax a bit more. A few of the animals, which Arkenthan thought of as the older ones, kept a watchful eye on the pair of them. The younger animals however, who hadn't had to survive for as long as the older ones, soon returned to their playing. Arkenthan slowly got up, and signalled for Greypaws to stay where he was. A strange birdsong arose behind him, but soon disappeared again. He put his weapons down beside Greypaws and said "Protect these for me please." *'That's it, I must've gone completely mad now. Maybe I've become the crazy old man from the forest,'* Arkenthan thought as he slowly made his way towards the lake. He looked back and saw that Greypaws had laid down again. Nodding, to both the wolf and himself, Arkenthan slowly lowered himself into the water. The animals around them seemed to pay the two of them a lot of attention, but all Arkenthan could think was *'This is so cool. I am actually in the middle of a pack of animals, in a huge forest, taking a bath.'* He sat down on a big rock in the lake, bringing the water up to his chest. The water was perfectly heated, and the sun was just past its apex, so Arkenthan knew it would stay like that for a long time. He let the water relax him as he sat there amongst the playing animals. Out of nowhere, a big crash was heard and suddenly a fjällbear stood in the clearing. Shocked, Arkenthan looked at the bear unable to understand what had happened. As the bear growled and the animals started bounding into the forest, Arkenthan pointed with two fingers at Greypaws who looked back at him. He turned and let the arm point at the bear. As the bear started towards the water, Greypaws bounded off the ground and landed in front of it growling, blocking its path. Arkenthan saw that the bear and the wolf were about the same height. He knew that

Greypaws would probably be a bit quicker than the bear, but the bear would be much stronger than the wolf. *I'll have to help in some way,'* Arkenthan thought and scrambled out of the water. As the growls of the two animals grew louder, Arkenthan ran for his bow. He picked it up and knocked an arrow onto the string. Turning, he saw the two animals dancing around each other, neither wanting to back off. *I don't want to hit Greypaws. What shall I do?'* he thought as he was unable to see where he could shoot the bear without the danger of hitting Greypaws. The bear swung its paw, hitting Greypaws in the side. The wolf tumbled sideways, and in that short moment before the wolf scrambled onto his feet, Arkenthan pulled the arrow to his chin, aimed and let go of the string. As if in slow motion, Arkenthan saw the arrow fly towards the bear. With the arrow still flying through the air, Greypaws had managed to get to his feet, and jump towards the bear. The bear stood on its hind legs, getting ready to bash Greypaws on the head, when the arrow pierced its front paw. The bear roared and lowered itself to the ground. This new turn of events must have surprized Greypaws, as he struck the bear's face with his shoulder. The shoulder itself hit the mouth of the bear, ripping open a big wound. Greypaws fell to the ground, and struggled to get back up. Arkenthan pulled his sword and, screaming, ran towards the bear. With its wounded paw, the bear turned its head and noticed Arkenthan. The bear looked back at Greypaws who was labouring his way back onto his feet. Arkenthan saw the bear look back at him before turning towards the forest and fleeing on three paws. Feeling guilty about the bear, wondering if it would survive with the arrow through its paw, Arkenthan slowed down. He dropped the sword and ran to Greypaws who was staggering upright. "Come on, you can do it. Stand up, and we'll get home to clean your wounds." As Greypaws struggled to get up, Arkenthan ran to get his things.

Getting home, Arkenthan hurried into the house, retrieving the potion he'd made with Johanna. Outside, Greypaws had laid down in his pen, and was trying to reach his wound with his mouth. Arkenthan came to the wolf's side, and tried to push his head out of the way. Greypaws didn't seem to like this, as he uttered a low growl, which made Arkenthan pull back for a bit. He sat down staring at the wolf, who was trying to lick the wound clean. He sighed and kept looking at Greypaws until the wolf gave up reaching the wound. When he did, and had put his head down, Arkenthan stood up and went to the wolf's side. He examined the wound to see if it needed any cleaning, and found that a tooth of the bear had broken off inside Greypaws' shoulder. Pulling it out, with barks and growls from the wolf, Arkenthan showed it to him and said "Is this what you were trying to get out?" He put the tooth in a pocket and made sure there were no more dirt or teeth in the wound. The potion had a red and orangey colour, but as he dripped drops of it onto Greypaws' shoulder it turned a green colour and Arkenthan thought *'Wow, I wonder if it always does that?'* After having coloured the entire wound green, Arkenthan stopped applying the potion and hoped it was enough. *'It is more than Johanna said I'd need,'* he thought and watched as the wolf seemed to be more relaxed. "I guess I'll have to get food for us both for a few days, won't I?" Arkenthan said to the now sleeping wolf. He sighed and went inside to prepare some food for them both. "I wonder how much he actually eats?" Arkenthan said to himself as he got a lot of meat out of his barrel. Some of the meat he hung above the fire to roast, but most of it he brought outside for Greypaws. The smell of the food seemed to awaken the wolf as he lifted his head looking at Arkenthan. "Here you go. It's almost the last of my food, so I'll have to hunt tomorrow. I hope this is enough for you," Arkenthan said, putting the meat down in front of Greypaws who answered by putting his tongue out before sniffing the meat. Arkenthan saw that the green wound was starting to turn bluish, and wondered if it was supposed to do that. *'I hope my muscles aren't as sore tomorrow, I have to hunt something,'* Arkenthan thought as he went inside to eat. After dinner, Arkenthan spent the rest of the evening reading his book. *'The king, Jonathan noticed, was much younger than he assumed a king should be.'*

Chapter 41
THE LAST OF THE THIRTEEN

Jonathan looked at the king, surrounded by guards, and thought *'He can't be more than ten years older than me.'* As they got closer, he noticed the guards were standing in a way which would make it very easy for them to fight if they had to.

The king rose from his throne and said "I hear you have urgent news? I am a busy man, but when one of my city's head guards guides you here herself I figure it's necessary to hear what you have to say. I can't seem to remember seeing you before, where are you from?" Boriam bowed, and as Jonathan noticed this he bowed as well. "We have travelled far" Boriam said. "I am from many places, but you have seen me before Myrtis. I remember you as a five year old boy, with your messy blonde hair full of mud from playing in the streets. I understand that you don't recognize me. This here is Jonathan. He's from Shadowtree, one of the hidden villages far to the west. He is following me on my journey. My name is Boriam, and as an old friend of your father, I had hoped to meet you as king bearing better news." Myrtis looked thoughtful as he said "I recognize the name Boriam from somewhere, but I cannot remember from where. I guess we will find out eventually, but please, tell me this news you have." Boriam nodded and explained their observations in Fisherman's Rest, their trip upriver and all the occurrences on the way until the great crossroads. He followed by explaining their assumptions on the hike from the army until they were attacked outside the city. "And you think this army is big enough to bring down my city? And why haven't I heard of this army gathering?" Myrtis said with one portion of concern and one of mockery in his tone. Boriam sighed, and said "I can see how this is hard to believe. The army is big enough to do great damage to this city even if you were prepared for it. As of right now, however, I wouldn't say you were very well prepared at all. Unless you start preparations immediately, it could very well be that the army will manage to take down this great city." King Myrtis looked thoughtfully out a window for a while before asking "How can I trust you? You say you have met me before, but I am still not sure about who you are.

Is anyone out there now trying to confirm this information you bring?" Boriam nodded and explained that the man named Miron was on the way there now to corroborate the information. "Or you've just sent one of my best men to his death," Myrtis pointed out, and Jonathan thought *Not easy to convince this guy, is it?'* Boriam and Myrtis talked back and forth for a while, but for every insurance Boriam offered, Myrtis had a counterargument. Jonathan sighed and sat down in a chair standing by the wall while they kept at it. Eventually, Myrtis said "I understand that you are warning me about an attack, and that preparing for it would do no harm if it were only this I had to prepare. If this army really is as strong as you say, and heading this way, I will have to call upon our allies to help us. If I do this, their cities will be empty, ready for the Council to strike there. I need something to convince me that you are on our side, and that I can trust you both." Boriam sighed and nodded before again pulling out his medallion. "Ah." Myrtis said. "That's where I have your name from. You are actually that Boriam?" Boriam nodded and said "I am Boriam of the Whispering Wind, the Sixth of the Thirteen."

Jonathan stared at Boriam thinking *The Sixth of the Thirteen? He's one of the Thirteen? But.. He's one of the Lions, not the Thirteen. I.. So that's why he agreed to me following him. My parents wanted me to learn from the Thirteen, and he is one of them?'* He felt like everything around him turned dark and he could see nothing but the thoughts in his head. All he heard was the drumming of his heartbeats in his ears, but eventually Boriam's voice cut through again saying "I am, unfortunately, the last of us Thirteen. I have one pupil left, and that is Jonathan. If you want to trust me now, I will aid in what I can. If not, then there's not much more I can help you with until the attack actually happens. If you will trust me on this, then Jonathan needs weapons training before this war. I had hoped your best man could help him with this. I will help to draft a strategy to defend this city while he is in training." Myrtis nodded and signalled one of his guards over while saying "How long do you reckon we have until they attack?" Boriam explained how he'd seen other guards in Fisherman's Rest, and assumed that they would take a few more days to gather at least. The king nodded again and gave a message to his guard. Stepping over to Jonathan, the guard introduced himself as Seth, and said "I will put you through rigorous training over the next few days while the others prepare for the attack. As a pupil of the Thirteen I expect you to learn quicker than most others. Come on, let's head out." With that, Jonathan looked at Boriam who looked back and nodded, silently saying "Follow him." Jonathan looked at Seth and said "Okay, lead the way." On the way out of the castle, the guard grabbed Jonathan's sword and looked at it before saying "I thought the Thirteen had better weapons than this?" Not wanting the man to look down on the Thirteen, Jonathan answered "Yes, they do. But not their apprentices. And besides, we left my home town in a bit of a hurry. We didn't have the time to wait for our smith to make me a better one." The guard nodded and said "We can practice with this, but when the battle arrives, I'll have to get you a better one." The guard noticed something red in one of the cracks and wondered if it was rust, but Jonathan took his sword back and said "It's probably blood. I should clean it I guess." The guard looked at Jonathan asking "Blood? You've actually hurt someone with this?" "Yes," Jonathan said and again felt the blood leave his face. "We were attacked by a group of army scouts when we turned towards Draios Strag. We had said we were heading to Il-something, so they followed us until the small crossing half a day southwards. Once we were there and turned this way instead of towards that city, they attacked us. Boriam held their arrows off as we ran, but they caught up to us eventually. Luckily those Linima archers helped us take them out. I killed the one I was fighting. I don't really know what happened, he lost his footing or something, but I didn't have time to think." Seth punched him in the back saying "Good job! Not many people would've been able to do that. Especially if they haven't had too much practice with a sword before." Jonathan nodded and pointed out that Boriam had been a good teacher.

They entered what looked like an arena. Everywhere there were wooden dummies, and round targets which Jonathan assumed were for archers. As Seth entered, the people practicing stopped what they were doing and turned towards him to salute. Jonathan didn't comment this, but followed the man towards a more open area with racks for weapons. Seth pulled out two wooden swords and threw one to Jonathan. As they prepared, Seth said "If I'm to teach you, I need to see how much you know. So get ready for my attack." And as he finished the sentence, Seth attacked. For some reason this all felt familiar to Jonathan. He'd grown used to suddenly being attacked, so the sudden turn of Seth's sword didn't surprise him. He easily parried the first strike, then turned and locked Seth's sword on the second strike. "Good, you know some things," Seth said in a mocking tone and jumped backwards before resuming his attack. As the difficulty of Seth's attacks increased, Jonathan felt more and more tired. He didn't complain or back down though, but focused on defending more than attacking. Eventually his sword flew out of his hands, and Seth pointed at his chest with his sword. "Dead," Seth said mockingly and pointed at the sword lying in the sand. "You're better than I had thought though, strong hits and good balance. But you're lacking the ability to push your opponent. Again. And this time, you attack me." Jonathan blinked thinking *Have I ever really been the one attacking?* He didn't say anything though, but picked up his sword and got ready. As he attacked, he immediately felt his foot slip, and only a few strokes passed before the sword again flew out of his hands.

215

Seth laughed quietly and said "I guess you haven't done that much. Okay, we'll start with what you know and work our way from there." Jonathan nodded and went to fetch his sword again. As he picked it up, he got a strange feeling. He quickly turned, lifting his sword and barely managed to parry Seth's attack. Surprized by the sudden parry, Seth hesitated for a second, during which time, Jonathan managed to get his sword under the guard's chin. Seth smiled and said "Good reflexes. How did you do that?" "It's pretty much the only thing I've been practicing. Boriam used to beat a stick on my head as I lay sleeping, telling me to always be ready for an attack," Jonathan said to Seth's apparent bemusement. "And it works?" He asked to which Jonathan answered "I don't know. I can't remember if I managed to stop any of those attacks, but apparently it taught me to be prepared at any moment I was awake at least." Seth nodded and returned to their battle area.

As the evening wore on their fighting became ever fiercer, and they started to attract a crowd. Jonathan was exhausted by this time, and during one of his attacks his footing slipped. Sprawling on the ground, Jonathan had a hard time getting back up again. Seth seemed slightly tired as well, but not as much as Jonathan. "Tired already?" Seth said mockingly. *'I'm not going to get annoyed by that now,'* Jonathan thought and staggered upright as Seth said "Very well, I'll guide you to the barracks. You can stay there." Jonathan nodded. As they exited the arena Seth said "I'll have to train your endurance I guess." But Jonathan pointed out that he had been running all day as well as fighting for his life, to which Seth asked "How did it feel?" "Umm... What?" Jonathan answered and Seth said "How did it feel to fight for your life?" The question made Jonathan's mind race, but he said "I was scared. Very scared. I am glad I had the training from Boriam, because my arms worked on their own." Seth sighed and said "Everyone is scared in their first fight. The question is, what will you do about it?" "What do you mean with 'do about it'?" Jonathan asked, and Seth thought for a while before saying "Some people give up and do something else entirely. Some people try again and again, yet stay so scared they get blinded by it. And then there are those who try again and manage to overcome their fear. They are still scared, but they don't get affected by it." Jonathan thought about this for a while as they walked down the white road, passing food stands in all kinds of colour. Eventually he said "Wouldn't it be better to not get scared?" Seth laughed and said "Every fight is for your life. Don't you want to be afraid to lose your life? The moment you're no longer afraid to die in a battle, is the moment you no longer want to live." Jonathan understood what Seth meant, and walked the rest of the way to the barracks in silence pondering this. When they arrived, Seth said "Ask the station chief for a bed, tell him I sent you. Tomorrow I'll push you even harder." He then turned and went back towards the castle.

The barracks were dark, lit by few torches and smelled of sweat. As he entered, a very small man, a good head shorter than Jonathan, approached him and said "Can I help you?" His voice sounded as if he was speaking through a metal pipe. "I'm looking for the station chief?" Jonathan said uncertainly, and the man answered "Found'im." "Right," Jonathan said being careful not to offend the man. "Seth told me to ask for you, and tell you to show me a bed I could have?" The little man looked Jonathan over before saying "So Seth told you that, eh?" He sighed. "Very well, follow me please." He then wandered off into the darkness of the barracks. Through a heavy wooden door were the sleeping quarters. At the back of the room there were three beds with no gear on them, and the chief pointed them out telling him he could take any one he wished. Jonathan made his way there and chose the closest one. Having put his things down, the man in the closest bed said "I saw you at the arena today." Jonathan turned towards the man and put a hand out saying "I'm Jonathan." The man's name was Seeley. "You must be pretty important, getting personal training by Brigadier Seth." "Brigadier? He never told me his rank. He's just a substitute trainer as my current one is helping the king with something." Seeley raised an eyebrow asking "With what?" *'Am I allowed to say anything about this?'* Jonathan thought and decided to say "If or when you are supposed to know, they'll tell you. I can't really say anything about it yet." Seeley kept asking about it, but Jonathan stood his ground. Eventually Seeley said "You're pretty good with the sword, but you lack a few things. How long have you been fighting?" Jonathan raised his shoulders saying "I don't know, have lost track of time. Two moons perhaps?" The guard blinked a few times and said "Only two moons? Wow, then I say you're doing really well!" Jonathan smiled proudly as Seeley said "Your other teacher must be good to have taught you this much, where is he from?" But Jonathan just shook his head and said "He never tells people where he's from. The closest answer I can give is that he comes from many places." Seeley nodded and stared at the roof. "Going for more training tomorrow?" he said eventually, and Jonathan confirmed this. "I guess I'll see you there, then," Seeley said as he turned around in his bed and went to sleep. Jonathan sighed and wondered what Boriam was up to before he too lay down in bed and fell asleep.

Chapter 42
THE ARENA

It was early morning when the men in the barracks were shouted awake by a voice declaiming "Okay, ladies, get up! We've got orders by the king himself to secure Draios Strag against an oncoming attack! This is not a drill, I repeat, this is not a drill! Is there a Jonathan in here somewhere?" Jonathan had jumped out of bed, sword ready for defence before he had even heard the message. He raised one hand and the shouting man said "The Brigadier's waiting for you at the arena. Everyone else, move out!" Seeley stood beside Jonathan and said "Nice reflexes. But you're pretty safe in here. Long time since we've been through an exercise where the city's being attacked. Too bad you'll miss it, could've been fun." Jonathan looked at Seeley and said "The man said it's not a drill. Doesn't that mean it isn't an exercise?" Seeley shrugged and said "They always say it's not a drill. It's just the way they do things here." Jonathan nodded and said "Don't be so sure about that. This is what I couldn't say yesterday. Boriam, my teacher, and I barely managed to get away from the Council's army yesterday. So don't take this half-heartedly. We need these preparations." Seeley stood still for a few seconds before saying "So you're saying there's actually an army on its way to attack this city?" But to this Jonathan only nodded and went out of the room.

Seth stood at the centre of the arena with a wooden sword in each hand. As Jonathan approached, he said "It would seem you spoke the truth. Miron returned early this morning confirming everything. Which means that you have some training to do. Miron said the army hadn't moved from where you said it would be yet, so I reckon we still have a few days before the attack. Here, get ready. This will be a long day." He then handed a sword to Jonathan and got in position. The fight quickly reached the fierceness and intensity of the night before, and Jonathan found he had to move in different ways when facing Seth to what he had while fighting Boriam. He even got a few strikes in. After each sparring finished, Seth gave Jonathan instructions on what he should try next. As the day wore on, Jonathan felt that he had greater control during the fights. In the evening, other guards came to practice, and a couple of them sat down to watch them fight. Jonathan felt tired as evening came on, and he wondered how long they were going to practice for. "Don't think about other things," Seth said as he struck the sword out of Jonathan's hands. Going over to pick up his sword, one of the guards watching had already done so, and was holding it out to him. "Seeley. Thanks," Jonathan said when he saw who it was. Seeley nodded and said "You could've had him there. Seth seems to expose his lower left side more than anything else. Just a hint." He then sat down again to watch. As Jonathan returned to the fight, Seth said "Got yourself a friend already? Maybe he can join in, so I could instruct from the sidelines." He shouted for Seeley and told him to take his sword. When the fight started, Jonathan found that Seeley was slower than both Boriam and Seth, but he struck a lot harder. This was more like the fight outside the city, as if he was trying to overpower him instead of outmanoeuvring him. Jonathan sensed the feeling from the real fight returning, and thought *What to do with it? I don't want to stay scared in these situations. Okay, let's hope this helps.'* He then jumped backwards to buy himself a few seconds to focus before Seeley was on him again. The few seconds' respite helped, and he now felt his heart pounding, yet his focus remained on the fight instead of on the fear. The two fighters knocked each other's swords out of each other's hands every now and then, and Seth gave instructions to both as they were fighting. Jonathan's feet weren't as easy to manage as earlier, and he felt the strength of his arms and hands fading. Seth saw this, and said "In a real fight you don't have time to rest. Keep going!" Seeley seemed to be tired too, for he stumbled every now and then as well. After an hour, Seth called "Seeley, switch with Rob!" Jonathan sighed as another man, well rested and ready to fight, took Seeley's sword. *What's he trying to do, kill me?'* Jonathan thought as the fight started. It didn't take long before his sword flew to the ground. "Run, kid! Get the sword and get ready again!" Seth shouted at Jonathan. His breath was heavy now, and sweat was running into his eyes. During the next fight Jonathan managed to hold on a bit longer before his sword skidded across the ground again. He stumbled and fell as he went to retrieve it. "Come on, kid! You're the pupil of one of the Thirteen, don't you have any tricks up your sleeve?" Seth shouted to gasps and whispers from the crowd. Jonathan looked angrily at Seth and thought *'I haven't learned that much yet! I wonder what I can...'* He then remembered the technique for restoring his energy, and thought *'Boriam said I shouldn't use it much, but this will let me keep fighting for a long time.'* He sat up and folded his hands in his lap. He got his breath under control and then forced his heart to stop. He coughed as it happened, his legs jolting out beneath him. He looked at Seth who stood staring at him. He then slowly stood up, got his sword and got into position. With everyone staring at him, apparently wondering what just happened, Rob attacked again. Jonathan thought Rob might have assumed he was still exhausted because the attack seemed weak and slow. After only a few passes Rob's sword was flying across the ground and Jonathan struck his revealed flank. Everyone grew quiet as Rob went to get his sword again. This time, he attacked much more fiercely, but again it didn't take long before his sword was on the ground. At this point Seth said "Okay, Rob, switch with me." This went on for a long time, and Jonathan made even Seth lose his sword a few times. "It seems you actually do have a trick up your sleeve. So what is it, you can never get tired?" Seth asked after knocking Jonathan's sword out of his hand. Jonathan shook his head and said "I can't do it often. I think it'll be a few days before I can do it again, it's very hard on my body." Seth pointed out that he saw his body shaking as it happened, and wondered why he did that. Putting his hand to his jaw, Jonathan looked at the sky and said "I don't know exactly, this is only the second time I've ever done it, but I force my heart to stop for a beat or two, then push every part of the stored energy into my muscles. It's hard to explain, but the sudden burst of energy makes the muscles jump. That's really all I can say." Seth stared at Jonathan saying "You actually stop your heart? Doesn't sound healthy to me." With this at least, Jonathan agreed. At this point hunger announced itself, and he said "The technique expends an incredible amount of energy, so right now I'm starving. Could we get some food?" Seth laughed and nodded before guiding Jonathan out of the arena.

Seth led the way into a tavern around the corner from the arena. Stepping through the door, Jonathan smelled the sweetest odours he'd ever smelled, and his stomach began to roar. The captain led the way to a booth near the window where they sat down. "What do you recommend?" Jonathan asked, and Seth said "We'll have to go back to training after resting a bit, so I suggest you get some solid meat. Beef, lamb or similar." There was a groove in the middle of the table with a metal grid above, and Jonathan wondered what it was. "Never had this before? Well, then I know what we'll have." The waitress approached wondering what she could get them. "Start this up, can you?" Seth said and pointed at the groove in the table. "And then we'll have a kilo of beef slices and just water for drinks, please." *'A kilo? That's a lot..'* Jonathan thought but went along with it. The waitress bowed and left the table. "We're going back to the arena after this? It's going to get dark soon, isn't it?" Seth nodded and said "We have lights in the arena. You need the training, but you've come a long way just today. I didn't think you would make me lose my sword, but you have developed a good technique. You're starting to become good enough with the sword for now. I am guessing you're going to focus on the sword in the future, but from tomorrow I'm going to push you through training in every other weapon we have here. Clubs, staffs, bows, pikes, axes, knives, we have them

all, and I want you to at least learn a bit for when, or if, you need it."
Jonathan sighed and when Seth asked what was wrong, Jonathan said "I've
been walking around with Boriam for what feels like ages. It's probably only
been two or three moons, but it's been a long time. Every day there was a
danger of someone catching up to us, catching us or finding out who we
were. I guess I won't get much rest before this battle either, but I am
looking forward to a long rest afterwards." Seth grinned and said "After this
battle, you've deserved a rest. But not before. Ah, our food!" The waitress
arrived carrying a lot of sliced raw meat. Behind her, two big men carried a
barrel with something in it. The men walked up to the table, lifted the metal
grid off the hole and tilted the barrel over the table. Burning coal poured
into the hole, and it immediately warmed Jonathan. Looking at the burning
pit in the middle of the table, then at the pile of raw meat, Jonathan
understood they were to fry their own pieces of meat. "Not bad. How long
should you keep the meat on there?" Jonathan asked and Seth grinned
widely saying "That's the beauty about it. Since it's meat from an ox, it is so
pure you can actually eat it raw. If that's what you like, of course. I hear
some people from the Wolf clans up in the mountains can eat anything raw.
Must be nice." "Wolf clans?" Jonathan asked. "Oh, yes, the wolf clans.
Never heard of them?" Seth asked, and when Jonathan said he hadn't, he
continued "They are half human, half wolves. Hairy people who can
actually change their shape into a wolf. Very handy to have in your army,
they can use weapons skilfully, with sharpened senses. When they lose their
weapons, they spend only about ten seconds changing into a wolf with
claws and fangs. But then again, they are completely vulnerable while
changing. Nice people, great sense of loyalty and honour." Jonathan noticed
Seth looking dreamily at the ceiling and wondered if he wished he was one.
He didn't say anything, but reached for some meat and put it on the grill.
The sound of the frying meat seemed to wake Seth up, and he quickly
grabbed a pile of food and spread it across the grill. "Put on enough pieces
to fill it up. They act as a lid which gives them a nice colour yet lets the
pieces keep their juicy taste. Here, pour this sauce onto the meat. It's a bit
strong, but it tastes good. Leave one piece bare though, so you can taste the
difference." Jonathan nodded and grabbed the bottle of sauce. As it ran off
the meat onto the embers beneath, flames appeared. Seth grinned, grabbed
a piece and cut it in half. "Needs a bit more for my taste," he said and put it
back.

After talking for a while, mostly Seth telling Jonathan what to focus on
during a fight, Jonathan grabbed a piece of meat. He couldn't remember
last time he'd tasted food this good, and the fight from the day before came
to his mind. *'If I'd died in that fight, I wouldn't have had this good food again,'*
Jonathan thought and felt sombre, but glad he'd managed to get through it.

At first he'd felt terrified about facing the men who were chasing them. When the others fell away, he'd felt slightly more confident in his own battle, but still scared enough so that he'd forgotten to move around. *'I'll have to learn to move around more,'* he thought, annoyed at himself. "What're you thinking about?" Seth asked, surprizing Jonathan so much that he got a piece of meat stuck in his throat, making him cough. "Sorry," Jonathan said. "I just thought back to the fight yesterday. I think I actually wouldn't have won without the other man falling. I was so terrified that I only stood in one place, swinging wildly. Moving around while I fight, that's what I should learn to do. Not just knowing that I have to do it, but to actually do it without thinking." Seth nodded and smiled. "You have a quick mind, and accept your faults. I can see why one of the Thirteen chose you as his pupil." Jonathan felt his face redden, and looked down at the food on the table. He grabbed another piece of meat, and received a slap on the back. Again the food got stuck in his throat, and another couple of slaps were needed to dislodge it. "Sorry about that, didn't mean to startle ya," Seeley said sitting down beside Jonathan. "Tell me, how did you do that thing?" Jonathan looked puzzled and asked what he meant. "You know," Seeley said "the sitting on the ground and then suddenly shake wildly before being completely fit for fight again. How did you do that?" Jonathan sighed wondering how to explain it, and without really telling him much about it, said "Two moons of meditation with the right guidance, and I'd managed it once before. I can't do it again for another few days at least, or it would possibly kill me. I have to be very careful about using it, but I figured the training was necessary." Seeley laughed and gave him another slap saying "I guess you're one of the patient ones, managing to meditate for two turns of the moon! I'll have a few problems there. Ooh, barbeque, mind if I join you?" He looked between Jonathan and Seth, and the brigadier gestured for Seeley to take some. "I'll have you help Jonathan onwards, so you need the strength," Seth said as Seeley grabbed a big pile of food. As the evening passed, before they returned to the arena, the two of them planned how to teach Jonathan the most effectively until the battle.

Chapter 43
DUNGEON THREE

Boriam looked at the map of the city, marked with crosses and letters everywhere. At the top of the map was the title "Operation Sealed Mountain" and Boriam wondered *Why do military people always have to arrange things like this into operations? Can't they just say "Defence of Draios Strag" or something like that?'* The king sighed and said "I'd been to only a few military meetings with my father. Never paid much attention back then, I figured he would be around for at least another decade. Enough time for me to learn things at a later time." Boriam smiled, and said "I guess no one could imagine he would be gone this soon." Pointing at the map, he said "I've never actually seen a map of the city before. I've been here a few times, and I've always thought that it's built wonderfully, or shall I say carved wonderfully?" The king grinned and Boriam continued "But this, this is amazing. The castle at the centre, five rows of houses built in concentric circles, tightly compressed. Only a few roads lead to the next circle, and you have to circle a big part of the city in order to find the next road inwards. Each circle is built higher than the one outside it, and another giant piece of stone can be lowered to stop the access through each circle of buildings. It's marvellous what the gnomes thought of when they made this city." The king looked at Boriam and said "One thing I've never understood, is: Why is it advantageous to have each circle of houses above the next one?" Boriam smiled and said "When you're defending the city from a huge attack, like this one, you want to position archers high up so they can reach further and see more. When you have several circles of houses with archers lining them, the front ones would block the view of the ones behind." At this point the king cut him off saying "So what you're saying is that with higher houses for each row, the archers behind the first ones are able to see the enemy and shoot where they want." "Exactly," Boriam said and continued, "these open squares within each circle I am guessing are for catapults?" The king nodded and explained that the squares were now small markets. "We'll find some catapults before the battle begins," the king said. Boriam raised his arms towards the map and said "Then I say your battle strategy is pretty much done." The king nodded and said "I think it's the same as it's been for a few hundred years. No one's ever needed to use it before though, so no one knows if it will actually work." Boriam put a hand on the king's shoulder and said "I feel confident in it, and I guess it's about time someone did test it out." At that moment, Lia pushed open the door carrying a piece of paper which she handed to the king. Myrtis turned to Boriam and said "I have the Linima running back and forth between scouts outside the Council's army and Draios. I'm getting reports each day about what they've been up to." Boriam nodded and indicated the paper. The king read it and said "They say more troops have joined them, along with some huge beasts which look like giant bulls. There is a little more activity in the enemy camp, but they haven't started to move yet." He thanked Lia for the message and sent her out of the room. The king paced a bit back and forth thinking aloud, wondering what their allies would say to the message he'd sent them. He sat down on his throne and sighed, saying "I wish my father was here. He'd know what to do about everything." Boriam looked at the map for a while before saying "I bet the gnomes will come to help us. This is the greatest thing they've ever made, so I doubt they want to let it be destroyed. The trolls will be harder to persuade, no one really understand how to trigger them into doing anything. The merfolk are many, but they can only fight effectively from the sea, which unfortunately only covers one side of the city. No, our best hope is to get help from the gnomes. Make a strategy for them and the humans, and hope that people from cities close by will come to our aid." The king nodded and wrote a few more letters. Having sent them off, he turned and said "I forgot about a couple of the smaller villages nearby. Maybe they can spare a few people as well. Oh, I don't feel ready for this at all!" He then started to pace around the room again. Boriam recalled his focus onto the matter at hand by asking how many provisions and weapons the city had in store. When the king didn't think they had enough weapons, Boriam asked "What about the armoury in the castle?" Myrtis looked up and asked "What armoury in the castle? I've been to all the halls, and I've never seen an armoury in here." Boriam nodded and said "That's not so strange. It was a secret between the gnomes and the Thirteen of the time. The knowledge has been passed down from the king to his son ever since, but only on the king's death bed. Did he say anything to you as he was close to dying?" Myrtis shook his head and said "He died so quickly, I got home from a long journey just in time to hear him say goodbye. Holding my hand, he passed away." Boriam nodded and said "Was there anything he showed you at some point? Something which was very important, perhaps, to keep safe?" Myrtis shook his head slowly, thinking. Boriam looked out of the window and noticed it was getting dark. Myrtis said he'd retire for the day, and

Boriam bade him good night as he went out the main door. Outside he bumped into captain Seth, who said "Hallo there. How is everything going?" Boriam told him about what they'd figured out, and asked how Jonathan was doing. "The kid's good," Seth said. "He's learning quickly, soon finished with his sword training. I'm starting him on different types of swords from tomorrow evening, and then other weapons as he begins to get an understanding for how the different weapons work. He's made himself a friend on his first day in the barracks. A brilliant guy as well, but not learning as quickly as Jonathan though." Boriam nodded and said "Good, I'm glad he's doing well. The king's gone to his quarters for the night. If it's very important I guess you can enter, but I would wait until tomorrow. He's got a lot to think about today." Seth understood and had just wanted to give an update on how things were going. Having asked Boriam to give the update to the king the next day, Seth turned and left.

The next morning Boriam was on his way to one of the city's new tunnels. Looking for the entrance, he thought 'Brown beetle outside... Brown beetle outside... Ah, here.' He entered the house and accessed the tunnel it was hiding. The king didn't look like he'd had much sleep, but he eagerly approached Boriam as he entered. "Boriam, good morning," the king said. "When I got back to my room I remembered my father having given me a note as he was dying. Here, take it." Boriam looked at the note the king gave him and read "eerhtnoegnud". The king nodded, and said "Dungeon three spelled backwards. I wondered what it was about dungeon three, and when I checked it at the time, I couldn't find anything special about it. So I forgot it, thinking it was an old man's ramblings. Maybe it could help you?" Boriam smiled at the king, asked him to show him this dungeon and soon they were hurrying along the long cellar tunnels. The dungeons were marked by a number of charred stones above the doorway, and in the dim light Boriam had trouble seeing them clearly. He let the king lead the way to dungeon three. Once inside the dungeon, Boriam stood looking at a wall covered in all the important, unimportant and forgotten symbols of the world. All the symbols were famous or belonged to some religion, both new and old. He saw the cross, the star, the yin-yang, the tower, the lightning bolt, the hammer, the lobster and he even saw the ball of yarn, which made Boriam laugh to himself. "Are all the dungeons like this?" he asked, and the king said "No, this is the only one like this, which is why I haven't used it for anything. Didn't want to make any potential god or deity angry." Boriam nodded and looked at the wall. It was covered in small tiles, and every tile had its own symbol. A ladder was mounted against the wall, and it seemed possible to slide it back and forth in order to reach the different symbols. The king said "I've got no idea what to do here, so I'll let you have fun with this." And with that he sat down on a barrel in the corner. Boriam spent a long time looking at the tiles until he found one marked with a lion's head. Smiling, he went over to it, and pressed it. The lion's head flipped and let a ray of light into the dungeon. The light struck the floor, and was fanned out across the ceiling in smaller beams. One of the beams hit another symbol on the wall, and Boriam proceeded to press this one. Another thick ray of light entered the room and hit the king's leg. Puzzled by this, Boriam told the king to get off the barrel. The king did so, and together they moved the barrel to the side. The corner behind the barrel was rounded and polished. Again the light was spread and struck several tiles. This chain went on for a while as Boriam pushed more symbols, and more light entered. Eventually, Boriam sighed and pushed a symbol of scales, the symbol of the goddess of equality, and the light hit seven stones in the wall to their right. The king had stepped towards the wall and raised an arm when Boriam shouted "Stop!" With the arm stretched towards one of the stones, the king refrained from pushing it, saying "What? Aren't we supposed to push the ones with light falling on them?" Boriam nodded and said "Earlier, only the tiles with symbols on them were lit. If we'd pushed the wrong one, who knows what would've happened? But now... Now several stones with no symbol on them are lit up. What if there's only one stone we are supposed to push now? What if all the others spring a trap on us?" The king sighed and said "So what do you suggest we do?" "I don't know," Boriam said, "Just let me think."

An hour had passed when a guard entered handing the king a note. Having read it, he looked at Boriam and said "There're some stirrings in the enemy camp. Our scouts say that something is changing in the enemy camp, and suspect they are starting to move very soon. We need to finish our preparations." He then gave the guard a set of instructions to ensure everything the city would need for the several weeks ahead were prepared. The guard bowed and left the room. Boriam sighed and shook his head. He looked at the tiled wall. Something seemed familiar about the lights. He tried to remember what it was, but was unable to. "There's something about the lights on the wall here. I can't recognize it, but the answer is there." He sighed and sat down on the floor looking at the lit wall. A long time passed before he recognized a small part of the lights, and turned his head to the side. "Hah! That's it!" he said and stood up. He went over to the wall and, from the left, counted five lit stones. He pushed the fifth stone and the entire room started shaking. *Was I wrong? But... Why?'* he managed to think before two rows of stones slowly slid back, revealing a hidden room. Boriam entered the room slowly, with an eager king behind him. "How did you do that?" Myrtis asked and Boriam said "The symbol of lights had been turned sideways. When I turned my head I saw that they pictured the old gnomish sign for the number five. Very clever. The number five is written very similarly to the numbers three and six. I am guessing that if we'd turned the wrong tiles earlier, one of those numbers would've come up." Behind the door and on the wall, pointy spikes were hanging from strange contraptions. They were aimed in between the cracks in the wall. Boriam pointed at them and said "Those would have been shot through the cracks if we'd pushed the wrong stone." The king was shocked by this, only managing to say "Really?" Boriam shrugged and said "I don't know that for sure, but I'm assuming so. Why would they be there otherwise?" They turned their attention to the room, lit the torches along the walls and found the room filled with weapons, armours, shields and other things to help secure the city. It was a big room, but unfortunately some of the things in it were rusty. "Have your weaponsmith come check out every single weapon in here to find what we can use. A blacksmith will be needed for the armours, and a woodworker will be handy for some of the shields," Boriam said to the king, who passed the message on to the guard outside the dungeon.

Walking through the room, Boriam picked up different swords and armour wondering how old they were. He picked up a curved long sword and thought '*A katana. I haven't seen these in a long time. It's more common in the far south than here.*' He picked up a sword which seemed very strong and light, swung it and figured Jonathan should have it. After an hour, when Boriam and Myrtis had started sorting the different types of items around the room, the guard returned with three people. Their faces were pale, and when the king asked them why, they said "When the king's guard tell us to follow him to the dungeons, you think unhappy thoughts." The king laughed and said "Not to worry, we need your knowledge." He had each person assigned to a pile, to start finding out what could be used, while Boriam kept sorting. He picked out a couple of items for himself and Jonathan, a few swords so Jonathan could decide which one he liked the best, a couple of shields and some armour. Myrtis didn't seem to mind this, as he glanced at the things he'd picked out and then returned to the smiths. When the pile was sorted, only a few of the things the smiths had managed to look through had to be thrown away. They made another pile of the things they could repair, and this pile was growing fast. "I'll bring this over to the arena where Jonathan is training, so he can find the gear he needs." The king nodded, and Boriam left the room. Carrying five swords, two shields and a helmet, getting out of the castle wasn't easy. Once outside, Boriam could finally breathe fresh air again. He took a few big breaths, then turned towards the arena.

Chapter 44
CELEBRATING A PROMOTION

Jonathan had dropped the long staff again and was about to pick it up when he saw Boriam entering the arena. He grabbed the staff and straightened up, waiting for him to approach. Boriam seemed to be carrying something, which made him walk slower than usual. As he approached, Jonathan saw what it was. Having exchanged greetings, Boriam said "You should look through these, try them out, and find which one you are the most comfortable with." Jonathan pulled out the different swords, and found that he could already exclude two of them. The three left were very different from each other. One was thicker in the middle than the two others, one was slightly curved, and one was slightly longer. He picked up the thickened one, and Boriam said "That's a gladius, very common for foot militia." Jonathan tested the sword on one of the training dolls before putting it down and picking up the second one. "That is a sabre. As it's curved it's easier to slash the enemy and perform quick flourishes with." Again Jonathan tested the sword on the dolls, but found that the curve of the sword confused him and put him off balance. "I could get used to this one, but I don't think I'll have time before this battle," Jonathan said as he put the sword down. He picked up the third one and Boriam said "That is the half longsword. Halfway between a gladius and a longsword." Jonathan nodded and felt that it was heavier, yet afforded him a better grip. When he swung it, the weight of the sword made it follow through, instead of him having to push it towards the target. He attempted a couple of quick strikes, and felt comfortable using it, so he looked up and told Boriam that this was the sword he wanted. Boriam said "The half longsword is a good weapon, it's slightly slower than a shortsword. It's quick enough to match the shortsword, if you're good, and it can deliver heavier blows. In addition to that, it can be used with one hand alongside a shield. If you don't have a shield, you can use both hands." Jonathan smiled, thinking he had made a good choice. Boriam gave him a shield and the helmet, and told Seth to teach him fighting using that. The shield felt uncomfortable to Jonathan. He wasn't used to the extra weight, so he made many errors he wouldn't normally make. A long time passed before he was able to muster any resistance against the attacks Seth made. Every time their fight ended, Boriam commented on what he should do differently, and with both Seth and Boriam there to instruct him, Jonathan learned to stay in control of the fight even with the unusual new weight.

Darkness was upon them when the training ended. "You have learned much in the last few days. For tomorrow, bring a full suit of armour from the barracks. That'll add even more weight, so you'll have to learn to fight using that as well," Boriam said as they exited the arena. "I'll be using a full suit of armour? Won't that slow me down a lot?" Jonathan asked, to which Boriam replied "You'll only use it in fights like this. When we're on the road, full armour weighs too much. Fighting without armour will make you move a lot quicker, but fighting with armour will ward you from blows. In this type of encounter you will have a greater chance of taking a stray blow from somewhere than if you were fighting a small mob on the road. And here you won't have to move very far, of course." He finished the sentence with a grin, turned towards the castle and left. Jonathan sighed and turned back towards the barracks. *If Boriam likes taking part in a war he's got to be crazy. I haven't been in one before, but from what I've heard, it's not a nice thing. I wonder what he's helped the king with?'* Jonathan thought as he reached the barracks.

Having opened the door, Seeley greeted him and said "Come on, Jonathan, let's get drunk. I have things to celebrate." "Wha... But, I..." Jonathan managed to say before Seeley grabbed his arm and pushed him back out the door. "You're young, and I have a feeling you haven't been drinking much in your life, so I'll tell you what. I'll get drunk, and you'll at least have a beer to keep me company," Seeley said, to which Jonathan felt he couldn't say no. As they entered the nearest tavern, Jonathan was reminded of the inn back in Shadowtree. *I guess most taverns or inns look the same,'* Jonathan thought as Seeley shouted an order to the maid, who curtsied and hurried behind the bar. "So what are we celebrating?" Jonathan asked and Seeley said "Do you see this here?" He stuck out an arm where a symbol of sorts had been sewn on. "A hooked line? What does that mean?" Jonathan asked, which seemed to shock Seeley. "You don't know what this is?" Seeley asked shouting. "This... This, is a sergeant's mark! Seth saw fit to promote me to sergeant! That's what we're out celebrating. Ah, the beer!" Seeley watched as the maid approached, hips swinging with each step, and put the two mugs of beer on the table. "Enjoy, boys," she said and winked at Seeley. "Thanks, Arina," Seeley said and held his mug up towards Jonathan. A second passed before Jonathan understood what Seeley wanted, but he quickly enough picked up his own mug of beer to complete the toasting. The first taste of beer felt horribly dry and spongy, and

Jonathan coughed, to Seeley's enjoyment. "And this is normal to drink?" Jonathan asked to which Seeley said "This is actually pretty good beer. Among the best in the city. Even the mugs are almost clean. So you be happy about this one." "So what's with you and um... What was her name? Aina?" Jonathan asked and Seeley quickly corrected him saying "Arina. What do you mean 'up with'?" But seeing the look Jonathan gave him, he said "Okay, well, I've kinda had my eye on her, if you know what I mean?" "Only your eye?" Jonathan asked and Seeley looked at the table, saying "Well, the time never seemed to be right." Now it was Jonathan's turn to laugh. "That's what every guy says. I didn't know a lot of people in my home town, practically no one really. I did, however, see how people acted around each other, and I heard what guys were talking about. Usually they talked about girls which didn't even notice them, but she," he indicated towards Arina, "has certainly noticed you before." Seeley looked up and said eagerly "Really? You think so?" Jonathan smiled and said "You didn't see her winking at you?" Seeley coughed and said "I guess things got a bit blurry as she approached. What do I do now? I don't know what to say, and I'm too shy to go over there." Jonathan gave a loud bark of a laugh and said "You're a sergeant now. You can't stay shy anymore, so man up. As for what to say: for every guy in every situation, a good start is 'Hi.'" Jonathan signalled Arina over. "Hi, I'm Jonathan, and this is Seeley. He was just promoted to sergeant, ain't that right, See?" Jonathan said, shortening Seeley's name. Seeley went slightly red and nodded quickly. "Ah, congratulations sergeant. Seeley was it? Out celebrating?" Arina said looking at Seeley. Jonathan stood up excusing himself, saying he had to go to the toilet. Having reached the far end of the inn he looked back at a still slightly red Seeley, but at least a talking Seeley. He stepped outside for a while, and caught some fresh air, before going back inside. He saw Arina putting a hand on Seeley's shoulder as she walked away from the table. When Jonathan sat down at the table again, Seeley said "You, my friend, are one mean bastard." Jonathan laughed, not minding the accusation. "So how did it go?" Jonathan asked and Seeley sighed saying "Well, it's hard to say, women are complicated. But she might want to meet me after her shift is finished. She didn't say that directly, but she did say it ended in about two hours." Jonathan smiled and said "Then I guess we'll stay here for a couple of hours, and then I'll be off." He lifted his mug and said "To a new sergeant with a new girl." "Hear, hear," Seeley said and drank. So did Jonathan, having forgotten how badly he thought it tasted. He crossed his face as the beer descended into his stomach. Sighing, Seeley asked "So what about you? Training more tomorrow?" Jonathan nodded and said "With armour this time. I got a sword today, so I'm going to get used to that. We'll see what happens. Seems Boriam, my teacher, is finished helping the king, so both he and Seth will be instructing me. I guess I'll learn quickly that way." Seeley looked up and said "Boriam? *The* Boriam of the Thirteen?" Jonathan heard an extra emphasis as Seeley said 'the', and asked why he was wondering. Seeley shook his head and said "I have only heard stories of the Thirteen, but Boriam was supposedly one of the more secretive ones. He was always the quickest in battle, which I guess might be why he's the only one left. And they said he had spies everywhere. Only to keep the world safe of course, that's why they were the Thirteen. But you always wondered if he got to know what you were talking to your mates about." Jonathan stared silently ahead, thinking *Boriam had spies everywhere? I mean, I've understood he's a bit secretive, but spies? I wonder if that is true, and what else he's been into?'* After sitting lost in thought for a while, Jonathan noticed Seeley had been trying to get his attention. "Sorry," he said "I didn't know he had spies or anything, so I was just thinking back to what I've seen and noticed so far." Seeley nodded his understanding and was about to say something when Arina came over and said "So apparently my shift was different today. I'm off now, if you boys don't mind me joining you?" Jonathan and Seeley looked at each other, and Seeley said "Not at all. Sit, please." She made as if to sit down beside Jonathan, but he stood up saying he had to leave soon. Arina seemed disappointed at this, but Jonathan had a suspicion she didn't mean it. They sat talking for a while as Jonathan forced his beer down. When he had finished it, he left the two others and headed back to the barracks.

The armour weighed Jonathan down as he carried it to the arena. Boriam stood outside the entrance waiting for him. "You know, moving around would be easier if you'd put the armour on before coming here," Boriam said as he approached. Jonathan looked at the set of armour in his arms and felt stupid for carrying it all the way. "I don't really know how to put it on," he said as an excuse, knowing that someone at the barracks could have helped him. Boriam shook his head and let Jonathan inside. "Are you finished helping the king? What had to be done?" Jonathan asked without expecting to get a decent answer. To Jonathan's surprize, Boriam told him everything they had done while he put the armour on. Jonathan got to know what defences the city had, what areas should receive more attention than others, and he even got to know about dungeon three. When Boriam had finished talking, Jonathan stood staring into space, thinking. When Boriam asked what was wrong, Jonathan said "You normally never tell me anything, and when you do, you don't tell me everything. It seems like you've done that now. I guess I'm just wondering 'Why?'." Boriam sighed and said "Really? Well, old habit I guess." Jonathan nodded and said "I heard a rumour about you. I don't know who said it, but it claimed that you had spies everywhere. In a good way, of course, but still. Is that why it's a habit to keep things a secret?" Boriam looked at Jonathan who quickly apologized. Lifting a hand to silence Jonathan, Boriam said "In my experience, every rumour has a lot of lie in it, but usually a little bit of truth as well. I did have spies around, but they've grown more and more quiet as the Council's been taking over cities. I see you're sceptical about me having spies, but before you judge me for anything, you'll have to know a bit about the Lions' system. Now, that will take some time to explain, and now you have to learn how to truly fight." Seeing Jonathan's disappointed face, Boriam said "I'll tell you what. Our system is a lot to take in. But I promise you, that if we make it through the oncoming battle, I'll tell you all about it. Now get ready to fight for your life." Jonathan nodded, half ran to the centre of the arena and pulled his sword. The armour was heavy, and he found it hard to grip his sword. *I should have learned to fight with armour from the beginning,'* he thought as Seth approached him with his sword drawn. It didn't take long before Jonathan's sword lay on the ground. *'So I have to learn everything from the beginning each and every day?'* Jonathan thought as he picked his sword up. He stretched his limbs and felt the armour set itself slightly differently, and his grip suddenly felt easier on the sword. He smiled to himself, and returned to the fight. This time the fight was slightly easier, but the armour along with the new sword made everything difficult. Jonathan gritted his teeth and kept on training.

Chapter 45
FIGHTING MAGIC

The king entered the arena bearing his sword, and headed towards the group teaching Jonathan. *'I guess it's getting close,'* Boriam thought and glanced back at Jonathan who was now training with this Seeley person. He noticed they'd got an easy tone with one another, as if they'd known each other for years. *'He'll need to build his own set of contacts, so this is a good start,'* Boriam thought as he instructed the both of them in how to handle their different types of sword. Seeley was much better than Jonathan technically, but Jonathan had been taught to be quick and precise with his strikes. Not many people were taught this, and a few of the techniques Jonathan had learned were secrets from the Lions. These seemed to help him a lot in his fights. The king arrived at the group, and greeted them all. He seemed happy to meet Jonathan again, and also greeted Seeley with respect. After looking at how far Jonathan had progressed in his training, Myrtis pulled Boriam and Seth aside. "The enemy has started moving in our direction. They have huge bulls pulling giant carts of gear. Now when I say huge, I mean really huge." Boriam interrupted the king and said "It's probably a Tauroxen. They have been used by the Council previously instead of battering rams. The bulls run straight into the gate, tearing it off its hinges or splintering the wood it's made from." The king nodded and said "We shouldn't have too much of a problem with that if we lower the guarding stones though. There is one more trick we can try as well. Did you notice a slight trench beside the road as you entered the city?" Boriam had not, and the king continued "Well, they lead to outer walls near the ocean. When these are opened, the trench is flooded with water. It will make raising ladders to scale the walls even harder. When the assault begins, I'll have them opened. They haven't been used for over a hundred years though, so I hope the mechanics still work." Boriam smiled imagining how the city would look like surrounded by water. He then asked "Have you heard anything from our allies?" The king sighed and said "Some have come from nearby cities, but as for the other races, only a few gnomes have marched in, some merfolk have answered the call, but not even enough for a single squad. Oh, and three wolfmen came lumbering into town in their lurching way." The king shivered and said "Something about them creeps me out." Boriam laughed and said "Trust me, there are far worse things out there. So, the preparations are going as planned then? Anything else we can do?" Myrtis shook his head and said "What you can do now, is teach me more. I have a lot of training, but I am still young and inexperienced. Please, if you don't mind?" Boriam shook his head and said that Seth should begin, as he'd been the one instructing the king earlier. The king agreed to this, and pulled his sword. The arena went silent. No one had seen the king fight before, and wondered what their leader would be able to do. Boriam noticed this, went over to Seth and quietly whispered "These men seem unsure about their leader. Make the fight hard, but let the king win the first bout. The men around the arena will feel better if their leader wins over one they consider to be among the best." Seth looked around at the men who were now sitting on the ground looking their way. He nodded and pulled his sword. The fight started slowly, but soon enough got more frenzied. Seth must have known what the king was able to stand up to, and Boriam was impressed by the level of swordsmanship the king possessed, when suddenly Seth's sword flew out of his hands, landing in the dirt next to some men. The arena cheered for the victor, and the crowd must have been satisfied by their king, as they soon resumed their own training. Boriam nodded and let Seth and Myrtis go at it again while he instructed Jonathan and Seeley.

They both got better through the course of the day, and when all five were weary, Boriam asked everyone to gather around him. Focussing first on Seth and Myrtis, Boriam asked "Have you ever fought someone who were able to use magic?" Myrtis had not, but Seth said "Once. Only luck got me through it." Boriam nodded and said "Well, then it's about time to learn how to fight it. There are a few things you should know about. Very few people are good enough with magic to activate it at a moment's notice. Some are able to prepare their magic while moving around, but most people have to prepare it while standing still. So usually, when fighting someone who can use magic, they will have to stand still and focus for some time before casting. In the Council's army, I believe the few who are able to use magic at a moment's notice are the Muriahs. They usually have a blood red armour with small spikes on their shoulders. No one else in their army has ever carried that armour, so it's a good chance it'll be the same now." The crowd had increased to about ten people now, who eagerly listened to Boriam talking. Everyone was sitting on the ground, and Boriam felt he was back at the school he had once taught at. More people arrived while Boriam kept talking. "For everyone else, when they are preparing magic, their target area will be charged with the spell before it takes effect. Those of you, if any, who are able to use magic, can cast your own magic, of the opposing element, at that area, and the spell will be interrupted, or greatly weakened. If you are in the area and don't know magic, you should run or quickly jump away." A hand was raised in the gathered crowd and the owner of it said "How do we know if we're in that kind of area?" Boriam blinked a few times before asking "Didn't I mention that?" The crowd shook their heads and Boriam explained "Ah, well then. When the magic is charged, there will be a tingling sensation and the hair on your arms, legs and neck will stand up. This will indicate that you're either in the area, or extremely close to it. Oh, and magic is strongest near its caster, so most magic wielders will try to get pretty close before casting anything. The stronger the caster, the stronger or better the magic. Now, I will charge the area you are sitting in, just so you will get a feel for how it is. That way you can hopefully notice it later and stay out of unnecessary trouble." Boriam looked inside himself in the standard way of charging magic, and focused on the entire area where the crowd had gathered. A few of them started scratching their necks or arms, and some smiled. A few didn't seem affected by it at all. *Maybe they know magic already? Or maybe they just accept what is happening?* Boriam thought and allowed the magic to die down. He nodded and said "All of you find a partner to spar with. I will stand in the middle of the arena and target random people while you fight. Either you jump away both from your fight and the magic, or you will be struck by it. Don't worry, I won't hurt you. Much." He then grinned and people started looking at each other. "Come on, we haven't got all day! Form into pairs!" he shouted and people jumped up and started taking up positions around the arena. Boriam smiled as he located one of the men who didn't seem to notice the magic earlier. He prepared his magic and focused on the man. Having waited an appropriate amount of time, Boriam let the magic fly forwards. He watched as the man was blown several metres to the side. Standing back up the man spat dirt out of his mouth and said "I know a bit of magic, and put up an aura of water magic against it, but it didn't seem to work." Boriam nodded and said "It was a good effort, but the strength of the magic is dependent on the strength of the caster. Apparently my magic is stronger than yours, even at this distance. My spell was weaker than I intended, yet strong enough to throw you away from your fight. Now do as I said, and jump away instead of trying to prevent it." A lot of people had been watching the discussion, but they quickly returned to their fights when Boriam turned towards them. When Boriam next tried magic on someone, the soldier quickly jumped backwards surprizing his sparring partner. The partner understood what was happening as soon as he saw a cone of dust rush past in front of him. He started laughing at it all, as the man jumping away lay in a heap on the ground trying to get up. "Jumping away from a fight is a good tactic at times, but only if you're able to land properly," Boriam shouted to the amusement of the other fighters. The next magic was directed at Jonathan, who jumped backwards effectively. He let the magic pass him, and then rushed back into the fight. The quick recovery surprised Seeley, whom he was fighting, and Seeley's sword soon lay on the ground. *'Good,'* Boriam thought, and threw a few blasts at some of the other fighters, along with the king who also reacted well.

Nodding, Boriam decided to confuse the fighters a little. He put his focus on three people. After a short while, they jumped away from their fights and he quickly shifted his focus to three others, then fired the magic. Two of the men managed to jump away, but the third was thrown far off. The man's partner was in the middle of a swing when the man was blown away. The sword passed the empty space, and buried itself in his own foot. "Sorry about that," Boriam said and went over to the man. He pulled the sword out of his foot, and gathered his energy to heal the wound. A little time passed, but eventually the wound started to close. The man sighed as the pain receded and soon the wound was completely healed. Boriam nodded saying in a joking tone "Let's hope that doesn't happen too many times." The man laughed and Boriam went back to the middle of the arena. The fighter who had been blown away returned to his partner and had to sit down to rest for a while. "I said that I wouldn't hurt you much," Boriam said, "not that I wouldn't hurt you at all." A few men gave a nervous laugh and continued their fights. They practiced like this for a long time that evening, and people sat down to rest every now and then. Jonathan and Seeley were among the last to take a rest, and Boriam figured he should let them get at least one break during their training. At a moment when most of the people who were training were sitting on the ground, one of the more rested ones stood up. He said "We have taken instructions from you all evening, but how do we know how good you really are?" Boriam saw Jonathan looking at him, raise an eyebrow and then shake his head. He pointed at his sword and then on the ground, and Boriam had a feeling he understood what Jonathan meant. He pulled his sword and put it carefully on the ground before saying "Look at my sword. Try it, if you wish. Tell me what you think of it." He then stepped back several paces and let the man approach the blade. The man sceptically looked at the blade saying "It looks very old, yet very new at the same time." He dug his hand into the ground and around the hilt of the sword and lifted it. At least, he tried to lift it. The man's face grew a dark red colour as he tried to lift it off the ground, and soon two more men came to help lift it. Unable to get the sword off the ground, the man let go of the sword and stood gasping for breath. Boriam smiled and said "Now take your own sword, and attack me." The man looked around at the crowd and then at Boriam who put his hands out showing that he held no weapon in them. Nervously the man pulled his sword, and Boriam nodded showing it was okay for the man to do this. The man lifted his sword and came running at Boriam. Boriam put his hand forward in a fist, pushed his little finger and thumb out to the sides and pulled his hand backwards. Boriam's sword flew past the charging man and into Boriam's hand. Turning around, Boriam delivered a powerful sweeping stroke, which impacted directly on the man's sword, throwing it high into the air. Using two fingers to point to the air he made three bolts of lightning strike the man's sword. Each strike altered the direction the blade flew, and after the third bolt of lightning the sword struck the ground right between the man's feet. With the colour draining from the man's face, he said "Wow." Boriam sheathed his sword and went back to the crowd where several sat gaping at what had happened. "That, is just a piece of what might meet you in this war. So get ready for practically anything. Equip an extra knife, or a sidearm baton. Something to pull quickly in case you lose your main weapon. It looks like you are all ready for the fight. Keep training, but make sure you get some rest as well. I believe we may have two more days of preparations before the battle occurs, so be ready by then." He could see motivation shining from several faces, fear mixed with focus in others. As they all seemed pleased with what they had been taught that evening, Boriam said "I believe I have taught you most of what I can before the fight, so I guess the rest will be up to you all. Good luck, and I'll see you at least in a couple of days." With that he stepped towards the king, who said "Shouldn't it, you know technically, be me giving this speech?" Boriam smiled and said "Your time will come. These are but a few soldiers, who right now had all their attention fixed on me. When you wish to motivate the entire army, a few minutes before the battle, that will be your job. These people won't even remember my speech at that moment." The king nodded and signalled for Seth and a few of his guards to join him at the castle. Boriam bid them farewell and turned his attention to Jonathan. "Nice speech," the boy said and Boriam laughed saying "I figured it was called for. So how are you doing? Feeling ready? Have you practiced more magic lately?" Jonathan shook his head and said "I feel more comfortable in a fight now, but I still feel there is a lot to learn. I have only had time to practice magic a little. I guess I'll have to do that mostly after this war." Boriam nodded and agreed to that. The rest of the night Boriam taught Jonathan a few more techniques which could be good to know before the battle. It was dark by the time they left the arena. "Meditate tomorrow before training, and then go here for a few hours, but don't spend the entire day in training. You need to rest before the battle." Jonathan nodded and said he understood, before heading for the barracks. Boriam nodded to himself before turning and heading down the street.

Chapter 46
CAPTAIN OF THE FORESTERS

Arkenthan yawned and noticed that it was late. He put the book in the bookcase and returned to the bed. He lay awake for a while wondering what was going to happen in the book. Having tried to imagine what was happening onwards, he finally started feeling tired. Arkenthan drifted in and out of dreams all night, some were of long haired men with pointy teeth who changed into wolves, and others were of calmer things like standing in the middle of a field with only trees around him. In one of these calmer dreams one of the small creatures he'd seen in the forest appeared. It looked like a human, but was small as a child. Its hair was unruly, with twigs and moss mixed into it. Its nose was small but longer than usual, and when it opened its mouth, a strange sound came, which woke Arkenthan up. He stared at the ceiling wondering what the thing was, when the sound appeared again. Jumping out of bed he went outside to look around. Greypaws was sleeping in his pen, apparently not bothered by the sound. Again the sound came, and Arkenthan thought that it might have come from one of the trees, yet this time it seemed more familiar. It went "Tok-tok-tok", and the next time it appeared Arkenthan thought '*A woodpecker. Of course, I should have recognized it the first time.*' He breathed out and returned to his bed.

The next morning he didn't feel as worn out as he had on the day before, and after eating what was left in his stockpile, he grabbed his bow and set out. Passing Greypaws on the way into the forest, Arkenthan said "You stay here and get well. I'll try to get enough food for us both." He began the route around his traps, and soon had three small game in his bag. He shot two more before turning towards home. On the way he passed the Dragon's Blood plant and noticed new leaves were starting to grow where he had broken off the last ones. '*Wow, already growing again?*' Arkenthan thought and thought it okay to pick two more leaves, thinking '*It seems like I'm going to need them.*' He also dug a little into the ground, trying to figure out how long the roots were, and found them to be actually very short. '*Maybe I can dig up a big area around it and bring the entire plant back to the house?*' he

238

thought as he left the plant.

Getting back home, he threw one of the small game towards Greypaws and sat down near the campfire pit to skin the rest. As the bones of Greypaws' food cracked, Arkenthan jumped a little. He smiled to himself and thought *'I should get used to that, I won't always be able to stay in my house, so when I am sleeping out in the forest, I'll have to hear him eat.'* Having skinned the rest of his catch he stored it inside the house. He rolled up the two leaves he'd picked and put them in his bag. He saw that the potion of Dragon's Blood was half spent from the previous fight and thought *'I should make as much as I can for now, always keeping a spare bottle of it, just in case.'* With that he decided to take a trip to town the following day. Arkenthan looked at his catch and figured he would need to have more meat for a trip to town than what he had now. Heading outside he applied some more potion to Greypaws' wound and headed out to hunt more. He came back with a small deer, and cut it into decently sized pieces so that Greypaws could have another small game that same night, and then a leg of a deer the following morning. Arkenthan figured that if he were to carry a lot of food into town, he would have to get all the help he could. Finding a thick branch on a tree Arkenthan cut it off and made a walking stick. He cleaned the handle, but let the bark at the bottom of the stick remain. During the evening he carved symbols he'd seen in the storybooks back home into the bark. When he felt the walking stick was well decorated, he leaned it against the wall and went inside to sleep.

The next day's hike was made easier by the new walking stick. Greypaws remained back at the house, and Arkenthan didn't feel as safe as he had grown used to. For this reason he kept to the side of the path. As he drew near to the clearing by the lake he heard the murmur of the river and decided to head in that direction. He knew it would take him closer to the village, and he didn't think he needed to sneak around the outskirts anymore. *'I guess most of the villagers know I come from the forest by now,'* Arkenthan thought as he drew close to the river. Pushing aside a bush leading up to the river, Arkenthan saw one of the little creatures he'd seen before and dreamt of. What he hadn't noticed earlier, was that the creature had a tail. It turned around looking directly at him with its round head and dark blue eyes. It blinked a few times as Arkenthan and the creature-person stood staring at each other, and then it ran off upriver. "Hey!" Arkenthan shouted and ran after the creature. It made a high screech like a scared bird as it kept on running. After a minute the creature turned up a hill from the river and ran off into the forest. Arkenthan followed and saw it running towards what looked like a clearing. It jumped over a bush just in front of the clearing, and Arkenthan was surprized by how high the creature could jump. Hurrying after it, Arkenthan crashed through the bush and scrambled into the clearing. He looked around the clearing and found nothing. There were trees lining the edges far away, and grass with some flowers covering the clearing, but no small person running across it. *'It shouldn't have reached the edge already. Where can it be?'* Arkenthan thought as he slowly made his way across the field, listening for the sounds of running. Having crossed the clearing a few times, Arkenthan could find no hiding place in the field, and no apparent path out of it. Sighing, Arkenthan decided that looking any further wouldn't be of any help, so he headed back towards the village. Crossing the river he spotted a fjällbear further down. It didn't seem to notice Arkenthan, and he decided it would be a bad idea to make any unnecessary noise. Instead, he slowly made his way to town.

As he exited the forest he met a team of scouts heading towards the woods. He put his hand up and said "Stop, you really shouldn't head into the forest right now." The lead scout looked at Arkenthan and in a grumpy tone asked "And why would we listen to your opinion?" "Because he," someone behind the party of scouts said, and Arkenthan soon realized it was Colonel Locke who finished his sentence saying "has been given an honorary rank of Captain. So whatever he says, Sergeant, you will do." The Sergeant looked from the Colonel to Arkenthan for a while with his mouth opening and closing before managing to say "Honorary Captain? I've never heard of anything like that before. Why?" Locke sighed and said "In a heartbeat he knew more about where to bring a wounded man in this village than several of my men, and even me. He saved the man's life. A few hours later, he singlehandedly stopped the attack of the great white wolf, and led it into the forest. The only reason he's an honorary Captain instead of an official Captain, is because this kid is not directly from this village. So, do you have any more questions Born?" Born blinked a few times and looked at Arkenthan before saluting. Perplexed at everything that happened, Arkenthan's mind raced *'Honorary Captain? Me? I have a command in this city even though I don't live here? But..'* He noticed the sergeant was saluting him, and he quickly raised his hand to return the salute. The sergeant understood the news had surprised Arkenthan as well, and nodded before saying "So why shouldn't our patrol head into the forest?" Arkenthan blinked a few times, having forgotten about the bear for a moment, before saying "Oh, you can head in there, I am guessing, in about an hour. Right now, only a half hour's walk straight into the forest, a fjällbear, that's one of the big ones but I assume you knew that already, is resting by the river. Give it an hour and I would say it's safer to head out. The bears tend to move on pretty quickly unless they're going to sleep." The Sergeant nodded and the Colonel seemed pleased with the information Arkenthan had given. Locke stepped past the scout team and said "Sergeant Born, have your squad stand down for an hour and then head out. Report this to the command post, and have the clerk there postpone every squad by one hour." The Sergeant saluted again and the squad returned to town. Arkenthan looked at Locke and said "Honorary Captain?" The Colonel nodded and said "I never got to tell you, it seemed like we missed each other every time. Follow me, I have some papers and things to give you." He then headed off in the direction of one of the towers. Hesitantly, Arkenthan followed the Colonel who said "Of course, you don't have any official command over anyone here. You don't have any military experience, so I can't let you start your career as a Captain. But when it comes to those who are heading into the forest, I want you to have priority, and for those soldiers you will be a Captain." That made a lot more sense to Arkenthan and he said "I was wondering about that. Captain is a high rank. Starting out there, especially at my age, will make some people angry." The Colonel nodded his understanding as he opened the door to the tower. "This is where the forest scouts stay. You can stay here if you want, or find your own lodging. This way, please," the Colonel said and led the way towards another door. Arkenthan noticed a few of the men from the squad he had met earlier staring at them as they entered the next room. The Colonel gestured towards the room as they entered. Arkenthan saw that it contained a desk, a lot of bookcases and a trunk. "This is the ranking officer's quarter," the Colonel said "We want the officers and the privates to get along well, so they all sleep in the same room. This, is where the ranking officer can sit and work, have some books or scrolls of information around as he performs his duties. You will mostly be the ranking officer in this tower, but at times others might come in and require the desk. There haven't been any problems yet with this system, so let's hope you will find it acceptable too. Anyways, here's what I wanted you for." Arkenthan saw a few things lying on the table and the Colonel picked up a scroll and unfolded it. Arkenthan said "You do know that I'm only here about once a week, right?" The Colonel looked at him and said "Oh, yes. Right. Forgot about that. That won't be a problem. The guys will just do as they normally do, and then there's a slight change whenever you have something to add." Arkenthan nodded and joined the Colonel at the table. The scroll was a document stating Arkenthan's rank and branch, and Arkenthan had to sign it in several places. "Right," Locke said. "Now you are a part of our town's woodland scouts. Your military branch's symbol is a tree. Whenever there's someone with that symbol, you will usually have superior rank. Then again, if you are in town and an attack or some other emergency occurs, you are obliged to help." Arkenthan nodded and thought *Well, I wanted to join the military, just maybe not exactly in this way. Let's see what happens. I'll leave at some point, and maybe this can help me get into the army.'* The Colonel gave Arkenthan a small badge and explained that he could keep it in his pocket in case he needed to give a quick order. For when he was in town, or wanted to enter the guards' towers, Arkenthan received an armband with two silver lines on it. It informed those around him of his rank in the military branch. Arkenthan nodded as the Colonel spoke, explaining what the rules were and what to do in different situations. When he had finished, the Colonel led the way into the main quarters to show him where the others rested. "Officers up front!" Locke shouted and four men stood up and came closer. Pointing out the different men, Locke said "These people are Born, whom you've already met, Jeron and Bear. Bear is a nickname because of his size and strength, his real name is Christopher. They are the sergeants of this branch, and are under the command of Lieutenant Karn here." Directing his attention to the men, the Colonel said "This is Arkenthan. He's a newly appointed Captain for this branch of the guard. I know it's unconventional to appoint someone directly to such a high rank, but I hope you will understand and respect the decision. Arkenthan, you have anything to say to your officers?" The four men turned towards Arkenthan and saluted. Returning the salute, the officers stood down awaiting any message. Arkenthan coughed and said "This all is pretty new to all of you, and myself as well. I got to know about this merely an hour ago, so I'm still a bit taken aback. I wish to see how you do things here, and I hope you won't mind my current lack of experience. Um... As far as I understand, you are the ones responsible for scouting out the forest, and I guess that is why I've been put in this position. The forest has grown more dangerous it would seem, but I hope I can give you a bit of my knowledge to help you get through your task more easily. Um... You might wonder why I am to help with anything forest related, and I guess that would be because, um... Well, let's be open with each other. I live in there. I have lived in there for some time now, and I'm still alive." At this point a few of the men got a surprized look on their faces and some looked at others as Arkenthan said "Please keep this to yourself, I don't need everyone to know that I live there, but I figured it would be best to let you, the officers, know. If you are ever driven far into the forest and don't think you'll make it back to town before nightfall, look out for the single mountain, and make your way there. At the far side of it is my house." The men nodded. Arkenthan looked at the Colonel and said "I think that's all for now. And I think we should find a system if ever I'm needed here." The Colonel gave a short laugh and said "They're your men, so you should dismiss them." Arkenthan stood for a second thinking before turning to the men and saying "Okay, I'll probably ask you about things a bit later on. How your systems work and so on, but for now you're all dismissed. Oh, and let your men know who I am. If they have questions for me, or about me, I'm happy to answer what I can." The men saluted again and returned to their respective areas of the tower. *I guess each sergeant has his own set of bunks where his men stay. Good to have order,'* Arkenthan thought before the Colonel said "Good enough. You'll have to work on how to speak to these men though. Develop a tone of authority, you know. Get them to respect you. Well, here's a silver coin, your payment for joining the guards, and then you'll receive a few copper coins each week you serve. The central tower near the square where you got rid of the white beast is the headquarters. That's where you can get food whenever you need as well. I am usually there, unless I'm on patrol. If there is anything you need, you should start by looking there." Arkenthan nodded and the Colonel left the tower.

Looking over the men who were now staring back at Arkenthan, he thought *'Oh gods, what is happening? I actually have what? Thirty men maybe under my command? I should at least not panic in front of them.'* He cleared his throat and said "I guess you all know who I am by now. I am not going to be here too often, so just keep doing what you have been doing until now. I will decide where I'm staying. Sometimes here, and sometimes I'll stay at a room I'm renting at the butcher's. If you have any important message for me, you should give it to the butcher, and I'll get it." One man raised a hand and when Arkenthan gave him permission to speak, he said "You're the one who brought the white beast out of the village, aren't you?" Arkenthan smiled, feeling proud and said "Yes. It's a wolf though, I've named it Greypaws." The man gave a quick laugh and said "You've met it before, have you?" When Arkenthan confirmed this, the man said "How many wolves or bears have you met in the forest?" At this, Arkenthan had to think for a while before saying "I can't say for sure, as the bears seem very similar. There's only one wolf of that size, as far as I know. I've run away from three bears, I think, at the same time. And then I've fought one bear." Seeing the faces of the men looking at him, he quickly added "I had help from the wolf to fight it off though, so I didn't do it on my own. That was just a few days ago." Some of the men seemed surprised and started talking amongst themselves excitedly. Born seemed to think that question time was over, and got up saying "If you'll excuse me, Captain, my group is heading into the forest now." Arkenthan nodded and said "Good luck, and stay safe." Born didn't need anything else said, and headed out of the tower with his men following. *'He doesn't like me very much,'* Arkenthan thought as he watched the men leave the tower. The Lieutenant came over, apparently understanding what Arkenthan thought and said "Don't worry about him. He's wanted a promotion for a long time, so he dislikes anyone who gets one before him." Arkenthan nodded and said "And I guess he dislikes me even worse as I don't have any experience in the guards until now." The Lieutenant grinned and said "Exactly. But it's his loss. If he can't accept others holding higher rank, he'll never reach a higher rank himself." The

Lieutenant shrugged and said "Welcome to the Foresters, anyways. That's what we call ourselves. We feel like we're a kind of special branch of the guards, as we're the only ones in town who venture into the forest." Arkenthan smiled and said "Glad to be here. I'll probably have loads of questions, but right now I have to go to the butcher. I have an errand at the apothecary tomorrow, so I'll probably be there all day if there is anything. I would like to know if there ever is anything out of the ordinary, or if you meet with any danger. If there is anything at all, write it down on a scroll and I'll see it the next time I get to town." The Lieutenant nodded and saluted as Arkenthan prepared to leave.

Chapter 47
NOISY SCOUTS

Arkenthan opened the door to the apothecary's store. The smell stung his nostrils, even though he was prepared for it. No one was behind the counter, so he half shouted a "Hello?" into the room. Soon, the door to the back room opened and Johanna looked into the store eagerly. She said "Hey, long time now, where have you been hiding?" Arkenthan smiled and said "A lot happened, and I can't come here every time I'm in town, you know." Johanna seemed disappointed and said "Many important things to do, I guess? So, what can I help you with today then?" Arkenthan explained how he'd fought the bear to an eagerly listening Johanna. Ending the story, he explain how he'd found that he should have more of the potion standing by, just in case anything happened. Johanna nodded and as Arkenthan put the two leaves on the counter, she said "The leaves will have to be prepared on their own, and as you know, the process will take a full day. Since I'm so nice, I'll help you out by preparing one of the leaves while you do the other." She then seemed to half dance towards the back room to fetch the instruments which would be needed.

Arkenthan found it fascinating to see the speed which Johanna worked at, even though she apparently slowed down in order for Arkenthan to be able to follow. The day passed in much the same way that it had when they had first made the potion. They were only interrupted once by lieutenant Karn, and Arkenthan had to explain to Johanna that he'd gotten a rather high rank in the guard, so he was receiving a report. The report said that a squad had seen a fjällbear by the river near the village, but nothing else of importance. As the rest of the day went by, Arkenthan and Johanna managed to make four small bottles of the Dragon's Blood potion. Thanking her for the help she had given him, he gave the largest bottle of the potion to her, and gave her a silver coin for the last three bottles. "That's too much for three small bottles!" Johanna exclaimed, but Arkenthan said "Then take it as payment for the bottles, the help you've given me, and also since I am taking most of the potion with me. You were supposed to have half, weren't you?" Johanna looked down at the desk for a few seconds and said "Yes, I guess so. But everything shouldn't cost more than at most eighty coppers, so this is still too much though." Arkenthan raised his hand to silence her and said "Really, take it. I must go now, so don't argue more about this." Johanna looked at Arkenthan, came around the counter and gave him a hug saying "Don't take too long to come back here, then." It all put Arkenthan a bit off his balance, and he cleared his throat before saying good bye and heading outside.

"Ho, military boy!" Jonas said when Arkenthan entered the butcher's store, making him feel slightly embarrassed. Jonas continued "There came a letter for you. I put it on the bed upstairs." Arkenthan blinked a few times thinking *'Another report?'* He then nodded to the butcher and went upstairs. The letter lay on the bed, and Arkenthan thought it looked different from a report. First of all it came in an envelope. The flowing writing didn't seem like something you wrote a report with. He looked at the front of the envelope again reading "Arkenthan". He recognized the handwriting, and soon remembered it as belonging to his mother. Tearing the envelope open, he quickly unfolded the letter reading it half to himself and half out loud to the room. "Dear Arkenthan. I am so happy to hear from you. I wrote a letter to your father saying that you had followed him, but he wrote back that he still hadn't seen you there. All kinds of thoughts passed through my head as I waited for some sign that you were alive. I would like you to come home, but I understand that you wouldn't come back even if I came there myself to drag you home. I just hope you are careful in that forest, it doesn't sound very safe in there." The letter went on about how she missed him and that his experiences seemed intriguing. It ended by asking Arkenthan to be careful and to send a letter to her every now and then, to let her know he was doing well. Arkenthan folded the letter, put it in his bag and wiped a tear from his cheek. He felt homesick wondering what both his mother and father were doing right now. After a while, Arkenthan went downstairs and asked for a few sheets of paper to write another letter. He wrote of what had happened since the last time, how he had helped a man of the guard and got Greypaws out of town. He also wrote that he'd been recruited into the guard, and that he'd got a high command in the scouts branch. He told his mother to let his father know that he was okay, and that when he was able to join the great army he'd find him. Having finished the letter, Arkenthan saw that it was only one sheet. "Better than the last one," he said laughing to himself. Going downstairs he gave the letter to Jonas so that he could send it. The butcher nodded and put the letter in his pocket.

The next morning Arkenthan headed to the Foresters' tower to see if anyone were heading out soon. *'Better to take a trip with someone than taking it all alone,'* he thought as he opened the door. Just inside the door stood Bear and four other men. Seeing who entered, they all saluted and Bear said "Morning Captain, we're preparing to head out into the forest now." Arkenthan smiled and said he'd join them. Bear seemed to understand why, but the others just seemed excited to have him along. They crossed to the edge of the forest and immediately he noticed how much noise the group made. *Wow, no wonder they never see anything out here, they must be scaring everything off,'* Arkenthan thought. After a few minutes, Bear turned around and said "I only heard the sounds of my guys behind me, so I thought we'd lost you." Arkenthan nodded and said "I did notice you were making a lot of noise walking around here. If you want to find out what's going on here, you should learn to be a little more quiet. The advantage of making sound, though, is that animals aren't surprized when you appear." The scouts stood still at this moment, and Arkenthan wondered what they were thinking about. They reached the river and Bear said that they usually went upstream. Arkenthan told Bear that he would have to head in the other direction, and Bear said that he couldn't remember the last time they went that way. "Maybe a change to the system would be good once in a while?" he said and Arkenthan smiled saying "I'll tell the others I'll be observing them from inside the forest. After a while, if they wonder where I'm at, tell them I went off somewhere. Oh, and I'll actually be observing for a bit as well. See how they behave in the forest when it's just you five around." Bear nodded and Arkenthan let the guys know. They looked a bit nervously from one to the other, but didn't argue with his decision. Arkenthan slipped into the forest and heard Bear give a command to move out. At first Arkenthan made an effort to make a bit of noise, but eventually he went as quiet as he could. The gradual change didn't seem to affect the guards, and he could soon see how they chose the broadest, most open paths along their route. *That's the easiest way, but that's what bigger animals will think as well,'* Arkenthan thought as he ran alongside the squad. He got to a bend in the river before the squad and saw one of the little human-like creatures. It seemed to have heard the squad and quickly jumped behind a bush. From where Arkenthan was standing the creature was completely visible, and by the way the group of people were moving, the creature seemed to feel safe. A few minutes later the group of five passed the area, without noticing anything out of the ordinary. Arkenthan almost laughed, but didn't want to scare the creature. *It shouldn't have to run straight into the scouts,'* he thought and snuck closer to the riverbed where the creature was stepping forth again. Lying down on his stomach, Arkenthan watched as the creature patiently stood looking into the river. He was lying widely open, but had been so quiet that the creature didn't seem to notice him. After a minute the creature thrust its hands into the river and pulled up a big fish. *Wow,'* Arkenthan thought and kept watching. The creature turned and noticed Arkenthan lying beside the river

247

upstream. Arkenthan waved to the human looking creature, and after a few seconds it picked up the fish and sceptically stepped into the forest. *I'll probably not find it now if I decide to run after it. Who knows, maybe I'll see it again soon,'* Arkenthan thought as he got up, dusted off and headed into the forest.

He quickly caught up with the squad who were taking a quick break in the clearing, marvelling at how nice it was there. At that point, Greypaws entered the clearing. As the men scrambled around preparing their weapons, the wolf got nervous and started growling. Arkenthan sighed and stepped into the clearing behind the scouts. When Greypaws noticed Arkenthan he sat down, to the scouts' surprize. A few of them were nervously holding their weapons in front of themselves. This time Arkenthan did laugh, and the men turned to look at him. "Stand down, he's not dangerous. At least, not while I'm here. I can't speak for when I'm not around, but I wouldn't think he'd hurt you even then," Arkenthan said and passed them. He put a hand on Greypaws' head and had each man reach out a hand so that the wolf could get used to their smell. A bird's warble was heard and Greypaws raised one ear. The men didn't seem to think much about it, but Arkenthan looked around the clearing uncertainly. At the far end of the clearing, at a branch high up in a tree sat one of the strange creatures looking at them. Arkenthan smiled and returned his attention to the group. He took Bear to the side, pointed in the direction he was going to go, and said "That way there is a direct line to the mountain I mentioned two days ago. This clearing is where I usually pass when I come from home, and from town. It's a useful point of navigating for getting back and forth." Bear nodded and Arkenthan returned to the men who seemed to be feeling a bit calmer around the great wolf. "Okay, guys, listen up. I'll have to take him somewhere else. So I'll be leaving you for now. Good job today, a bit noisy for my taste though. I noticed you scared off a couple of animals unnecessarily, but practice and it will get better." A few of the men laughed a little and Arkenthan turned towards Greypaws and said "Come on, you. Let's go." Greypaws stood up and turned towards the mountain. Glancing back, he saw the little creature jump from the top of the tree onto the ground behind some bushes. Again Arkenthan smiled and thought *'Maybe I can make that one get used to me as well?'*

The trip home went easily enough. Having left the guards, Arkenthan put a bit more potion onto the wound in Greypaws' shoulder, but it already looked a lot better. Upon getting home, Arkenthan went around his traps and found a couple of smaller game which would be enough for that day. Having got the fire in his house burning well, Arkenthan made another fire outside his house. The night was warm and after having eaten, he lay down in the grass beside the fire. Greypaws lay in the grass chewing what was left of the dinner. The chewing noises made Arkenthan drowsy and soon he fell asleep. He woke up in the middle of the night as it was raining. With his clothes soaking wet, Arkenthan ran inside and hung them in front of the fire. *'I hope they dry by tomorrow,'* he thought as he went to bed again. Having trouble falling asleep, Arkenthan lay thinking of how to be able to get a message to or from town when he was at home. He thought of making some kind of lights system, and thought *'Then I'd need to go up to the mountain every night, I guess.'* His thoughts turned from the village to him joining the militia, and with that his thoughts trailed towards the book. *'I wonder what's going to happen now,'* he thought, and seeing how he wasn't tired anymore he went into the cave to get the book. Getting back out to the house he lay down in bed to start reading.

Chapter 48
THE CRAZY OLD MAN

The next morning Arkenthan woke up with his head in the book, not remembering if he'd actually read anything. Sighing he thought *'I'll have to read more soon, but I can't right now.'* He got dressed and went outside. Greypaws lay soaking on the ground, and as Arkenthan approached, the wolf stood up and shook the water out of his fur. It felt like it was raining again, and in a joking tone Arkenthan said "Greypaws, my clothes were almost dry." The wolf responded by tilting his head to the side. Arkenthan looked up and saw that the sky was clear, and the sun was on its way. He brought his sword out from the house and thought *'I could probably get a better one from the guard tower. I'll have to ask captain Locke what I can have.'* Bringing a few of his scrolls with him, Arkenthan practiced several new techniques. He noticed that the training Johannes had put him through afforded him more control over his movements, and now he could more easily pretend to have an opponent. With his new experience Arkenthan also found it easier to learn several of the techniques that the scrolls were illustrating. After a long workout, leaving him tired but with dry clothes, Arkenthan got his bow and said to Greypaws "Come on, let's take a trip up the mountain. I have to check something." He then walked down the path to the mountain, but Greypaws decided to head into the forest instead. *'Strange,'* Arkenthan thought. *'I guess he has his own things to see to as well.'* Preparing an arrow on the string, Arkenthan made his way up the mountain path. After an hour he found a good campsite overlooking the forest towards town. After looking towards town for some time, Arkenthan noticed a small tower standing a bit taller than the rest of its buildings. *'There. That's what I should use,'* Arkenthan thought and wondered how easy it would be seen in the dark. He lay down and tested the breathing technique the book had talked about. *'Breathe in for seven seconds, hold the breath for three seconds and breathe out for seven seconds,'* Arkenthan told himself as he lay on the ground, arms outstretched and took deep breaths. Soon enough his head started tingling, and his arms felt numb. Losing focus every now and then, Arkenthan eventually managed to arrive at the feeling described in the book. The tingling filled his entire body and after a while, when the feeling was so strong that he felt it wouldn't get any stronger, he started focusing on an area in the middle of his chest. After a while the tingling, pushing feeling started to compress where he was focusing. While watching the energy inside him, Arkenthan started to see colours shift and turn, and his body felt strange. He compressed the energy into a ball which turned blue. After a while he felt like it changed to a green colour, and then a light brown. While the colour changed every few seconds, Arkenthan kept watching the ball, doing the exercise as he remembered it from the book. What felt like ages passed, until the small ball of energy inside him seemed to stop at a very strange feeling. Trying to imagine what colour it was, Arkenthan couldn't find anything which felt right. He tried thinking back to the book and remembered Boriam talking about a golden colour. Arkenthan got the feeling that this was not right for the ball of energy inside him. Eventually he thought *'it would have to be silver coloured. That feels right, for some reason.'* Having discovered the colour of his energy, Arkenthan opened his eyes and took a deep breath. Sitting up, he still had a tingling feeling in his arms. As he gripped his bow, Arkenthan could feel how every finger worked its grip individually. *'Whoah, that is a crazy feeling,'* Arkenthan thought as he flexed his fingers. He put an arrow to the string and pulled the bow effortlessly. Smiling, Arkenthan lowered the bow again and started on the way down. As he walked, everything seemed much brighter, and he could easily see where he should put his foot for his next step. Arkenthan started wondering what the other steps of the meditation were, imagining what the book would teach next.

He arrived at his house and fetched a piece of paper and some charcoal. He quickly drew a small house and marked it with a circle. He noted down where the lake was, the clearing he'd first been chased by Greypaws, where the Dragon's Blood plant and the beehive was, and also where he thought the big tree stump was. Bringing his map, Arkenthan entered the forest. Every time he found berries, herbs, animal tracks or small paths he drew them on the map. Soon the map was filled with notes and drawings of what was where. Using the map to locate different things, he spent the rest of the evening gathering roots, herbs and berries. With his bag full of edible plants, Arkenthan headed home. On the way there he heard some strange sounds nearby. He snuck into the bushes and saw a small wild pig eating something. Oblivious to Arkenthan, the pig made a lot of noise digging something out of the ground. Without fear of being noticed, Arkenthan fastened an arrow and drew the string. Guided by the new sensation he'd got after the meditation on the mountain, Arkenthan didn't really need to aim for the pig. As soon as he'd pulled the string, he felt as if a small part of the pig started glowing, and he knew that the arrow would hit where he saw the glow. As soon as he had shifted the glow to the pig's neck, Arkenthan let go of the string. He watched as the arrow flew through the air and struck exactly where he intended. The pig gave a quick squeal, and fell over. Stepping calmly over to the pig, Arkenthan noticed it was a rather small animal, but he assumed it would last for a few days at least. "Right. Let's get you home, and get you cooked," Arkenthan said ignoring the fact that he was alone. *'I'm allowed to be a little crazy when I live alone in the forest,'* he thought and lifted the pig.

The pig filled Arkenthan's stomach completely, and he sat sighing outside when Greypaws returned. He was carrying a big branch and put it on the lawn before settling down. "Hey Greypaws, what have you been doing all day?" Arkenthan asked and continued "Is that your chewing stick?" Greypaws tilted his head, but didn't bite the branch. Too tired to get up, Arkenthan lay in the grass for a while watching the sky as it turned darker. Eventually, Arkenthan went inside and brought out a small piece of meat for Greypaws. Arkenthan watched as the wolf ate the whole piece in a single bite, and then he went inside to sleep.

The next morning a bird was sitting outside the window singing. Stepping outside and feeling the air, Arkenthan thought *'It must have been raining last night as well.'* Droplets of water hung from the branches of the trees. He noticed that Greypaws had gone again, and the bed where he slept was wet, so Arkenthan assumed he'd been away all night. The branch was still lying on the ground where the wolf had dropped it. Arkenthan went over to the branch to look at it. *'It's a small branch for him to chew on,'* he thought as he picked it up. Turning it around, Arkenthan saw strange carvings in the wood, like the symbols he'd made on his walking stick. *'Strange. I wonder where he found it?'* Arkenthan thought and brought it inside. Looking through the scrolls in the bookcase, Arkenthan was unable to find anything about the symbols on the stick. He found another piece of paper and noted down the symbols from the stick. He put the paper on a shelf along with the map he'd made the day before. He decided to get a bit more hunting done, if the rain was going to come more often it would be nice to have some more food in stock. His traps yielded three small game, and he shot a couple of other small animals. Starting to feel like he had got enough to survive for a while, Arkenthan headed back home. Taking a slightly longer route, Arkenthan found a badger and thought *'Why not? Just to be sure I have enough.'* He loaded an arrow, pulled the string and heard a loud snap. The top piece of his bow broke off and hit him hard in the forehead. The sound scared the animal off, and when Arkenthan felt his forehead, his fingers came away red. *'Crap,'* Arkenthan thought as he ran towards his house. By the time he got there, one of his eyes were closed from the blood dripping down his face. He hurried inside and used a bucket of water to clean the wound and see how deep it was. He found it to be dripping steadily, but it didn't look too deep. He took a cloth and wiped it off, before dripping a few drops of his potion onto the wound. It stung badly as it hit the wound. *'I understand why Greypaws flinched when I applied it to his wound,'* Arkenthan thought as he watched the potion turn green in the wound. The bleeding stopped a few seconds afterwards, and with a beginning headache Arkenthan lay down in bed. Waking up a few hours later he examined the wound again and saw that it had turned a yellow colour. *'I wonder what that means?'* he thought and applied one more drop to the wound, which turned green, then blue then yellow. Nodding to himself, Arkenthan thought *'I guess it's supposed to look like that then.'* Stepping outside he found the broken bow and sighed. He tried to remember where he'd found the wood for it earlier, but quickly thought of the bows the guards in town were carrying. *'Maybe I can get a bow from the city guards?'* he thought and remembered thinking that he should ask for a sword as well. "I might just as well ask soon," Arkenthan said to himself, and decided to head to town the following day. After making a quick dinner, his head started pounding again, so he went to bed early.

Arkenthan woke up early the next morning, when the sun was still below the horizon. Looking out the window, he saw Greypaws lying in his pen and he thought *'If I get him to come along, the journey won't be as dangerous. And if I leave now, maybe I can actually get back before the day is done?'* Arkenthan nodded to himself having made the decision. When Arkenthan came out of the house, Greypaws slowly lifted his head and yawned. The great wolf stretched its limbs and stood up. "Come on, Grey. Want to follow me back to town? I'll only be there for a few hours, so I'll be getting back by tonight." Greypaws gave another yawn and followed Arkenthan up the hill. At night the forest seemed much scarier than during the day. Everything seemed quiet, and then out of nowhere something jumped across the path, or a birds nest started chirping. A few times Arkenthan heard some loud noises sounding like howling and growling coming from the darkness, and then it all went quiet again. He knew it was close to morning, and the thought of the sun rising to bring light to everything cheered him up. The patting of Greypaws' paws calmed him down and made him feel safer.

The sun stood high in the sky when Arkenthan arrived at the little lake. He sat down on the log which lay there, and let Greypaws settle down for a bit. As he sighed, Arkenthan could hear some voices coming through the forest, and he thought *'They really need to learn how to be quiet out here. I hope they do that when it's dark, at least.'* He could hear them come closer, and started wondering who it was. Greypaws lifted his head and followed the sound until the five men appeared. As Arkenthan sat behind Greypaws when the men appeared, the five men jumped as they noticed the big wolf.

Arkenthan could see it was sergeant Jeron who led the men on their patrol, and after letting the men panic for a few seconds, Arkenthan stood up and walked around the wolf. "'Morning," he said and the men seemed confused about what was happening. Jeron gave a quick laugh, saluted and said "I thought you wouldn't be back for about a week! What are you doing here now?" Arkenthan sighed and said "My bow snapped yesterday. Gave me this cut on my forehead." He pointed to the cut and said "I was wondering if the guards would equip me with a bow and a sword perhaps?" Jeron opened and closed his mouth a few times before saying "You're saying that you've walked through the forest along with the huge wolf there without a weapon?" Arkenthan lifted an eyebrow and said "What's wrong with that?" A few of the men laughed a little and Arkenthan remembered "You guys should really learn to be quiet out here though. I could hear you for five minutes before you got here." He knew it was an exaggeration, but they didn't. The men fell quiet and Arkenthan directed his attention to the sergeant and asked "So do you think I can get a bow and a sword in town?" Jeron nodded and said "Go to the main tower and ask for the Colonel. He should give you what you need. Now if you'll excuse us, we should be on our way for the patrol." Arkenthan saluted the men, and said "And you should really not be afraid around Greypaws. It might make him nervous, but he shouldn't attack you without reason." A few of the men looked sceptically at the great wolf and then turned and walked after their leader. When they had disappeared into the forest, Arkenthan smiled and turned towards Greypaws saying "Okay, you know what to do, stay here until I come back." Greypaws sat down, and Arkenthan nodded before turning towards town.

Half an hour later Arkenthan entered town near where the tower he'd seen from the mountain stood. *'Hmm. I wonder if anyone is in there?'* Arkenthan thought and knocked on the door. An elderly man opened the door and said "Ooh, it's you! Um. Hello, can I help you with anything?" Sceptically, Arkenthan asked "What do you mean by 'Oh, it's you'?" The elderly man sighed and said "Forgive me. I've been snooping. Come in, I'll tell you, forest-boy." Blinking a few times, Arkenthan followed the old man into the tower. Having asked how the old man knew he came from the forest, the old man grinned and said "Follow me to the top of the tower. I have something to show you." As they made their way up the winding stairs, the old man explained. "I have made this invention. It's a tube with pieces of crystal inside, which lets me see over great distances. It's a bit hard to see everything, and it's quite big, but I'm trying to make a smaller one these days. With this, I usually look at the night sky, but one day I was looking towards the mountain, and I saw a young man walking back and forth. Every now and then I've seen this man, you, on the mountain, and that's how I knew you were from the forest." They reached the top floor, and Arkenthan understood what the man meant by 'quite big.' The tube occupied half the room, and was pointed out the window towards the mountain. When he looked into the tube he could see exactly where he had decided to make his latest camp site. He imagined himself being at that camp, and understood that the old man could recognize him. He wondered how the tube worked, but didn't dare ask right now. He said "That is a fantastic invention. And you are trying to make a smaller version of it?" The man nodded eagerly, and said "Yes, yes! I have almost managed to do it. Yes, the last one I tried making exploded, but I'm getting there." Again Arkenthan didn't dare ask, and instead said "I was wondering about something." The man nodded and Arkenthan continued "I have been enlisted in the guards here, commanding the forest scouts." The old man interrupted saying "Ah, the Foresters. Great branch of the guard. I used to be a Forester, you know." Arkenthan felt a story coming and nodded. The old man seemed to pick himself up and said "Oh, sorry, I almost dragged you into something else entirely. What were you saying?" Arkenthan breathed out, relieved, and said "As you know I live in the forest. Right where you have your looking-tube pointed, I've found a small camp. I was wondering if the Foresters could borrow your tower in case an emergency arose? Lighting a bright light will make me see it from that camp, and if I then see a great light I know there's something I'm needed for in town. That way I can come as soon as I'm needed, instead of people waiting for me for several days." The old man stood thinking for a while and said "Okay, I guess that's possible. I'll work on it right away. A temporary light should be no problem to make, but I'll try to find something better." Arkenthan nodded and thanked the old man. He gave a strange laugh, and shoved Arkenthan towards the stairs saying "Off you go now, I have work to do. You can find your own way out, can't you?" Without being given the chance to respond, Arkenthan suddenly stood at the top of the stairs, and the old man was on his way back to his desk. Laughing to himself, Arkenthan thought *Crazy old man.* He then walked down the stairs of the tower.

Chapter 49
EQUIPMENT

When Arkenthan got to the main tower he had to go through a labyrinth of corridors and stairs in order to find Colonel Locke. When he finally found him, the Colonel wondered why he was back so soon, and Arkenthan explained what had happened, and asked what equipment he might get from the city guard. "Forgot to give you equipment, did I? Oh, well, follow me," the Colonel said and led the way through another maze. Eventually Arkenthan was so confused about where he was that he had to ask the Colonel. Locke laughed and said "We've come two floors beneath the ground now. This room here is where we store all our equipment. Come." Arkenthan was still surprized by the fact that they'd gone beneath the ground. When the Colonel opened the door to a huge room, Arkenthan noticed it was parted into several sections. Several walls were standing separately in the room in rows. Each wall had its own type of weapon, armour, shield or different types of arrows. Arkenthan stared around the room as the Colonel walked towards the wall holding swords. "New recruits generally get one of these swords here," Locke said and pointed at a big stack of swords standing out from the wall. "But you are an officer, after all, and so you are allowed to choose any of these four types of sword here. The last two types are for higher ranking officers." Baffled by all this, Arkenthan went over to the four swords the Colonel had pulled out. He noticed they were taken better care of than the recruits' swords, and they were gilded more to look better. He picked up one after another and noticed that the shape was slightly different for each one. The weight varied too, and he asked if Locke could tell him anything about any of them. The Colonel nodded and said "This here is heavier, to enable you to strike harder, forcing the enemy back. I'm thinking this is more for big guys who generally are a bit slower, like Bear. You wouldn't want this one." He picked up another one and said "This is a very standard sword, decent weight and not too flashy, if you understand what I mean. It's made to fight, but that's it. Many choose this sword as it is good in any situation, as long as you know a bit about sword handling. This along with the last two is more up your alley I guess." Moving on, Locke explained how the next one was suited for a quicker technique, where the owner had to change stance and direction of attack very quickly. "Not too many choose this sword, as it requires more precision and a refined technique," he said and moved on to the fourth one. "Another good general sword, fit for any situation. A bit heavier than sword number two, so it requires a bit more strength to wield properly. That's it, really. Test the swords on the dummy over there, and see which one you prefer." Arkenthan quickly discarded the first sword. The second and fourth seemed pretty much the same, which was what the Colonel had explained, but the third sword seemed to want to slip out of his hand. Trying to wield the third sword, Arkenthan started laughing at the strange way the sword acted. He looked up and said "I think this sword has some grudge against me." Locke laughed and said "As I said, not too many choose that sword." Arkenthan noticed another stack of swords and asked "What are those?" The Colonel looked over and said "Oh, I completely forgot about those. Can't blame me though, as they require a very old technique to use properly, so no one I've met have ever chosen one. It is much lighter than all the others, so it won't lend the same force to the blows, but I have a feeling it can be one of the more efficient swords as long as you know the technique. I don't know of anyone who know this technique any more though, so the swords will probably just rust away." Arkenthan asked if he could look at one, and the Colonel brought a couple of them out to find the one which was the least worn out. "Here, have fun," Locke said and gave the sword to Arkenthan. The guard was red, and the grip was blue with golden circles on it. At the end was a small golden pommel. He slipped his fingers around the grip, and could feel the sword rest perfectly in his hand. *'Feels like it's holding onto me instead of the other way around,'* Arkenthan thought and walked over to the dummy. "Old technique, eh?" he said to himself and decided to do a couple of flourishes from the scrolls in his house. Soon a chunk of the dummy lay on the floor, and Arkenthan hadn't even felt he'd needed to use the sword. The Colonel stood staring at the piece of the dummy for a few seconds before saying "How did you do that?" Arkenthan laughed and said "I don't know, it's just the way I've learned to fight." Locke nodded and said "I guess I've finally found someone who actually want that sword." They then went on to the bows and arrows, and Arkenthan found a bow which he figured would blend well in with the forest. Choosing a leather quiver of arrows with much the same colours, Arkenthan fired a couple of shots at the dummy and felt good about the bow. The Colonel nodded and guided Arkenthan out of the tower again. Once outside, the Colonel gave Arkenthan a coin token and said "Give that to the blacksmith and he'll sharpen your blade for you. The woodworker is the one supplying us with arrows, so if you run out you can ask him for some more." Arkenthan put the coin in his pocket and headed towards the smithy.

Horace seemed happy to see Arkenthan as he entered, and Arkenthan could almost see a smile in the big man's beard. "Hey Horace, how have you been?" Horace grinned and said "I was more worried about you, boy. The last time I saw you, you were fighting the big white wolf. What happened after you left?" Arkenthan sighed and said "Everyone makes it out to be such a big deal. I already knew the wolf well, and knew that as soon as I could make it realize who I was, I would get it out of town easily. Everyone just kept scaring it, so it kept defending itself. When I came here a few days ago, Colonel Locke said that since I knew the forest and had the wolf under my control, I was given an honorary command in the forest scouts." Horace congratulated him and said "So I guess you won't be able to help me out anymore, eh?" Arkenthan laughed and said "I'll try my best. I do like being in a smithy, but I have a feeling a lot of my time will have to be spent elsewhere." Horace nodded and asked what he could help Arkenthan with this time. Arkenthan pulled out his new sword and said that he needed to get it sharpened. Horace looked at the sword and said "I have probably sharpened every sword the guards use. Until now I have never seen one like this. It's so light, will it do what is needed?" Arkenthan nodded and said "Apparently I'm the only one here with a weird enough technique to wield this type of sword." Horace laughed and headed towards a big stone wheel. "It seem very old, and very unused. Didn't have any newer ones did they?" the smith said and Arkenthan sat down sighing. Horace nodded and started working. He explained that usually he would use two types of grindstone, where one was used to remove the worst dents, and then the second to make it sharper. With Arkenthan's sword he had to use a third one to get rid of the green and red rust which had appeared in various places on the sword before he could use the two other stones. The smith seemed to find it interesting to sharpen the sword though, as he kept looking at it in the light. He said "This sword has some very strange shapes etched into the metal itself. It looks like the rings on a tree go through it. The edge is shaped in a way which makes sharpening a bit harder to do, but I think it will stay sharp for longer than other swords. Arkenthan didn't really understand what the smith meant, but let the man ramble on as the sword was sharpened. Having finished the sword, the smith led Arkenthan outside into the sunlight and showed him his sword. The blade itself seemed to have a brown colour, and along with the red guard, the blue grip with the golden circles and pommel, the sword seemed to shine in the sunlight. "Wow," Arkenthan said and Horace nodded saying "You can say that again. Beautiful blade. Take care of it, now. And if anything happens to it, bring it back here and I'll see what I can do for you." Arkenthan thanked the smith for all his help, and gave him the token. Horace nodded, put the token in his pocket and returned to the smithy.

Looking up the street Arkenthan saw the carpenter's store and hurried over. When he'd knocked on the open door, he said "I think I might owe you for a bamboo staff." The carpenter looked at Arkenthan and said "Ah, yes. I was wondering where it went. It is rather expensive though, it's from the far west which, I guess you would know, we're in war against." Arkenthan sighed and asked if he could pay him back in instalments, and the carpenter laughed saying that that could work and that he'd knock off a bit of the price. "Since you got the big wolf out of town," he said and asked "Was it the bamboo pole you used back then? Quick thinking. I didn't recognize it, I was pretty far back in the crowd." Arkenthan smiled and told him how he remembered the carpenter having said the bamboo was very strong. The carpenter smiled at this, and Arkenthan gave him almost all of his money before turning towards the Foresters' tower.

As he passed guards on the way to the Foresters' tower, several turned and looked at the sword hanging from Arkenthan's side. Feeling a little on display, Arkenthan increased his speed and quickly entered the tower. Inside Born was standing getting ready to head out. Arkenthan sighed and said "Every time I enter this tower it seems like someone is about to head out on a patrol." Born nodded and said "Want to join us captain?" Arkenthan shrugged and said "I have a few things to do first, but I'll head out shortly after you, so maybe I'll find you in there." Born nodded and told the men to head out. The Lieutenant approached Arkenthan after the group had left and said "Nice sword. Never seen anyone choose that one before." Arkenthan explained what had happened when he had tested it, and the Lieutenant seemed surprised at this saying "You actually cut a piece off the dummy? Bear did that as well, but other than him I haven't heard of anyone doing that." Arkenthan looked at Bear lying in his bunk. 'He does look like a bear,' Arkenthan thought and asked "Anything to report?" As the Lieutenant said that nothing appeared to have changed, Arkenthan told him about the old man's tower. "And each night, as darkness is approaching, I'll head up the mountain to look for a signal. If there is a signal, I'll get here the next day. We should find a way of declaring if it's an urgent emergency as well. That way I would know that I had to get here the same night." The Lieutenant nodded and said he'd speak to the man in the tower. They agreed to test it out the day after the current one, and then Arkenthan headed out of the tower.

Stepping into the forest, Arkenthan wondered if he would get home before it got dark. He followed the river downstream towards the clearing, keeping his eyes open for the little human-like creatures. He found no creature along the river and, getting to the clearing, Arkenthan sighed wondering where Greypaws was at. He turned towards his path home and started walking. After a few minutes, already deep into the forest, Arkenthan heard a scream. *'That sounded like a human,'* he thought and ran towards where it had come from. Arkenthan could hear several men shouting now, and he wondered what was happening when a branch tripped him up. *'Come on, Arkenthan, get up and get moving!'* he thought and started running again. The shouts grew louder and he soon came crashing into a clearing where he stopped and stared at what was unfolding before him..

Chapter 50
BATTLING A BEAR

In front of Arkenthan stood two huge fjällbears facing the other way towards Born's group of men. One of them was lying on the ground, holding his arms around his leg, and the four others stood in front of him with their swords drawn. Arkenthan thought *'Oh, no. I have to do something, but what?'* One of the bears bounded towards the group, but as there were four of them they managed to hold it off. When the other bear prepared to attack, Arkenthan instinctively picked up a rock and threw it at the big bear's head. Confused, the bear turned towards Arkenthan and growled so loudly that it felt like the sound itself would grind his bones to dust. The four standing men seemed equally surprised at seeing Arkenthan, but kept their attention on the bear attacking them. Throwing another stone at the second bear made it turn towards Arkenthan and bound towards him. "Shit," Arkenthan said and ran into the forest. He could hear the bear crashing through the forest after him, and Arkenthan thought *I wonder if I'll ever not need to do this? At least the others should manage to take care of the one bear. Now what should I do?'* As he ran through the forest, the bear kept coming closer, then falling further behind before starting to catch up again. A tree came crashing down behind him and he gave a short scream as he kept on running. He knew the bear would catch up eventually, but he wanted to keep that from happening for another while. Several birds flew into the air as the two of them crashed through bushes and knocked down trees. *'Maybe they always fly when a bear is around?'* Arkenthan wondered, but figured they didn't really get scared when a bear just walked through the forest. He dashed into a clearing and thought *'Oh, no.'* Knowing the bear would catch up to him before he could cross the clearing, Arkenthan ran for a short while, then turned pulling his sword. He was out of breath, his legs were shaking and he could barely stand upright when the bear came running out of the forest. To Arkenthan it was all happening very slowly. The big brown beast crashing through a bush at the edge of the clearing, scaring two birds into the air who flew wildly into the branches of the neighbouring tree, and Arkenthan thought *'I'm going to die, aren't I?'* Sitting down, Arkenthan sighed

FREDRIK B. LUNDE

and prepared for a quick stab of pain when a white blur shot out of the forest and crashed into the bear. Arkenthan blinked a few times as the brown and white heap of creatures rolled sideways, and it took a few seconds before he understood what had happened. Still tired after running, Arkenthan tried the meditation the book had mentioned. He felt the lump in his chest burning, expanding and soon he felt a shock go through his body. His muscles jumped forcefully, making his limbs stretch out before returning to his chosen way of sitting. Regaining the feeling of his limbs, Arkenthan felt completely refreshed. Standing up, he grabbed his sword and ran towards the two fighting creatures. "Greypaws!" Arkenthan shouted, and the wolf ran around the side of the bear and joined Arkenthan. Pointing to the left, Arkenthan ran to the right. Greypaws apparently understood what he meant, as he ran to the left and started to attack the bear again. The bear, not knowing what was happening, struck its paw out towards Arkenthan and strafed his stomach. A big wound appeared across Arkenthan's stomach, but he forced himself onwards. The wound wasn't too deep, and using the sword as a shield to block the bear's attacks, Arkenthan got closer for each time Greypaws struck the bear. *'It really is huge,'* Arkenthan thought looking up at the bear. Swinging the sword, Arkenthan cut the bear in several places, but for each cut the bear received, the more enraged it became. With ever harder strikes from the bear, Arkenthan started to grow very tired. The lump in his chest started burning, and the feeling made Arkenthan feel sick. *'Can't focus on that now,'* he thought as he kept swinging his sword. Greypaws howled and Arkenthan saw that the wolf had got a big cut across its ribs. Starting to get angry, Arkenthan swung his sword faster, but failed to parry the bear's attack. The claws of the bear struck his leg and made a deep wound. With the wound in his leg, Arkenthan found it harder to move around. The little moving he did pained him, and the pain made him feel extremely warm. At one point he was so warm it felt like he was back at the smithy in the Black Village. The bear struck Greypaws' head, and the wolf rolled to the side. Watching, Arkenthan couldn't see Greypaws trying to get up. He got so angry he jumped towards the bear screaming. He landed on the wounded leg and the pain welled up in him as he forced the blade into the bear's hind leg. Pushing the blade as hard as he could, suddenly a white light appeared in front of Arkenthan's eyes. Focusing on the feeling of the blade pushing into the bear's leg, suddenly the bear howled, and jumped away from Arkenthan. Arkenthan fell and caught himself just as he hit the ground. While lying on the ground, the white light disappeared from his eyes. Arkenthan watched as the bear crashed into the forest with what looked like a burning leg. One of the human looking creatures stepped into his view and jumped to one of the trees. It looked at him and smiled. Then he fell asleep.

262

A wet nose prodded Arkenthan's cheek, waking him up. Exhausted, Arkenthan barely managed to turn his head and saw Greypaws standing beside him. "Hey," Arkenthan said weakly "I was afraid you'd died. I can't get up." He tried to turn around, but a pain shot up his leg and across his stomach. He looked along his body and saw the big wounds both on his stomach and chest, and on the leg. "Ow," he said and laughed to himself. "Now what? I need to stop the bleeding, but I can't get up." He sighed and started grabbing the grass in front of him when Greypaws lay down in front of him blocking his path. "Move, I need to get some leaves or something to stop my bleeding." The wolf moved slightly towards Arkenthan and pushed his head under Arkenthan's arm. "You want me to hold on to you?" Arkenthan asked and stretched his arm around the wolf's neck, grabbing the opposite side. Standing up, Greypaws lifted Arkenthan off the ground. By sitting down and standing up again a few times Greypaws allowed Arkenthan to get a good grip around his neck. Most of his bodyweight lay on top of the great wolf. Greypaws bounded through the darkening forest without Arkenthan knowing in which direction. A long time passed, where Arkenthan fell asleep and woke up several times before they suddenly appeared at the house by the mountain. This time Greypaws entered the garden and set Arkenthan down by the front door. "Thanks, Grey," Arkenthan said weakly as he opened the door to his house. The fire was still keeping the house warm. Just inside the door his bag lay, where he knew the potions were, and after some fiddling he got the bottles out. He poured a lot of the potion onto the wounds, and a searing pain shot through his body. Thinking *'Ah, why not?'* Arkenthan drank a bit of the potion as well, and immediately fell asleep.

When he finally woke up, Arkenthan lay on the floor just inside the door. The wounds had stopped bleeding, and had started to heal, but he still couldn't walk on his leg. *'That is a powerful potion,'* Arkenthan thought and noticed that it was sunny outside. He suddenly felt like he was starving and thirsting. Looking at the fireplace he noticed that it had gone cold. *'It shouldn't go cold for at least a couple of days, how long was I sleeping?'* he thought and drank a bucket of water. Feeling a little refreshed, Arkenthan jumped on one leg towards the fireplace to try and light it again. An hour passed before he managed to get the fire going again. He put a piece of meat on a spit and hung it over the small flame. As the fire built, Arkenthan sat on the floor resting his leg, when something struck the door. *'Nothing ever enters the garden. Except Greypaws when he carried me here,'* Arkenthan thought and wondered what it could be. Using the branch Greypaws had brought some days earlier, Arkenthan supported his damaged leg on the way to the door. He opened it, and was surprized to find Born and Karn standing outside ready to give the door another knock. With a surprized look, the lieutenant said

"So you do live here. The men were all worried about you." As Arkenthan was unable to understand what they meant, Born said "It's been a week since you took off into the forest with a great bear on your tail. You didn't respond to the light signals we sent from the tower, so we were wondering what had happened to you." Arkenthan blinked a few times and said "A week?" The two guards looked at each other, then nodded to Arkenthan. "Come in, please," Arkenthan said and hopped into the room. "Can't really walk on my leg, so excuse me for not holding the door for you." He sat down on one of the beds and gestured towards the next. Karn and Born sat down asking "What happened to you and the bear?" Arkenthan sighed and said "Actually, it would seem I haven't had anything to eat for a week, could one of you check the meat over the fire there?" Confused, Born went over to the big piece of meat and found it to be done. As he ate his food, Arkenthan told them about what had happened, except for the fire and the strange human-like creature. Ending the story, Arkenthan said "I have this nice little potion which heals most wounds pretty quickly. When I dragged myself into the house after the fight, and having put the potion onto my wounds," he pointed at his leg and took off his shirt, "I drank a bit of the potion, and fell asleep. I woke up today, just a few hours before you two knocked on my door, actually." Shocked, the two men sat staring at Arkenthan's leg and stomach, until Karn said "Born and his men had enough trouble with the one bear they had to fight. Good job on fighting off the second one, even though you did get some help from a giant wolf." Born nodded and said "You truly saved both me and my men's life that day. A couple of them are in the infirmary at the moment with some injuries, but they'll live. Is there anything we can do to help you?" Arkenthan shook his head and suddenly realized "There is one thing I will need. My leg is unusable right now, could one of you tie a branch or something to it? The extra support would help diminish the pain. And I'll need some food to survive, so if it isn't too much to ask, it would be nice if one of you could hunt something for me." The requests left Arkenthan feeling slightly helpless, but Born gave a short laugh and said "Sure thing, I'll head out now. Karn, look to the boy's wounds, would you?" He then stood up preparing to head out. At that moment a loud thump came from the door and the three men jumped in unison. They looked at each other and Karn asked "Expecting someone?" Arkenthan shook his head and Born pulled his sword before opening the door. Buried tip first in the door was Arkenthan's sword. Having looked around outside, Born said "I don't remember this being here earlier? Can't see anyone outside either." The two guards looked questioningly at Arkenthan who shrugged. Born barely managed to pull the sword out of the door, but after some time he put it down beside Arkenthan saying "It looks burnt, I wonder what's happened to it." Arkenthan nodded and Born left the house bringing a bow.

A couple of hours passed and Karn was looking at the scrolls on the bookcase when Born entered the house again saying "I guess you know your way around here, but finding the way back was a nightmare." Arkenthan laughed and Born put two big animals onto the table. Finding the cooking area, Born and Karn started working on one animal each saying "You deserve a decent meal after all this. We'll make you something nice." Arkenthan smiled and said "In that bag over there are a lot of herbs and other things, if you want it." The lieutenant nodded and started rummaging through the bag. "And could you cut off a piece of meat in case Greypaws appear? I like to give him something when I'm eating. Feels like he's at the table with me," Arkenthan said and the two guards looked at each other before cutting off a big piece of meat. One of the animals was cut into decent sized pieces and the meat was put into the barrels, while the other animal was turned into what Arkenthan thought to be a rather fancy meal. Arkenthan hopped to the window, and looking at the sky said "It's getting late, you won't make it back before it gets dark. Why don't the two of you stay here until tomorrow and leave in the morning?" Karn came up to the window and said "We can do that. It's safer that way. We actually prepared for that event. I should go up to the mountain and light a small fire letting the old man in the tower know we're ok. I told him to tell the guard that if we light a fire there, we'll stay until tomorrow." Arkenthan nodded, grabbed the branch in one hand and the walking stick in the other and hobbled outside to explain the way to the path up the mountain. When Karn had left, Arkenthan went back inside, watching as Born cooked the meal. "There's a crack in your wall over there," Born said. "Behind the bookcase, see it?" With his mind racing, Arkenthan said "Yes, I know. It's just a small crack though, and it's supported from the other side, so I can't repair it more." Born nodded and returned to the meal.

An hour later Karn returned saying "I just made a small fire and headed back. Maybe he'll see it. There's no point in me staying up there for long anyways. Besides, it felt like something was watching me." Arkenthan smiled, thinking of the giant lizard. "And dinner is done!" Born said proudly. Setting out bowls and plates, the two guards sliced up pieces of meat and poured a soup. Looking at the table, Arkenthan's mouth started to water. Even though he'd just had a big piece of meat, he felt strangely hungry. While eating, Born and Karn talked about how people were starting to talk about him. Most people in town had already heard about how he'd brought Greypaws out of town. "But some of the men," Born said eagerly, "have spoken about how you took on a bear on your own, and the story seems to be spreading pretty quickly. This is a small town, you know. Not very often something exciting happens." Arkenthan nodded with his mouth full of food, feeling slightly embarrassed about everything. Eventually, he managed to say "I don't want that much attention, though." The two guards laughed and said "A bit too late for that now. But give it some time and things will quieten down. You should take a trip to town soon though, or the stories will spread even more, and probably grow more fantastical." Sighing Arkenthan said "Can it wait a couple of weeks? I would like to be able to use my leg a little first." Karn nodded and said "Take the time you need, of course. But I believe the captain would like to hear what's going on." Arkenthan nodded and looked out the window. Something white sat at the edge of the forest, and Arkenthan wanted to run outside. Forgetting about his damaged leg, he fell flat on the floor, and the two guards wondered what was going on. Laughing, Arkenthan said "I have to get outside. Greypaws is there. Could one of you bring the meat for me?" He then grabbed his sticks and made his way to the door. Outside, Arkenthan shouted "Hey Greypaws, missed me?" The wolf howled and stuck its tongue out of its mouth. He tilted his head as the two guards came out of the house, but Arkenthan went straight towards Greypaws. Having petted the wolf a little while, Arkenthan signalled to the two guards that they should bring the meat over. Greypaws sniffed the meat sceptically and looked at Arkenthan who said "Go on, you've earned it." As Greypaws started eating the piece of meat, Arkenthan sat down in the grass beside him. The guards stood a little distance away looking at them, and after a while they sat down in the grass as well. "I see how you can like it here," Karn said to Arkenthan who nodded and said "For some reason, animals don't enter this garden. I don't know why, but when Grey first chased me, he stopped at the edge here, apparently afraid to enter. I've seen other animals do this as well, so as long as I'm in the garden I know I am safe even if I fall asleep outside the house." This surprized the two guards and Born asked "Animals are afraid to enter this garden?" Again Arkenthan nodded and said "I've found one more spot in the forest where animals seem afraid to enter, but I don't know that for sure. There was nothing important there, so I couldn't figure out why." Greypaws finished his meal, lay down in the grass and fell asleep. The three men sat talking until dark, when they went into the house. The next morning Arkenthan was woken up by Born dropping an armful of lumber into the bin. "Sorry," Born said, "I figured you'd need some lumber as well. We're heading off now, you get well and drop by town when you can." Arkenthan sat upright in bed and nodded. "I'll see you soon. Let people know I'm okay," Arkenthan said as the guards said their goodbye. Having watched the guards leave, passing Greypaws who were lying on the ground resting, Arkenthan turned towards the room. He noticed the book was still lying in the bookcase and he thought 'Strange. Shouldn't the book be back in the cave by now?' He picked it up and thought *'Well, if I'm going to stay here for the next week I'll probably get a lot of reading done.'* He opened the book and noticed he was nearing the end. *'I can't be this close to the end of the story?'* he thought and started reading. *'Jonathan looked over the walls of the castle at the approaching army.'*

Chapter 51
A DANCE OF ICE

He figured there were thousands of flags and banners, and he didn't even dare imagine how many spearheads he saw. A few more gnomes had arrived before the battle, and a couple of trolls had dropped by as the city was being locked down, but Jonathan still felt there were too few trying to defend the city. Looking down from the wall, he could see the trenches where the water would flow, and saw small pikes sticking out of the ground. "What are they for? They don't seem to be very tall," Jonathan asked, and Boriam said "They are not for blocking the enemy's path, but so that the enemy will have to watch their steps. The pikes are sharpened, and will slow them down." Jonathan nodded and glanced at what he could see of the city. Archers stood ready on the roofs and walls at the front of the city. He looked at Boriam and said "What should we do now?" Boriam sighed and said "Now we wait and let the archers do their job. If the enemy breaches the first wall, we'll have to help hold the enemy back. Although, if the enemy does break through, we're probably going to be forced back behind the next wall. We want to be behind it before the second gate is shut. After that, we'll wait and see if they can breach the second gate. If for some reason everything should go badly, we'll fall back into the castle. Once inside the castle, it will be easier to control the flow of enemies." Jonathan nodded and sighed saying "And we are currently all the way at the front, because?" Boriam laughed and said "Someone has to be. Besides, we're on the first wall. If the enemy breaches the wall, it's technically the ones on the ground just behind the wall who are all the way at the front." Jonathan looked back at all the men standing ready, with armour polished and swords sharpened. He found Seeley, who nodded back at him. Knowing Seeley wasn't too far behind him, and knowing the man would have his back, calmed Jonathan slightly as he awaited the oncoming army. All the women and children had been led into the castle, and all men were issued a sword and whatever armour the city had available.

An hour passed before the army stopped marching towards the city. A loud horn blasted through the air, and the enemy army roared. An answering call sounded from the horns of the city, which were so deep and loud that the walls and the ground shook. Some of the people in the army looked at the ground and Jonathan thought '*I wonder if any of the women or children felt that?*' Some men from the army seemed to ride back and forth preparing the troops and Jonathan thought '*Why doesn't anyone do anything?*' Asking Boriam, the old man said "This is a psychological part of the fight, where the two sides try to scare each other, or boost morale in their own ranks. Don't worry, it'll start soon enough. Oh, of course they've brought those." Jonathan looked at the opposing army and saw giant ladders being brought to the front. "They're going to try to scale the walls, buying time for the teams who attempt to tear them down," Boriam said and shouted to the archers "Focus fire on the ladders! Do not allow them to be raised!" The archers lifted their bows, showing Boriam they had got the message. "As soon as the army starts moving, we should open the flood gates. Maybe we can wash some of the militia out to sea?" Jonathan hoped they could wash most of it out, so the fight wouldn't last for too long. Another trumpet blast sounded from the army, and the troops started forward. Boriam pointed at the rear tower which controlled the flood gates, and it slowly started to open. The gate itself surprized Jonathan. He expected the gate to be raised, but instead it seemed to be pulled backwards, into the city itself. "So that if the tower is taken, they can't just cut some ropes to close it," Boriam said. Water rushed around the walls of the castle, and Jonathan saw one ladder being carried off underneath the bridge of the city. A few soldiers were washed away, but apparently not as many as Boriam had hoped. Jonathan heard the old man say something in a different language. It didn't sound like a happy sentence, so he assumed it was a curse.

The water made the army's movement a lot harder, and the soldiers spent a long time before they reached the wall. Many soldiers stepped on the now concealed pikes underneath the water, and had to retreat. The archers did what they had been told, but for every man who fell, another jumped in to carry the ladders across the water. Something heavy crashed into the main gate. Jonathan turned and saw several of the giant oxen the king had mentioned battering the gate with great force. The first ladder was being raised, and most of the archers focused their shots on this one. As the ladder fell again and again, the bulk of the army seemed to shift sideways to where another ladder was being raised. Archers were working on this as well, but there were two trolls raising the ladder, who didn't seem to get hurt by the arrows. Some of the king's magicians were casting several spells on them, and after a long time one of the trolls fell. There were several ladders going up now, and the archers were struggling to keep up. A blast from a trumpet issued from the army, some of their soldiers seemed to shift around for a few seconds, and soon a volley of arrows was in the air.

"Shields up!" Boriam shouted, and as Jonathan lifted his shield, he looked at the army behind the wall. It looked like a floor of metal and wood had appeared above the heads of the guards below. As the arrows struck, Jonathan saw only a few of the men beneath the floor of shields fall, but several of the archers were hit. An arrow struck his shield with surprizing force. When Jonathan lowered the shield he kept looking at the arrow protruding from it. Suddenly there was a wavelike motion in the crowd on top of the wall, and Boriam said "It seems like someone have managed to get onto the wall. Come on!" He then ran towards where the wave originated. Jonathan got there just in time to see one of the enemy militia falling off the wall, and a ladder being pushed off again. Suddenly there came three loud thumps coursing through the wall, and then a loud crash. Jonathan saw Boriam signalling something to the men on the ground, and suddenly they were running towards the second wall. *This is it,'* Jonathan thought *'They have breached the front gate.'* They started running on the makeshift bridges between the two walls, and soon the enemy was pouring into the first space between the walls. Seeing the oxen, Jonathan noticed some small creatures leading them. *'Gnomes controlling the oxen?'* he thought and dared to shout "Archers, try to hit the gnomes leading the oxen." Boriam turned to him and said "Quick thinking, good suggestion. Come, we'll have to pour the oil." *'The oil?'* Jonathan thought as he ran after the old man.

Every now and then both the enemy and the defending guards would fall. Jonathan didn't like the feeling of seeing so many get killed, and he started to feel a bit sick. Another crash was heard and Boriam stopped, saying "They shouldn't have reached the second gate yet. What's going on?" They hurried along the top of the wall and saw a gnome pointing an ox directly at one of the houses. *'Why would they do that? They just want to break things?'* Jonathan thought and watched as the ox ran through the first wall of the house. He told what he'd seen to Boriam who stared blankly ahead for a few seconds before saying "Of course! The houses are a part of the walls, which means that where there is a house, the wall is thinner." Soon, oxen ran rampant behind the second gate, jumping out from holes everywhere and then turning to another house in the third wall. Everything happened so quickly Jonathan barely had time to see it. Troops from the enemy army were suddenly everywhere, jumping through the holes in the walls. Boriam pointed at the sky, then at one of the gnomes, and a lightning bolt struck the gnome. A nearby ox suddenly stopped in its tracks, looking around itself. All the noise and confusion seemed to scare it so much, that it started running back and forth within the enemy army. A cone of empty space spread out behind the ox as men were thrown to the sides. This seemed to cripple the army within that wall, and Boriam quickly took out two more gnomes. Jonathan ran between the edges of the wall and looked down at a bull in each street, running wildly around. Suddenly an arrow from below glanced off the side of his helmet, and he jumped away from the edge thinking *'Have to be more careful than that.'* He looked around and saw that six enemy soldiers had got onto the wall, and Jonathan shouted "Boriam? Over there!" Boriam turned and nodded before saying "Come on, Jonathan, let's help take them out." Jonathan followed Boriam towards the enemy group, and he saw one of the enemy raising a bow. Boriam threw his sword at the group, but they all ducked beneath it. A few of the city guard had reached the enemies by now, and the archer was unable to fire any arrows. What the enemy didn't expect, was Boriam's sword's desire to return to its owner. One of the men was killed and thrown far forwards by the returning sword, and the rest of the group looked around confusedly. This was enough for Boriam, Jonathan and the three guards to take out the last five easily enough. Jonathan felt a slight panic as he recognized this to be his first kill in the war, and he started breathing heavily. "Relax, keep your breathing under control. Level one, remember?" Jonathan blinked a few times before nodding and noticing another group of enemies along the wall. This group was a big one, and quickly made their way along the great wall. Boriam said "They've killed one of the bulls, and are starting to regroup down there. Come on, we should move towards the centre of the city." Jonathan nodded and followed Boriam towards the next wall.

When they were almost at the next wall, they were stopped by an enemy group, and forced back towards the previous one. They stood amongst fifteen guards of the city now, and fought off wave after wave of enemies, until they were forced to retreat further along the streets of the city. "Jonathan! Over here!" a voice shouted, and Jonathan saw Seeley waving at him. Waving back, Jonathan suggested they joined Seeley, and the group of now eight men agreed. Boriam started swinging his sword in a circle while pointing it at the enemy, and soon a small tornado materialized at the centre of the enemy group. "Wow. That is amazing!" Seeley said as they reached him. Boriam nodded and said "It won't last for long. Something that size is hard to maintain." Seeley understood this, and prepared for the next wave of enemies. None came, and Seeley asked "Is it normal to have to wait for an enemy attack this long in a war?" Boriam shook his head saying he had no idea what was happening, and that he needed to get onto a wall to get an overview of the field. Seeley nodded as something started tickling inside Jonathan. "Magic!" Jonathan shouted and threw himself to the side along with the rest of the group. A second later a huge explosion erupted where they had been standing. Looking up, Jonathan saw five men with their arms raised towards the group. He shouted at the guards, making them get up quickly. Behind the five magicians, the street was filled with enemy soldiers. A couple of enemy archers were at the front of the enemy group, and another group stood on the walls preparing their arrows. A bolt of lightning struck one of the enemies, and Jonathan saw that Boriam had taken up position in the middle of the road. He hurried to the old man's side and held his sword up. "Where're the king's magicians?" Boriam whispered as one of the enemies sent a ball of fire flying along the road towards them. Boriam pushed Jonathan to the ground and ducked under the fire. He then dropped his sword and put his hands out to the sides. Taking a deep breath and closing his eyes, Boriam started moving his arms and hands in ominous patterns, and Jonathan saw how uncertain the enemies became. The balls of fire they sent towards the old man seemed to vanish as they got close to Boriam. Eventually, a cloud of water appeared in front of Boriam. Continuing the hand movements, Boriam sorted the water into small pointy shapes, then froze them to ice. This went on for a while, as Jonathan and the others kept the old man safe. Looking back, Jonathan saw Boriam had constructed a wall in front of him of these small shards of ice. Fireballs struck the wall of shards again and again along with arrows both from the ground and from the walls. Jonathan saw Seeley managing to stick a shield above Boriam's head just as an arrow was soaring towards him. As the arrow bounced off the shield, Boriam still didn't speak or open his eyes, but he changed the way his arms moved. After another while, Boriam clapped, opened his eyes, and started a movement which reminded Jonathan more of a dance than anything else. Shard after shard flew out of the icy wall. A stream of ice shards flew down the street towards the enemies. Some shards flew towards the walls, and some even flew backwards past the guards of the city. A minute went by with a continuous stream of ice flying around the area until everything went quiet. Jonathan could hear broken pieces of ice hitting the ground like glass. "Again, wow," Seeley quietly said looking at the now empty area around them. He then turned to everyone saying "Okay, let's regroup and get back on top of the wall. Then we can see what we're up against."

Chapter 52
RETREAT FROM THE DARK

Boriam was breathing heavily as they sped up the tower. "Are you okay?" Jonathan asked. Boriam used the wall for support as he said "Well, the spell is very demanding. When we get onto the wall, let me sit down to rest for a bit. I will need to save the rest of my energy." Jonathan nodded and helped the old man up the rest of the tower. He soon found himself on top of the first wall overlooking the field below. "There seems to be no end to the enemy," Boriam said. Many soldiers were still crossing the water with ladders, and over half of them had to retreat because of the small spikes. As Jonathan cheered, Boriam pointed out "They might have to sit this battle out, but that means the Council will still have a big army for later." Suddenly, a volley of fireballs soared towards them from the army. Everyone braced themselves and put up their shields. One shield broke and the unfortunate guard was thrown backwards, but he only suffered a smaller burn to his arm. The rest of the shields held out, and because of the great distance to its caster, the size and heat of the flames were small. The ground beneath the wall was starting to fill up again, with both city guards and enemy soldiers, and Jonathan figured it would only be a matter of time before full chaos returned. Arrows whistled past the group, and they ducked behind the low wall. "How many archers do we have here?" Boriam asked and Seeley pointed out three men. Nodding, Boriam said "Go to the next tower over there." He pointed along the wall, towards where the enemy was attacking. "Jonathan and I will join you to cover the stairs. The rest of you should head down this tower here, and hold it. Make sure no one gets into this tower." The men nodded, and Seeley slapped Jonathan on the back before turning towards the tower. Boriam, Jonathan and the three archers ran across the wall to where the bulk of the enemy were. Getting to the door in the tower leading up to the wall, Boriam said "Fire your arrows. Take out those who seem to be in command, but stay hidden in the tower here. Make the best use of your arrows, don't just fire wildly. Better to fire five arrows which hit, than twenty which nearly do so." The three men nodded and spread out between the two doors of the tower. The winding

273

stair came up in the centre of the room, where Boriam and Jonathan stood ready. It didn't take long before arrows started to fly in through the doors, and Jonathan could hear voices shouting at the bottom of the stairs. The archers took their time when choosing and aiming at their targets. Jonathan could hear the archers mumble "hit" and "miss" as they fired arrow after arrow. He counted considerably more hits than misses before his counting was interrupted by militia coming running up the stairs.

Thanks to the stairs, Boriam and Jonathan managed to hold off the enemy for some time before starting to be forced backwards. As they had to fall back, the tower slowly filled with enemy soldiers. One of the archers fell, and the others turned to help hold the enemy off. The group of four were forced back onto the wall where they met Seeley who said "I think we're losing the tower soon. I see things aren't going too well on your end either?" Jonathan laughed and glanced over the wall. A steady stream of enemies pushed their way across the bridge leading into the city. Looking down the other side of the wall, he saw a group of gnomes swinging their picks and axes wildly, giving the enemy a hard time moving forward. The sight of the gnomes facing the enemy army was close to comical, but Jonathan felt it would be wrong to laugh, so he quickly looked back at the oncoming enemies on the wall. A fireball struck the side of the wall, sending a wave of heat across the small group. On the ground, Jonathan saw a dark skinned man with orange eyes looking in their direction. "Arnkhand," Jonathan said, looked at Boriam, and whispered to one of the archers "You see the dark man with the almost glowing eyes down there?" The archer nodded and Jonathan asked "Can you hit him?" The archer looked from Jonathan to Arnkhand and slowly nocked an arrow. Jonathan watched as the arrow flew through the air towards Arnkhand who merely smiled. Ten meters before striking the man, the arrow started burning and veering towards the side. As it reached Arnkhand there was nothing left of the arrow, and the soot from it was scattered by the wind. "Good shot, but you can't take him out with an arrow," Boriam said still focusing on the oncoming enemies. He looked at Jonathan and said "Thanks." Jonathan nodded and attacked one of the enemies. Having taken out the soldier, Jonathan looked back at Arnkhand. The man was moving his arms just as Boriam had while preparing the ice shards. "What is he doing?" Jonathan said and Boriam looked over the wall. Jonathan watched as Boriam got a blank expression on his face and he seemed to become even paler than his age had made him. "We should get off the wall," he said and shouted "Now! Get off the wall!" The guards stood wondering what was happening as Boriam and Jonathan turned and sprinted towards the tower that Seeley's group was defending. They got inside, and Seeley followed with one of the archers. The second archer was still out on the wall when the entire section of the wall collapsed. The last archer along with several enemy soldiers plummeted to the ground along with the pieces of the wall. Looking out of the tower, Jonathan could see Arnkhand gasping for air while a big portion of the army rushed across the flowing water. "What in the gods' names was that?" Seeley asked and Boriam sighed "He made several signs which were obvious magical patterns. I felt earth magic being focused on the wall. I understood he wanted to do something about it, but make it all collapse? He's even stronger than I imagined." Seeley looked at Boriam saying "Than you imagined? You know this person?" Here Jonathan jumped into the conversation saying "Let's not get into this now, but let's get out of here before we're flooded with enemies." He then looked at Seeley who stood a second before nodding.

Having sprinted down the tower, the group had to force their way out onto the streets, joining several other guards. An ox rushed past them, knocking both allied and enemy soldiers to the ground. "We need to stop the oxen," Seeley said and Jonathan agreed. They had been useful when they were running amok in the midst of the enemy soldiers, but now that they ran wildly around town, everyone were affected by them. The ox which had just passed them turned and ran through the wall of a house where it became stuck. Immediately, several arrows flew towards it. As the arrows struck the ox, it seemed to gain renewed strength. The ox was soon back on the streets running, almost trampling the small group. As Jonathan was the furthest into the street, he was forced some way down the road towards the enemy. As he turned around, an enemy jumped towards him with his sword raised. Unable to move, Jonathan watched as the man landed and swung his sword towards him. He heard the sword strike the top of his helmet, and then the man was forced sideways by something blurry. Jolted out of his trance, Jonathan grabbed his sword and prepared for another attack. Two wolves with long yellow fur walked past him. Jonathan noticed the blur which had saved him was a brown and red furred wolf as well. *Wolfmen?*' he thought, and said "Thanks." The wolf looked up at him and nodded before joining his two kinsmen in attacking the enemy. Their attacks were so swift that a chill went down Jonathan's back. *I'm glad they are on my side,*'Jonathan thought before joining the fight.

They managed to hold the enemy back for a while, but eventually they were forced backwards. As they reached the rest of the guards, an ox came running along the street from behind Jonathan. It was as if the war was forgotten for a few seconds as people, seemingly politely, stepped to the side and waited for the ox to pass. Jonathan could see a lot of enemies where the ox was coming from, and he knew that there were a lot of them where it was running towards. "We're trapped. See how many enemies there are over there? There's at least as many the other way as well," he said to Boriam as the ox ran past. Boriam cursed under his breath and blocked another strike from an enemy soldier. The group of guards in the street had started out rather large, but as the pressure of the oncoming soldiers increased from both sides, their numbers quickly dwindled. When one of the wolfmen along with over half of the guards had fallen, the ox came running past again. "Finally," Boriam said and Jonathan thought *'Finally? you've been waiting for a giant bull to trample us?'* As the entire street took a step to the side, Boriam took a deep breath and made a huge ball of fire in front of the running bull. It skidded to a stop and started to turn, when Boriam made a ball of fire on the opposite side. Looking back and forth between the inner wall of the street and the group of guards, the ox turned towards them. Boriam sighed and said "Sorry," before making a wall of fire between the group and the bull. Jonathan couldn't hear any fighting and looked around to see every soldier and guard staring at what was happening. He was about to laugh, thinking *'It's too strange that we're in the middle of a war and no one is fighting.'* At that moment a loud crash was heard and the flames died out. Some of the men started clapping and cheering. Jonathan looked around and saw both city guards as well as enemy soldiers clapping before realizing where they were. "Go!" Boriam shouted and ran towards the hole in the wall. After hesitating for a second the group understood what was happening, and they followed him through. On the other side of the wall they watched as both guards and soldiers were struggling to get up again. A lot more allied guards were in this section of the wall, and Jonathan was starting to feel a bit safer. The soldiers they had been fighting came leaping through the wall, and soon there were big fights throughout the entire street.

The streets were bathed in an orange light, which Jonathan would have thought pretty if it hadn't been strewn with fallen men. As the sky turned red, the press of soldiers started to subside and Jonathan wondered what was happening. A group of enemy soldiers, with which they were currently fighting, suddenly stepped away and started sprinting down the street. The fighters who were left in the street stood baffled, wondering what was happening. As an archer fired an arrow after the enemy soldiers, Boriam ran towards a hole in the wall and peered through. "The next street's empty," he said as Jonathan approached. "Why? What are they planning?" Jonathan asked, but Boriam just shrugged and stepped through to the next street. Following close behind, Jonathan saw a couple of soldiers leaving through the great gap in the wall. He looked up and down at the empty street and followed Boriam towards one of the towers. Gazing out past the wall, they could see a line of archers standing on guard outside the wall as soldiers ran out of the city. "They're making camp," Jonathan said and Boriam nodded saying "A popular rumour claims that the Council tend to be afraid of fighting in the dark. They once suffered a great loss against a small city because the citizens knew where to hide in the dark. There's a rumour that they have never attacked a city during the night after that. It appears to be true." He sighed and Jonathan looked at the still huge army gathering in front of the city. After a while, the sun dipped behind the horizon. A few seconds after the sun had gone down, two soldiers came running out from the city towards the besieging army. Immediately, five of the army's own archers raised their bows and shot them. "Why'd they do that?" Jonathan asked staring in shock at the two soldiers. "I guess they wanted to make sure none of their enemies were attacking as it got dark," Boriam said and looked towards the centre of the city. "Come on, let's find out how many people we have left." He then started down the tower.

Chapter 53
A HOWLING BUBBLE

As they approached the main square, Jonathan could see several groups of people standing around talking. King Myrtis came down the street. As he approached, he asked what was going on, and Boriam told him what they had seen. The king nodded and turned to the general walking beside him. "Have groups of your men search the city. Kill whatever enemies are left, and tell the guards who are spread around town to gather here." The general nodded and left for the bulk of people in the square. "I really hope we're more men than this," the king said as he looked across the mass of people. Boriam sighed and sat down on a nearby barrel. Jonathan asked how he was doing, if his earlier exhaustion still troubled him, but Boriam smiled and said "Thank you for the concern, but I could have fought for a long time yet. But now I guess I can rest a little, and then I might find enough energy for another round tomorrow." Jonathan looked at the ground and asked "What will happen if you use a spell like you did earlier, but don't have the energy for it?" Boriam shrugged and said "I'll probably do it up to a certain point before falling asleep like you did earlier. Or I might lose energy so fast that I go into a coma, or maybe even die from it." Jonathan looked up and asked "You can die from casting spells?" "Oh, yes," Boriam said "If you cast a big spell without being strong enough for it, the energy you use might drain so fast that you stop your own blood from flowing. Then you'll die. Or, if you try magic you don't know and it backfires. I've seen some bad outcomes from that." Jonathan blinked a few times and said "Like what?"

The king approached again and said "What are we going to do? This doesn't seem to be a lot of people, and my scouts say at least half the enemy army is left." Boriam shrugged and stared at the group of people in the square. Every now and then one or two guards would come from one of the streets and settle down somewhere in the market. "I can imagine several scenarios," Boriam said, and after explaining to both the king and Jonathan what a scenario was, continued by saying "One, we can lock ourselves into the castle. I think that's what they expect us to do, but if we bunch together in the hallways they will just send in one bull, and we're gone. Two, we can make barricades out here in the streets and hope they will hold off both men and bulls, but their archers can easily shoot us. Three, we hide inside buildings and alleys, silently taking out those who come looking for us. This probably won't work in the situation we're in. Or four, we give up." At this the king said "I won't give up. We should do the second one. Barricade the streets. If we prepare our archers around the corners from the great holes in the walls, we can shoot many before they reach deep into the city." He then signalled one of his officers over and explained what to do. The officer nodded and hurried towards the crowd in the marketplace. "Hey, where's Seeley? Did you see him when they fell back?" Jonathan asked Boriam, but the old man shook his head and stood up. Boriam followed a group of guards heading down one of the streets to help secure everything, and Jonathan was left alone by the market. He looked around the groups of soldiers for any sign of Seeley, but couldn't find him. Starting to dread what could have happened, he turned his attention to one of the groups heading down one of the roads. *They'll need all the help they can get,'* he thought and started carrying a couple of logs.

Jonathan could almost see out through one of the gaps created in the outer wall. He was glad he couldn't, as he knew there were archers outside who would shoot if they saw him. Their newly erected barricade was waist high, with sharp spears pointing towards the gap in the wall. *'No one will want to run into this,'* Jonathan thought as he started preparing the next barricade. They found many spears from fallen soldiers, and eventually they had three rows of barricades they could cover behind if the first ones were overrun. "Jonathan!" someone shouted, and as he turned around he saw a small group of men coming down the street. "Seeley! Where have you been?" Jonathan said as the man approached. He noticed Seeley had a slight limp, and wondered what had happened. "I joined this group chasing the enemy out of the city. At one point I was alone and when the enemy noticed, they turned and ganged up on me. I had to hide inside a house under some blankets in order to survive." Jonathan slapped Seeley on the back saying "I'm glad you did." He turned to the barricades and explained what they knew both about the enemy and the situation in the city. Seeley nodded, listening eagerly. When Jonathan finished, Seeley stood thinking for a few seconds before turning to the rest of the men. "Okay, gather round!" He shouted, and as the men bunched together, he continued "Right. I see we're about twenty people. I am guessing there'll be about five hours of darkness, which mean we should camp here and keep four men on watch for one hour at a time. Two on this side of camp, in case the enemy suddenly attacks, and two on the opposite side in case there are any enemy soldiers left in the city." The men nodded as Seeley split them into their teams. He put himself along with Jonathan for the first team with two others Jonathan didn't know. The two other soldiers positioned themselves on the far side of camp while the rest of the men tried to get some sleep. "I don't know if I'll be able to sleep," Jonathan said and Seeley pointed out "At least while you are thinking that you can't." Jonathan nodded and sat down next to the wall hoping nothing would happen that night. The hour dragged on slowly. Jonathan heard celebrations and cheering from outside the wall and started wondering if the enemy was going to attack the next day or not. As he talked to Seeley, the hour went by and eventually they woke up the next team to keep watch. The night passed with Jonathan waking up every now and then. Each time a new set of guards were woken up, Jonathan woke up as well. When the fourth change of guard happened, Jonathan noticed the sky was starting to grow a little brighter. He sat up and quickly woke Seeley. "What? Morning already?" he said and Jonathan pointed to the sky saying "It's the beginning of the fifth shift, but it's starting to get brighter. I figured we should wake up before it all starts." Seeley grunted and said he would have liked to sleep in, but he got up and started waking everyone up. "Get up, get warm and get ready. Who knows when these buggers are going to strike," he said as he wandered through their camp. Several men had joined them during the night, and some were a lot more tired than others. Jonathan noticed most of them had bows, and he could also see several archers coming down the street. He looked at the first barricade and said to Seeley "We should have three rows of archers behind each barricade. A little behind the archers we should have swords and spears ready to keep the enemy back for a bit. If we're lucky the enemy will fill the streets, so it'll be easy for the archers to hit. As the first row of archers falls back, the fighters can hold the enemy off, and the second row of archers start firing." Seeley nodded and shouted the message to the guards standing ready. One of the men stepped up to Seeley and said "Good job sergeant, I'll take command from here. Good suggestions, but I'll move people around a little." Jonathan noticed the man was of a higher rank, and Seeley stepped down without arguing. The officer came up to Jonathan and said "I heard you suggesting the setup. Who are you? I'll send in a recommendation for you." Jonathan stood silent for a few seconds wondering what he would get a recommendation for, but understood soon enough. "I'm not from town, so that's not necessary." The officer creased his eyebrows and asked "Where are you from then?" Jonathan answered "I can't really say I have a home anymore. I abandoned my town when the Council attacked it. I followed Boriam of the Thirteen here as his apprentice." The officer looked him over and said "So you're one of the Thirteen? A bit young, aren't you?" Jonathan sighed and said "There's only one left of the Thirteen. I'm his apprentice, so I'm technically not one of the Thirteen yet." The officer nodded and started commanding people around. "Then I'll treat you as one of my soldiers for now. So get moving." Jonathan smiled and found his position. Seeley was placed in the same group as him, and then they stood awaiting what might come. *'I wonder where Boriam is,'* Jonathan thought as he waited, imagining what would happen. He hoped the enemy would be scared by their new barricade, and fall away again. More people kept joining the guards waiting by the third barricade, and Jonathan started to get his hopes up when a trumpet rang from outside. The trumpet was answered by a blast from the city which made Jonathan smile and think *'No use showing we're weakened.'* What happened next flashed by so quickly Jonathan didn't really understand any of it.

Several of the enemy soldiers poured through the razed outer wall, filling the street. As the archers started firing their arrows, Jonathan saw an ox bursting through the outer wall and a loud crash was heard. As the enemy soldiers started to fall to the arrows, some of them started running towards the archers, and some turned back. It looked as though the enemy was very confused about the situation. As the first archers retreated, Jonathan helped hold back the rushing enemies. The street was starting to fill up with soldiers, and he could see arrows flying by as the second row of archers started firing. Soon the enemy army started returning arrows, and Jonathan didn't know how prepared the guards further back were. He heard arrows hit shields and armour, and he turned to see how everything was going when the inner wall behind the guards suddenly exploded outwards. As the stones and dust settled, Jonathan saw an ox standing in the middle of the road flaring its nostrils towards the guards. "Oh, shit," someone said near Jonathan. He started sprinting towards the back of the guards and along the way he grabbed an archer. As they neared the end of the row of guards, he could see a small creature walking through the hole in the wall. "There! Shoot him!" Jonathan shouted to the archer who fumbled with the arrow before nocking it on the string. The ox crouched and prepared to charge. The archer pulled the string back. As the archer let go of the string, the ox started running. For a short moment, the gnome's eyes widened as both he and the arrow disappeared from view behind the ox. For a second the ox kept on running, and the men prepared to jump out of the way when the ox suddenly shook its head and stumbled. As the ox rose from the ground and started staring at the mass of people, Jonathan shouted "Make a lot of noise!" Then the group nearest to the ox started screaming and waving their weapons in the air. The ox turned and ran down the street as several soldiers came through the hole in the wall. *'This will never stop, will it?'* he thought and got the ranking officer's attention. Having pointed towards the soldiers appearing behind them, the officer twisted his face into a grimace and shouted some quick orders. Soon everyone was moving slowly past the new hole in the inner wall. Some of the archers ran into a tower and started shooting the enemy soldiers from above, but they were soon struck down by enemy arrows. Another group of guards came down the road to join them, and Jonathan saw Boriam among them. "How are things in other parts of town?" Jonathan asked the old man who said "Pretty much the same as here. Enemy soldiers keep jumping out of holes in the walls everywhere, and it's hard to maintain control in any one place at a time." Jonathan nodded and asked "How many guards do we have left?" But to this Boriam shrugged and said "Everyone's spread so far across town it's hard to tell, but it's not many. Let's get up top and see how many of the enemy there are left outside." Jonathan nodded and signalled to the ranking officer that they were going up the tower.

A group of men had joined them up at the top of the wall. Seeley was one of them, and when they peered over the wall he just stood there, staring. Outside the city, masses of tents were set up, and groups of armoured soldiers were running back and forth. "That... is a lot of soldiers," Jonathan said and sat down behind the low wall. Looking down at the street, it was hard to tell enemies from allies, except by the direction in which they were heading. A couple of enemy soldiers had got onto the wall and were running towards them. As the group of guards prepared for the fight, the battlefield suddenly grew dark. Everyone stopped what they were doing and stared towards the sun. Squinting at something floating in the air, Jonathan thought it looked like a bubble. Seconds passed where nothing happened. City guards and enemy soldiers all stood staring at the strange sight. Then the bubble burst. A loud noise like a wolf's howl muffled by water exploded across the battlefield. Some people creased their eyebrows, some put their hands to their ears. Boriam grinned and looked over the wall. Jonathan followed his gaze and understood what Boriam was grinning about. Fish appeared to be jumping over the bridge. Fish with knives and swords, Jonathan noticed. "It would seem the merfolk finally received our plea for help," Boriam said, applauding. Chaos erupted outside the city as merfolk knocked soldiers off the bridge, pulling them out to sea. The soldiers standing in the water suddenly disappeared, and instead the water became filled with sharp teethed, dagger wielding merfolk. The soldiers who were left outside the city pulled away from the water as the merfolk sunk into the water and started circling the city. Whenever anyone tried to cross the bridge, a merfolk jumped out of the water and took the soldier down. As the press of oncoming soldiers eased, the soldiers in the streets started to run backwards and through the holes in the inner wall, trying to escape the fight. This confused the rest of the soldiers in the street, and it didn't take long for them to be overtaken. The soldiers on the wall understood that their assault was over and put their swords down. Boriam nodded, saying "No need to kill those who don't want to kill us, is there?" He then got a hold of some rope from one of the towers and tied the enemies' hands. Jonathan leaned towards Seeley and said "Hold this area and let me know if anything happens. Boriam and I will go further into the city." Seeley nodded his response, and picked a team to hold the area.

Chapter 54
AN ACQUIRED TASTE

The fighting was still heavy further into the city, and the bulls were raging wildly through the streets. Jonathan and Boriam arrived just as one of the bulls fell, and one of the guards asked "What's going on now? We still have a lot of enemies up ahead, but the pressure seems to be gone." Jonathan looked at the guard and said "No more enemies are entering the city." The guard raised an eyebrow and Jonathan explained that the merfolk now surrounded the city. The guard shouted this to the others who gave off a loud roar before running as a group up the road. Boriam and Jonathan looked at each other questioningly before following the group.

They ran to the next part of town where a big fight was still going on. Magicians as well as swordsmen made the whole area one big brawl as fireballs flew everywhere, swords flew across the ground and spears waved frantically in the air. Boriam sighed and started battling the magicians while Jonathan helped the swordsmen. It felt like hours passed before the fight started to calm down, and one of the guards said "There're still some enemies in the next road, a bull broke through there some time ago. The king's there, so someone should go help him." Quickly, Jonathan turned towards the breached wall and ran to the next road. He forced his way between enemies and allies, getting a few cuts on his arms and legs. Emerging at the next road, the whole place suddenly seemed deserted. *'What's going on?'* Jonathan thought and ran to his left. It didn't take long before he found a group of soldiers battling a small group of the city guard. Jonathan had a feeling the guard had the fight under control, so he decided to try something out. He searched inside himself for the ball of energy and started feeling very warm. *Maybe I can use a bit of magic. Just make my sword hot or something?'* Jonathan thought and started forcing the heat out through his sword. He saw the blade start to turn red. When he felt the blade was hot enough, he attacked one of the enemies. As they all stood with their backs to him, he wanted to make sure that he struck well on the first swing. He located a breach in one of the enemy soldiers' armour, and focused on it as his blade entered. Immediately the enemy soldier burst into flames, shocking both Jonathan and the enemy group. This allowed the guards to take control of the brawl and take out the few enemies who were left. Jonathan felt his legs buckle in on themselves as the last of the enemy fell. '*I did magic. Okay, I set someone on fire, which is pretty sick, but I did magic!*' he thought sitting on the ground. Myrtis approached saying "Good job! If you hadn't come, I don't know what would've happened." Jonathan nodded and yawned. "Not exciting enough for ya?" The king asked and Jonathan laughed saying "I did magic! I still can't believe it. It takes a lot of energy though, so I'm pretty tired now. Can one of you help me up?" One of the guards offered a hand and Jonathan was soon back on his feet, feeling somewhat shaky. "What is happening out there?" The king asked, and Jonathan sighed saying "They're mostly just cleaning up the remainder now. The merfolk came, swimming through the river around the castle. They hold the outside of the city, and no one gets past them. As long as we manage to clean out the last of the enemy inside the city, we seem to have won." The king opened his eyes wide and said "We've won? Really? Wow." Jonathan nodded and started back past the last wall when the bull which had made the breach came running around the corner. "It's been running around for a while now. Should get pretty tired soon," one of the guards said, and Jonathan found him to be right. The bull noticed the group looking at it, stopped and dropped to the ground. It didn't do anything as Jonathan approached, and when Jonathan looked at the great bull, it seemed to be asleep. "I guess you've got yourself a new pet," Jonathan said to the king who laughed. A great horn sounded through the air, and Jonathan said "Oh, what now?" He ran to the last wall where the fight was still raging. Most of the enemy soldiers seemed to drop their weapons and sit down on the ground. Someone came running up the street shouting for Jonathan, who recognized the man as one of Seeley's men. Jonathan ran to the man asking "What's going on! Is Seeley okay?" The man put up a hand saying "Yes, yes. I have a message for you. Seeley says the enemy is falling back! Retreating! We've won!" The men standing around Jonathan started cheering. Looking at the men, with others still fighting in the background, Jonathan still couldn't understand all that had happened. Seeing the king talking to Boriam, Jonathan ran towards them. Interrupting the two men's conversation, Jonathan said "Seeley's saying the enemy is retreating! I have a feeling we're more men inside the city than there are enemies. Does that mean we've won?" Boriam smiled and said "In one way, we've won, and in another we've lost." Jonathan didn't understand this, and Boriam explained. "To everyone else, we've won. But for us, me as a Thirteen and you as the apprentice, this was no victory. A lot of lives were lost here, and that's never anything to celebrate." Jonathan blinked while looking at the old man before saying "Right. So we've won, then?" Boriam laughed and said

"Sure." Jonathan turned and ran down the street shouting "We've won!" Everywhere he ran, people started cheering. He ran out to the next wall and found some people still fighting, and seeing one of the city guard being killed, his excitement quieted. *This isn't won yet,'* Jonathan thought as he realized there were still enemies fighting inside the city. Pulling his sword, Jonathan was soon in the middle of a fight once more.

Sorting out the fighting and rounding up the last of the enemies took the entire evening. By the end of it, Jonathan was exhausted and was sitting on the first wall looking down into the city. "Mind if I join you?" a voice said. Looking up, Jonathan saw Seeley holding a bag of something. Pointing at the bag, he asked "What's that?" Seeley grinned as he sat down and said "Tobacco. Best sort. Found it on a dead enemy. Want some?" Jonathan blinked, saying "I've never tried it before. Everyone does it though, so I don't know why not." Seeley packed a pipe full of the grass-looking tobacco and lit it. He sighed and offered the pipe to Jonathan. Taking the pipe, Jonathan filled his lungs with the smoke. It burned in his throat and he coughed hard. Seeley laughed and said "Okay, tobacco is what you would call an acquired taste." Still coughing, Jonathan said "Like beer?" "Like beer," Seeley said and added "and coffee." Jonathan could understand that one as he'd tasted coffee some times, and found it better after a few cups. They sat quietly looking at the sunset above the city, passing the pipe between them. Jonathan coughed a few times, but still tried to get used to it. "What will happen after this?" Seeley asked and Jonathan shrugged. After thinking for a while, Jonathan said "I guess the Council still wants this city, but it will take some time before they're able to gather an army this large again. Boriam and I will be heading off I guess, to adventures unknown. Unknown to me at least." Seeley laughed and sighed "But this is a good evening. We'll have to celebrate later on." Jonathan smiled and nodded, knowing it probably wouldn't happen. The sun went down behind the city before they moved. There were small fires spread across the city. They were used both to light up the streets, and to burn the fallen men. Some people were looting the fallen enemies, but the king's guards soon stopped this. "It's not honourable to steal from the fallen," they said and confiscated what they found. Boriam seemed to have disappeared from the clean-up, but Jonathan didn't mind that. *I'll have to listen to his stories again soon enough,'* he thought as he cleared bodies away from the streets. It was early morning before they were allowed to return to the barracks to rest.

Chapter 55
THE SYSTEM OF THE THIRTEEN

They were awakened at midday by one of the king's guards. "Come with me," the guard said to Jonathan and walked out of the room. Jonathan looked at Seeley who shrugged before going back to sleep. Sighing, Jonathan got off the bed and felt all his muscles screaming. He slowly made his way outside and followed the guard to the castle. "Your friend didn't want to join us?" the guard asked and Jonathan replied "You told me to follow you, not us. So he went back to sleep. Why?" The guard shook his head and said "No one seems surprized if you two go everywhere together. I was directed to the barracks by people saying 'they're resting at the barracks over there'. Yes, they actually said 'they're' instead of 'he's'." Jonathan coughed and silently followed the guard straight to the castle. Some women had started washing the houses and roads, but it was still very dirty everywhere. "No tunnel to get to the king?" Jonathan asked and the guard shook his head saying "I guess he figured the worst is over by now."

Outside the throne room, Jonathan was told to wait for a few seconds as the guard announced his arrival. The doors soon opened to let him in, and the king came down the room to greet him. "Thank you, again, for saving me and my men yesterday." Myrtis reached out a hand which Jonathan shook. Boriam came up to them saying "Myrtis has told me how you saved them. You actually did magic on the battlefield? Brave of you to try it out there." Jonathan smiled to himself and said "I didn't really mean to do the magic like that. I figured a hot blade would be more intimidating, so I made the fire heat the blade before I attacked. I didn't know the man would burst into flames." Boriam nodded and said "If you put enough focus on the soldier while you were heating your blade, it doesn't surprize me that you set him on fire." The door opened and a man ran up to the king with a message. After hearing it, the king said "Oh, good! Send him in." Jonathan looked at Boriam who shrugged. The door opened and in wobbled an old-looking merman. He had a long moustache which swung back and forth as the man slowly made his way across the floor. "Great Orichlin. I thank you for coming to our rescue," The king said and bowed to the merman. The merman bowed and the king pointed at Boriam and Jonathan and said "This is Boriam, the last of the Thirteen, and that is Jonathan, Boriam's last apprentice. This," the king gestured to the merman and said "Is king Orichlin, the leader of the merfolk." The three men bowed to each other, and the merfolk king's voice was deep and bubbling as he said "Last of the Thirteen. Thank you. And apprentice, learn well, for the world will need it." Again Boriam bowed and Jonathan followed. Myrtis turned to the two and said "If you'll excuse us, I have a lot to discuss with the king of the deeps. I will seek your counsel again soon." They took their leave, and left the room.

Outside the throne room, Jonathan said "Merfolk don't talk very much, do they?" Boriam grinned and shook his head. "You owe me a bit of a story," Jonathan said, and Boriam looked at him questioningly. "About the Thirteen, or Lions or whatever you guys are. Your system and everything." Boriam looked at the ceiling and said "I won't tell you everything, but you are right. I did promise to tell you about the Lions' system. But I can't tell you here, too many who could hear." He then turned down a corridor. Jonathan followed the old man for a long time. Suddenly Boriam stopped outside a door and opened it. Inside were a table, two chairs and a bed. "This is where I've been staying since we arrived. It's not sound proof, but it's better than talking in the halls." Jonathan nodded and sat down on one of the chairs. Boriam sat down on the other chair, sighed and said "Where to begin?" He thought for a while, then started talking. "The first Thirteen were hailed as the heroes who, through calm and patience, brought peace between gnomes and men. That peace was eventually broken many years later, but by then the Thirteen had made a name for themselves. They worshipped the combination of the spirit, the mind and the body, and through that became strong, quick and wise. Many wanted to know their secrets, and the Thirteen would teach those who asked. This was a problem for a long time. Many evil men gathered to learn from them, and eventually war broke out. As the years passed, the Thirteen, along with many others of course, won the war. But the Thirteen became wary, not wanting to teach any more evil men. So they made a system. 'The' system. Every member of the Thirteen would teach twelve followers. Some called them pupils, like me, and some called them disciples. You will probably hear different words for their followers. Anyways, these twelve again would help teach others of the world and the life the Thirteen would lead. At one point, some hundred years ago, there were thousands of followers in total. The Thirteen had several layers of teaching, with a foundation in the meditation I've been teaching you. They knew that when someone passed the thirteenth level, that person would be fit for joining the Thirteen.

This system, where one person taught twelve followers, created a division of labour in the Thirteen. Each member had an area of responsibility. The first branch was responsible for weapons handling, the second for trade, the third for peacekeeping with the gnomes, the fourth was responsible for processing intelligence from around the world. They were responsible for finding out where something was happening, so the eighth branch could act upon it and prevent war. Where was I? Oh, the fifth, was responsible for keeping peace with the trolls. Then there's the sixth, which is my branch. We were responsible for gathering any information, rumour and knowledge from all over the world. This is why I did have a lot of spies everywhere. We gathered all the information we could, so that the fourth branch could find out where trouble was brewing. The seventh was responsible for securing the peace with the merfolk, the eighth as I mentioned earlier was responsible for acting on the suspected information to find out if it was true, and so prevent another great war. The ninth was responsible for securing provisions and materials for all of the thirteen branches. The tenth was responsible for keeping the peace with the birdmen. This group lost their purpose in the system the day the birdmen disappeared. No one knows where they went, but they're gone from the world we know. The eleventh made sure the human cities didn't wage war against each other, and the twelfth was responsible for making sure messages to and from the Thirteen arrived where they should. The thirteenth branch was a dark branch, with the members operating in the shadows of the world, taking swift action if they heard anything. They were the ones who got something done if the eighth didn't. And they were the leading voices at the great meetings. So those are all the different branches of our system. When one of the Thirteen would fall, or choose to retire, the other twelve would test that member's followers. From this they would find which member had come the furthest in their teachings, and let him or her become a Lion. None of the followers knew who the group of Lions were, but through their training they would hear about all the things the Lions had done. This system was established some hundred years ago, and until the Council managed to slip through the system of knowledge, peace had reigned the world. About seven hundred years ago, the weapons were handed out. Remember I told you about those? The troll asked all the Thirteen to come, bringing their preferred weapons, and the troll made similar ones to the weapon they brought. My branch brought a sword similar to mine, so this is what it got." Boriam put his sword on the table. "I'll teach you how to make one of these yours later. The weapons became a symbol of the branch you were in. Each branch specialized in the weapon type of the branch leader. As an additional proof of being a member of the Thirteen, everyone wore medallions like this." He then took out his medallion. It had some waves on it, and a rune. "The rune is the number thirteen in gnomish, and the waves display the number six in the merfolk language. Six is for the branch I'm leading." Jonathan blinked a few times before pulling out the chain and medallion he'd been given in Tresponts. "How'd you get that?" Boriam asked accusingly, and Jonathan said "A woman owned a shop in Tresponts. It was filled with old shields, weapons, armour and other old things. I like old items, so I entered. She couldn't speak, but signed with her hands about something, and then went into the back room. She brought this out and gave it to me before I was pushed out of the store." Boriam squinted as he looked at the ceiling. "We'll have to go back there then. She seems to have got hold of items belonging to the Thirteen. Maybe she's got something we need. A shield perhaps." Jonathan looked at the old man and asked "You have magical shields or something?" But to this Boriam only smiled and said "You'll see when we find my shield." He then pointed at the amulet in Jonathan's hand and said "That bears the number thirteen in the merfolk language, so it belonged to branch thirteen. Fits well, we'll have to stick to the shadows from now on." Jonathan felt proud as he looked at the amulet. "Where are we going now?" Jonathan asked and Boriam shrugged saying "We'll go to Ilsberg, you'll have to see that city. After that, we should take a trip to Uppheim. That's the centre of thievery, not a nice place, but if anyone has got a hold of things belonging to the Thirteen, it'll probably be there. After that, we'll have to see how far your training's progressed. You've been moving much faster through this training than any other follower, but I believe you can keep up, so I'll keep pushing you." Jonathan sat staring at the table when Boriam said "I like that you've made a good friend in this Seeley. In my branch we need all the information we can get, and for that we need to trust those who can give it to us. Seeley, I would say, is the first of your contacts. If you need word of what is happening in this area, he'll be the one you should ask." Jonathan nodded, understanding what Boriam meant. He then said "So I'll need to make friends, but only to get information?" Boriam sighed and said "They are your friends, you experience things with them, like you and Seeley have been through a battle together now. You will talk about it many years from now. And you will ask about information from them when the conversation steers in that direction. You will come to understand that there are few people you can truly trust, and most of what everyone is saying is just a rumour." Jonathan looked at Boriam and said "And all rumours have a lot of lie in them, yet some truth as well?" Boriam smiled and nodded.

Someone knocked at the door. When Boriam opened, a guard entered saying that the king wanted them. They looked at each other and followed the guard. Soon they were standing in front of both kings, of the humans and the merfolk. "I bring word," the deep king of the merfolk bubbled. "From Thundir. He's very happy to hear that you are still alive, and that you have one following you. He hopes to see you again soon, and is wondering if you have found anything that can help our cause." He turned to Jonathan and said "You have found us another ally, which is good, but is it good enough?" Jonathan sighed and said "I don't know what I can do, but I will do what I can." The king smiled with jagged teeth bared, and Boriam said "He's a quick speaker. I have some things. Jonathan's parents had one item which I will bring when I come by next time. Other than that we're out looking now. I believe we'll be leaving this city in very few days. When that happens it will be hard to find us again until we visit." The merman bowed his head and stepped to the side. Myrtis stepped forth and asked "Who is Thundir? Is there anything Draios Strag can do to help?" Boriam sighed and said "Unfortunately, there's not much more Draios can do for now. You can let Jonathan keep the sword he's grown used to. Other than that, I suggest you gather the weapons and armour from dungeon three and put it back. Maybe put in a bit newer items as well. Close the dungeon until it's needed again." The king nodded and signalled to one of his guards who nodded and left the room. "Thundir," Boriam said "is a half gnome, half human who is leading the resistance against the Council. I had no time to send him a message about this attack, but I am glad the merfolk answered." Myrtis thought for a while before saying "There is a resistance against the Council? Where?" But Boriam shook his head saying "It is better if fewer people know at this point, but when Draios Strag is needed we will send for you." The king nodded and said "And we will come." As the conversation moved towards an end, Boriam said "Jonathan and I have a lot of packing to do before we leave. We'll need provisions for a long journey." The king nodded and led them out of the room telling them who to ask for provisions. Boriam thanked the king, and hoped they would return soon. Then they left the castle. "We'll get provisions tomorrow then, and leave the next morning. We should start early." "As always," Jonathan said and Boriam laughed saying "As always."

Chapter 56
A CHAIR WITH WHEELS?

Arkenthan turned the last page of the book and read 'You have now read the beginning of Jonathan's journey on the Lion's path. The next part can be found in the Cave of the Night.' And then the book ended. Arkenthan turned it over a few times and thought *That's it? What's this Cave of the Night?'* He looked at the bookcase and wondered if that was the Cave of the Night, but something told him it wasn't. His leg was still unusable, and he used the sticks to make his way to the door. He brought a piece of meat outside and gave it to Greypaws. The wolf had stayed by the house for several days now, and Arkenthan was happy that he had. As it ate, Arkenthan hobbled over and sat down next to the wolf. He sighed and said "I wonder how long my leg will keep hurting?" Greypaws sneezed in response. Arkenthan sat staring at the sky for a while thinking about the story in the book until Greypaws stood up. "Hey, can't I sit next to you? Okay, just give me a minute to get up." The wolf crouched down again and Arkenthan wondered if anything was wrong. "What is it?" he said, but the wolf stood up, then crouched again, giving a low bark. Looking at the wolf, then around the garden, Arkenthan couldn't imagine what was happening. After standing up and crouching again a few more times, Greypaws went and stood behind Arkenthan, put his snout beneath his legs and lifted him. "Aah! Wha.. You want me to sit on your back? Okay, put me down again then." Greypaws lowered his head again so that Arkenthan could get back on the ground, then crouched down once more. Arkenthan hopped to the wolf's side and spent a long time climbing onto Greypaws' back. When Arkenthan had finally got onto the wolf's back, Greypaws stood up abruptly, which almost made Arkenthan fall off again. Getting a firm grip on the wolf's fur, Arkenthan said "Woah! I'm not used to this, okay? So take it slowly." The wolf then jumped across the lawn and ran into the forest. Arkenthan screamed as he was led deep into the forest.

They passed the small lake near his house, and continued into the forest. Arkenthan did everything he could to hold on to the beast's fur. "What are you doing? Where are we going?" Arkenthan shouted, but

Greypaws just kept on running. After an hour, Arkenthan began feeling that the ride became easier, and he didn't have to strain so much to hold on. Then Greypaws ran down a steep hill to more screams from Arkenthan. They turned and followed a river and by now Arkenthan was so lost he knew the only way of getting back would be for Greypaws to show him. As the wolf slowed to a halt beside a small puddle, Arkenthan wondered what was going on. Greypaws sniffed a few times back and forth, drank some water and rushed into the forest again.

Arkenthan had a feeling that several hours passed. He managed to change his seating so it was a bit more comfortable, and when he finally had started to feel better about his ride, Greypaws stopped. "What now?" Arkenthan said and Greypaws tilted his head and looked at him with one eye. "Don't ask me, I have no idea where we are." Greypaws sneezed, which sent tremors through Arkenthan's body. It stung his leg, but he didn't have time to scream out as Greypaws bounded onwards through the forest, jumped and landed heavily on a doe. Several animals jumped away from the area, but Greypaws only focused on his catch. Picking the doe up with his jaws, Greypaws pulled the animal with him to a clearing where he lay down showing that Arkenthan should go off. *I really hope he doesn't leave me here,* Arkenthan thought as he climbed off the beast. Greypaws then used his claw to pull off a piece of meat which he pushed towards Arkenthan with his nose. He then sat down to eat the rest of the animal. "You eat quite a lot, don't you?" Arkenthan said as he picked up the piece of meat and thought *Ugh, raw meat is never a good idea. Let's hope I don't get sick.* He then buried his teeth in the piece. They finished their meal almost simultaneously, and again Greypaws crouched showing Arkenthan that he should climb onto his back. After struggling for a while, Arkenthan finally sat comfortably. The ride seemed a bit more comfortable now, but the wolf still ran wherever he wanted. A long time had passed when they suddenly ran in front of a fjällbear, which roared and started running after them. It soon gave up as the wolf was a lot quicker, and Arkenthan thought *I am glad we're this quick, I would've been bear food if I'd been walking at my own pace.* He then sighed and leaned forwards onto his stomach. They soon passed a clearing and Arkenthan thought *That looked familiar.* Greypaws then suddenly dug his claws into the ground, sliding into the garden by the house. Having been surprized by the sudden stop, Arkenthan gasped for breath after Greypaws' shoulder had pushed itself into his stomach. He coughed for a while, then looked around his garden. *Okay, so we're back now. Let me try this.* He then pointed towards the road up the mountain and said "Greypaws, up there." Nothing happened. He pointed again and again, growing slightly annoyed, but still nothing happened. After a while Greypaws crouched slightly and growled, and Arkenthan stopped trying to push the wolf forwards. He straightened his back, took a deep breath, then closed his eyes. Sitting atop the wolf, Arkenthan could feel himself calming down, and he thought *'Let's try this one more time.'* He then opened his eyes, took another deep breath, and looked at the path up the mountain. With this, Greypaws suddenly started running. Holding the wolf's fur tightly so he wouldn't fall off, Arkenthan realized Greypaws was running where he wanted. Soon, they were at the campsite where they could see the town, and after some shouting and waving of his arms, Arkenthan got Greypaws to stop. He lowered himself to the ground, and jumped towards what was left of the fire. It took a long time to light the fire, but as the sky grew dark around him, Arkenthan managed to get a small fire going. Sitting on the mountain looking at the town, he could see a small light winking on and off at the tower. Arkenthan smiled and said "Seems like it's working, Grey. We'll have to visit town soon. Think you're ready for that?" Greypaws gave off a strange growl, and Arkenthan turned towards him. "Are you asleep?" he said to no response from the wolf. He sighed and thought *'I guess we'll find out.'*

The next morning Arkenthan packed his bag and brought his sword along with his bow and arrows. As he came outside, he noticed that Greypaws had wandered off somewhere, and he thought *'Great. Not going to town today then?'* He sat down on a rock outside his house. He looked at the bow and wondered if he'd be able to fire it from Greypaws' back. *'I'll have to try that some time,'* he thought and sighed. The air felt colder than it used to, and again Arkenthan wondered if this was the beginning of winter. He'd lost track of the time he'd spent in the forest, so winter could come at any moment. He stood up from the rock and was about to go back inside when the bushes on the other side of his garden rustled. Turning around, he saw Greypaws returning with some food for himself. "Hey, thought you'd wandered off for the day," he said, and watched as Greypaws ate his food. When the wolf had finished, Arkenthan pointed upwards, and Greypaws stood up. *'This is so cool,'* Arkenthan thought smiling. He then went and stood next to the wolf, and Greypaws crouched down. Once atop the wolf, sitting on his sticks to keep them with him, Arkenthan sighed to calm himself down, then looked towards the path to town. Greypaws bounded across the garden and up the hill. As they came around the mountain, Arkenthan looked towards the town and put his hand on the wolf's back. Greypaws turned and ran into the forest. While the forest flew by quickly, Arkenthan wondered how he could make Greypaws walk more slowly. He tried many things, shouting commands, but nothing seemed to work. He then put his hand on Greypaws' head and immediately the wolf skidded to a stop. "Okay, so that's how I stop you?" he said and the wolf looked up at him. Arkenthan smiled and looked forwards again, and again Greypaws started running. They got to the lake before the road in less than an hour, but Arkenthan's back was extremely sore. He climbed down and had to lie on the ground for a while before being able to get up. Eventually he sat up and said "I don't think I'll take you into town today, we need to calm you down a little first." As an answer to this, Greypaws sat down, tilting his head. "Yes. Exactly that. Now for once, please stay here," Arkenthan said as he got ready to hobble the last part of the way using the sticks for support.

The last stretch of the way took about the same amount of time as the entire trip on Greypaws' back had done. Arkenthan laughed silently, hoping his leg would be well again soon. A guard stopped him wondering if he needed any help, and Arkenthan said "Could you go to the Foresters' tower and get me lieutenant Karn? Tell him to bring a trolley or something." The guard looked at Arkenthan's foot and asked "And who shall I say asks for him?" Arkenthan, annoyed, looked at the guard and pulled out his captain's badge. The guard opened his eyes widely and hurried off towards the tower. Not long after, Karn, Born, Bear and Jeron all came running towards him. Bear was carrying what looked like a chair on wheels, and Arkenthan wondered what it was for. "There's the hero!" Karn said as he approached, then all four men saluted quickly before gesturing for Arkenthan to sit down in the chair. He did, and Bear pushed him towards the main tower as they talked. "How did you get here? With that leg, it must've taken a long time," Bear asked and Arkenthan said "Well, I got some help from a friend of mine." The men laughed a little and asked where he was, but Arkenthan shook his head and said "I didn't feel that he was ready for entering town again just yet." After some time, they arrived at the guards' main tower where they called for the Colonel. Locke clapped as he arrived and said "I've heard what you did. Stupid, but brave. I am glad you're alive. The guards have seen fit to throw a party tonight, if you'll stay?" Arkenthan felt blood rush to his face as he thought *'A party? For me?'* He slowly nodded and said he'd stay until the next day. "I have some people to meet, but could one of you help me get around?" Arkenthan said.

"What have you done this time then?" Jonas said scowling at Arkenthan who shrugged and said "I might have poked the wrong bear." The butcher blinked a few times thinking before saying "You actually did poke one of the great bears, didn't you?" Laughing, Arkenthan nodded. "Go on, then, what happened?" Jonas said eagerly, and Arkenthan told him what had happened. "Huh," the butcher said when the story ended. "You do know how to find trouble. Good thing your wolf helped you." Arkenthan agreed to this, and mentioned there was going to be a celebration later on. The butcher nodded and said "I've got a big order for meat, but I can't boast of much from the forest at the moment." He looked at Arkenthan's leg and added "For some reason. But I'll join the festivities, definitely." This pleased Arkenthan and he looked up at Jeron who was pushing his chair and asked "There's a man who lives opposite from the smithy. He's been teaching me to fight with a sword, and should be at the party." Jeron twisted his face into a grimace and said "You mean Johannes? That grumpy old sod, how'd you get him to teach you to fight?" Arkenthan looked questioningly at Jeron who said "Well he is grumpy." Arkenthan laughed and said "You're right there. He didn't want to teach me, then I brought exactly the herb which was needed to save his life at the apothecary's store. So I saved his life, and in exchange he taught me to fight. He's still going to teach me more, but I think I'll need a better leg first." Jeron laughed and said "So that was you? Tell me, who haven't you saved in this town?" Arkenthan looked sheepishly ahead as he was helped along the road. "Careful though," Jeron said. "You don't want too many people owing you too much." *'Where did that come from?'* Arkenthan thought but nodded politely.

Soon, Jeron was knocking on Johannes' door. It opened quickly, and Johannes said "Jeron. What are you doing here?" Jeron put up a hand and said "I'm not here for you. He is." He then pointed at Arkenthan. Johannes looked at the sitting boy and asked "What happened?" *'Pleasant as always,'* Arkenthan thought and said "Fought a bear." Johannes looked at the wound and said "You mean the sergeant Bear, or one of the big ones in the forest?" Arkenthan sensed a joke in there, but couldn't quite find it before saying "One of the forest ones. It was attacking some of the scouts, so I drew its attention. Apparently there's a party tonight for that, and since you taught me how to fight, I thought you should be there." Johannes looked between Arkenthan and Jeron and said "I'll think about it." He then slammed the door shut. "You two seemed to have a good tone going," Arkenthan said but Jeron just grunted and pushed the chair down the road. After a while, Arkenthan asked "So what's new?" Jeron shrugged and said "Once a day we practice how to be quieter in the forest. The bear attack made us realize just how dangerous the way we do things now can be." Arkenthan nodded and said "Good. Because you guys were loud." Jeron laughed. After a while, he asked "The bear you were fighting. Did you kill it?" Arkenthan shook his head and said "I must have wounded it enough to scare it off." Jeron nodded and said "So it's probably angry then?" Arkenthan shrugged and said "I don't think animals hold grudges. Besides, the bears seem to be angry no matter what." Again Jeron laughed and stopped the chair. Arkenthan noticed they had arrived at the Foresters' tower, and Jeron said "You want to go inside, or stay out here? I have some things to tend to, so I have to leave you now." Arkenthan thanked him for helping him around, and said "I'll just sit here for a bit." Jeron nodded and said "The party will probably not start for several hours." Arkenthan nodded and said "Is there anything I can assist with?" But Jeron just shook his head and entered the tower. Arkenthan looked towards the street at all the people wandering by. He tried to imagine what they were on their way to do. There was a woman with a basked, whom he thought were going to the market. There were men carrying logs, and he thought *Maybe they're going to sell the wood to the carpenter?'* Arkenthan found it fascinating how a lot of people seemed to have so little time going to and from places, but they still spent a lot of time talking to the friends they met. A few of them glanced at Arkenthan, some in a questioning way, and some in a more annoyed, angry and scared way. Suddenly everyone turned towards him, then started running in different directions. *'Oh, no. What now?'* Arkenthan thought, and slowly turned around.

Chapter 57
DANCES, SONGS AND A BIG FIRE

At the edge of the forest, Greypaws was standing looking at the town. The great wolf seemed unsure if he should enter or not. "Ho, Greypaws! Once again, you didn't stay where I told you. Didn't think you wanted to come back here for a while," Arkenthan shouted and Greypaws turned towards him. Arkenthan noticed people staring through windows and doorways as the great wolf cautiously made his way to Arkenthan's side. People started shouting at each other, wondering if they should come to Arkenthan's side to scare the wolf away, but as soon as Greypaws lay down beside Arkenthan, everyone grew quiet. A few seconds later, the officers came running out of the tower. "What's going on? Oh!" Karn said and started laughing. "No wonder people were shouting. Hello Greypaws, how are you?" he said and petted Greypaws on the head. As people saw this, they started coming out of their houses looking at the group. "Don't let all of them come up at the same time. Might scare him," Arkenthan said and the officers nodded and went up to the groups of people who'd started to gather. After some explaining, groups of two people at a time were led to Arkenthan's side to meet the wolf. At first Greypaws gave a low growl and the people were unsure of what to do, but Arkenthan calmly said "No, Greypaws. They should meet you, so that they're not that afraid of you." He then put a hand on the wolf's head which made him stop growling. After a while a few kids came over wanting to pet him, and at first Arkenthan was unsure if he should let them. *'I don't want him to eat any of them,'* Arkenthan thought, but after a few pleas he said "Okay, but don't make any sudden moves. I don't want you to get hurt." The kids carefully petted the wolf, and then ran back to their parents laughing. Arkenthan smiled, and one of the parents, a father, came over to him saying "Is that the same wolf which attacked the town some weeks ago?" Arkenthan opened and closed his mouth a few times trying to find a way to explain it. He ended up saying "In a way he was attacking, but in another way he just lost his way into the town, and was scared by all the people." The man nodded and looked at the wolf before asking "Is it safe to have it here?

Amongst all the children, I mean." Arkenthan smiled and looked the man in the eyes before saying "As long as people remain calm around him, he should be calm around them."

Bear came over and said "I think everyone's met Greypaws now. Anything else you need done?" The man looked at Arkenthan and said "Greypaws? Fitting name. So who are you really? You with these guys?" *'I wonder if he's always this sceptical,'* Arkenthan thought before saying "I am from out of town, but I spend a lot of time here as well, and I know the forest. I give commands to the forest scouts when it's needed, but I'm not in command of anyone else." The man shrugged and must have accepted the answers he'd got, as he turned and went back to his family. The officers came up to Arkenthan saying "There're a few more hours to go before the party, but we have a lot to prepare so we're heading off. At least one of us will be in the tower at any given time, so just shout if there is anything." Arkenthan nodded his thanks, and watched as Born entered the tower while the three others headed off. The people still looked unsure about what was happening, and even though they seemed a bit more relaxed, a lot of them still stared at Arkenthan and Greypaws. "I guess they wonder if you were the one who hurt my leg." He sighed and said "Okay, let's head into the forest and we'll come back in a while." He stood up and hopped to the door of the tower. Struggling to keep his balance, Arkenthan spent some time trying to get the heavy door open. Having finally prized it open, Arkenthan shouted into the room "Born, I'm taking Greypaws for a trip into the forest. People keep staring, so I think they're nervous about him. I'll come back in a few hours." Born came over and said he understood. "I'll let the others know, in case you're a bit late for the party." Arkenthan nodded, then the heavy door slammed shut. "Grey, stand up. We're taking a trip." Greypaws stood up, then crouched for Arkenthan to climb up. As he did so, several people gasped and looked away. Having finally found a comfortable seat, Arkenthan took a deep breath and looked towards the forest. Greypaws didn't linger, and they were soon out of town.

When they reached the river, Arkenthan put his hand on the wolf's head, and soon enough they came to a stop. "Okay, we need to be able to walk at normal speed. If you run around like this, people in town will be terrified," Arkenthan said without any response from Greypaws. *'Okay, think. When I calm down and look around, he runs that way. How can I make him walk instead?'* Arkenthan wondered. He took another deep breath, put his hand on the wolf's head, and looked along the river. Greypaws shot off at his usual speed. Arkenthan straightened up, lifted his hand from the wolf's head then put it down again, and Greypaws stopped. Arkenthan stretched his arms and legs. The sudden stops and starts were starting to wear on him. He leaned back and lay down on the wolf's back. Greypaws lay down as well, which made Arkenthan roll off his back and fall into the river. "Ugh. That, I wasn't prepared for," Arkenthan said and looked at Greypaws who seemed like he was grinning. "Yes, yes, you laugh all you want. Now I'm going to come to the party wet as a fish." Greypaws tilted his head at this, and Arkenthan sighed before crawling out of the river. He noticed his leg didn't hurt as much while he was crawling on his knees, but as he stood up, the pain shot through him. He almost fell into the river again, but managed to lean forwards and landed on Greypaws. The wolf yelped as Arkenthan fell on him, but didn't do anything else. "Sorry. But it was partly your fault," Arkenthan said, starting to climb back onto the wolf's back. As he got on, Greypaws stood up again. He barked a few times into the air, and Arkenthan looked up. One of the human–like creatures sat in the tree looking down on him. Arkenthan waved to the creature, but quickly wondered why. The creature smiled and raised a finger as if to show the number one. Then it jumped into the forest and disappeared. Arkenthan sat staring at the now empty tree for a while wondering what was going on. *'It's as if it understood me a little, and tried to make some sort of contact,'* Arkenthan thought. *'I wonder what it was trying to say.'* He sighed and leaned slightly backwards looking along the river where they'd come from. As he did so, Greypaws started walking in that direction. It took a while before Arkenthan noticed that they were moving, but eventually he sat up saying "You're walking! This is much better!" Greypaws then suddenly started running again, almost throwing Arkenthan off. Stopping the wolf again, Arkenthan said "Now what was that about? Suddenly you start running again?" He sighed as Greypaws looked up at him with a grin. Arkenthan made circles in the air with his hand as if to say "Yes, grin all you want." *'I made him walk once, so I can do it again,'* Arkenthan thought and started thinking back at what had happened. After a few attempts where Greypaws started running, Arkenthan again leaned backwards, took a deep breath and looked along the river. Greypaws started walking, and Arkenthan gave a loud cheer. When he leaned forwards, Greypaws started running. When Arkenthan leaned backwards, Greypaws slowed down and started walking again. "So that's your secret. You do understand what to do, just in a slightly illogical way." Arkenthan made Greypaws run to the clearing by the lake, and then slowed down to a walk, circling the lake a few times before stopping. *'I wonder how he knows so well what I want?'* Arkenthan thought as he climbed off the great wolf. He sat down in the grass wondering what to do. He looked at his bow and thought *'Why not?'* Getting up, he prepared his bow and arrows, and said "Let's try something." Greypaws tilted his head but Arkenthan pointed towards the wolf and then upwards. Greypaws stood up and as Arkenthan came to his side, the wolf crouched again. Having finally found his seat, Arkenthan nocked an arrow and thought *'I should let him get used to the sound before I start firing as he walks around.'* He pulled the string and aimed at a tree. Greypaws shot off towards Arkenthan's target, which made Arkenthan fall off his back, and the arrow fly far into the forest. He landed heavily on the ground, knocking his breath out. After a few gasps of air, Arkenthan managed to get up again, scowling at the wolf. *'I guess I'll have to get used to riding before starting to fire the bow,'* he thought as Greypaws returned to his side. The sun warmed him as he lay in the grass, and Arkenthan thought *'Maybe I can manage to dry a bit before going back to town?'*

When they entered town again, the sun was approaching the horizon. Greypaws was walking calmly, and Arkenthan's clothes were almost dried. "Nice ride. You're just in time, they're lighting the fire now," Bear said as they reached the market square. Everyone stopped and looked towards Arkenthan, but he had a feeling they were really looking at Greypaws. He sighed and asked where his seat was. Bear pointed to the centre of one of the long tables. "Could I sit at one of the ends? So Grey can stay close by?" Bear looked at the table and thought for a while before leading him to one of the smaller tables. Once there, Arkenthan climbed off the wolf and sat down at the table. While most of the townspeople stared at Arkenthan and the great wolf beside him, some continued lighting the fire. The bonfire was huge, and the heat hit Arkenthan strongly. Greypaws turned away from the fire and lay down looking along the street. Arkenthan noticed a lot of tables were set out, and he wondered if everyone in town was invited. *'Any excuse for having a party I guess,'* Arkenthan thought as Colonel Locke came over. He looked sceptically at Greypaws, but just shook his head and welcomed them to the party. Arkenthan said "Sorry I'm not standing up at the moment, it's a bit hard to do that right now." Locke raised a hand and said "No matter, you've finally managed to get here. In a rather alternative way, I am guessing?" Arkenthan grinned but didn't answer. "Arkenthan!" a thin voice squeaked. Turning around, he could see Johanna running towards him, but she stopped as she noticed Greypaws was looking at her. Arkenthan smiled and gestured for her to come over. She walked around the wolf at a slight distance, but was soon standing in front of Arkenthan. "What happened to your leg?" she exclaimed as she saw the sticks he used for support, and a bit of the wound. Arkenthan said "I'm fine, so it doesn't matter." She scowled at Greypaws and Arkenthan laughed saying "No, he didn't do this." He then told Johanna what had happened, how the scouts had been attacked, and that he'd made one of the bears come after him. He didn't tell her about the creature in the clearing, but he did tell her about the potion's effect on him. Johanna stared at him and then said "You drank a lot of it? I haven't heard of anyone who's done that before. Let me see your leg." She then sat down and started folding up the leg of his pants. Arkenthan felt a bit awkward sitting there, but Johanna didn't seem to notice. She looked at the wound and said "No wonder you can't use it. You've torn open the muscles in your lower leg. This will take a long time to heal, even with the potion. You shouldn't move around much." Arkenthan sighed and asked "You don't have anything to help it get better?" Johanna shook her head and said "I've read in old books about something which could help, but I can't remember where or what. Sorry." Arkenthan shook his head and rolled down the leg of his pants again. "Don't you live really far away?" Johanna asked. Arkenthan nodded and said "Have you seen the single mountain deep into the forest?" Johanna nodded and said "I used to climb onto the roof of our house when I was smaller. I remember the mountain." Arkenthan continued saying "I live about that distance away from here." Karn laughed a little and Arkenthan noticed he'd been listening in on the conversation. The Lieutenant quickly stopped laughing and walked away. Johanna looked confusedly at Karn, and said "That's really far, did you have a cart to ride here?" Arkenthan smiled, shook his head and looked at Greypaws. "He brought you here?" Johanna asked, but before Arkenthan could answer, the colonel interrupted them. "How's the leg doing? Getting well soon?" Johanna scowled at the colonel, but Arkenthan couldn't understand why. Looking up at the colonel, he said "It doesn't seem like it. Johanna here said it will take a long time to heal." The colonel looked at Johanna and nodded before saying "We all hope you will get well soon. Let's get this party started, shall we?" Johanna clapped, stood up and ran towards the bonfire. "I understand if you don't join us," Locke said and as Arkenthan watched, everyone gathered around the big fire. After the colonel had joined the crowd, they started singing, then dancing around the fire. A long time passed as the crowd cheered, sang, danced and clapped around the fire. Arkenthan found it all very well rehearsed, and wondered how many times they had done this before. The sounds seemed to have gotten Greypaws' attention as the great wolf sat upright with its head tilted to the side looking towards the crowd. After an hour of song and dance, everyone went to their own seats at the different tables.

Chapter 58
THE LITTLE GIRL AND THE WITCH

The Foresters sat at Arkenthan's table. While eating, they threw a small piece of meat to Greypaws every now and then. The wolf seemed to be calm around the crowd which had once tried to scare him off. Arkenthan wondered about this for some time until the sergeants started to tell jokes and stories of older days. Everyone who listened laughed copiously as the evening went by. After dinner, music started up and some people started dancing and singing again, while others sat together talking. They moved closer to the fire, where Born started to tell a story. He said "This is a myth about our close friend, the forest. Once upon a time there was a little girl. She lived with her parents here in Garani. The forest at that time was not as dangerous as it is now. Back then the kids liked to play in the forest. One day when the girl was looking for her friends, she met an old woman. The woman said she knew where the girl's friends were, and asked the little girl to follow her. Ever deeper into the forest they went, until they came to a field. In the middle of the open field was a huge tree, and when I say huge, I mean really huge. The tree was as wide as a house. The old woman said the girl's friends were playing inside the tree. When the girl examined the tree, she noticed that it was lifted off the ground by the roots. The girl looked up at the old woman who smiled, nodded and pointed towards the entrance. The little girl ran eagerly to her friends. Her parents never saw her again. The old woman is rumoured to be a witch, and people have different endings to this myth. Some say she ate the little girl, some say she taught the girl to become a witch. What I do know, is that several people claim to have seen a little girl running around the forest late at night, and that she was gone when they tried to follow her." Several of the listeners gasped and some shook their heads. One of the listeners said "Now, I don't believe that." Born looked at him and said "And why is that?" The man stood up and said "I know that as a child, most of us climbed up onto the roofs of our houses and sat looking over the forest." Several people nodded and the man continued "I have never seen a tree that size. What I mean is, the tree would almost be as high as the mountain, wouldn't it?" Born shook his head and said "What if someone had gone into the forest and cut it down?" As Born and the man started arguing about the myth, Arkenthan's mind drifted to the stump of the huge tree he'd found in the forest. He was pulled from his daydream by Jeron saying "Hey, Arkenthan, you all right?" Arkenthan looked at the sergeant and Jeron said "You look a bit pale, are you feeling well?" *'Am I feeling well? What do you think? A witch might live close to my house, and you wonder if I feel well?'* Arkenthan thought, but said "Yeah, I'm good. Just… full." Jeron laughed and slapped his back "Good food, eh? Jonas truly knows how to cook." Arkenthan smiled and looked towards Greypaws. He saw a couple of kids had started climbing on the great wolf, but he didn't seem to mind them. *'Still calm, eh?'* he thought as one of the kids, a girl, fell off with a small scream, to her friends' laughter. The wolf turned its head and looked at the kids, and all the kids screamed and ran to hide under tables and behind chairs. Some of them started laughing, and their parents seemed to breathe a collective sigh of relief as they understood that everything was all right. Arkenthan smiled and returned to Jeron who'd apparently said something. "Sorry, had to check on what was going on with Grey. What did you say?" "I asked what you thought of the party." Arkenthan looked around and said "It looks like everyone's enjoying themselves, as am I, but I get a feeling you've done this before?" Jeron laughed and tapped his nose. "We hold this party every year. It's a celebration to end the autumn, and welcome winter." Arkenthan nodded and said "So when you said it was going to be a party celebrating that I had saved those men, you meant?" "Well, we do hold this party every year. But we don't hold it until something great happens that we can celebrate. Last year practically nothing great happened, so by the end of autumn we were getting a bit desperate. I think we celebrated that the scouts came home from the forest without an incident. I can't really remember." Arkenthan smiled and nodded. As the party wore on, to more stories of the forest, Greypaws eventually stood up and left for the forest, while Arkenthan stayed behind.

It was early morning before Arkenthan was helped to the Foresters' tower, where he had unruly dreams about witches, werewolves, little girls and, for some reason, sitting in a barrel on a huge river. He woke up by falling out of bed, slamming his head on the floor. One of the guards there saw this and started laughing before helping him up. Arkenthan grunted as he got up and felt his leg sting. Someone brought him a plate of food, which he eagerly accepted. "How long was I asleep for?" Arkenthan asked, and the guard shrugged and said "I just got here, but the party ended half a day ago." Arkenthan looked at the guard thinking *'Half a day? I wonder if Greypaws will help me get home?'* "Yes?" the guard said, which pulled Arkenthan out of his thoughts with a "Huh?" The guard looked at him and said "You were staring, so I wondered if you needed something?" Arkenthan looked blankly ahead before saying "Umm. No, it's okay. Thanks." Feeling slightly embarrassed, Arkenthan turned to his food and ate it quickly. He found his sword and bow on the floor beside the bed, and the sticks he used for support was leaned against the wall.

Eventually he got outside to soaking rain, and thought *'Great. I wonder when someone is heading into the forest.'* He turned and entered the tower again. "Hey!" he shouted, "When's the next patrol heading into the forest?" A couple of people shuffled across the room to the far wall, and one of them shouted "The lieutenant is taking a group in about an hour." "Right," Arkenthan mumbled to himself and headed for the office. As he entered he noticed two rolls of parchment on the desk, and thought *'Why not?'* He sat down, sighed and started reading. One of the scrolls reported what Arkenthan had told Karn and Born when they had visited him. The other described what had happened to the squad that was originally attacked. He read how the first man was suddenly struck down by the bear, the other bear coming to join the fight, and how everyone had thought their days were at an end. *'We managed to fend the bears off for a while, until Arkenthan jumped in and got one of the bears to follow him,'* Arkenthan read silently. *'With only one bear left we still struggled, a few men were injured, but we had the control of the situation. When the bear was dead, we saw that Yurg had received a big wound, and needed to be brought back to town quickly. Some of the men wanted to go after Arkenthan, and it was decided that Born and Liris should search the area for Arkenthan. Robin and Storm were ordered to help Yurg back to town. After half an hour's search we found a trail of the bear running heavily on the ground. We followed the trail until we came to a clearing where dirt had been dug out of the ground and the tracks stopped. Having searched the area for some time, and considering the danger in only being two people, we decided to call it off and head back to town.'* Arkenthan looked at the ceiling thinking, imagining what they were doing in the forest. He sat staring blankly ahead for some time until someone knocked on the door. Karn put his head into the room and said "They said you wanted to join us into the forest?" he said, to which Arkenthan nodded and got up. "Are you even fit to enter the forest?" one of the men said as they came outside. Arkenthan looked at him and said "I wanted to enter some time ago alone. Then I figured I might be a little safer if I joined the next team heading in. I want to head towards the clearing by the lake, and see if Grey appears." The men nodded and Karn said "I was going to go upstream, but I guess we can get you to the lake first." Arkenthan smiled and followed the lieutenant outside.

Once in the forest, Arkenthan noticed how hard it was to get around when he only had one leg to really use. They spent a long time getting to the river, and an even longer time getting to the lake. Arkenthan had to half climb over obstacles and take longer detours to avoid falling into the river.

'I really hope my leg gets better soon,' he thought as he jumped on one leg over a log.

Eventually they got to the lake where Arkenthan shouted for Greypaws a couple of times before sitting down. A couple of the scouts shouted as well a few times, then Karn said "Okay, we should get going. We have to get back in decent time as well, or the others will worry. Don't need them to send out a search party, especially when we've walked in the wrong direction." Arkenthan nodded and said "Okay, I'll stick around here. When you get back, tell the next group to check if I'm gone. If I'm still here I'll probably go back to town by that time." "What're you going to do if your wolf appears?" one of the guards asked, and Arkenthan answered that he would be heading home. The guards nodded, said goodbye and left by the river route again. *'Now what to do?'* Arkenthan thought as he looked around. He sighed and tried some meditation. *'I hope I'll find the next book, I wonder what the next part of the meditation is,'* he thought and then quietened his mind. Meditation was easier than it normally was, and he soon felt the lump in his chest again starting to grow stronger. *'I guess I pushed myself while I fought the bear,'* he thought at the same time as he heard a crash from the edge of the forest. He opened his eyes saying "Greypaws?" He was looking at a great bear with no fur on one of its legs. It had wounds where its fur should be, and it seemed to have a hard time walking as it went back and forth a few times, looking at Arkenthan. "Looks like I wounded you less than you wounded me," Arkenthan said to the bear and sighed, wondering what would happen now. At that moment Greypaws came wandering into the clearing, and as the bear saw the two of them together, it decided to head back into the forest. Arkenthan looked at the wolf and said "Great timing Greypaws, great timing." He staggered upright and made his way to the wolf's side. As he got on top of the beast, he checked that he could still make the wolf walk calmly, before setting off into the forest. Greypaws was quick to start running, as usual, and Arkenthan almost fell off when they started on the trip home. He gripped the fur on the wolf's neck and held on. The trees rushed past them as they got deeper into the forest. Every now and then birds flew into the air, scared by the rushing wolf. A low branch almost knocked Arkenthan off Greypaws' back, but he managed to regain his balance. "Watch out! Remember that I am up here," Arkenthan shouted with no response from Greypaws. After about an hour, Arkenthan's back was so sore that he had to get off. He lay down on the ground stretching his limbs and noticed that his leg didn't hurt when he moved the foot. *'Maybe it's starting to heal?'* Arkenthan thought and sat upright. Moving the foot back and forth he still didn't feel any pain in the leg, so he stood up. As soon as he put any pressure on the leg though, the pain shot through his entire body once more. *'Okay, far from well, but hopefully on its way there,'* he thought and turned to Greypaws who was waiting patiently. "Why are you always helping me?" he said suspiciously. "You always wait for me, you always know what I want done, yet at the beginning of all this, you tried to kill me. We haven't been around each other that long, so why don't you try to eat me these days?" Greypaws responded by putting his tongue out and then give a loud sneeze. Greypaws shook his head, and Arkenthan started laughing. Hopping to the wolf's side, Arkenthan was still laughing as he climbed back onto the great wolf's back. As soon as he focussed his attention on the mountain, the great wolf started running.

Chapter 59
CAVE OF THE NIGHT

By the time Arkenthan arrived at his house, it was starting to grow dark. He went inside and got the fire going again. After cooking a big dinner for both himself and Greypaws, Arkenthan went outside with the meat for the wolf. He sat eating his own dinner outside until he started to feel cold, at which time he stood up and turned towards the house. He looked up at the mountain and again saw what looked like a cave, and he thought *'The next book is in the Cave of the Night, eh? I've only ever seen that cave when it gets dark.'* Sighing he thought *'I guess I'll have to check it out.'* He turned to Greypaws and said "Get up, we're going up the mountain." Greypaws tilted his head, but as soon as Arkenthan had grabbed his bag from inside his house and hopped to his side, he stood up. Soon they were speeding up the mountain to the camp where Arkenthan had fallen asleep not long ago. As soon as they reached the camp, Arkenthan made Greypaws walk more slowly, back and forth up the mountain. Eventually Arkenthan could see a dark area of the mountain and steered Greypaws towards it. When he got closer he could see the dark area went into the mountain and Arkenthan looked back down the mountain. Far below he could see his house and thought *'I should be able to see this from my garden, so what is this? The cave only appear at night? And how is that possible?'* Greypaws didn't want to go inside, so Arkenthan had to get off and use his sticks for support as he jumped to the mouth of the cave. He could hear a few noises coming from the cave, but he couldn't understand what might be making them. He took a deep breath and started to walk. The cave was so dark that he had to use his hands to follow the wall inwards. He tripped and fell a few times, and struggled to get back to his feet. After what felt like an hour of walking in darkness, Arkenthan turned a corner and discovered some small rocks in the wall of the cave which gave off a weak light. The rocks led further into the cave where Arkenthan could see the light growing stronger. Finally able to see where he was going, Arkenthan had an easier time moving through the cave. He soon turned another corner and, far ahead, he could see a table shaped like a lion. The head appeared to have been broken off, and Arkenthan wondered why

308

as he stepped towards it. When he got close to the table, Arkenthan noticed that the back wall was moving. He slowly took the last few steps towards the table and saw a book and a key lying in special recesses in the table. The key and the lock on the book were of a brown colour, but the book was so dusty that Arkenthan was unable to see the name or the colour of the book itself. *'Great. I'll have to clean it off,'* he thought and looked up from the book. A silver-coloured eye was staring directly at him, and he gave a small scream of shock. The lizard crawled from the back wall up to the ceiling, from where it kept its attention riveted on Arkenthan. Looking around, Arkenthan saw that one of the small glowing rocks had dropped from the wall. He put the book and key in his bag and picked up the stone before making his way back outside. The glow from the stone made his trip through the dark cave a lot easier. Once outside, Greypaws started growling at him. "What's wrong?" Arkenthan asked, but noticed that the wolf was staring at the glowing stone in his hand. He quickly put it in a pocket, and soon Greypaws started to calm down. "Don't like these, do you?" Arkenthan said trying to calm the wolf down further. After a long time, Greypaws let Arkenthan climb onto his back and then started down the mountain. *'I wonder why he started growling at the stone?'* Arkenthan thought as they entered the garden. He climbed off the wolf and went inside. The fire burned nicely, and Arkenthan threw a few more logs on before getting a rag. He dipped it in some water and wringed most of it out again. He started cleaning off the dust, and revealed that the book had a deep green colour, with copper letters and a copper lock. As he finished cleaning the book, he was about to bring it to some light when something knocked hard on the door. "Visitors now?" he said to himself and stood up. He put the book in the bookcase and went to open the door.

Arkenthan was looking at two of the human-like creatures he'd seen in the forest. One had long green hair with blue eyes, which were twice the size of a normal human's. The other had grey hair and grey eyes and was supported by a cane. It looked like a very old man, just very small one with big eyes and a big nose. What appeared to be the younger one looked at the elder, pointed at Arkenthan then whistled a bird's sound and said "Tok-tok-tok". Then it ran away leaving the older one staring with big eyes at Arkenthan. "Umm. Hello?" Arkenthan said which seemed to startle the creature. It cleared its throat and said "H-hell'o?" Arkenthan looked from the older creature to the forest, where the younger one had disappeared. He looked around his garden, wondering if there were any more out there. Seeing no one he said "You want to come inside?" The creature made a gesture as if writing words in the air with his finger before saying "No-o?" Feeling a bit awkward about the whole situation, Arkenthan said "I'll come outside then. There're some rocks over there we can sit on." He guided the

309

creature to a couple of rocks in the garden and sat down on one of them. The creature had apparently decided to stand. Arkenthan coughed and asked "Who are you?" A few more swirls in the air before the old creature said "I, am Norin. Ve-e, are vetter." *'Vee? We maybe?'* Arkenthan thought before asking "You're wetter?" Norin looked angry when he said "No-o, not v-vater thing, the'ey are other. No, shar'p v, Vetter." He coughed and continued "I-i am old. One of not man'y, who kno'v this-s speech. I kno'v not all," he made a few gestures in the air before saying "vords, but I vill try." Arkenthan watched fascinated as the old vette slowly spoke "I'it is decided, say to you th'at ve-e are. I vill not say a'll about us-s no'v, but ve-e vill se'end for you vhen it is-s time." Arkenthan blinked a few times before asking "Send for me? To go where?" Norin smiled and said "To our, place?" As nothing else was being said, Arkenthan used his sticks to stand upright, then stretched out his hand to greet him more politely and said "I guess I'll just have to wait for a message?" Norin turned to a small bag he was carrying and soon shoved a bowl into Arkenthan's hand. Looking at the bowl, Arkenthan noticed it was half filled with green berries with blue spots and small orange leaves. He looked at Norin questioningly who pointed at his leg saying "For leg'g, it vill help." Arkenthan opened and closed his mouth a few times before thanking Norin. The vette bowed and turned towards the forest. When he had almost crossed the line of trees, Arkenthan shouted "Wait!" Norin turned and looked at Arkenthan who said "Why did you guys save me from the bear?" Norin raised what Arkenthan assumed to be an eyebrow and said "vh'at bear?" Gesturing with his hands, Arkenthan said "The one who did this to my stomach and leg. The one that one of you set on fire." Norin looked at the sky for a few seconds before saying "Ah, that ve-e did" he made another few spelling motions in the air before saying "not." He then disappeared into the forest. Arkenthan looked at the spot where Norin had disappeared for a long time, wondering what the old Vette had meant. Eventually he yawned and went inside. He threw another log on the fire while the conversation with Norin buzzed around his head, and lay down on the bed. "What did he mean? By any of it really?" Arkenthan said half to himself and half to the gloom of the fire before falling asleep. In his dream he was running through the forest. He didn't know away from or towards what, but he knew he had to run. As darkness started to surround him, he entered a clearing with a huge tree stump. He knew exactly where he was, but he wasn't alone. An old woman stood hunched over a crooked cane, glaring at him. The old woman started laughing a shrill laugh which made Arkenthan's bones feel cold. He was suddenly dragged into the darkness under the tree, and as he was engulfed by the darkness Arkenthan woke up. He sat breathing heavily in bed thinking *'Why did Born have to tell that story? He knew that I live out here.'* A while passed before he got out of bed to make some breakfast. He saw the bowl of berries he'd gotten the night before and sighed, thinking *'Why not?'* He took a handful of the berries, but quickly spat them out again. The taste was sour and the berries themselves were so chewy that he was unable to eat more than three at a time. Sitting beside the fire, Arkenthan ate several berries before starting to get a stomach ache. *'Maybe I shouldn't eat so many at the same time?'* he thought as he hurried outside. The mist lay heavily over the ground, and Greypaws was nowhere to be seen. He coughed a few times before moving on. As he got back inside, he stood looking at the bookcase with the green book in it. The book itself had a kind of glow to it where it stood outlined against the dark brown wood of the bookcase. His fingers were tingling as he reached for the book. He slowly brought the book over to the window for more light, and read the title. He looked out the window repeating the title in his mind, and saw Greypaws coming out of the misty forest. He smiled, tossed the book onto the bed and made his way outside.

Fredrik Bjønnes Lunde started writing his first book "The Lion's Cub" in 2011 as a part of the book series "The Lion's Path". When he was still in school he did not see the joy in writing. This changed when he saw the movie "The Neverending Story" and he felt that something was missing. A story, where he could make the rules himself, started brewing in his head and after a few years he started to write some of the thoughts down. All of a sudden he couldn't stop writing, and his writing career had started.

His early years was spent on an island just outside Oslo, Norway. He has lived his entire life in Norway, except a semester abroad in Victoria, B.C. Canada. He graduated in 2011 with an engineering degree in chemistry and biotechnology. He now lives in Oslo where he has a full-time job besides his writing.

FREDRIK B. LUNDE